COPPERHEAD

ALSO BY ALEXI ZENTNER

The Lobster Kings
Touch

COPPERHEAD

———◆———

Alexi Zentner

VIKING

VIKING
An imprint of Penguin Random House LLC
penguinrandomhouse.com

LIBRARY OF CONGRESS CATALOGING-IN-PUBLICATION DATA
Names: Zentner, Alexi, author.
Title: Copperhead / Alexi Zentner.
Description: New York : Viking, [2019] |
Identifiers: LCCN 2019001145 (print) | LCCN 2019003008 (ebook) |
ISBN 9781984877291 (ebook) | ISBN 9781984877284 (hardcover)
Subjects: | BISAC: FICTION / Literary. | FICTION / Coming of Age. |
GSAFD: Bildungsromans.
Classification: LCC PS3626.E445 (ebook) | LCC PS3626.E445 C67 2019 (print) |
DDC 813/.6--dc23
LC record available at https://lccn.loc.gov/2019001145

Printed in the United States of America
1   3   5   7   9   10   8   6   4   2

Set in Baskerville MT Std
Designed by Cassandra Garruzzo

For my mother.
For all of the obvious reasons
and for some of the less obvious ones, too.

Dear Reader,

When I was growing up, my mother was a prominent local activist fighting against anti-Semitism and racism. She and my father were both clinical social workers, and they had a private practice in an old Victorian next door to our family house. Often, I'd come home from school and find my mom meeting with another activist or an official from the community. My mom was tiny, but she was fierce; I saw her scare the hell out of men three times her size. My dad was just as tough. My parents believed in standing up to bullies and fighting to make sure everybody got a fair shake.

But the year I turned eighteen—after years of threats and menace—my parents' office was firebombed by a neo-Nazi group. We rebuilt the house and my mother doubled down on her convictions. Then the office was firebombed a second time. No arrests were ever made.

What happened to my family felt extreme back then, but the dog whistle of white supremacy and hatred is a straight-up shout today. With *Copperhead*, I wanted to look more closely at how our sense of morality both mutates and crystallizes as we come of age. I wanted to explore how hatred can complicate love, how love can make us blind to the danger around us, and how racism and hate are at work even in the lives of those who don't think they've chosen a side.

I've been thinking about this story practically my whole life, and the place and time we're living in propelled me to write it now. Doing so hasn't brought me much certainty, but it has helped me articulate the questions that have dogged me. Is hatred as complicated as love? What if I had been another boy? What would my life have been like if I'd been raised with a different lodestar? Would I be able to step out from under the haze of bigotry? Who would I be now, as a man? What does it take to be good? And on the road to good, what mistakes will we make, what scars will all of us then bear?

Thank you for reading.

Alexi Zentner

COPPERHEAD

T-MINUS ZERO

He spins the wheel hard, angry. He cannot pull away from the house fast enough. The truck lurches forward. A bee-stung horse. Snow and ice spit out from under the wheels, like a curse from a teacher's mouth, like buckshot scattering through the air and bloodying the breast of a duck flushed from the water. The back end of the pickup, light and bouncy, skids wide and loose.

When it happens, he feels the sound of the impact as much as he hears it: like a soda can crushed by a stomped foot. But it's two distinct sounds: the heavy thud of the boot and the gossamer crinkle of metal folding on itself.

Except the sound does not come from a soda can crushed by a foot. He knows what it is immediately. He stomps hard on the brake pedal, the truck stopping as violently as it started. He sits. The stereo is loud in the stillness, so he thumbs it off, but the windshield wipers squeak, so he turns them off too and then stops the motor.

It is too quiet. If everything were going to be okay, there would be a word. A voice. A sound. Something. Anything. But the only sound he can hear is an echo, a memory, the undertone that came with the thud and crumple of metal: the inevitable weakness of a body. He wishes it had simply been an empty soda can. But he knows it was a human being.

He gets out of the truck. He moves as slowly as he can force himself to.

He hit a deer once, more than a year ago, not long after he got the truck running, but that was different. The animal bounded out in front of him. Dumb-eyed and desperate. He barely had time to touch the brake before his fender tore open the deer's belly. When he stopped the truck and walked back to where the deer was crumpled on the shoulder, it was still alive. A sort of miracle.

But the wrong sort of miracle. Guts spilled onto the asphalt, the slow sodium light of the streetlights washing everything down. The doe's breath a desperate whistle of blood. Her right hind leg scraping weakly against the ground as if she was still trying to stand. He watched her like this for a minute or two and then went back to his truck. If he'd had his hunting knife with him, he could have been merciful, but there was nothing to do other than head home to hose off the blood and gore. He had to use a pair of pliers to fish out a chunk of the doe's skin that was lodged in the creased fender.

Now he walks the long way around the front of the truck, touching the hood and then looking at the memory of the deer imprinted on the front fender; the metal still bears an ugly kiss.

When he has made his way around the truck, he looks. The body is ten, twenty feet behind the bed of the truck. He knows it is a person, but in the shadows and the false light coming from the house, it could be anything else. He wants it to be anything else. A soda can. A doe. But it is, and always will be, stubbornly, a dead body.

MINUS TEN

Halloween come and gone. It's the month of November, and it is a miracle: Jessup is still playing football. The first time in forty years that Cortaca High School has made the playoffs. Jessup is a senior. Seventeen years old and big. He was athletic even when he was small, but he's grown into himself. Played all four years on varsity. Four years of snot and blood. Freshman, sophomore, junior year they got bounced before the playoffs, but this year they've only lost two games. Tonight they play Kilton Valley High. Win or go home.

His cleats click and splash on the wet cement as he jogs to the stadium. Rain started in the middle of the night, and it's been near freezing all day; he could smell the coming snow before he even walked out of his house this morning. A wet bruise on the air. All day, during school, sitting in math or English, the familiar itch of game day making his knee bounce, Jessup kept looking out the window, waiting for the sky to decide it was time to turn from rain to snow. Now, with the sun down, the sky has decided on neither: sleet. But he can feel the temperature still dropping. The sleet will make the transition to water-heavy snow soon enough.

He's in the middle of the pack of boys heading to the stadium. He steps off the sidewalk as they cut across the asphalt parking lot. There's a puddle of slush that the other boys jump over or dance around, but not Jessup. He's on a straight line. He's not moving for nothing. Steps right in the puddle. The icy water splashes his ankle, soaks through his sock. He doesn't care. He'll be soaked soon enough.

Only a few days earlier it was warm. In Cortaca, mothers make sure that children pick Halloween costumes that can be worn with winter jackets, hats, and gloves. More years than not, the ghouls and goblins can see their breath in the air. This year, however, the jack-o'-lanterns spit shadows into a fall night that held a heat that seemed like it would last forever. Jessup's sister, Jewel, is eleven. Twelve in February. Sixth grade. Old enough to almost be too old to trick-or-treat, old enough to go with just her friends, but Jessup tagged along. Drove her into town in his truck. Walked with them but stayed on the sidewalk as they sprinted up to houses. Comfortable in his T-shirt despite the end of October. Just there to keep an eye on you, he said. I'm not asking for candy, not hitting the doorbells, Jewel, so I don't need a costume. Jewel rolling her eyes, she and her friends dressed as zombies. Zombies never go out of style, Jessup thought. He helped her with her makeup. Mom's eyeliner, ketchup for blood. By the end of the night she was sweaty from running, hopped up on sugar, and cranky, the makeup smudged. She let Jessup have all her peanut butter cups.

It stayed warm like that all week. As if winter were just a rumor. At practice, the smell of falling leaves and cut grass mixed with sweat. It was hot enough that it felt like an echo of summer. Practice in full pads, but only light hitting. Lots of water breaks. Coach, mindful of the heat, wanted them fresh for the playoffs. Yesterday, during practice, the first hint of chill. And overnight, things changed. Summer gone and skipped past the crispness of fall. This is the cold drudgery of sleet. The temperature dropping.

Tomorrow, Jessup knows, will be winter. Tomorrow it will be snow. Tomorrow, when he goes deer hunting, the woods will be a different world from the one that exists today. It will be ice and snow and the magic of whiteness, the crunch of his boots, the quiet hush of blanketed woods while he waits for a clear shot, for a buck with a rack worth taking. Fill the freezer with good meat they can't afford to buy. His girlfriend, Deanne, has asked to come but he's said no. The whole point isn't the hunt but the wait. The quiet. To be in the trees, alone. Nobody looking at him and thinking about Jessup's brother and his stepfather in prison. It's been four years since Ricky beat those two boys to death. Black boys. His stepfather didn't touch anybody, but he was there, and he has a history. History is everything in a town the size of Cortaca.

Ricky has another sixteen years, at least, if things go well. His stepfather, David John Michaels, was supposed to serve five, but he's out early. Today. Jessup's mom drove up north this morning to bring David John back. She brought Jewel with her, since she's David John's kid. Jessup argued that Jewel shouldn't miss school, but it wasn't a real argument. The kid's only in sixth grade, and besides, she's smart as hell. Smarter than Jessup, even. Honor roll in her sleep. A day of school won't make a difference. There was never a question of Jessup going along as well. Even if he didn't have football. They're supposed to be back by now. Sitting in the stands. His stepfather up there with Jessup's mother and Jewel. They'll be expecting him to go out for dinner with them after the game. He'll do that and then head to the party and, after that, what he's really looking forward to tonight: time with his girlfriend.

But tomorrow, tomorrow Jessup can be alone.

MINUS NINE

That's tomorrow. Tonight, it's football. The sleet is starting to gather. It's the kind of cold wet that makes certain kids wish they'd picked a different sport. Cortaca High School is a mix of kids. Poor whites like Jessup living outside of Cortaca on country roads, hills, and hollers, right off county highways or buried back down dirt roads, in trailers or beaten-down houses with missing windows, sweat-equity additions finished only with Tyvek, with months or years before siding goes up. Woodstoves if you're lucky, the constant whine of a chainsaw or the thunk of a maul giving you a house warm enough to make you sweat. If you're not lucky, propane, the house at forty-five degrees all winter, balls freezing under thin blankets, sleeping with your clothes on because nobody, not even Treman Gas, will fill your propane tank on credit. The poor blacks mostly living in Cortaca proper, up in the housing complex on East Hill, East Village—Jessup calls it the Jungle, but so do all of the blacks and the poor whites, with only the rich whites calling it by the proper name, too scared to give it its due—and the rest of the poor blacks near the downtown core, old houses once proud but now subdivided into two, four, eight apartments. Only a few of the poor blacks are out in the country like Jessup, but there are enough poor whites in town that there's a lot of crossing of color lines there. The kids who aren't poor are all affiliated with Cortaca University or in that orbit. Professors' kids. Professionals'. Or just come from money. Moms available for birthday parties and carnival night during elementary school, dads who can take the day off to chaperone the middle school field trip to Hershey Park in the spring, parents who insist on honors and AP classes in high school, who know how to procure and pay for tutors when their darlings can't handle the math or Spanish or chemistry. Jessup is in the classes dominated by rich kids and doing fine, top 10 percent of his class for grades.

Not valedictorian, but within spitting distance, not bad for no tutors, for playing three sports and having a part-time job, for helping to raise his sister, top 10 percent of his class something to crow about, a ticket out of here. Beat the drum and check your numbers, teachers never quite believing he can hold his own. Not with a camo hunting jacket and what everybody knows about his brother and his stepdad. Small town, small town, small town. No way for a clean slate.

The Kilton Valley team comes from an hour away. Rich kids in a commuter town. There will be a few boys like Jessup on the team—everywhere, there are boys like him—but mostly the kids from Kilton Valley live in houses with epoxy-coated garage floors, four-bedroom homes with gas fireplaces used only for decoration, thermostats set to seventy-two in the winter, sixty-eight in the summer, cedar fences to keep the golden retriever in. Jessup has heard that the Kilton Valley team practices on an indoor field when the weather is bad. There will be boys on the Kilton Valley team who are already looking forward to getting home before the game has even started, thinking about warming up and drying off instead of the ritualized brutality Jessup loves.

As he jogs through the parking lot, the stadium lights seem too bright for the weather. He can see fat, furious dollops of ice and rain coming in streaks. The wind has kicked up, too. It's sharp, cutting. The hit of skin on skin, helmet on skin, skin on turf is going to burn. It's going to burn now, but worse, it's going to burn later, under the hot showers. Around him, most of the other boys jogging to the field are wearing long sleeves under their pads. Not Jessup. Just his jersey. Bare arms. He wants the boys from Kilton Valley across the line to think about the cold. He wants them to think about what it means that Jessup isn't hiding from the weather, what it means that it doesn't bother him. It won't bother him. Not during the game. He accepted, long ago, that to play football is to understand pain. Both to give and to receive. It is one of the reasons he is good at what he does. Because the secret to being a linebacker is not just the willingness to punish and to accept punishment alike, but to revel in it.

MINUS EIGHT

There's still real grass and dirt on the fields surrounding the stadium, but they play their games on synthetic grass. He grew up playing Pop Warner football on rec-league fields. The grass torn into mud by October, standing water after a rain, no way to run without stumbling in ruts and divots. By contrast, the turf at the stadium is immaculate. The football field is perfectly flat, the plastic grass a smooth mat, the seams sewn together and invisible. The school district rakes the plastic fibers and sweeps the field clean regularly. The rubber pellet infill mixed with some type of sand means that even when it is raining, the water drains quickly. But the sleet is starting to stick. It's coming down hard enough that the Kilton Valley Cougars aren't going to risk throwing the ball. Which is good for the Cortaca High School Bears. Injuries have meant relying on a third-string quarterback. The Bears have won with defense the whole year. They aren't going to win a shoot-out, so anything that keeps the ball on the ground for the other side is a net win as far as Jessup is concerned. Another ten minutes like this and a thick slick of sleet will cover the lines. It will be slippery. Straight-line running. Bloody-nose football. Ugly football. Jessup is excited.

They jog into the stadium to muted applause. The stands are nothing like what you'd find in Texas. Not even big enough to fit two thousand people. And today, with the weather, even though this is a playoff game, the first in forty years, the first home playoff game in even longer, the stands are only half full. There is no history of excellence. Jessup's stepfather played, and he only had one winning season. Jessup's brother played, too, and they were winless three out of four years. Both Ricky and David John write regularly, follow the team best they can from prison. Living vicariously. Ricky wrote this week to say how much he wished he could be there to see

Jessup suit up for the playoffs. Loves that Jessup wears his old number. Brothers. But if he can't be there, at least David John is going to get to see Jessup play tonight. Can hardly believe Cortaca is in the playoffs.

Jessup can believe it. Both his freshman and sophomore campaigns were marked as three-win seasons. But between his sophomore and junior years, Cortaca High School hired Coach Diggins and the team got good. They missed the playoffs last year by a shanked field goal in overtime, a pain so keen that Jessup actually cried on the sidelines. This year, though, it's been clear that they were headed for the playoffs. They are still not a favorite to win, but most people think they have some chance. There's energy. It doesn't translate to a full stadium, however. Call it twelve hundred people, but the crowd is big enough for Jessup. He looks for his mother and Jewel and David John, but he can't find them.

They've already done warm-ups and then gone back to the locker rooms for last-minute pep talks, reminders of assignments, a final chance to take a piss or squeeze out a nervous crap. Some of the boys puke before every game. But now there are only a few minutes before the whistle. Jessup takes a couple of runs up and down the field, getting a feel for how slippery it is. He sees Coach Diggins chatting with one of the referees.

Diggins should have picked Jessup as one of the four captains—Mike Crean, whom Jessup is friends with, is a good player but not as good as Jessup, was named one of the captains—but he didn't. Took Jessup into his office the week before the first game of the season and said that it wasn't just about how good you were on the field. It wasn't enough to be the best player on the team. Leadership. Jessup doesn't talk enough, Diggins says. Loners don't make good leaders. Oh, Jessup talks during games; he calls out formations and changes the defensive read. All off-season, Jessup was one of the group of players that Diggins had come to his home on Sunday afternoons to do film study so that they understood the game better. He's taken to it. His junior year he was good, but this season he's been a stud. He's a late recruit, but colleges have come calling. Part of it is that he's big and fast, but it's more now—because all that time in Diggins's office has meant that the game's slowed down for him. Doesn't matter if he's playing strong side or

weak side, he's directing the defense. Should be the middle linebacker calling it out, except that even though Damian Greene is a solid player, he can't
read the offense quick enough, so it's Jessup's job to play traffic cop. But
even though Diggins has occasionally named other players as additional
captains for a game, an honor given out, he's never named Jessup.

"Hope you understand, son," Diggins said in his slow Mississippi drawl.

MINUS SEVEN

Jessup doesn't argue with any of what Diggins says. It's true. He doesn't talk much in groups, doesn't talk more than he needs to in class. Gives answers but keeps them short. He keeps to himself too much. He knows that. He isn't a follower, but he isn't a leader either. He's just Jessup. But it gets under his skin that he isn't a captain. Plus, the college coaches recruiting him—mostly starting this year—have asked why he isn't in a leadership role. How come the best defensive player on the field, the best player on the team, doesn't go out to call the coin flip?

What's Jessup supposed to say to the college coaches? That Diggins is black and there's no way he's going to pick Jessup to be a captain? That Diggins has never brought up Jessup's brother and stepfather or their church, has always acted like none of it matters, but of course it matters?

Diggins is a big man, but not as big as Jessup would have expected for somebody who played in the NFL. Though Coach is quick to point out that he was on the bubble for all eight years he played pro. "The only reason I stayed in the league as long as I did was because I was smart," he likes to say. "I couldn't make myself any faster, but I could learn the game and see it faster. All the same"—and with this he'd always grin—"best player or worst player on the team, you all get a ring." National championship his junior year in college at Alabama, when he was one of the better players on the team, and Super Bowl ring his last year in the pros, when he didn't take a snap until his team was already up four touchdowns. He's a good coach, even a great coach at the high school level, but he's not a lightning-and-thunder guy. He rarely raises his voice except to be heard. Work hard, do your job, understand the game better than the boy across the line from you.

Jessup watches Diggins shake hands with the ref and then trot over to the sideline and up to where the fence separates the bleachers from the field. His wife, Melissa, leans over for a kiss. Diggins is born and raised Mississippi, played college in Alabama, and bounced around in the pros. He met Melissa while he was playing in San Francisco. Coach is late forties, Mrs. Diggins a couple of years younger but looks midthirties. She's a California girl: white and blond and an athletic kind of skinny, like her job is to work out, except that her actual job is doing something up at Cortaca University. Jessup doesn't know what, except that she's the reason the Diggins family moved here, the reason why Coach Diggins was willing to try to turn around Cortaca High's football team.

At least that's what Deanne says. Deanne is a junior and Coach Diggins and Mrs. Diggins's daughter. Coach is dark and Mrs. Diggins isn't, and Deanne is a mix of the two of them. She gets mad at him when he compares her skin to food, says he's exoticizing her, but it's become a joke between the two of them. At least he thinks it's a joke. They've been dating for four months. Jessup worked at the golf course doing grounds six days a week over the summer, worked at the movie theater six nights. Gave up the golf course when football started but still works at the cinema, Saturdays and some Sundays after film study at Coach's house. Needs the money. Deanne worked at the movie theater over the summer and has kept it up during the school year, Saturdays and some Sundays, too, schedules in sync. They'd met before that, but they'd never spent real time together. He's still not exactly sure how they started dating. In any case, they've kept it discreet. Deanne's told her friends, and word has gotten around at school. Jessup's quiet, but he's not low profile. And Deanne's black. That means something with his family history. Mrs. Diggins knows they're dating, but he's pretty sure Coach doesn't know. If he does, he hasn't let on to Jessup.

He watches Deanne lean over the fence, too, kiss her dad on the cheek, and then straighten up. She looks at him and gives him something approximating a smile. They're going to meet up later, at the party, the two of them planning to sneak off and park somewhere. They slept together for the first time about two weeks ago, and he thinks he might love her, but that's something else Jessup shouldn't be thinking about right now.

Behind Mrs. Diggins and Deanne, two rows up, he sees an assistant coach from Syracuse University. This is the second game he's been to, and a scholarship offer is forthcoming. That's what Jessup has heard. He's not good enough for big-time football schools, but he's good enough to get offers from the bottom-feeding Division I schools. More important, his grades combined with his play on the field means the Ivies have started calling. An assistant coach from Brown University is at tonight's game, and Yale and Princeton have both been recruiting him. If he didn't play football, he'd be unsure about getting into Ivy League schools on his own merits, but he does play football, so the Ivy League coaches are salivating. His grades and SAT scores are high enough that he's an easy sell to administrators. The Ivies don't offer athletic scholarships, but he's poor as shit, so they'll give him a full ride. His mom wants him to stay home and play for Cortaca University—though she'd be okay with Syracuse, only an hour away, if that comes through, or the University at Buffalo, which offered already, too—but Jessup wants to put some miles between himself and Cortaca.

He knows the Cortaca University coach thinks he's in the bag, and he's pretty sure Syracuse feels the same way. Local kid? Why wouldn't he want to stay? But that's just it. He doesn't want to stay. He wants to get as far away from Cortaca as he can, and he wants to make sure he never has to come back. He hasn't said this out loud yet. His mom doesn't know he applied early decision to Yale. He'll hear at the beginning of December. If that doesn't work out, he's got applications out to Dartmouth, Brown, and Princeton, and just last week he got a scholarship offer from Duke. Bye-bye, upstate New York.

He takes another quick scan of the stands. His mom usually sits right in the middle, up high, her back against the fence, but there's a group of kids from the high school already there.

He doesn't see her, but they haven't kicked off yet. She texted him and said that the pickup at the prison went fine and that she'd be at the game. He's not worried. She's always there. She works days as a cleaning lady and a few nights a week at Target on the register, but she's always been clear with her manager that if she has to choose between taking a shift on a Friday night and losing her job, well, in a town like Cortaca, there are plenty of places she can work part time making a dollar and fifty cents an hour more than minimum wage.

MINUS SIX

He sees one of the Kilton Valley Cougars high-stepping. Kid named Kevin Corson. He's a running back. Good player. They've overlapped at a couple of one-day football camps. Never talked, which makes sense, since they play on opposite sides of the ball. Corson is already committed to play for Syracuse. Real dark skin—hide-in-the-night kind of black—but not one of the poor blacks. Six foot, two hundred pounds, fast in the flats with a good first move. He keeps himself low to the ground when he runs, shoulder down, ball tucked high and tight. He runs with purpose. His mom is an optometrist and his dad works at a bank or something. Money. Even from here, Jessup can see that he's wearing a brand-new pair of Nike turf shoes and pro gloves. The shoes go for something like $130 a pop, the gloves $60. Must have bought them just for this playoff game. He's heard Corson has worked with a personal trainer since middle school. He looks like it, all fast twitch, no fat. Could be the assistant coach from Syracuse University is here to take a last look at Corson, too. There's a part of Jessup that hopes so.

He's watched a lot of film, and he thinks he's got Corson dialed in. Corson's got a tell when he's going to cut left. Jessup will be able to contain him, keep him mostly bottled up, but if he plays it perfectly he'll be able to blow Corson up at least once. With a little luck, he'll jar the ball loose. Even if he can't make a highlight-reel hit, it's going to be a running game the whole night. Jessup will be able to take some shots. Maybe one of the guys on the line will stand Corson up so Jessup can go in hard and take his helmet off early on. Send him to the bench thinking about whether or not he really wants to keep going. That's the kind of thing that can tilt a game.

Corson sprints and takes a few quick shakes, getting a feel for the turf. It's sloppy, and it looks like Corson isn't happy. The kid glances up and sees

Jessup watching and gives him a big wink. Jessup doesn't smile. Doesn't look away. Thinks, I'm going to put you on your ass. A kid like Corson *likes* to play football while Jessup *needs* to play.

He feels a hard slap on his shoulder pads. Derek Lemper plays nose guard. He's a junior. Dumb as shit, but nice, and a tank. Dad's out of the picture, but Mom is the sales manager at the Honda dealership. She's a little hefty but still attractive. Nothing like Derek. Derek is close to three hundred pounds, his belly rolling over, head like a watermelon. He's got a girlfriend who looks like she came out of a gumball machine. Lot of jokes about her being crushed to death if Derek ever falls asleep after sex.

"Ready, Jessup? Kick some ass?" Derek has his hand out for a bump, and Jessup tags him.

"Kick some ass," Jessup agrees.

Derek grins and does a shimmy that makes Jessup laugh. He turns to see Wyatt Dunn doing his own sort of dance. He's been best friends with Wyatt since David John first started taking the family to church. Met him at church but went to the same elementary school, too, same middle school, same high school, Wyatt like a brother even if they don't go to church together anymore. Jessup hasn't gone to church since David John and Ricky were arrested, but even though Wyatt took a fair number of Sundays off to go hunting or just to sleep in when he was in eighth, ninth, tenth grades, he's started going regular again with his parents, every week, just like Jessup's mom and Jewel. Wyatt plays tackle. He's got a scholarship offer from UConn. Doesn't expect any more to come his way. The Huskies only won two of their twelve games last year. Wyatt's under no illusions, but he figures it's better than paying for college.

Wyatt reaches around him with his meaty arms and pulls Jessup in for a hug. He presses the side of his helmet into Jessup's. "Saw you watching Corson warm up. Knock the shit out of that son of a bitch, okay? Let's teach him a lesson, man. Teach him where he belongs." Wyatt squeezes Jessup and then says, "Jesus loves you and I love you, brother. Let's light 'em up."

Jessup says it back. Rituals. Jesus loves you and I love you, brother. Light 'em up. And together, Jesus keep us safe from harm. The same thing before every game since freshman year.

A couple of other defensive linemen have drifted over, and he goes through the routine with them, too, tapping fists, kick some ass, protect this house, stop them cold. The coaches are gesturing for them to head over to the bench, so they break it up.

In the few minutes since they've come back out from the locker room, the field has garnered a scrum of slush. It's a haze on the plastic grass. He looks up at the lights. The sleet has started to fully give over to snow. It comes down tracing the arc of winds and gravity, the pure glow of the lights turning every snowflake into a falling star. If he didn't have a game, he'd be happy to stand there forever. But he feels a few other hands slapping his shoulder pads, so he jogs over to the sideline, each step careful and testing, getting a sense of how his shoes are going to bite. He feels good. Loose. He got home from practice last night, helped his sister with her math, finished his own homework, and was in bed by ten, asleep so quick that he could have been drunk. He doesn't remember dreaming. People would pay good money to sleep like that.

Kilton Valley has elected to kick off. That means they'll start the second half with the ball, but right now it means that Jessup is going to have some time before he hits the field. He sits down on the bench, the wet metal cold, but it gives him a minute to deal with his shoes. He likes starting the game with everything perfect. It doesn't matter that the exercise is pointless; the rubber pellets on the turf cannot be conquered. He knows as soon as he's back on the field he'll have them gathered in his shoes. Once he hits the ground for the first time, they'll be worked up in his pads, too, in his socks, his hair. You can't escape them. He's got rubber pellets embedded under the scab on his elbow. He unlaces anyhow, shakes out his shoes, and has them laced back up in time to watch the kickoff.

But he misses the kick, because he catches sight of his sister and his mom at the end of the field, wending their way up the steps. And right with them, his stepfather. David John out of prison.

WHEN IT HAPPENED

Jessup at thirteen. Eighth grade and still hadn't grown yet. Hoping he was going to grow. Not that he was a shrimp, but he was on the smaller side. Mom always told him that his dad was a big guy, she'd say six two and solid. An engineering graduate student at Cortaca University. Either way, he was a drunk—that's what Jessup's father and mother had in common—and he killed himself in a single-car accident before Jessup was even born. From what his mom said, it didn't seem like things would have stuck between them anyway; they came from different worlds, and it wasn't much more than a fling, the two of them partying together, Jessup the only good thing to come out of it. She doesn't have a lot to say about Jessup's father, and they aren't in contact with that side of the family.

Ricky's dad, Pete Gilbert, was around here and there, though right now he is serving time at a state prison. Different prison than Ricky. Pete did okay as a dad when he wasn't in jail, usually remembering Ricky's birthday, showing up for football games despite how bad the team was, dropping by every few weeks. Doing his best to do right. Scrawny guy, and Ricky took after his dad. Pete and Jessup never talked much, but not a cross word, either. Nothing wrong with Pete except that he was just a kid when he got Jessup's mom pregnant. She was only fourteen, right at the end of her freshman year, when she had Ricky, Ricky's dad one year older but already dropped out of high school. What passed for a relationship between Pete and Jessup's mom was over long before Ricky could walk. By the time David John had become a going concern, Pete was just some guy who occasionally looked in on his son. No beef between the two men.

Ricky was already ten when David John came on the scene, but Jessup was only five. He doesn't remember what it was like before his stepfather. Nothing concrete. His life might as well have started the day David John walked through the door. Ricky's told him stories about what it was like before David John, but they seem unconnected to Jessup's life. Theoretical. Even though Jessup knows that it's true—his mom still goes to meetings every few weeks and calls herself an alcoholic—it's hard for him to believe. They don't keep alcohol in the house and Jessup doesn't have a memory of his mother ever having a drink. But he knows that's his stepfather's doing.

From Ricky's perspective, David John is the best thing to happen in his life. David John made good money as a plumber, and with him around, Mom stuck to cleaning houses. Dinner on the table every night. A full re-frigerator. Ricky no longer making grilled cheese for Jessup because their mom was working double shifts, cereal for dinner, school breakfast and lunch okay during the year, but things lean in the summers and on holi-days. The nurse at school keeping a food pantry and Ricky bringing food home to make sure he and Jessup had something to eat.

Neither Ricky nor Jessup was the kind to make excuses—David John wasn't one for excuses, and they'd learned to own up to their actions—but in letters the brothers had written back and forth, Ricky had been remark-ably forgiving of their mom.

Not like Grandma or Grandpa were much help. Can't have been easy. She was just a kid herself.

Which was true. Ricky at fourteen, Jessup when she was nineteen. By the time she met David John and they'd married, she was only twenty-five. And her parents. Grandpa was okay. Stubborn bastard, but he didn't say much. He liked spending time in the garage. He helped Jessup fix up his pickup, the only occasion Jessup can think of when he's ever spent much time with his grandfather, the truck a beater that Jessup bought for six hun-dred bucks and brought back from the dead. But his grandma, his mom's mother. Jesus. The old bitch had never been happy a day in her life. Hand the woman a pile of cash, and she'd complain about getting paper cuts. They kicked Cindy out when she was seventeen, Ricky only three. You're on your own, girl.

So David John was a lifeline, and Ricky grabbed hard.

Not Jessup. He didn't know why. Ricky was calling David John "Dad" by the time Jewel was born, but Jessup never got there.

"Mr. Serious," his mom called him.

"Doesn't matter none," David John said, because it didn't matter none to him. He treated both Ricky and Jessup like they were his own boys. Plenty of Jessup's friends didn't have fathers around, and plenty of the ones who did would have been happier without. If Jessup struggled to remember what it was like when his mother was drinking, all he had to do to get a sense of that life was to look around. Their closest neighbor had a boy near Jessup's age, just a year older, and his dad was a drunk and mean and quick with a fist. Mostly they played at Jessup's.

SEA CHANGE

No, Jessup doesn't remember what it was like before David John came along, and he doesn't think much of it, either. It was what it was, and then David John and his mom got together, and then it was something different. And the different was good. David John didn't drink and didn't allow it in the house. He believed in hard work and discipline and Jesus Christ and family, and he taught both Jessup and Ricky what it meant to be a man. They helped him with cutting and stacking wood, with fixing up the house, went with him on plumbing jobs during school breaks and dug up sewage lines. Learned to work a shovel, a chainsaw, a splitting maul, learned to say "Yes, sir" and "Yes, ma'am" and to make their beds and clear the dishes. David John was always patient, always willing to take the time to teach them how to do something properly. "If you're going to do something, you might as well do it right." Taught Jessup how to get his pads on, got up early with both boys to run and train for football but told them they weren't stepping on the field if their grades weren't up.

"Can't be lazy," he'd say. "The world ain't what it used to be. You need a college degree to get anywhere now, and they've got all kinds of quotas that you boys don't fit into. You can't just check a box and get into college. So study up unless you want to be working knee deep in crap your whole life like me." Said it with a grin, but even though Ricky was set on following in his stepfather's footsteps, Jessup liked school, and David John encouraged both of them. "You're smart, but the world's tilted against white boys like you nowadays. We live out here in the country in a trailer, and when they look at you, they're thinking white trash. Teachers don't expect much, so you've got to show them."

After dinner, television off and sit at the kitchen table. David John and Ricky and Jessup working over math and English and anything else they'd brought home from school. Ricky needed the help and Jessup didn't, but either way, David John was there at the table with the two boys. What he didn't know, he learned, just so he could give Ricky a hand. No college, but that didn't mean he was dumb. Mom cleaning up and taking care of baby Jewel. Nothing stronger than iced tea for her.

They went to church on the regular, too. That was something else that was new. David John's brother a preacher. Ten minutes farther out of town, toward Brooktown. Two hundred wooded acres. A compound. "No trespassing" signs ringing the acreage. The church in an old barn that'd been fixed up.

Blessed Church of the White America.

CORTACA AND SURROUNDING

But first, Cortaca and surrounding areas.

Glacial remains carved out a string of lakes in upstate New York, and Cortaca sits at the head of Cortaca Lake. The lake is thirty miles tip to tail, a mile across. There are gorges cut throughout the land around here, steep walls and rivers and creeks sawing through. Can't walk anywhere without passing a waterfall. Something like 150 waterfalls in the area. There's one almost across the street from the high school that has to be twenty stories tall and just as wide. The city prides itself on the waterfalls, but that's not what most people know about Cortaca. What people know is the university.

The joke is that Cortaca University is your Ivy League safety school if you're rich enough to buy your way into Harvard but not smart enough to stay there. For most kids, though, Cortaca University is a first choice. Fifteen percent admission rate, expectation is that you're near the top of your class. Ivy League doesn't come easy. Or cheap. Not all of the students at Cortaca University come from money, but sometimes it feels that way. Mommy and Daddy dropping a quarter million to buy a condo for their precious to live in with friends because it's just a smart investment, and besides, have you seen the rentals in Collegetown? The school is big enough that you can feel it when the students are gone. Every August, the grocery stores suddenly stocking microwaves and minifridges, new students accidentally driving the wrong way down one-way streets.

The university has its own gravity—it's the largest employer in town—but it's not everything. There's a whole other world in Cortaca that's fallen through the cracks. Thirty-five percent of the county is under the poverty line. Used to be lots of good jobs, but it's the same old story as any other Rust Belt town. Not as bad as Syracuse or some of the other towns that got hollowed out and had to rebuild, but bad enough. Empty factory buildings on East Hill, the ground contaminated from years of lax standards. Too expensive to clean up, so no hope for new construction. The skeletons of the buildings laid bare, roofs collapsing, windows knocked out, good places to go drink and party, make a fire, the light laying bare the rot. Jessup's grandfather worked fifteen years assembling washing machines at one of the factories, but it closed up about the time Jessup's mom was ten. From then on, it was three years here, two years there, nothing with staying power. Each new job a cut in pay. Assistant manager at a body shop now. The owner's a good guy, let Jessup and his grandfather use one of the bays on the weekends to finish up Jessup's truck. Paint job at cost.

Not every job is gone. There's still the Cargill plant and the salt works, and if you can catch on at either one, it's a good paycheck. Solid work. A furniture-manufacturing plant past the university employs close to two hundred people, but there've been rumors about a move overseas. Made in America costs too much. The auto-parts plant near the municipal airport—six flights a day, two each to Washington, Detroit, and Philadelphia—has more than a thousand workers, but that's owned by a multinational, so most people are just counting the days until it folds. Erkman's Power Transmission makes bearings and couplings and employs nearly as many people. It's locally owned, but the work is hard and the pay isn't much better than you could do elsewhere. Starts at minimum wage plus two.

Even with the decay, it's a town that looks pretty in pictures and makes visiting parents feel good about sending their kids. Without the students, the Cortaca metropolitan area still has a population of about fifty thousand people. Big enough that there's a Target and a Walmart and a whole string of chains lining the main road that cuts through town. But if chain stores aren't your thing, at the foot of the hill, below where the university sits, there's a pedestrian mall, two city blocks closed to traffic. The pedestrian mall is full of one-offs: local restaurants, small stores selling sheepskin clothing, antiques, outdoor gear. Boutiques. It's picturesque. You have to go out of your way to stumble into the poor parts of town. Easier still to pay no attention to what happens when you get a little outside, in the surrounding areas. If you stay on the county highways, you'll see trailers and run-down houses, but unless you take the county lanes, you don't see the sheer numbers. Most of the country people keep some privacy. People like Jessup might as well be invisible.

He doesn't mind it, though. Likes not being seen. Likes being outside of Cortaca proper. Their trailer isn't much, but he can walk out the back of their property and cut through the trees until he meets the deer trail, and from there it's only a few minutes until he's on public land. Forty minutes of good walking takes him to wetlands, not bad for duck hunting. Their trailer is set back off the road, not that there's much traffic anyway. Midlake Road isn't a shortcut to anywhere. In the winter, it gets plowed late. His mom has a rusted-out 2005 Ford Focus that she drives when the weather is good because it gets better gas mileage, but when there's snow she takes David John's work van, which is four-wheel drive. Jessup manages okay in his truck. At first he had trouble, because with the weight of the engine up front and the empty bed in back, he kept spinning, but David John wrote and told him to keep a two-by-six wedged across the back of the truck bed and then drop in a couple of sandbags. The two-by-six keeps the sandbags in place, and the weight from the sandbags keeps the back end from fishtailing in the snow. With the change in the weather, tomorrow he'll have to put the two-by-six and the sandbags back in place before he heads out to keep the truck from sliding on him.

Jessup knows that Cortaca isn't a bad place to live. With the university and a history of good jobs—even if many of them are gone—the schools are solid. And for a kid like Jessup, who likes the outdoors and doesn't have a lot of money, it's a wonderland. But he's ready to get away. As soon as he graduates, he'll be gone.

Too much history here.

THE FIGHT

It's not his history. He doesn't share a last name with either Ricky or his stepfather, but it doesn't matter. Cortaca's too small a town for people to stay out of each other's business.

The whole thing played in the papers and on television. Not just local, either. Story was national. Jessup doesn't talk about it, and his friends know to steer clear of the question. Not that he has that many friends aside from Wyatt. Teammates, sure. Football in the fall, wrestling in the winter, runs the one hundred and two hundred in track and field in the spring. Buddies, really, which is different from friends. Plus, now, Deanne. And she's never asked him about what happened with David John and Ricky in the alley. It's a hole they could fall into. They both know that.

Jessup's just glad it never went to trial. That would have been an even bigger circus.

An emergency job on the pedestrian mall. Saturday night turned Sunday morning, closing in on two o'clock. Ricky's nineteen at this point. Out of high school and officially apprenticing with David John. During the days they both wear Dickies short-sleeve shirts, a DJM Plumbing patch above where their names are embroidered. David John liked to say you could charge an extra ten bucks an hour if you looked like you were a real business instead of just some idiot with a truck. He has tattoos himself, but they were out of sight: back, shoulders, chest. He made it clear to Ricky that if he got ink where you could see it while he was working, Ricky would spend his days wearing long-sleeved shirts.

But emergency job, and Ricky coming from his girlfriend's house. Stacey and her parents congregants at Blessed Church of the White America themselves. So Ricky wearing jeans and a tank top, heading to the van, parked in the alley behind the pedestrian mall, near the back door of the restaurant. The van, "DJM Plumbing" a phone number, and "On call, on time. Your local plumber" stenciled on the side. David John's text to Ricky:

already inside. Uniform on front seat.

It's a warm night. Early in September. A few days before the full moon, so even if the alley wasn't lit, and the interior dome light from the van didn't spill out over him from the open passenger side door, it would have been plenty bright enough to see Ricky pull off his tank top. He's shirtless, holding his work shirt and ready to slip it on as the boys walk by.

Two of them. Both Cortaca University students, cutting through the alley on the way home from a bar. Black kids. One from Atlanta, the other from Buffalo, both seniors, both twenty-one. Jermane Holmes and Blake Liveson. They'd both snuck their beers out of the bar with them. Bottles of Yuengling, TopFloor Bar running a special.

Right there on Ricky's back, "Blessed Church of the White America" circling a flaming cross, the whole thing about the size of a sheet of printer paper, six hundred bucks' worth of tattoo. On his right shoulder, "eighty-eight" and on his left shoulder, "pure blood." Impossible for Holmes and Liveson to miss.

Sometimes Jessup wonders what would have happened if it had been him standing in the alley instead of Ricky. At seventeen, Jessup is six foot two and weighs in at 240. He's chiseled. His face shows his age, but he's got a man's body, and all you have to do is see him walk to understand that Jessup is built for certain kinds of violence. But two different dads mean two different boys, two different bodies. Ricky thought of himself as lean—even though he played football—but he looked scrawny, like his dad. He was strong and never had trouble keeping up with David John at work, but when they arrested him, he was five eight and a buck sixty. Not imposing. Holmes and Liveson weren't particularly big themselves, and they might have kept walking if they'd seen somebody Jessup's size. But it wasn't Jessup. It was Ricky.

The black kids come at him. Ricky said he told them he didn't want trouble, was just there to do a job, but words were exchanged. Names called.

Liveson, the bigger of the two black students, hits Ricky with his bottle of Yeungling—the booking photos show a deep bruise seeping down from Ricky's eye and a cut across his cheek, could have lost an eye—and according to Ricky, the other one, Holmes, the one from Atlanta, has a knife. Ricky reaches through the open passenger-side door, grabs a loose pipe wrench from the floor.

Self-defense, Ricky said.

Eighteen inches and five and a half pounds of steel. Swings the pipe wrench as hard as he can. Takes the jaw off Liveson. Kid spins and flops to the asphalt. By this time, the yelling's brought David John out into the alley. He's grabbing the back of the second black kid's shirt, Holmes, the one Ricky claims has the knife, when Ricky swings the wrench a second time. Connects right on Holmes's temple. Staves his head in. Dead before he hits the ground.

The bar has a video camera on the back entrance, but it's low quality and doesn't capture everything. Jerky, shooting at 7.5 frames per second, and grainy. The whole fight captured. Liveson twitches for thirty, forty seconds before going still, but it's not clear when he actually dies. As for Holmes, only his body from the knees down are in the frame, and his legs don't move at all. There's no sound, but you can see Ricky sit down and lean against the front wheel of the van. He drops the wrench and slumps over, rests his head on his hands. He's still shirtless. David John stands in front of Ricky for a full minute, his back to the camera. Then he turns and looks around. After a few seconds, it's clear that he spots the camera. He stares at it, and then David John is in and out of the van—you can't see what he's doing, no way to prove he's grabbing a knife, wiping it clean of prints—and walks past Holmes's body. There's a herky-jerky movement, shadow falling into the frame, and then Holmes is rolled over, still only his lower legs in the frame, his sneakers now turned so that he's on his back. Another minute, and then David John comes back into the frame. He says something to Ricky and pulls his phone out of his pocket. Calls the cops and then sits down next to Ricky.

THE AFTERMATH

The video shows Liveson hitting Ricky first, but there's no angle that shows whether or not Holmes is holding a knife before David John turns him over. Holmes's got a knife in his hand by the time the police and the ambulance arrive, that's for sure, but there's only a single set of fingerprints on it, as if somebody had wrapped Holmes's fingers around the handle. It's a cheap folding pocketknife, the kind sold at hardware stores for twenty bucks. This model comes from Home Depot. Something a contractor—or a plumber—might carry, but there's no way to tell who bought it. No audio, so no way to prove what the black kids said to Ricky, what word Ricky might have said back.

It's a messy case, the kind that's a no-win for the prosecutor. David John's record is pretty clean—he's never done time—but his brother, Earl, is the preacher and the face of the Blessed Church of the White America, and David John has his own tattoos. Affiliations. If the dead kids were white, you could settle it as self-defense, give a slap on the wrist, call it a day, but with two dead black kids, both students at Cortaca University to boot? Holmes's dad a police chief in one of Atlanta's suburbs, his mom a kindergarten teacher, Liveson's parents both lawyers and moneyed. It hits the national papers, CNN and Fox News and MSNBC sending news trucks, Jessup's mom having to chase at least one reporter off their property. Protests at the church—Jessup hears this from his mom and Wyatt, because he refuses to go—with signs and chanting and eggs thrown at congregants' cars. It plays on the news for weeks.

The whole thing is high profile, but it's not open-and-shut: with the video, and with both Ricky and David John sticking to their stories, there's too much room for it to go off the rails if the prosecutor takes it to court. The victims drinking, Ricky claiming self-defense, the video showing Ricky getting hit first. If the boys had been empty-handed, it would have been a disproportional response, but with the beer bottles, with a knife found in one of the black kid's hands? It's the kind of case that can kill a political career if it goes poorly. The prosecutor decides to deal.

Jessup's mom wants them to fight, but the court-appointed lawyer—they can't afford any better, though there's some talk of a collection at the church—explains that her son and her husband aren't going to find a sympathetic jury. Not here. The mayor of Cortaca, a former Cortaca University student who is only in his midtwenties, is incensed. He's calling it a hate crime, calls it a crime against the community. He's asked the Department of Justice to open a civil rights investigation. The mayor is earnest, but there are other politicians getting in on it, grandstanding. It's a litmus test.

The lawyer, frustrated, tells them that if they risk a trial, Ricky might spend the rest of his life in prison, David John along for the ride. It's not going to look good. White-power tattoos and two dead black college students?

They take the plea bargains. Rock and a hard place and all that. Ricky lucky to be able to walk out of prison when he's nearly forty, half his life gone by. That's a good deal for killing two men, the lawyer tells them, and David John's only doing five years. Less if he behaves himself.

He behaves himself.

David John skates after four.

KICKOFF

David John is walking behind Jessup's mom and Jewel. From thirty yards away, Jessup recognizes his stepfather, but can't see if the man looks any different. Jessup's been good about writing back to both David John and Ricky—both men write him at least once a week—but he's refused to visit either. He doesn't know why.

The hum of the crowd swells as the kicker for the Kilton Valley Cougars runs at the ball. Everybody's watching the field, the way the kicker plants his foot and swings through, the ball tumbling high in the heavy falling snow, spinning up into the darkness and then back down, dropping near the ten. The first wave of Kilton Valley players crashes against the Cortaca High players, and even though he's looking away from the field, at his family, Jessup can hear the grunts and the crack of pads and helmets. Everybody is watching the kickoff except for David John. His stepfather's eyes have found him, and he gives Jessup a nod. Jessup nods back.

He turns in time to see the Kilton Valley gunner—a white kid who plays tight end when he isn't tasked with head-hunting the Cortaca High kick returner—cut in and take Simeon Lesko down at the seventeen.

Five of the players on the kick-return team are also starters on offense, so it's a piecemeal swap of players for Cortaca High. Kilton Valley fills the box, ready to stop the run. They know what's coming. Cortaca's starting quarterback, Jonathan Choo, could sling the ball, but he broke his clavicle the second game of the season. There's a chance he'll be back for next week's game if the Bears make it through. In the same game Choo got hurt, the backup—a mouthy, arrogant senior named Jayden Carlisle, who resented having to sit behind Choo—got his knee torn up. Since then, it's been Phillip Ryerson. Kid is fourteen, a true freshman, looks milquetoast, but tough as heck. Not a great arm, but smart and only had five turnovers for the season.

All preseason with Choo, they practiced Diggins's plan to have them run and gun. With Jonathan at quarterback, they figured they'd be able to score four, five touchdowns a game. All the defense had to do was keep it close and let Choo do his thing. But plans change; they have to, otherwise two injuries over three quarters sends the season down the tubes. With Ryerson back there, the plan has been grind it out. Three yards and a pile of bodies. Live and die by the defense. Ryerson only throwing eight, ten times a game, just trying to keep the other team honest.

But it isn't enough to keep the other team honest. When the Bears have the ball, opposing teams fill the box. And that's what Kilton Valley does on the first play. Nine men up front, both safeties crowding the line and ready to corral the run.

Of course, that assumes Cortaca does, in fact, run the ball.

They practiced it all week. It isn't the play that is the issue; it's selling the run. Ryerson has to keep his head down, look back at Mike Crean playing fullback and Pearce Trion at running back behind him, motion them over a foot or two. And split all the way left, Trevell Brown, looking like he's half-assing it.

Ryerson barks in cadence, pauses and motions to his right, pulling everybody but Trevell to the line. Kilton Valley is playing a six-two, but the middle linebackers are almost close enough to touch the offensive line, and the free safety is right in the middle, barely five yards back. The cornerback on the right side has drifted in with his assignment, and even from his spot on the sideline, Jessup can see that the cornerback covering Trevell has already turned his hips to the inside. It's one on one with Trevell. No backup for Kilton Valley if Trevell can get past his man: it's clear to Jessup even before Ryerson has the ball in his hands that Kilton Valley has bit on the play.

The crowd in the stand recognizes it even as the two lines smash into each other, a throaty roar washing over Jessup as he watches Ryerson taking a seven-step drop, Crean and Pearce rushing up to keep a pocket around him. Jessup has to admit it's a ballsy call by Coach Diggins. They ran it at least twenty times in practice, and even with a soft defense, they only pulled it off half the time. Trevell's got straight-line speed, but he's also got hands of stone, and it's not like Ryerson can just drop it in the breadbasket. And tonight, with the cold and the sleet turned into heavy, fat snow, a thousand sparkling candles in the floodlights, Jessup figures it for a wasted play. Best case, it gets Kilton Valley to play receivers like they are a real threat for a while, give a little space for Cortaca to run the ball.

But good Lord, Trevell gets the jump on the cornerback. By the time he's five yards off the line of scrimmage, the cornerback is just starting to turn. Trevell has got his man beat easy, wide-open field in front of him. He's running flat out, head down, not supposed to even look for the ball until he's twenty yards off the line. And Ryerson finishes dropping back and then cocks the ball back and steps forward, all his weight behind the ball. He gives it everything he's got.

It's an ugly throw. Slow-motion highlights from college and the pros always show the ball in a tight spiral, spinning through the air like a bullet, but this ball is wobbling and a floater. And yet it's clear that despite how wounded the ball looks, Ryerson has overshot. He's thrown the ball forty, forty-five yards. A hell of a throw. Trevell still hasn't looked up, and he's got at least ten yards on the cornerback now. Finally, he turns his head, and even though Jessup is across the field, he swears he can see Trevell's eyes popping out of his skull. He's got a bead on the ball, and he takes one last step before laying himself full out in the air, the ball nestling perfectly into his fingers. He pulls the ball in to his chest and twists as he comes down, landing on his back on the Kilton Valley thirty-five and sliding a good ten yards in the mess of snow and slush. When he comes to a stop on the Kilton Valley twenty-five-yard line, he holds the ball up and there's an explosion of noise from the stands behind Jessup.

SEVEN TO THREE

One minute and forty-four seconds left in the second quarter. The temperature has dropped at least two degrees. It's full snow now. Still wet and heavy, but no longer sleet, and there's at least half an inch coating the field. The line markings are invisible. A couple of middle school kids with brooms sweep the sidelines clean every time the play stops, but on the field, the yardage markers might as well not exist.

After that first play, they moved the ball down the field in two- and three-yard chunks, Coach Diggins deciding to go for it on fourth down when they were on the Kilton Valley eighteen, converting, and again when they were on the one-yard line, punching in for the touchdown. Up seven zip before Kilton Valley touched the ball. Other than that first pass, however, it's been bruising football. The punters on both teams getting a lot of work. Cortaca hasn't even gotten it past the fifty-yard line since the opening series. Kilton Valley only on the board because their kicker is a senior and committed to playing at Colgate University. Not a football powerhouse, but still, a Division I school is a D-I school. Despite the weather, their kicker hit a forty-seven-yard field goal at the end of the first quarter. The score has been stuck at 7–3 all of the second quarter.

But now, with less than two minutes until halftime, Kilton Valley is on the Bears' eleven-yard line. Third down and three to go. The Cougars have been riding Corson hard. The running back is already over a hundred yards for the day. He's only broken one run, for twenty yards, and Jessup brought him down from behind, but there have been a couple of others that have been close. Sooner or later, with the ground the way it is, Corson is going to go long. Jessup knows this, but mostly, at this moment, he's only worried about short yardage. There's the eleven yards between the line of scrimmage and his end zone, and there's the three yards between the Cougars and a first down. If Corson picks up the first down, the Cougars have three more shots at the end zone before settling for a field goal. But worse, playing to protect only those three yards leaves Cortaca vulnerable for the whole eleven. The problem is that it's not just Corson Jessup is worried about; the Kilton Valley quarterback has been throwing, no matter the snow. Short throws, but it's meant Jessup has had to stay on his toes, calling out defensive alignments and shifts. He's broken up two passes, but he can tell by the way his teammates are moving that they're gassed. On their last possession, Cortaca punted from the fifty, the Cougars taking the ball inside the ten; they've backed the Bears eighty yards down the field.

And then he sees it. The quarterback has Kilton Valley lined up for what will be an obvious rollout to the left side. Anybody can see what the play is going to be. The whole offense is tilted left: there are two receivers split wide, the tight end looking back, and the fullback with his body angled to clear space for the quarterback. When the center snaps the ball, the quarterback is supposed to run left and then either keep the ball himself or toss it into the end zone. Except that there's a reason Coach Diggins has them watch so much tape.

If Kilton Valley runs the play correctly, as the entire offense swings left, the quarterback paced by the fullback, the receivers flashing open, the defense follows suit, swallowing the play hook, line, and sinker. The whole thing is a feint. As the play starts, Corson, the running back, jams right against the tide, and instead of keeping the ball or throwing to a receiver, the quarterback turns and zips a fastball across to the other side of the field, where Corson has a wide corridor into the end zone.

Jessup looks over his teammates and sees that none of them have recognized it. They are all about to bite hard on the play: every single player on defense is oriented toward the overload, ready to protect the strong side. The smart move here is for Jessup to yell it out, make a defensive shift. He can call for a weak side pickup—peel the strong safety and the outside linebacker out, doubling Corson—or make the shift himself and cover Corson as he runs. Either option would take away Corson as an option. It would mean trusting the corners and the free safety to cover the tight end and the receivers in the end zone, forcing the quarterback to keep the ball himself.

Best-case scenario, somebody takes the quarterback down behind the line of scrimmage, fourth down, and the Kilton Valley Cougars settle for the easy field goal, Jessup goes into the locker room at halftime with his team up seven to six.

His job is to recognize what the offense is doing, to make the call and shift the defense, but he decides against it. It's a huge gamble, but he figures if nobody else on his team has recognized the play, maybe Corson and the Kilton Valley quarterback won't realize Jessup has sussed it out.

He creeps up to the line, showing blitz. Let them think he's coming hard at the quarterback. He's on the weak side, the side Corson is going to be rolling to, and Jessup is careful to keep his eyes on the quarterback. As the quarterback puts out his hand, he takes one more quick scan of the field, and Jessup sees the gleam in the boy's eye; as far as he can tell, the entire Cortaca High School football team is about to make a huge mistake.

The quarterback hits his cadence, "hut, hut, hut," and the center snaps the ball. Immediately, the quarterback and the fullback and the entire offensive line start sweeping left. The defense follows. But not Jessup. Jessup has pivoted and is running hard away from the play. He's following Corson.

He doesn't even bother looking for the ball. He's watching Corson. The running back sprints to the right and then stops and pivots. Corson is locked in, tunnel vision on the quarterback. The quarterback has already turned and is slinging the ball across the field, but with the wet and the cold, the ball is high. Corson has to jump, his hands up above his head. He's a full yard behind the line of scrimmage as the ball comes to him.

Jessup times it perfectly. He's fast. He runs the one hundred and two hundred in track and field for a reason. He's running full speed as he propels himself. Corson's locked in on the football, doesn't even see what's about to happen.

Jessup blows him up.

He absolutely murders Corson.

FOURTEEN TO THREE

It's a bang-bang play. Jessup freight-trains Corson just as the ball arrives. Catches him right in the sternum with his shoulder. Jessup's launched himself, so his entire body weight, 240, hits with a sickening crunch that he'll hear like an echo for the rest of his life. He follows through, lifting and dropping, bringing Corson onto his back with Jessup driving down with his shoulder. Corson hits the turf so hard his helmet pops off, but Jessup isn't watching: he's after the ball. The football has bounced off Corson's hands and hits the ground spinning backward, two, three yards.

It all happens behind the line of scrimmage, so it doesn't matter that Corson couldn't hold on: it's a live ball no matter what. Jessup's scrambling, pawing at the ground, shoes sliding in the wet snow. He risks a glance toward the center of the field. He can see players from both teams rumbling toward him, but he's already scooping up the ball.

Clear sailing to the end zone. Closest player is one of his own, ready to block for him, but still ten yards back and with nobody on defense even within fifteen yards of him by the time Jessup waltzes in for the touchdown. He stands in the end zone savoring it until he's dog-piled by most of the defensive players on the field. He ends up on his back, and once his guys start peeling themselves off, he takes a second and does a quick snow angel, expecting the whistle, but the ref lets it go.

He knocks helmets and bumps fists and takes hugs on the sidelines. He doesn't bother watching the point after or the kickoff. He's looking at Corson across the way. His teammates had to help Corson get off the field, and right now, while Jessup's watching, Corson pushes away the athletic trainer so that he can puke in a trash can.

Jessup wasn't head-hunting—it was a clean hit, football done the right way—and he didn't want to injure Corson, but no way that boy will be the same if he comes back in the game.

Wyatt calls his name, and Jessup gets up and jogs back onto the field. Kilton Valley is on their own twenty. There isn't enough time left in the half for them to do anything, so they just kneel down three straight plays, run out the clock so they can head into the locker room and lick their wounds, the score fourteen to three.

At the whistle, the Kilton Valley boys walk off the field, while the Cortaca High School players jog. Jessup is smiling when he looks up into the stands. David John and his mom are sitting down—at least he thinks they are, since he can't really see them—but Jewel is standing up on her seat and waving at him. He waves back.

The two of them are tight. He doesn't mind that she's eleven. She tags along with him as much as he lets her. Since Ricky and her dad have been in prison, he's stepped into David John's role: helps her with her homework, makes sure she brushes her teeth before bed, that she's got clean clothes for school, that she's eating right. They weren't exactly rolling in it when David John was home, but since his stepfather went to jail, it's been rough. Money is always tight, Mom doing best when she gets paid cash for cleaning houses, the extra shifts at Target means she brings home groceries, but David John was strict about the family eating real food, not crap from a box. And no microwave in this house—do you really believe the government is telling you the truth about those? On the nights his mom is working, Jessup cooks. Nothing fancy, but fresh vegetables, pasta, chicken, everything homemade. Venison and duck he hunts and packs in the freezer. Jewel usually does the dishes after dinner so that he can finish his own homework.

Normally at halftime, while he's in the locker room, she'll go find her friends, head to the snack bar for a hot chocolate if Jessup slips her a few dollars, but tonight he figures she'll stay with Mom and her dad.

She waves again and then blows him a kiss, and he reciprocates before heading out of the stadium and into the parking lot. It's transformed. The open asphalt looks like a Dalmatian's back, mostly white, but with black spots where the snow hasn't stuck yet. The cars and trucks in the lot are blanketed, all but the most recent arrivals with a good coating of snow. Hope you remembered to throw the scraper and brush back into your car.

All of the snow has brought a quiet with it. The boys are shouting and talking as they jog toward the main building and the locker rooms, but Jessup realizes that the click of his shoes has been muted, that the sound of the traffic passing by the high school on Route 13 is a muffled echo. In the morning, when he goes hunting, the woods are going to be a church.

HALFTIME

A piss and then position group meetings, and then Coach Diggins gathers them around and tells them to keep doing what they're doing. The old coach was a rah-rah guy, but no good with *X*'s and *O*'s. Coach Diggins is more reserved, but he commands the room: he's earned their respect. Every single one of these kids, Jessup included, would lay their body out on the field for Coach Diggins.

In the same way that Coach Diggins isn't rah-rah in his halftime speeches, he isn't rah-rah about Jesus, either. The prayers are supposed to be nondenominational, but a quarter of the kids exit the room or hang out on the edges when the team circles up for the prayer. There are a couple of Jews on the team—Steve Silver is a good player, an anchor on the offensive line—one player who's a Muslim, two other players who are Indian or Pakistani or something and Jessup doesn't know what they are, plus a few more who it's just not their thing. The professors' kids, not that there are that many who play football, always decline. Jessup knows that in the South it's full-on praise Jesus and pastors and preachers brought into the locker room, but the Bears usually just stick to "Dear Lord, please protect our players and our opponents, keep us safe in your arms and your heart, amen," and then twenty or thirty seconds of silent prayer.

Wyatt occasionally gives Jessup a hard time about his absence from church. For the last year or so, Wyatt has been attending regularly, and he means it when he says he worries about Jessup's soul: come on brother, you don't want to burn, I love you and Jesus loves you, and Jesus has to be your lord and savior. Wyatt believes in eternal salvation, Jesus's love, and the Blessed Church of the White America.

Jessup's mom has never been hit-or-miss on attending church like Wyatt was, but even though she's not happy about Jessup's absence, she leaves him be. She still takes Jewel to church, though, every single Sunday, never fail, never miss, the two of them usually eating lunch out at the compound. Once or twice a month, David John's brother, Earl—Jewel's uncle, his mom's brother-in-law—comes to the trailer to join them for dinner on a Saturday night. Jessup tries to be out those nights. Nothing he can point to, no mornings he's woken up to Earl slinking out of the house, and if anything, the man always keeps too much physical distance between himself and Jessup's mom. He slips her some money now and then, but there's something about him that leaves Jessup cold.

In almost every letter David John writes, he encourages Jessup to return to the fold: *Church is family, and you don't walk away from family, Jessup. You can't turn your back on your family. Family first and always. I worry about your soul, of course. Don't you believe that Jesus died for your sins? But I worry about your place here on earth, as well. It's important to spend time surrounded by the people who are like you, with no outside distractions, nothing to dilute the purity of Christ's love. These are your people. Your tribe.*

Just because Jessup doesn't go to church doesn't mean he won't pray, however, and he kneels down between Wyatt and Mike Crean. They all clasp hands, bow their heads, say "amen" to the idea of being kept safe, and then stay quiet.

He doesn't know what the coaches and the other boys are thinking. Probably praying to win the game, to stay healthy, for God to grant them personal favors. Jessup usually prays for Jewel to be happy, for things to be a little easier for his mother. He prays with fervor; he has not lost faith, even if he doesn't attend church.

After fifteen minutes inside, the night feels cold. His pants and jersey are soaked, a mix of sweat and hitting the wet, snow-covered turf. Jessup figures there might be three or four inches on the ground by morning if it keeps up. In the stadium, the middle school boys have done their work with shovels and brooms, and the sidelines and yardage markers are clean for now.

Jessup is middle of the pack as the team jogs into the stadium. Some of the boys head straight to the bench, and some go onto the field to warm up again while the scoreboard ticks off the last two minutes until the start of the second half, but some of the boys stop to talk to friends or girlfriends or moms and dads. Jessup peels off and walks to where the chest-high fence meets the bleachers. His mom, Jewel, and David John are waiting for him.

THE TRIBE

David John is shaking his head and smiling. He's wearing a heavy work jacket that's unzipped, showing a blue hooded sweatshirt. His hair is cut short, almost a buzz cut but enough for Jessup to see that there is white in the hair that isn't because of the snow. His stepdad has one hand shoved into a pocket, the other free so that he can keep his arm wrapped around Jewel's shoulder. Jewel is leaning into him, a fat grin on her face, Christmas morning having her dad back in the house.

David John leans over now and smacks Jessup's shoulder pad. "Hell of a hit there, son. You saw that coming, didn't you?"

"Yes, sir. Been doing a lot of film study."

David John straightens up and then lets his head fall back and his eyes scrunch tight as he calls out, "Whoo-hee! You lit that boy up." His voice is loud enough that people standing nearby glance over. "You put a hurting on that boy."

There's a group of parents a few feet over, and they do more than glance. They stare. Two of the couples are black, and Jessup sees one of the women whisper something to her husband. The visitors all sit in the stands on the other side of the field, so these are Cortaca parents. He's not sure he recognizes them, but they sure seem to recognize him and David John. Jessup knows the word "boy" comes out loaded from David John's mouth, even if he doesn't think his stepfather means anything by it.

At least, not right in this moment.

It's hard to tell sometimes. David John doesn't allow swearing, doesn't use epithets, isn't calling Corson "boy" to stir up trouble. Jessup doesn't understand how his stepfather's devotion to his family, his gentle politeness, reconcile with his tattoos, with his belief in the Blessed Church of the White America, a place where certain words are used with casual violence. But can anything be reconciled? Where does Jessup stand in any of this? Because he loves his family, no question, but he also loves—yes, he thinks, loves—Deanne, even Coach Diggins, the boys on the team, too, absolutely he'd say he loves all of them, brothers sometimes, like he thinks of Wyatt like a brother, football flattening everything, the color of the jerseys the only thing that matters, and when he put Corson in the dirt right before halftime, in that moment, it was only about football.

Except it can't be about just football anymore, can it? Not with David John here. Not with what happened in the alley.

He misses the way it was before.

The ability to believe in an uncomplicated manner that his stepfather is a good man.

His sister can still do it: even with all that's happened, she can't conceptualize David John as anything other than her father.

If only it were that simple for Jessup. He's tried to avoid addressing the question—avoiding it altogether, refusing to visit both his stepfather and his brother and refusing to talk about why—but there are some things that you can only put off so long, and David John has brought the question home.

Jewel takes his attention back, says, "We're going to Kirby's"—a burger place on Route 13 that David John likes—"after the game. Celebrate having Dad home. Well, and celebrate the game, too. You going to meet us there, or at home?"

Jessup takes a quick look at the scoreboard. Fifty seconds ticking down. He puts his helmet on. "Let's wait to celebrate the game until it's over, okay? And I'll meet you at Kirby's. I've got plans later, though. After that. Can't stay long. Meeting up with Wyatt and some of the guys. I won't be home until late."

His mom and Jewel are happy, juiced up on David John's presence and on the score of the game, but Jessup can see a quick squint from David John. Disappointment that he's not going to stay in with the family. But it's there and gone.

His mom says, "Is there going to be drinking?"

"It's a party, so probably." Jessup shrugs. "But not by me, and I'll drive myself. I'll be careful."

David John leans over the railing again and taps him on the top of the helmet. It's a familiar gesture. The tribe of football. "Go teach those boys what they get when they come into our house," he says.

Jessup turns and heads to the bench. Kilton Valley kicked off to start the game, so that means they are going to receive, and Jessup needs to start the half on the field.

He looks back over his shoulder and sees his mom and Jewel already climbing up the bleacher steps, but David John is watching him. There's a part of Jessup that wants to apologize, wants to say that he knows it's a big deal that David John is home and he'll cancel his plans. But only a part.

He does have plans, but not with the guys. Oh, after he leaves Kirby's he'll stop by the party, and Wyatt will be there. But if it were only that, he'd go home with his family, spend the night soaking in the quiet comfort of his mother's and sister's happiness.

No, he's going out because Deanne's coming to the party, too. They'll make the rounds and then leave as soon as they can get away with it, drive out to one of the forest preserves and leave the truck running so there will be more than just the heat of their bodies to keep them warm.

WINNER WINNER

Jessup's hair is still wet from the shower, but he doesn't feel cold. Lots of yelling and jumping in the locker room after the game, coach quieting them down to remind them that they need to get back to work for next week, but it's all good feelings; Kilton Valley didn't put up much of a fight after halftime, final score 20–6.

Diggins singles out plays, players, all good, all good. And then he holds up a football. "We've never done game balls since I've been here, but then again, we've never had a playoff game, either." His smile an electric charge sparking around the room. "I think we all know who this game ball is going to." He turns to Jessup. "You were the beating heart of this team, and you deserve this." Lots of huffing and hooting and "yes, sir" and clapping as Coach Diggins tucks the game ball into Jessup's gut, the two of them hugging hard, and in the noise of the room, it's only Jessup who hears Diggins say, "I'm proud of you, son."

They end their embrace and Diggins continues to address the room: "You sent a message, but we've got another game coming on us fast. Now, smart decisions this weekend. I don't need you doing anything stupid. No practice tomorrow." Boys nodding, some serious, some smiling at the news. "Rest up. Get your bodies right. No practice tomorrow, but regular time Monday. I want you full of energy on Monday. This is the playoffs, baby! It's win-or-go-home time now. And remember, film study at my house Sunday afternoon at four. You know who you are. Mrs. Diggins will have snacks for you." He holds out his hand. "Bring it in."

PARKING LOT

J essup isn't the first one out of the locker room, but he's hustling. Wants to get over to Kirby's as soon as possible. Can already see the poorly hidden disappointment on his mom's face when he leaves for the party. David John won't say anything, but Jewel will whine a bit.

He reaches into the truck and tucks the game ball behind his seat. He grabs the scraper and is working on the windshield when he feels the finger poke into his shoulder blade. It's Kevin Corson, the Kilton Valley running back. Mostly, when Jessup has seen the kid, Corson has been smiling. He's not smiling now.

"That was bullshit," Corson says. He jabs his finger into the center of Jessup's chest now, right on the bone between his pecs. It hurts, but Jessup doesn't flinch.

"Hold on to the ball next time," Jessup says.

"You hit me early."

Jessup's got two inches and forty pounds on Corson, and he looks over the running back's shoulder. Kilton Valley players are heading out of the school and onto the bus that's idling at the edge of the parking lot.

"I didn't hear a whistle."

"Syracuse was here tonight."

"I saw. Heard that's where you're going."

"That's right. And you know what? After the game, Coach Trevor came up to me and laughed about that hit. Know what I said?"

Jessup shifts a bit, turning his hip so that he can feel the truck behind him. He tries to give himself a bit of space to move. Corson has that look, and even though Jessup knows he can take him, no point making it easy. He shakes his head.

"I told him about your dad and your brother. Said you come from a family of Nazis and that kind of thing might not play well in the Syracuse locker room. Came as a surprise to him. If I were you, I wouldn't be holding my breath for a scholarship offer."

Jessup doesn't say anything, tries to keep his face still, but in not saying anything, he must be saying something, because a smile flits across Corson's face.

"Oh. You think I didn't know? Think that's the sort of thing that stays quiet?"

From across the parking lot, Jessup hears Corson's name being called. A woman's voice. Corson turns and waves. "In a minute," he yells. There are two people over by a clump of cars. Corson's parents waiting for him. But he and Corson are in their own private bubble right now. By the look on his face, Corson is trying to decide whether or not to swing at Jessup, and Jessup considers his options. Not a punch but a takedown. As soon as Corson swings, step in and bring him to the ground. Even if he didn't have a weight and height advantage on Corson, Jessup wrestles in the winter and he's good at it. Not college scholarship good, but good enough that as soon as they're on the asphalt, Corson will start regretting his actions. Jessup would bet whatever is in his wallet that Corson's never been in a real fight. Sure, on the practice field, or more likely stuffing some freshman in his locker, but not the kind of fight where there's no one close enough to stop things. Jessup thinks of the grainy video from the alley, of the way Ricky swung the wrench.

Corson goes to poke him in the chest again, but Jessup grabs his wrist. "You do that again, and I'll lay you out," he says. They both stay like that, rigid, Jessup's hand on Corson's wrist, Corson's arm outstretched. Jessup notices the cop car idling in the corner of the parking lot, the cop looking over. At the same time, Corson's mom calls him again. This time there's a note of worry in her voice, and Corson lets a smile rip through. His arm loosens up, so Jessup releases his wrist. Corson pats him on the shoulder. "This isn't over, boy," Corson says. He turns and starts walking away.

"Maybe," Jessup calls, "but your season is, *boy*."

Corson stiffens, stops, turns. Jessup tips his chin. He's the one smiling now. He gets in the truck, starts it up, and starts to pull out.

He feels the thump, hears the crack of broken plastic. He stops the truck, looks in the driver's-side mirror. Corson is standing by the back of the truck bed, looking pleased with himself. And now Jessup has to decide: beat Corson's ass or walk away. Cop car right there. High school parking lot and all that comes with getting in a fight. No way he'd get to play next week. Suspension at least. Possibly worse. Thinks David John. Ricky. The alley. Thinks Corson's black skin. Thinks jail. Thinks of Ricky spending half his life in prison, David John already done his four years, thinks of the nights his mother cried hard enough to shake the trailer.

Thinks his own hands are shaking on the wheel.

Drives away.

KIRBY'S

By the time he's turning onto Route 13, his hands have stopped shaking. He turns the music up loud. The stereo, even though it's a cheap piece of crap—the only good thing about it is he can play music off his phone—is the nicest thing about the truck. Pulled it out of a totaled Subaru in the junkyard, ten bucks, though he's still using the truck's factory speakers. He mostly listens to alternative country, old Springsteen, Johnny Cash. His last girlfriend turned him on to upbeat indie folk music, and he listens to that when he's in a good mood and wants something easy. Since they've started dating, Deanne has had him listening to pop music, and when Jewel's in the truck, she makes him put on 103.7, WQNY, country top forty.

On the drive to Kirby's, he's got Eric Church's *Chief* on shuffle. He likes Eric Church because Eric Church, particularly with his old stuff, has the right kind of beautiful rawness. The speakers in his truck rattle when he cranks it, but he wouldn't upgrade things even if he could afford something better; the music is real to him this way. When he pulls into the parking lot, Church is singing about Springsteen and being seventeen, and Jessup, for the first time, understands that even though he can't wait to get out of Cortaca, there will always be a piece of him left behind. He wonders how he can be nostalgic for a place he hasn't departed.

Kirby's is busy, though Jessup isn't sure he's ever been in the restaurant when it's been slow. He ends up backing into a spot that opens up when a white Toyota hatchback pulls out. Thinks about bringing in the game ball but decides to leave it in the truck. It's his. Not something he's ready to share yet. But on his way in, he stops in the lobby and hits the ATM, takes out sixty dollars. He looks at the slip—seventy-six dollars and a few cents left in his account—and then crumples it in his hand and shoves it in his pocket. He puts twenty into his wallet, putting him at about forty-five bucks there, keeps the other forty in his hand. His sister, mother, and stepfather are waiting for him in a booth near the back. David John sees him first and pops to his feet. He's grinning at Jessup like they share a secret, and David John grabs him and hugs him hard. Jessup remembers his stepfather as solid, and he still is—David John might as well be carved out of oak, clearly spent his time in jail keeping fit—but Jessup is startled to realize that he almost looms over his stepfather. He's easily got fifty pounds on David John. If the two of them fought, Jessup would kick his ass.

"Mom wouldn't let me order until you got here," Jewel says. She's bouncing on the seat, her hands pinned under her thighs like she's afraid her arms will flap her away if they aren't trapped. "Uncle Earl gave us some money, so we can order whatever we want. Mom said I can get a milkshake. Or should I get a malt?"

Jessup knows he should be grateful to David John's brother. He's seen his mom buying gas one or two gallons at a time, handfuls of quarters and nickels and dimes, returning cans and bottles so she can buy five bucks' worth of gas so she can get to the next house she cleans, the wife apologizing because she forgot to leave a check the week before—oh, you know how it is with the kids, and everything can be so crazy when school is on holiday—but not really understanding that Jessup's family *needed* that hundred dollars, that to go without that money meant they had to go, well, without. Taking Jewel to the thrift store every week until they come across a pair of snow boots that fit, his sister never once complaining about how her friends get everything new from Target or online from L.L.Bean. Sure, every time Earl gives his mom a few hundred dollars it's a kind of salvation, but it feels . . . What? Capricious. It feels capricious, he thinks. That's the word he's looking for. The money unpredictable. What they really need is somebody to get his mom a new car, somebody to pay the utility bills, some regularity, a chance to plan ahead for once. And he can't help but feel like there's a catch with the money Earl offers. He's never seen the hook at the end of the line, but he knows it's there.

PLANS

T ell you what," Jessup says, easing into the booth next to his sister. "Special occasion. We're celebrating your daddy coming home." He's still got the two twenties in his hand from the cash machine, but they aren't needed with Earl's money. Instead of putting the bills on the table and offering to treat, he stuffs them into the pocket of his jeans. David John is watching him, so Jessup gives a nod, but there's something changed about his stepfather and Jessup can't read it.

He slides all the way across, into his sister, bumping her friendly with his hip. "You get a shake and I'll get a malt, and we can share." Jewel smiles broadly and Jessup looks more closely. "You finally lost that tooth."

Jewel rolls her lips up and thrusts her face toward him so that he can get a good look at the gap. "Wiggled it out during the third quarter."

He rolls his eyes back and sticks out his tongue so that she giggles. "Come on, now," he says. "Nobody here wants to see your gross, bloody gums. Put your lips back down."

David John slaps his hand on the table lightly. "I'll tell you, Jessup, your mom said you'd gotten big, and I knew you'd turned into quite a player, but whoa. You were something else on that field. You done good, kid. That hit right before halftime." Something that sounds like a laugh seems to catch in his throat. "Knocked that kid so hard you got him throwing up. Bet he wished he'd stayed home tonight. Taught him a lesson for sure."

Jessup wonders what David John would say if he told him about Corson confronting him in the parking lot after the game. He knows what David John's brother would say. Even if Jessup hasn't gone to church since Ricky killed those boys, his mother keeps trying to get him to go, tells him about what Earl's been preaching. A big one is standing up for yourself, about how the only way to protect yourself from savagery is to stand your ground.

At church, Ricky and David John are held up as heroes. Stand for your race or you stand for nothing.

David John has his arm around Jessup's mother's shoulder, and she's leaning into him like all she wants is for them to be one person. Four years, Jessup thinks. Four years they've been apart. He doesn't want it in his head, but he knows it's been a long time for the two of them, and the walls are thin in the trailer. Jewel can sleep through anything, but Jessup's glad he'll be out late tonight. He doesn't like sleeping with his headphones on.

They order burgers and fries and shakes and malts, his mom and step-father sharing an order. David John talks about how things are going to be now that he's home. He's already got a couple of plumbing jobs lined up. Old customers who can see past his time in jail and congregants from the Blessed Church of the White America who will pay cash. "It'll take a while to get up and rolling full speed again," David John says, "but things will be back to normal soon enough."

Not for Ricky, Jessup thinks, but he doesn't say it.

"Monday I'll start working. Got some good leads. Going to have to sort through my tools. Cindy said you've got everything out in the shed?" Jessup nods. "Well then, that's good. But tomorrow, well, tomorrow I think we all need to go out for some ice cream as a family. What do you think about that, darling?" he says, winking at Jewel. "And Cindy, how about some fried chicken for dinner? In the afternoon, Jessup, you can take the recliner and I'll cuddle up on the couch with my two girls and watch some college football. And just so you all can plan ahead, know that if you want to take a shower, you best get started early, because I'm aiming to use up all of the hot water. I'm going to take a shower so long that you'll start to worry I've pruned up into nothing. Jessup—"

"I'm hunting in the morning," Jessup says. It comes out quicker than he expected, but if David John minds having his words stepped on, he doesn't show it.

"Hunting?"

"Deer hunting. Freezer's empty. And I'm working tomorrow afternoon and night. Two to eight."

The waitress has delivered their drinks, so Jewel is going at her shake already. His mom can't seem to stop herself from smiling, but David John is looking at Jessup evenly. Not angry, not happy. Just figuring things out. There's a blankness there.

For a second Jessup feels like a little kid again. "Sorry," he blurts out. "Wasn't thinking. Should have gotten out of work this weekend so I could have been at home."

David John shakes his head, but the blankness is gone. He's smiling now. "Nope. I'm proud of you, Jessup. Most kids your age, they work, that money goes into buying a new phone or making their car shiny or new clothes or whatever, but your mom's been telling me how you've been pitching in." Jessup can feel the crumpled bills in his pocket, pushing against his wallet. "You did good. We ain't welfare queens in some ghetto. We're good country people and we work for what we get. I'm sorry that things have been hard the last couple of years, but what's past is past. I'm here now. What you earn is yours from now on out, Jessup. You're a teenager, and you should have a chance to act like one. You spend that money on something fun. You and Wyatt should get yourselves up to a little trouble. You got that?"

"Yes, sir," Jessup says.

"And Sunday," David John says. "You'll be coming to church?"

It sounds like a question, but it isn't a question.

The waitress brings the burgers to the table. David John reaches out to take his wife's hand and Jessup's hand, Jessup reaching for Jewel, Jewel for their mother, the four of them linked in an unbroken circle.

"Dear Jesus," David John says. Jessup bows his head and closes his eyes.

CHERRIES

They walk out together. Jewel between him and David John, holding each of their hands and talking nonstop. The adrenaline from the game has worn off, and Jessup is starting to feel sore. He's got turf burn on his left forearm, a decent bruise on his right thigh, and the general sense that when he wakes up tomorrow morning he'll know that he played football the night before.

The Cortaca PD cruiser is double-parked outside of the entrance. David John goes stiff as soon as he sees it. The reaction of a man who is afraid of going back to jail, Jessup thinks.

The car is running and there's a single cop, a woman who Jessup hasn't seen before, sitting in the passenger seat. She's young and good-looking. A lesbian, he figures, with her short hair. Why else would she want to be a cop?

"Excuse me." The voice behind them is bright and cheerful and, as they part, a cop brushes past them.

No, he doesn't brush, Jessup thinks. The cop waddles. He's five ten, five eleven, but he's shaped like a beach ball. There's a layer of hardness under the fat, but Jessup can't imagine this cop running a mile in under ten minutes or doing push-ups or passing any fitness test. He's carrying a paper takeout sack and holding a drink tray with three drinks on it. Three drinks? Two milkshakes and a soda, Jessup realizes, and then wonders if the fat cop is going to drink both shakes or if one of them is for the woman.

The cop smiles at them as he walks by and nods at Jewel. "You all have a good night, now. Drive safe with this snow."

The four of them stay still for a minute, watching him lever himself into the car, the cruiser settling on its springs a bit as his weight hits the front seat. When the car pulls away, they move again. Jessup wonders if he held his breath. His mother touches David John on the back of his neck. "You okay?" she says.

"Just skittish. I'm sorry. It's not going to be like this every time I see a cop," David John says quietly.

"I know." His mom might be trying not to cry, or she might just be happy. Jessup can't tell, but she steps into her husband and hugs him, nestling her face against his neck. "I'm just so tired of all of it, you know?"

Jessup looks away.

Jewel is starting to crash already by the time she's in the backseat of the car and buckled up. Jessup's mom takes the passenger seat, leaving David John to do the driving.

David John pauses a second before getting in the car, looking up at the sky, letting the snow drift down on him. Jessup looks up, too. He loves watching the white kiss through the parking lot's lights.

"We'll have to do something about your mom's car. Work van is no good for taking the family out, and your mom's car ain't exactly suited for the snow. A good SUV, or a pickup with an extended cab. I'll ask around at church and see if anybody's looking to sell and willing to work out some financing until we're back on our feet." He turns to Jessup and offers his hand.

It's an odd thing for Jessup. He can't remember ever shaking David John's hand. He knows that's the way with some families, but David John's always been affectionate with Jessup and Ricky and Jewel. He's a strict dad, but not in a bad way. Get your work done, do your chores, do the right thing, and there are consequences for talking back or failing to live up to expectations, but he was always quick to pull the kids in for a hug, to wrap an arm around you, always kissing Jessup's mom. Telling all of them that he loved them.

Jessup shakes David John's hand. It's a firm grip, but he's surprised by how cool his stepfather's hand feels. They shake, and then David John clasps Jessup's one hand with both of his and looks him full on. "You've turned into a man while I've been gone, Jessup."

"Yes, sir."

David John is still clasping his hand.

"And I'm proud of you, the way you've stepped up. I'm sorry for how much I've missed. But it's good to be home." He lets go of Jessup's hand now and then winks. "Enough already. I know you're itching to see your friends. Go have some fun."

David John lets the windshield wipers clean off the new snow, and Jessup steps to the back of the car, pulls his gloves out of his jacket pocket, and uses his hands to clear the rear window. Wants to make sure they get home safely. Once the car pulls out, Jessup walks over to his truck and does a good job with the brush, making sure everything is cleaned off. Gets in, peels off his gloves, tosses them onto the passenger seat, pulls out of the parking lot.

He's been driving a couple of minutes and is just near the edge of campus when he sees the cherries light up in his rearview mirror. A quick blat from the siren.

He pulls over, rolls down the window, and waits.

WARNING

Y
ou know why I pulled you over?"

"No, sir."

"Broken taillight."

Jessup tries hard to keep his face from showing anything, but he knows he's gripping the steering wheel tight. Corson must have smashed the taillight. Should have gotten out of the truck and kicked his ass. No. Can't do that. Not in the school parking lot. Not in front of the cop. But he should have looked when he got to Kirby's. Got to the restaurant, backed it in, didn't think about it. Corson's out there somewhere driving Mommy and Daddy's luxury car, and now Jessup has a broken taillight to fix. He'll have to stop by the auto-parts store tomorrow. He thinks about the forty dollars still crushed up in his pocket, money he thought he could hold on to. The bulb will only run him two bucks, but the lens will be closer to thirty-five. Cheaper to go to the junkyard for the lens, but he'll have to get lucky and it will eat up time.

The cop leans in a bit, squinting, and Jessup, who always figures it's best to look domesticated, keeps his head tilted down.

"I know you," the cop says.

Jessup looks up now. He doesn't recognize the cop, but he doesn't not recognize him either. That's the sort of thing that happens in a town the size of Cortaca.

"License, registration, insurance."

Jessup pops the glove box and grabs the paperwork. He digs out his wallet—the two crumpled twenties coming out, too—and pulls out his license, hands the pile over to the cop. Name tag reads "Hawkins." Hawkins. Hawkins.

The cop reads the information on Jessup's driver's license and then narrows his eyes, crosses his arms, and leans on the windowsill. "Collins?"

"Yes, sir," Jessup says.

"Thought you were a Michaels."

Jessup feels something shift in his stomach.

For the most part, the cops have left them alone since David John and Ricky went to jail. Every few weeks a cruiser from the sheriff's office will do a drive-by on their trailer, but nothing that could be construed as outright harassment. Jessup's mom keeps her head down, does her work, keeps quiet. Jessup has learned by example. Sticks to the speed limit, doesn't push his luck.

"No relation, then? David John Michaels? He's not your father?"

A pair of cars go wide around them. Jessup listens to the wet thrum of their tires on the road, a mix of asphalt and packed snow, more snow coming down slow and steady now.

Hawkins doesn't pay any attention to the cars going by. He's looking directly at Jessup, but Jessup can't read him.

"Stepfather," Jessup says. He says it reluctantly, and he's ashamed that he's ashamed to say it. Ashamed that he feels the need to correct the cop. Should be willing to own David John as his father. Might as well have been his father. But he knows something hangs in the balance here. The cops may not have bothered them since his brother and stepfather were sentenced, but in the time leading up to the plea deal, they were a constant presence in Jessup's life, and not a good thing. Tossed the whole trailer. Did it twice. Warrant and all that. Got word that they were trying to get a warrant to search the compound, too, but that one was denied. Which was a good thing. Uncle Earl talked big, said he would have liked to see the cops try and serve a warrant. "Time for another Waco," he said. Second Amendment.

The cop nods. He slides the registration and insurance card back into the little plastic pouch and holds the pouch and Jessup's license between his thumb and forefinger. He holds them out, but not far enough that he's giving them back yet. "If I run Jessup Collins through the computer, am I going to find anything problematic? What are you"—he looks at the license again, squints, does the math—"seventeen? Still a juvenile?"

"No problems, sir," Jessup says. "This is the first time I've been pulled over. Never gotten a ticket. And I'm sorry about the taillight. Happened tonight. I'll fix it first thing in the morning."

"You hit something?"

"No, sir."

What gears would be set in motion if he told Hawkins what happened? Make a complaint against Corson? No, too messy. How's that going to look, Jessup complaining about a black kid kicking out his taillight? Small town. Family history. It would blow up. No way.

"What happened, then?"

"Don't know what happened. I had a football game and when I came out afterward . . . Somebody must have broke it."

Hawkins nods. The cop is late twenties, something like that. Buzz cut. Short, but has muscle packed on him, Jessup can tell even though he's wearing a Kevlar vest. Every cop Jessup sees nowadays is wearing a Kevlar vest. Makes a small man look bigger. Maybe that's the point, Jessup thinks, looking at Hawkins. He's puffed up, inflated. Spends his free time lifting weights, but already starting the slow slide toward middle age. He looks like . . . a cop. Reminds Jessup of a kid who likes hazing, scaring freshmen, pretending it's all a joke but you know it isn't. Except there's something off in the way Hawkins is talking to Jessup. No bullying there. Like he's trying to be friends. He reaches out fully now, handing the license and paperwork back. "Been a long time since Cortaca made the playoffs, huh? I played, but not here. Safety. You?"

"Linebacker."

"Good stuff. I miss it. Nothing like laying somebody out. You guys win tonight?"

"Yes, sir."

"I like hearing that." Hawkins straightens up. "You got any tattoos, Jessup?"

Jessup is shoving the insurance and registration into the glove box, and he tries not to let on that he's confused by the question. "Sir? Uh, no, sir. No tattoos."

"No Celtic cross? No eighty-eights? No fourteen or Sieg Heil? None of that white power bullshit?"

100%

The cop asks the question, but Jessup is thinking about walking with Deanne last Sunday. They were up in the university's bird sanctuary, holding hands. Still warm. Leaves on the trees. The path didn't have any discernible reason for twisting this way or that. They stopped deep in the woods and Deanne sat on a downed tree that formed a natural bench. Jessup was standing between her legs, kissing her, his hand under her shirt, when he felt something watching them. He opened his eyes and saw a big buck barely fifteen feet from him, the kind of rack you mount and display as a trophy. He wished he had his rifle. He whispered to Deanne, and the two of them just stared at the deer until, after thirty, forty seconds, the buck turned and walked away. He thinks of the way the buck sized them up, trying to figure out if they were a threat or not. He can't decide how he feels about this cop, so he closes the glove box and sits up straight. He keeps his torso forward, puts his hands back on the wheel, turns his head to look at Hawkins, keeps his voice flat.

"No, sir. No tattoos." Thinks of David John's tattoos. On his back, "Blessed Church of the White America" circling a flaming cross—the exact same as what Ricky got, a big deal when he was old enough to get one to match David John's, Jessup for years thinking he'd get one, too, when David John said he was old enough, though with both him and Ricky, David John expressed some doubts—an iron eagle complete with swastika high up on his stepfather's right shoulder, double SS lightning bolts on his left pec with "fgrn"—For God, Race, and Nation—inked below, over his heart. Wonders if David John got any new tattoos in prison. Ricky wrote that he'd had a spiderweb tattooed around his elbow by one of the guys in his crew. "Not yet."

"You don't remember me, do you?"

There's a flicker, something approaching a memory, but Jessup can't place it.

"That's a good thing, then. Not the worst thing to blend in. Piece of advice for you, Jessup. Skip the tattoos. Makes it too easy to flush you out. You get yourself a big old one hundred percent on your shoulder and then try to join the army? Put a swastika on your forearm and then try to become a cop? They look for that stuff. Pride is important, but it's not always a bad thing to work in the background, keep your head down until you're needed." Hawkins has one hand resting on the windowsill, has the thumb of his other hand tucked into his belt, above his gun. "Tell you what. I'll write you up a warning. No ticket, no fine. You get that taillight fixed first thing in the morning. And tell David John that Paul Hawkins says welcome home and that I expect I'll see him at church on Sunday."

MINUS FIVE

He has to sit for a few minutes and wait for Hawkins to write up the warning. Hawkins hands over the piece of paper, tells Jessup to drive safe, and then saunters back to his cruiser. He pulls out and is past Jessup before Jessup starts driving. Jessup holds the warning in his hand. It's not a ticket, but he's not really sure if he can just throw it away, so he places it in the slot above the stereo.

By the time he gets to Victoria Wallace's place, the party is well under way. The house is out past the university, out in the country a few miles, but not the kind of country that Jessup lives in. Victoria's house is set on at least twenty acres. It's the property that you buy when you can afford not to have neighbors. The house is at least two hundred yards from the road. As he turns off and heads up the driveway, he takes in the view: the university, the town of Cortaca, the lake. The property is on a rise. There's an open field that starts flat but then turns steep off the city side of the driveway, dropping headlong into a thick corset of forest. The house and the driveway sit high enough up that it's a clear view for a dozen miles.

The house itself is all glass and metal, but it's built to resemble a farmhouse. Resemble, but Jessup thinks it's only a passing resemblance. It looks like what a man who'd never worked on a farm would build. Beautiful in its way, easy to imagine it on the cover of one of those home magazines one rack over from the outdoor magazines at the bookstore. It's the kind of house his mother cleans, but he can't imagine ever living in a place like this. With all those windows, the gas bills in the winter must run more than what Jessup's mom pays for the mortgage and taxes combined on their place.

Victoria is a junior. Her mom is a professor at Cortaca University—of what, Jessup doesn't know—and her dad does something that lets him work from home. Whatever it is, they're rich. Victoria drives the smaller, high-end, Volvo SUV. Brand-new. This after she totaled her first car, a Honda that had also been new. Jessup is friends with her boyfriend, Aaron Burns, and he's been in the Volvo a couple of times with them. Leather seats and wood trim, chrome on the outside. He looked it up: close to sixty grand the way she was rolling in it.

Victoria's parents are in the city for the weekend—they have a two-bedroom condo there and go down most weekends, so this isn't the first time Victoria has thrown a party—and there are at least seventy kids inside the house already. Jessup figures another fifty before the night is over. Cortaca's football team only carries forty guys, and most of them will come out, bringing girlfriends and buddies, and Victoria's friends and people who just heard about it. Jessup will know everybody here.

NEAR DARKNESS

There's a long line of cars and trucks off the high side of the driveway, and Jessup does a K-turn before parking his truck so that he's set up to head out when Deanne is ready to leave the party. He pulls the warning from the slot, looks at it again for a second, then returns it to the glove box and gets out of the truck. Before closing the door, he reaches behind the seat and touches the game ball. Wishes Deanne had seen her father hugging him like that. *I'm proud of you, son.*

It's dark as shit where he is. The lights from the house don't even come close to cutting through the darkness. He's on the high side of the driveway and he takes a few seconds to look across and out, the way the grass runs down like a ski slope, steep into the woods, the view over the city, the water. The house is oriented to take advantage of the views, so most of the windows are turned away from the driveway, but the house is still a beacon on the hill.

He pulls out his phone to use it as a flashlight. The snow is rutted on the driveway and deep enough in the grass where he's parked that his feet would have gotten wet if he wasn't wearing his Timberlands. The boots are in rough shape, but he got them at the university yard sale at the beginning of last year for six bucks. Maybe now that David John is back, Jessup thinks. Save up his paycheck from the movie theater for a couple of weeks and buy a pair brand-new. What would that run him? One twenty? One fifty? A splurge. He walks to the back of the truck and looks at the shattered taillight. Forty bucks right there. Asshole. Before heading into the house, he shrugs off his jacket and tosses it on the passenger seat where his gloves are. Doesn't bother locking the door. Could leave the keys in the ignition and nobody would steal the thing.

He's cold by the time he gets to the house, the walk from his truck up the driveway a hundred yards, near darkness the whole way except for the light from his phone. Wishes he'd worn his coat. Inside, he stomps his boots clean in the entrance hall, a thicket of coats and bags on the floor. Bumps knuckles as he walks through, Mike Crean wrapping him up in a hug designed to pop your ribs. A lot of "atta boys" for the fumble recovery and touchdown. The front hall leads into a single, giant, open room. The kitchen is separated from the living space by a counter made of dark stone, and the appliances look they come from the future. Jessup bets the dishwasher costs more than his mom earns in two months. The dining area is simple, just a sideboard and a table that isn't overbearing. Instead of a massive landscape for candelabras and two dozen guests, it's a table that has chairs for eight, a sleek piece of glass and steel, the glass looking like it's floating. Victoria has the table loaded up with bowls of pretzels, chips and salsa, cookies, a vegetable tray on a silver platter. Napkins fanned out like something from a magazine. Parroting the parties she's seen her parents throw. The sitting area has a sectional and a couple of chairs, one of them leather and beat-up-enough-looking that Jessup wouldn't have bothered stopping to pick up if it was free on the side of the road, but it's evidently a piece of vintage furniture, cost five grand. The large, open room is easily twice as big as the double-wide trailer Jessup lives in, except that the ceiling jumps two stories high, and there's floor-to-ceiling glass so that you can see the whole of Cortaca laid out below. Victoria lives in a castle.

There's a keg out on the deck—somebody's older brother came through—but he's not a drinker. Ricky made him promise. Jessup might not remember much of his mother's drinking, but Ricky does. Doesn't bother Jessup to abstain. He's taken sips of beer here and there. Tastes like dog piss. Wyatt tells him you grow to like it, but Jessup figures, what's the point of learning to like something nasty? He steps out, takes a cup, but then brings it around the counter to the kitchen sink and fills it up with water. He likes having something in his hand.

He's standing a few steps out of the kitchen area, looking around to see if Deanne is there yet, when he sees the gang of boys and an equal number of girls come through the door. The boys, five of them, are all wearing Kilton Valley jackets. Kevin Corson in the front.

MINUS FOUR

He's decided to avoid trouble and just leave the party—text Deanne and meet her somewhere else—when he feels a hand slap down on his shoulder. Wyatt.

"Kind of ballsy, huh?" Wyatt moves his hand from Jessup's shoulder and clamps it on the back of Jessup's neck. This is his way of being friendly. He looks across the room with Jessup at the crowd of boys and girls from Kilton Valley. The boys move slow, looking around, casing it out, but the girls come in bubbly and chatting, colliding with five or six girls from Cortaca High in a pileup of hugging and kissing. "Aaron said that Victoria goes to camp with one of the girlfriends and they all know each other or something, so she invited them to the party. Don't think they would have been dumb enough to come if they'd won, but nobody's going to bother stirring up trouble with the losers."

"To the victor go the spoils," Jessup says.

Wyatt gives a rough squeeze. "Now, don't go doing that sort of shit, Jessup. I hate it when you go all gnostic on me. What do you mean, 'To the victor go the spoils'? I know what it means, but what's it supposed to *mean*?"

Jessup slides out from Wyatt's arm. "You know, just because you learn a new word doesn't mean you need to use it all the time. And if you are going to use it, at least use it right. I took AP Global same as you. You can't just slide in 'gnostic' when you mean mystic or mysterious. Beside which, you ever think that you not understanding something might not be because I said something cryptic? Maybe you don't understand it because you're dumb."

It's an old joke, which is why it's still funny, and Wyatt ruffles Jessup's hair. Which he knows Jessup hates. Which is why he does it. Which is why that's funny, too. Wyatt doesn't get it as bad from the teachers as Jessup does in school, but that's because Wyatt flies below the radar. His mom's a bookkeeper and his dad works steady as a mechanic. He lives in Cortaca proper, on city sewer and water, and even though he loves to hunt and can bag a deer from four hundred yards no problem—he's the best shot of anybody Jessup knows—he doesn't wear camo to school. Gets B grades across the board. Not interested in anything better than that. That's good enough to play football at UConn, and he's already looked into dental school: only needs a B+ average in college for that. Does just well enough that the teachers ignore him, Blessed Church of the White America or not, though it's not a thing you can tell just by looking. Jessup thinks of that and then thinks of the cop, Hawkins, telling him not to get tattoos. If it weren't for what Ricky did, Jessup could fly below the radar, too, but what's done is done, and the teachers get angry at Jessup all the time, as if it's some sort of insult to them that he's earning A grades, like they can't understand why he isn't as dumb as he's supposed to be.

"Eh," Wyatt says, "fuck 'em. We won, they lost. What are they going to do? Lose again?"

MINUS THREE

Before he can think better of it, Jessup tells Wyatt what happened in the parking lot between him and Corson. He sticks pretty close to the truth. Makes himself sound a little better, Corson a little worse.

Says, "I would have kicked his ass, but there was a cop was sitting right there."

"Come on," Wyatt says. "Need more beer."

Jessup follows Wyatt onto the deck. The snow has slowed down enough that it might as well have stopped. There's a cluster of boys from the team leaning against the railing and looking out at the lights of Cortaca dripping across the landscape below. Cortaca Lake is a dark spill of ink. Derek Lemper is holding two beers and laughing. He's topless for some reason, despite the cold, his gut spilling out.

Wyatt reaches for the tap to fill his cup. "Sweet Jesus, Jessup, can you think of anything worse than Derek topless?"

Jessup takes a sip of his water. It's refreshing out on the deck. "Worse than Derek topless? Derek without pants is no picnic either."

They both laugh. Jessup puts his cup on the railing and then places both his hands flat while Wyatt messes with the tap, trying to get more beer than foam.

The sky is dark with clouds, but the city and the university are a galaxy of stars, dorms lit up and stadium lights tunneling out of the darkness by the soccer fields, the hotels near the downtown core with gap-toothed grins, open and closed curtains, people getting ready for a late night out, others already in bed for the evening, streetlights and houses lit up, the sparkling blue of a snowplow clearing off Route 13.

"It's not too late to grab him and beat the crap out of him, you know. Teach him his place."

Jessup doesn't turn around. He feels Wyatt move up and then sees his friend lean on the railing, too. Yes, he thinks, I want to beat the crap out of Corson. Wants to put him on the ground and smash out those white teeth, find the car he's driving, throw a brick through the windshield. He doesn't say anything, but Wyatt answers anyway.

"I know," Wyatt says. "But don't worry. He'll get his when the time comes." He nudges Jessup with his elbow. The corner of his mouth twitches. "Rahowa, bitches."

Jessup can't stop himself from laughing, though he knows it wouldn't be funny to anybody else. Rahowa. Racial holy war. The elders at the Blessed Church of the White America have been promising a racial holy war as long as Jessup can remember. Jessup hasn't been to church in four years, but according to Wyatt, the racial holy war is still just around the corner, same as it always has been. Jessup can't joke about it with his other friends—the Blessed Church of the White America doesn't make people laugh—but that's one of the things he likes about Wyatt. They share a language. Wyatt at McDonald's—"After rahowa, they won't keep putting pickles on my burger when I asked for no goddamned pickles"—or running wind sprints during two-a-days in the heat of August—"I'm calling rahowa on wind sprints," he'd say, which made Jessup laugh even though what he really wanted to do was puke—or under his breath so only Jessup can hear him when Mrs. Howard, their AP European History teacher, has them split up to work with a partner—"Why the hell is *European* history being taught by somebody from Africa? Rahowa, bitches."

He doesn't tell Wyatt that he likes Mrs. Howard, thinks she's a good teacher. Keeps him intellectually engaged, treats the class like it's full of individuals instead of a monolithic entity. Makes him think. And even though she's black and he's sure she has to know about his brother and stepdad, about the Blessed Church of the White America, she treats him the same as everybody else. He wants to say that to Wyatt sometimes, to tell him to knock off with the jokes, to give Mrs. Howard the respect that is due to somebody who does her job well. He doesn't tell Wyatt to stop, however, because he doesn't want to have that conversation. And also, Jessup knows, because he doesn't want to have to reckon with it himself.

It's easier to laugh at the joke.

Though Jessup has to wonder how much of Wyatt is joking when he jokes about a racial holy war. Wyatt likes the AP European History class, seems to like Mrs. Howard fine, but Jessup knows that there are plenty of people going to Blessed Church of the White America who take it seriously, who believe a racial holy war *is* just around the corner. That being said, it's clear that Wyatt is joking right now, and part of what makes it funny is that they both know Brandon Rogers would never say it as a joke.

BRANDON ROGERS

Brandon is two years older than Jessup and Wyatt. He's studying at Cortaca University. Majoring in government. Lives off campus because of safety concerns but has a weekly radio show—internet only, but more than a quarter million downloads a month—and has more than once said, "Let them come for me. I'm not afraid to be a martyr for the cause."

He's twenty and there's a lot of talk that he's going to be *the* face of white nationalism. His nickname is "The Prince." His father is the heir to an industrial fortune, has put money into a baker's dozen of magazines and think tanks, but is most well known for bankrolling the Jewspiracy and TakeBack websites. The latter in particular has gone mainstream, treated like a bona fide news organization in some quarters. Brandon moved here for school from Florida, an Ivy League–educated spokesman just another way to bring white nationalism to the center; he's been groomed from birth to be the future of the movement. The only question is how quickly the future is coming. Over the summer, the *Washington Post* did a feature on him. Five thousand words, front page. Talked about how Brandon doesn't swear or smoke or drink, how he's promised to wait like a good Christian until he's married to have sex with his fiancée, how he wears a suit and tie to class every day because he wants to show his professors he's serious about his studies. He's handsome, hair neatly groomed, fingernails clipped short, television-ready, a safe guest for political shows looking for somebody who's edgy but won't get a show canceled. Has the language down for cable news talking heads: global interests, social justice warriors, elitist intellectuals, pride in my identity, don't blue lives matter, shouldn't all lives matter, not just black lives, isn't it natural to want to be with people who are like you? At least once a week he manages to pop up on television somewhere.

Brandon is at the church every Sunday, too, helps lead the youth group,

Uncle Earl occasionally trotting him out to speak to the whole congregation, backroom talks with the elders, but Jessup has only met him once. Uncle Earl brought him to the trailer near the end of Jessup's sophomore year, driving Brandon up in Earl's Ford F-150. Brandon was wearing a slim black suit, blood-red tie. Told Jessup's mom that David John and Ricky were heroes, that their actions protected the future for children like Jessup's beautiful, pure sister.

"Your son and your husband, Mrs. Michaels, are the kind of men we need. Men we can count on. When the racial holy war starts, it's going to be men like Ricky and David John who keep us safe. When the time comes, we'll need them."

Jessup was on the couch, headphones in his ears, but no music. Social studies textbook open on his lap. Hadn't said anything, but the words just popped out. "When will that be?"

The way Brandon looked at him let Jessup know that even though he'd kept his head down, he hadn't been invisible. Brandon saw him. Looked at him harder than Jessup had ever been looked at.

Never told Wyatt about that moment. Even though Wyatt makes fun of Brandon plenty, he also often sounds like he admires Brandon; Jessup doesn't know how to explain the hardness in Brandon's stare.

Instead, he goes along with it when Wyatt makes fun of Brandon, and he goes along with it when Wyatt talks deferentially about the man. Jessup goes along with a lot of things. You have to with a friend like Wyatt. Poking, needling, teasing. That's Wyatt's way, Jessup thinks. Besides, Wyatt doesn't really ever mean any harm. At least not toward Jessup. He's a joker.

Jessup thinks Wyatt is joking now about Corson getting what's his when the time comes. Hard to tell with Wyatt sometimes. He's got a mean streak. Sometimes, when he talks about racial holy war, Jessup thinks Wyatt is hoping for it, waiting. But he's known Wyatt his whole life, best friends. Wyatt likes to say Jessup is his real brother, even though he *has* two younger brothers. They spend a lot of time together, and otherwise, Wyatt's life revolves around football, Blessed Church of the White America, and his girlfriend. Speaking of whom . . .

KAYLEE

D on't you drink too much," Kaylee says, slipping between Jessup and Wyatt, ducking under Wyatt's arm so that it's around her shoulder. She presses her body against him, kisses him with an open mouth. Jessup sees the flash of tongue. She tilts her head, shoots Jessup some teeth. "Nice game, Jessup. Hear you got the game ball."

"Why not?" Wyatt says. "There's plenty of beer, and you're driving."

"Because, honey, I don't like it when you get drunk." She reaches out and pats Jessup on the cheek. "You keep an eye on him for me, Jessup. Okay? It's cold out here. I'm going back inside."

The pat on his cheek is gentle, sweet. Kaylee Owen is a gentle and sweet girl. Her parents have a farm in Brooktown, near the compound, and they sell organic produce and meat at the Cortaca Farmers' Market. They're gentle and sweet, too. Mrs. Owen brought lasagna over the night Ricky and David John were sentenced. Mr. Owen gave them twenty pounds of steak for the freezer. Jessup likes Kaylee. He'd admit to being a bit sweet on her when he was younger, but she and Wyatt have been dating since eighth grade. They're planning to get married after graduation. She's going to move with him to Storrs and work the first year while he's at UConn. "My grades are on the bubble, so what's the point of applying? Maybe if I check the box that says I'm black or if I pretend to be liberal, but screw that." She's planning to go to community college the year after. She wants to be a nurse.

She kisses Wyatt again and then slides open the glass door and walks over to where a couple of her girlfriends are sitting on the couch. Jessup and Wyatt drift inside, out of the cold. They talk for a bit with a couple of guys on the team, Jessup endures some teasing over his GPA—Cortaca's a good high school, and plenty of kids on the football team make the honor roll, but

Jessup isn't a professor's kid; he rolls into school wearing his camo hunting jacket, a litmus test of sorts, but has a real shot at an Ivy League school anyway—and then they move to the table.

"Got to love rich girls," Wyatt says. "High school party and she's got snacks out." He scoops a chip into the salsa and crams it in his mouth. "Think her mom went grocery shopping for her? She's got a freaking vegetable platter here."

"They're called crudités when it's fancy," Jessup says.

"Oh, you're going to fit in just fine at Yale, asshole."

But Jessup isn't really paying attention. He's noticing that the Kilton Valley boys have spread out a bit. Two of them are out on the deck—he can see them through the glass doors—holding cups of beer and chatting with the pack of guys from the Cortaca team. All smiles. One of the Kilton Valley boys, a big side of beef who gave Jessup a couple of hard blocks during the game, is telling some sort of funny story. He moves his hands while he talks. He's got a small afro and a shit-eating grin. He finishes his story and is rewarded with a burst of laughter that Jessup can hear from outside.

"That boy's eyeing you," Wyatt says. He lifts his chin, and Jessup glances over to the kitchen, sees Corson on the other side of the counter.

Corson is standing with two girls. One of them is leaning into him, arm around his waist, obviously his girlfriend. She's a small thing, pale, but with dark slashes of makeup penciled in around her eyes and a T-shirt that rides up and shows a pierced belly button as she gets on her tiptoes and moves her arm around his neck to pull him down for a kiss.

Corson is holding a beer, and after he's done kissing his girlfriend, he chugs it down.

"She's got jungle fever," Wyatt says under his breath. "Just like you."

MINUS TWO

J essup tells Wyatt to go fuck himself. Wyatt laughs, like Jessup isn't serious.

Is Jessup serious? He doesn't know if he is or isn't.

Whenever Deanne is around, Wyatt makes himself scarce, but he hasn't
said much to Jessup about Deanne. And he *has* toned down his language
since Jessup and Deanne started dating, but Jessup can't tell how much of
that is simply to avoid an argument. Kaylee has been less shy. One minute
she's bubbly and friendly, the next minute she's calling him a race traitor.
"It's one thing if you're just messing around with that girl, Jessup, if you
want a taste of it, but don't be ridiculous. You need to commit. One hundred percent, Jessup. Nothing less. Have some goddamned pride. Stick to
your own. I know plenty of pure white girls who—"

But Jessup is good at changing the subject. He's good at pretending
everything is okay. A survival skill.

Wyatt drifts away and Jessup's phone buzzes. Deanne.

can't come

why not

dad says no

why no?

snow. roads are bad. doesn't want me driving

what? no snow in mississippi? jk

I want to see you. I miss you

me too

tomorrow night? after work?

Jessup puts his phone away just as Alyssa Robinson corners him. They are working on a presentation for English that they are supposed to give the week after next. He likes Alyssa. She was in his kindergarten class and then in other classes off and on through now. He's pretty sure she doesn't like him—she lives near the university, comes from the kind of family that doesn't mix with Jessup's kind, that calls the housing complex on east hill "East Village" instead of "the Jungle"—but if she has a problem with him, she's kept it hidden. She's the sort of kid who grows up to privilege in Cortaca. Math and Spanish tutors even though she's got straight A grades, plays lacrosse and goes to lacrosse camps during the summer, does volunteer work at the SPCA and the food pantry, has known she was going to Williams College, her parents' alma mater, since she was in kindergarten. Everything easy for her, but she works hard anyway because she doesn't know how else to be. He agrees to meet her Wednesday morning in the library before school so they can game-plan. That satisfies her. She knows that Jessup will do his share of the work.

For the next hour, Jessup moves around the room, bullshitting with guys on the team. He moves easily through the room, always aware of the way Corson, beer in hand, seems to keep himself at maximum distance. At one point, Jessup chats for a few minutes with one of the players from Kilton Valley, the kid with the small afro, football talk, the kid saying, as long as you beat us, hope you make a run of things. Played a good game. He doesn't sit, doesn't stay in one place long. A little before eleven, he texts Deanne:

still not coming?

no. sorry. you know how my dad is

he making you run wind sprints?

very funny

a little. I miss you

me too. see you at work?

Okay. goodnight, babe

If he'd known Deanne wasn't going to make it, he would have just gone home with his family after they left Kirby's, spent the night at home, celebrating David John's release. Eleven o'clock isn't too bad, though. He'll get to bed at a reasonable hour. Knows he'll spend the night dreaming of the way Deanne feels against his body. Good dreams. Easy to sleep with that in his head. He goes out to the deck, where Wyatt is hanging out with Kaylee, tells them he's taking off. Wants to get up early to go hunting.

He's back inside, about to leave, edging his way into the entrance hall when he hears Corson calling his name.

SAY IT

But calling him would mean that Corson just wants to talk. Corson wants more than that. He wants an audience.

That's not what Jessup wants. He lifts his hands, palms out, a gesture of supplication, a gift. Whatever you want, Corson, I don't want to argue. "Heading home, man."

"You called me *boy*."

The room is suddenly quiet. There's music on, but it's low, something with an acoustic guitar, some sweet flower girl talking about love and what it feels like to be in high school.

"I don't think so."

There's something akin to electricity in the room. Derek Lemper, wearing a shirt now, lumbers up from the couch. Trevell is leaning against the kitchen counter, next to Jayden and their girlfriends. Jayden has his big knee brace on. Jessup glances through the sliding doors to the deck. The lights are on outside, a throng of people, twenty, thirty kids out there, and Jessup can see Wyatt with his coat on, standing with Kaylee, the two of them kissing, oblivious to what's going on inside.

"You called me *boy*," Corson says again. His voice is thick from beer. "But that's not what you wanted to say, was it?"

Everybody in the room is looking at Jessup and Corson now, back and forth, waiting, watching. Derek has a dumb look on his dumb face, smart enough to know something's wrong, that a fight is in the air, too dumb to understand anything more.

"You kicked out my fucking taillight," Jessup says, but even he knows it comes out wrong. There's something else he needs to say, but that's not it.

"Am I black?" Corson's voice is tight. He's loud.

Jessup blinks. "What?"

"I said. Am. I. Black." The Kilton Valley players have pulled into shape around Corson, the guys from Cortaca High starting to shift a little. It makes Jessup think of electrons and protons.

Corson's girlfriend steps in front of him. She looks like a glass of milk next to him. "Come on, honey. You're drunk."

Corson is gentle but firm, moving her aside. "I'm not talking to you. I'm talking to Mr. White Power here."

"I'm not—"

Cuts Jessup off. "Saw you talking to your dad at halftime. Fresh out of jail, huh? But your brother's still doing time."

His girlfriend tries again. "Corson."

"Everybody already knows," Corson says. "His dad and his brother killed two black kids. Brother's out around town with Nazi tattoos, gets in a fight, beats them to death with a wrench."

"Corson!"

"Everybody already knows," Corson says again. "Their whole family goes to that white power church out in the country. No secret there."

Jessup looks around the room. It's true. Everybody knows. He's hoping he'll see someone, anyone to save him. A life raft, a float, a rope, a log, anything he can grab onto to stop himself from drowning. But it's just faces looking back. He locks eyes with Trevell. The receiver breaks it off.

People have been talking. Not just now. His entire life.

TELEPHONE

He can see it, Trevell's girlfriend friends with Aaron's girlfriend, Victoria. Those girls friends with the girls from Kilton Valley. Go to summer camp together. Parents dropping five grand so their darlings can sleep in cabins and do overnight trips in tents, sit around campfires, canoe, hit the archery range, an expensive way to have your kids feel poor for a month. Nothing in common except parents who can afford it, which means they have everything in common. No tribe except money, skin or no skin, talking about David John and Ricky and that night in the alley and the way that blood begets blood and Jessup, no matter what he does on the field, no matter what he does in school, will always have been born into the wrong family, will always be on the wrong side of that divide.

The way all the kids at the party are looking at him, Jessup knows there's no win for him here. If he hits Corson, he proves the point. It's an impossible situation, and it makes him want to scream. A few weeks ago, Wyatt was bitching about reverse discrimination and quotas, how it's bullshit that libtards will do anything to get blacks and Mexicans into colleges but nothing for white kids like him and Kaylee and Jessup, how being white means they have to work twice as hard to get half as much as the Left *hands* out to people just for being colored. Jessup argued with him, saying it's more complicated than they make it out to be at the Blessed Church of the White America, but Wyatt shut him down. Said Jessup was only whistling that tune because he was sticking it to an ebony girl, and even though Jessup wanted to punch him, he didn't do anything or say anything because there was no win there either. All he could do was bury the comment, pretend like Wyatt never said it, convince himself that Wyatt was making a joke.

There's never a win. Not for somebody like Jessup. He didn't get to choose what he was born into, didn't choose the Blessed Church of the White America. And what kind of choice can he make now?

While Jessup has looked around the room, Corson has kept his eyes straight ahead. "So, I'll ask again. Am I black?"

"I don't want trouble," Jessup says. "I was just leaving."

Derek steps forward, a spark in his eyes. "No, man. This is our party. You can stay. You guys," he says to Corson and his buddies, "get the fuck out of here." Steve Silver is standing behind Derek and grabs his arm, says something into Derek's ear. The spark in Derek's eyes goes out.

Corson ignores everything around him. Points at Jessup. "I'll answer the question for you. No. You don't look at me and think 'black.' You don't think 'African American,' either."

The girls in the room all seem to be fading back, some of them pulling on the arms of boyfriends, but this is a roomful of football players. There aren't enough peacemakers. The boys are leaning forward.

"You kicked out my fucking taillight," Jessup says again, but again it's the wrong thing said the wrong way. He can hear that it sounds weak.

"Why don't you just go on and say it?" Corson has moved across the room now, with the deliberate gait of somebody who has been drinking. He gets close enough to crowd Jessup. "Say it."

"I'm not saying shit."

Corson's voice is loud, he's playing to an audience. "You look at me and you're thinking 'jigaboo.' You're thinking 'big ol' buck,' aren't you?"

Jessup shakes his head. There's nothing he can say.

"No?" Corson laughs now. "Oh, Mr. White Power is all quiet when I get up in his face."

ISLAND IN A STREAM

H e knows what Brandon Rogers would say about it, can hear his words as if he's watching Brandon on one of the political talk shows: you've got to stand your ground, argue with intelligence, the political correctness police are always trying to get us to say something that proves we're full of hate when all we're trying to do is be racial realists, and if you can be proud to be black or Latino, why can't you be proud to be white? But Jessup knows that none of what Brandon Rogers would say makes sense here, and while Brandon Rogers might believe, Jessup feels like he's tied up in knots, so he tries to keep his expression still. Flat. But that's not what Corson sees.

"You got your face all scrunched up!" Corson laughs. "You're angry, aren't you? Go on. Just say it." He opens his arms up now, taking in the whole room. "You got that word just ready to burst out of you, don't you? Go on, now. Say it. Say the word. Call me 'nigger.'"

The air disappears from the room. There's an absence of sound. Breath sucked into lungs. It makes Jessup think of the moment of kickoff at a football game, when the ball is at its apogee. Everybody is just waiting for it to come down.

Except this isn't a game that he wants to play. This isn't fair. He didn't do anything. Didn't say anything. But he can't say that. Can't call a time-out.

Corson's girlfriend tugs at his arm. She's crying. The dark slash of makeup is running off her eyes. "Please. You're drunk."

Corson reaches out, slow, careful, not pointing so much as shaking his finger at Jessup, scolding him. "You'll call me 'boy' when it's just us in a parking lot, but how about now? You thinking of it now? Nah. You're not thinking 'boy.' You're thinking 'nigger,' aren't you? Just say it. Call me a nigger."

Jessup stays quiet.

Corson lowers his arm and then shakes his head. He's got a big smile on his face, his teeth showing wide. "Didn't think so, bitch."

One of the Kilton Valley players, the kid with the afro, steps up and grabs Corson's elbow. "Come on, man. Let's get out of here."

For a moment, Jessup thinks Corson is going to shake his friend off, but then he accedes. There's an odd stillness from the rest of the room as the Kilton Valley kids, boys and girls alike, shuffle out and through the grand entrance, stopping to grab varsity jackets, bags, a couple of them finding boots they'd pulled off when they'd come in. Jessup stays where he is. Derek Lemper shakes his big melon head, purses his lips, but doesn't come over. Stays with Steve Silver. Nobody talks to Jessup. Wyatt is still out on the deck with Kaylee. Missed the whole thing.

As the kids all head outside, Jessup ends up drifting along, watching. There's a mob of Cortaca kids outside, too, the girls saying good-byes, the guys standing more off to the side. Jessup is an island. He sees them get in their cars in twos and threes. Corson is fighting with his girlfriend. The girlfriend leaves in a huff, gets in a car with two other girls. One of Corson's friends holds out his hand for the keys, but Corson shakes his head once, twice, gets into a dark sedan by himself. Car slides a bit as Corson gets it off the grass onto the driveway. He shouldn't be driving, Jessup thinks, beer in his hand all night. But that's not Jessup's problem.

MINUS ONE

He wants to leave. Head out into the night, fire up the truck, go to sleep in his own bed. Wake up in the morning with a fresh day, the snow covering the fields, everything clean. But he can't. To leave now would be to acknowledge what Corson was saying, to have every word be true.

He doesn't want it to be true.

It's awkward. Somebody tells Wyatt what happened, but having Wyatt in his corner doesn't exactly help his case. Jonathan Choo, who came to the party after the action was over, breaks the ice, tells Jessup he did good in the game today, wishes it could have been him slinging the ball instead of Phillip Ryerson, but still. He's close to being back, he says, just waiting for doctor's clearance. With any luck, in time for next week. Somebody turns up the music. People start talking and milling again. Derek Lemper brings Jessup a beer, calls Corson an asshole, and even though Jessup doesn't drink, he takes the beer and chokes it down. He notices that Trevell and Jayden don't come over. Steve Silver doesn't either. None of the black players do, none of the Jews. Only a few of the white boys. Most of the girls keep their distance, too.

He forces himself to drink two more beers over the next fifteen minutes. After that, he slows down a bit, but soon enough he's finished his fourth beer, and he's pretty buzzed when it's twenty to midnight and he feels his phone vibrate. Deanne again.

you still out?

yeah. about to go home.

come pick me up?!!

thought you couldn't come out

can't. sneaking out

really?

want to see you. pick me up and we can go to state street diner.
megan and brooke are going with boyfriends. we are meeting them
there ok?

Megan and Brooke are Deanne's best friends. He won't say anything
about it to Deanne, but he thinks that Brooke is dumb. She's Vietnamese or
Chinese or something, adopted, complains that everybody expects her to
do well in school because she's Asian and that there are quotas now at some
universities because there are too many Asian students, says Deanne is
lucky because she's black so every school wants her. Deanne laughs and
calls her a bitch and Jessup doesn't say anything; if he said the exact same
thing, he'd be run out of town. He likes Megan: she's sharp, wants to be a
lawyer—mom's a lawyer—does debate and runs cross-country and track
with Deanne. Megan's been dating the same guy, Josh Feinstein, since the
end of last year. Given his name, Jessup is not surprised that Feinstein is
rich, both parents doctors. Nerdy as hell but funny, and Jessup likes the kid
despite himself. Brooke's boyfriend has only been in the picture for a few
weeks, kid named Stanley who's new to Cortaca this year. Stanley's fine,
not a guy he'd necessarily hang out with, but he makes Brooke more bear-
able to be around.

okay. leaving now.

**text when you get here. don't park in front
of house**

why?

because I'm SNEAKING out dummy! park in
front of church on pearl street and text and
I'll come over

okay

!!!

He sees the "..." bubble of Deanne texting something else to add to her triple exclamation points, but then it disappears, her thought never finished. He wonders what letters she typed and thought better of. He looks at the keyboard, types in "I lo—." Deletes it. Tries again:

I'll text you when I'm there

He isn't thinking about sneaking out of the party. Doesn't plan to make a big thing of it, either, but one of the girls corrals all the football players, lines them up for a picture on and around the couches. It only takes a couple of minutes—they're smart enough to make sure there's no alcohol in the picture—and when it's done, Jessup's out the door.

T-MINUS ZERO

It's snowing again. Steady. Temperature has dropped a couple of degrees, and he starts shivering immediately. Why did he leave his jacket in the truck? The cold is good, though. Wakes him up. He can taste the sourness of the beer still. Knows he shouldn't be driving, but figures it's fine given his weight. Won't get stopped twice in one night anyway, will I? Why didn't he skip the party, stay home with his sister, his mom, David John? Because he wants to see Deanne. She makes it all worth it.

He walks past parked car after parked car. The neat line of cars and SUVs clogged up, cars on either side of the driveway now, two wheels on snow-covered asphalt, two wheels on the grass. He won't be surprised if somebody on the downhill side of the driveway ends up getting stuck in the grass.

There's a quarter inch of snow coating the windshield of his truck. He pulls his jacket and gloves off the passenger seat and starts the truck. The heater's cranky. Won't be blasting on him until he's halfway to Deanne's. The windshield wipers do a crappy job of clearing the snow. Iced up on the glass. He grabs his scraper, glad of the gloves. They're thin, but better than nothing.

He mostly has the windshield cleaned off when he sees the headlights. He doesn't know how he knows it's Corson, but he knows it as sure as he's been sure of anything. The car, a dark-colored sedan, pulls over and slides to a stop in the grass across the road, nose at an angle, pointed down at the edge of the steep slope that leads toward the trees. Corson puts it in park and sets the brake. The car is ten feet ahead of Jessup, but off to the side, out of his way.

Corson gets out of the car. With the door open, the interior lights show that he's on his own, and though Jessup knows he could take him in a fight, he can't stomach the idea. He just feels tired. Tired of all of it. All he wants to do is see Deanne. All he wants to do is feel her body against his. He wants to tell her that he loves her.

Corson is moving slowly and deliberately. Trying not to act drunk. It gives Jessup plenty of time. He's feeling like he's sobered up. He hops into the truck, closes and locks the door. He rolls down the window, though.

"Not interested."

Corson either hears him or he doesn't, but he doesn't acknowledge Jessup's voice. Doesn't change course, either. Walks right past Jessup to the back of the truck. Jessup puts it in gear, but before he takes his foot off the brake and starts moving, he feels the hard thud, hears the crunch of Corson's boot. Asshole is kicking the truck again. Same place. The plastic lens over the brake light brittle, the thin crunch of metal. He looks in the side mirror and sees a shadow moving, Corson coming toward the cab of the truck.

Jessup stomps down on the gas. He spins the wheel hard, angry. He cannot pull away from the house fast enough. The truck lurches forward. A bee-stung horse. Snow and ice spit out from under the wheels, like a curse from a teacher's mouth, like buckshot scattering through the air and bloodying the breast of a duck flushed from the water. The back end of the pickup, light and bouncy, skids wide and loose.

When it happens, he feels the sound of the impact as much as he hears it: like a soda can crushed by a stomped foot. But it's two distinct sounds: the heavy thud of the boot and the gossamer crinkle of metal folding on itself.

Except the sound does not come from a soda can crushed by a foot. He knows what it is immediately. He stomps hard on the brake pedal, the truck stopping as violently as it started. He sits. The stereo is loud in the stillness, so he thumbs it off, but the windshield wipers squeak, so he turns them off, too, and then stops the motor.

It is too quiet. If everything were going to be okay, there would be a word. A voice. A sound. Something. Anything. But the only sound he can hear is an echo, a memory, the undertone that came with the thud and crumple of metal: the inevitable weakness of a body. He wishes it had simply been an empty soda can. But he knows it was a human being.

He gets out of the truck. He moves as slowly as he can force himself to.

He hit a deer once, more than a year ago, not long after he got the truck running, but that was different. The animal bounded out in front of him. Dumb-eyed and desperate. He barely had time to touch the brake before his fender tore open the deer's belly. When he stopped the truck and walked back to where the deer was crumpled on the shoulder, it was still alive. A sort of miracle.

But the wrong sort of miracle. Guts spilled onto the asphalt, the slow sodium light of the streetlights washing everything down. The doe's breath a desperate whistle of blood. Her right hind leg scraping weakly against the ground as if she was still trying to stand. He watched her like this for a minute or two and then went back to his truck. If he'd had his hunting knife with him, he could have been merciful, but there was nothing to do other than head home to hose off the blood and gore. He had to use a pair of pliers to fish out a chunk of the doe's skin that was lodged in the creased fender.

Now he walks the long way around the front of the truck, touching the hood and then looking at the memory of the deer imprinted on the front fender; the metal still bears an ugly kiss.

When he has made his way around the truck, he looks. The body is ten, twenty feet behind the bed of the truck. He knows it is a person, but in the shadows and the false light coming from the house, it could be anything else. He wants it to be anything else. A soda can. A doe. But it is, and always will be, stubbornly, a dead body.

He's even with Corson's car now. The door is still open. The car is running, the soft chime of a warning that the key is in the ignition. The sound is elegant, and Jessup can't help but notice it's a Mercedes. He closes the door, the chiming stops.

He's still shivering, but he doesn't feel cold anymore. He reaches into his pocket and pulls out his phone.

Can he call the cops? Thinks of Ricky. Thinks of David John. Ricky in the alley, didn't do anything wrong. Doing twenty years for defending himself. Jessup is only seventeen. The scholarship from Duke. The chance to go to Cortaca, Yale, anywhere. All of that gone. His whole fucking life sucked into a whirlpool, like his brother and his stepfather are reaching up from the depths of the ocean to pull him down.

He's breathing fast. Gasping in air. Wind sprints. Dizzy from the heat during two-a-days. The smell of the mats in the wrestling room, head smashing into the ground on a bad takedown, three weeks keeping his headaches and the nausea hidden from his mom. Sprint training during track season, hundred meters on, hundred meters off, run until he pukes.

He's squatting. One gloved hand on the ground in front of him, bracing himself. Doesn't remember squatting.

Looks back at the house. It's a jewel box, sparkling in the night. Only a few windows peer out over the driveway, and they are empty. Nobody looking out, and even if they are, too far away, not enough light to see him, to see what he has wrought. He catches a gentle burst of music, and then it's cut off again, somebody going out onto the porch, closing the door behind them. Follows the line of the driveway with his eyes, sees the ribbon of light turn to darkness, and there, on the snow-covered asphalt, the deeper darkness of Corson's body.

He feels his phone buzz and he stands up and pulls it from his pocket. Looks at the message on the lock screen:

never mind about diner. told m and b we will see them tomorrow. want to go somewhere private instead. just the two of us. come get me!

Can't think. Doesn't unlock the phone. Just puts it back in his pocket.

Too young, they'll try him as a juvie. But he's seventeen. Is that close enough to be tried as an adult? And there's Ricky and David John, all that history. The mayor calling for a hate crime investigation. The prosecutor trying to make up lost ground. There are no accidents. Not in this world. Nobody will believe it was an accident. He'll be an old man by the time he's out.

He looks again at Corson's car. It's angled a bit, the nose pointed down the slope. Clear line to the woods, forty, fifty yards. The trees a dark mass. No lights down there. The clouds hiding the moon, the snow a thin curtain making the house seem hazy in the distance.

He walks toward Corson, keeping an eye on the house. The entire house is built to take advantage of the views of Cortaca, the lake, the university, not to look out over the driveway.

He gets to the body and steels himself. It can't be worse than a deer: split the skin, slide the knife, the blood hot on your hands, the smell like nothing else.

But Corson is whole.

Nothing spilling out of him. If it weren't for the way his neck is bent, the dent in his skull, for the utter stillness of Corson's body, Jessup would think he was simply sleeping.

Somehow, that's worse.

Jessup is suddenly overcome, runs and stumbles off the side of the driveway, falls to his knees, heaving. He empties his stomach once and then once again, a mix of puke and snot and he's crying and gasping, and he has the image in his mind of Corson on the sideline after the hit, puking, too.

He can feel the wetness of the snow leaching through the knees of his jeans, his thin gloves, and he scoops a clean handful up and uses it to wipe off his face. The sour taste of sick echoes in his mouth and throat.

Slowly, unaccountably afraid that Corson will suddenly shudder back to life, he approaches the body. He nudges him with his toe. Nothing.

"It was a clean hit," Jessup says. Or he thinks he says it. He gives Corson's chest a soft tap with his boot, and says, clearly, deliberately, "It was a clean hit."

A bang-bang play. Muscle memory and reaction. The ball and then Jessup's shoulder into Corson's sternum. The sound of the hit an echo still in Jessup's head. He didn't do anything wrong. Nothing to deserve this. Nothing to deserve Corson kicking his taillight in, nothing to deserve Corson calling him out at the party, nothing but bad luck rolling over on Jessup. He knows he didn't do anything wrong, but he knows that's not how the world works.

Ricky didn't do anything wrong either. Changing into his Dickies work shirt in an alley, doing things the right way. People out there sucking off the government's tit when good white people are working their asses off, that's what Wyatt says, Ricky leaving his girlfriend's in the middle of the night to wade in literal shit with David John so that the fine people of Cortaca can eat out without having to worry about what happens when they flush the toilet. Ricky minding his own goddamned business when Jermane Holmes and Blake Liveson jump him. Ricky taking a bottle of beer across the face and then facing off two black kids. If he hadn't grabbed that pipe wrench, what then? Wyatt asks. It would have been Ricky laid out on the cement, Jessup and Jewel and David John and Cindy crying over a cheap casket, and Holmes and Liveson's parents ponying up for the fanciest lawyers money can buy.

Bad luck. Bad timing. If Ricky had his shirt on thirty seconds earlier, if he'd lingered in bed with his girlfriend, Stacey, for another minute or two, Liveson and Holmes would have walked on by. Instead of spending twenty years locked away, right now Ricky would be married, Stacey popping out a boy, Jessup an uncle, David John never gone, the business doing well enough that Ricky could have his own van, money for Jessup's mom to fill her gas tank until the handle clicked off, instead of paying for two gallons at a time. And Jessup wouldn't be standing here, over the body of a dead black boy.

He can't call the cops. He knows that. They'll never believe it was an accident. And if he just drives away, what then? Somebody will find the body soon enough, and then there will be all kinds of fingers pointing at him. He can't just leave Corson's body here on the driveway.

He knows what he has to do, but he hesitates. No going back from it.

But he knows he doesn't really have a choice.

Sink or swim.

Jessup dimly realizes that Corson's skin is still warm enough to melt the falling snow—his face is wet, but there's a crust of snow gathering on his clothes. Jessup grabs the collar of Corson's jacket—his Kilton Valley letter jacket—with one gloved hand and reaches under his armpit with his other hand. Corson is solid. Dead weight. Literally, Jessup thinks, and he has to stifle a laugh. It's not funny, but he can't stop himself from snickering.

Jesus Christ, if this were Texas, they'd give him the chair for this. No. Not for this. Not for a black kid. Not in Texas.

But this isn't Texas. It's Cortaca.

No way for Jessup to say it was just an accident tonight, Corson was drunk, Corson was kicking his truck and all Jessup tried to do was drive away, nothing malicious; that's not something anybody will believe.

The hardest part is getting Corson's body into the car. Jessup opens the door back up and then ends up hoisting Corson onto his shoulder and dumping him into the driver's seat, straightening him up. He tries shifting the car into neutral, but the lever won't move. Brake pedal. Have to push down on the brake pedal. He shoves his foot in, his leg sliding over Corson's, but then he stops. The car is on. Will the air bag go off if the car is on? Will the car brake on its own? This is the type of expensive car that has collision avoidance, all the bells and whistles. Jessup pushes down on the brake pedal, shifts it into neutral, and then he turns off the car. The air bag might still go off, but it will roll free with the engine off, won't it?

He jumps back and slams the door shut, but nothing happens. The car might as well be a rock.

Parking brake. He opens the door again.

As soon as the parking brake is off, the car starts to move, slowly at first, slow enough for Jessup to close the door and stand back, but then it starts gathering speed, down the hill, the slope getting steeper with every foot the car moves. Jessup figures it's going close to fifty miles per hour by the time it hits the trees.

He's surprised by how quiet it is. There's a metallic disturbance, glass breaking, but it barely carries to him. With the music and people talking, they won't hear it on the deck.

He realizes he's just standing there, staring at the woods. He can't see the car. Can't see anything. The trees are a dark mass, swallowing everything. An absence in the night.

He waits for another few seconds, but there's no sound or movement from the house. He could be in another universe. It's possible none of this ever happened.

His phone buzzes again. He looks at the time. It's only been a couple of minutes since he walked out. How did time move so slowly? It's the same message on the lock screen, insistent, reminding him that he hasn't replied, demanding his attention:

> never mind about diner. told m and b we will see them tomorrow. want to go somewhere private instead. just the two of us. come get me!

All he wanted to do after the game was see her, but after what has just happened, he doesn't know if he. . . .

come get me!

He can't go home. Not right now. It's been, what, five minutes since he walked out of the party? Less? Everybody saw him leave. There's the picture with the guys from the team, and that's posted online, easy to confirm date and time. And the texts from Deanne. Only a small, small window for what happened with Corson. Everything that happened, his whole life out the window, three minutes since Corson rolled up? All he has to do is account for that small gap of time. All he has to do is be able to say that he had nothing to do with it, that everybody saw Corson drinking, what does it matter if he and I were arguing, the guy drives drunk and bad things happen, his girlfriend and buddies trying to get the keys off him but they're the ones who let him drive away, so how is that my fault, and besides, I was here and then I was with my girlfriend, no, what happened with Corson was the obvious, a tragic accident, a lesson to all the other kids out there about the perils of alcohol, and what does that have to do with me? But if he goes home, there's the whole night wide open, hours and hours when anything could have happened. If he picks up Deanne, then every minute is accounted for. That's what he tells himself, but it's not true. What's true is that he wants to see her.

come get me!

Needs to see her.

already on my way. snow sucks. slow driving

don't text while you're driving

I'll text when I get there

Jessup gets back in his truck and drives away.

PEARL STREET

He parks a block over, on Pearl Street, in front of the church. He's got acid in his throat from puking, and he digs through the glove box until he finds a tin of Altoids, throws a handful in his mouth and starts chewing.

He leaves the truck running, the heater blowing, and texts her. Turns off the lights. The truck is old enough that there are no automatic lights, and there are no streetlights on Pearl, so it's a heavy darkness. He wishes there were streetlights: he likes watching the snow fall through the artificial light, the way each piece is its own individual thing but also part of something larger.

There are a couple of parked cars along the way, but it's basically deserted. A few porch lights are on, but the houses are all sealed up tight for the night. A good neighborhood with good people, the kind of people who are asleep after midnight on a Friday night, Saturday a day for errands and taking the kids to practice and the library and finally getting around to fixing that loose stair tread, why don't we bake cookies this afternoon, go see a movie, do you need help with your homework?

He gets out of the truck and walks over to a row of bushes beside the church. He's got to take a piss, the beer working its way through him. It's a relief letting go. His hands are shaking. He can't stop his hands from shaking.

He finishes and then walks back to the truck. He puts his hand on the door handle and then hesitates, looks back at the bed of the truck. What would he see if there were streetlights, if he took a look? The back corner of his truck. Broken taillight and what else? But before he can pull out his phone to turn on the flashlight, he sees Deanne rounding the corner and heading to him.

She's on him quick, sliding her arms through the open jacket and around his waist. She's all cinnamon gum, her lips warm, tongue flicking against his teeth.

She pulls back. "Have you been drinking? You taste like mint and beer. It's gross."

"I had a couple of beers. And some Altoids." At least he's covered the worst of his sins.

She's got her hips pressed against his, and his arms are over her shoulders. His back is against the driver's door, solid, propping him up. He likes the way she leans into him, like she's his and he is hers, and he realizes his hands have stopped shaking.

Her hand snakes up under his T-shirt, her fingertips cool on his lower back. "I thought you didn't drink."

"I don't," Jessup says. "Not really."

She crinkles her nose but she's smiling, full of theatrics. "Your breath stinks. Blech. Beer." She reaches into her purse, a canvas satchel, and pulls out a pack of gum. She pops a piece into his mouth, and once he's taken a few chews, she kisses him again, both of them tasting now of cinnamon.

"You don't mind blowing off Megan and Brooke?"

"Would you rather go to the diner, or would you rather go park in the woods somewhere and have sex?"

"Yeah. Well."

"You're shivering."

Shaking, not shivering, Jessup thinks, but he says, "It's cold out here. But it's warm in the truck."

She giggles and then kisses him. "I told them we'll meet tomorrow after work. Unless, you know, you'd really rather . . ."

"No, no, no," he says quickly. "I'm fine with skipping the diner."

SOFT

He can't believe it's only twelve fifteen by the time they're pulled into the woods. It feels like it's been a thousand years since he walked out the door of Victoria Wallace's house. But it's a completely different world here, parked in the woods with Deanne. Here, he can believe that nothing happened, that everything is going to be okay.

In the summer, he wouldn't come here—there's a trail down to the reservoir, where high school kids and college students go to swim and drink beer even though there's signs everywhere warning that it's dangerous, and every once in a while, the cops break things up—but with the snow and the cold, they'll have privacy. The dirt road runs fifty feet off the main road into a gravel parking lot. With the trees, once you're parked, you can't even see the main road.

"Leave the truck running, okay?"

She's not the first girl he's slept with. Claire Reynolds in ninth grade was the first. They dated from Christmas through the end of the summer. Then last year, for a couple of months, Marissa Wells. Nice enough girl, hot as hell, but being with her was too easy. She never seemed to have any opinions of her own, and he could tell she was only sleeping with him because she thought that's what she was supposed to do. After that, off and on, Emily Bell. They were never really dating, but by then he could drive and had his truck, and her parents were never around. She'd let him come over and do whatever he wanted as long as he did what she wanted in return, her red hair dripping over his stomach, splayed on the pillow, telling him where to touch and how.

And yet, for all of that, he's always taken by surprise by how soft girls are. Deanne's just finished cross-country season—she's good enough that if she wants to run for a D-III college, she can—and she runs distance during track season, so she's strong and lean. But still. She leans back her seat as far as it will go, pulls him across. He tries to keep his weight on his elbow, knows he's twice her weight, runs his hand up under her shirt, her skin radiating heat, and even though he can feel the muscle under her skin, when his hand passes over her ribs and over her bra, he's stunned once again at the give of her flesh.

She's got one hand around the back of his neck, pulling him in to kiss her, her other hand working at his jacket, pulling it off. He props himself up, shrugs off the jacket, and then she's peeling off his T-shirt. She slides her hands up his sides, brings one hand across and over, traces his nipple, then leans forward and touches it with the tip of her tongue.

It's awkward, of course, simply because of their ages and because they are new at this—Deanne's only slept with one other boy, and that was only a couple of times—and because they are new at this specifically with each other. It doesn't help that Jessup's truck doesn't have an extended cab, that there's no backseat, that the passenger seat only reclines so far, a forty-five-degree angle. They kiss and touch each other, Deanne's shirt and bra off, and then struggle to turn, so now Jessup is on the bottom, his back against the seat, Deanne letting her full weight press down on him. He can't believe how warm she feels, her breasts against his chest.

He reaches down, slides his hand past the waistband of her leggings, loves the way she takes a sharp breath when he touches her, the wetness against his fingers. She's got her mouth against his neck, moves it up against his ear, and then lets him peel her leggings and underwear off. They're frantic now, her hands scrabbling at the button of his jeans, he helps to push them down around his ankles, and then there's a pause.

She pulls a condom out of her bag, tears it open. She's looking at Jessup and Jessup's looking at her, and she laughs a little as she tries to figure out which way to unroll it. He can hear himself let out a moan as she puts it on him, and then she straddles him, reaches down and guides him inside her.

She has her eyes closed now, and he watches her. Loves the way she bites her lip a bit, the way her eyes aren't just closed but are clenched. She starts slow, moves faster, grinding herself against him. He reaches down like Emily Bell taught him to—not that he'd tell Deanne that—and helps her along.

Soon enough they're both gasping, Deanne shuddering and letting out a small cry, Jessup right behind her.

They stay still for a few minutes. Deanne is panting, her breath coating his neck, her lips occasionally touching his skin, tickling. He's got his arms wrapped around her back, likes just staying there, inside of her, the two of them with nowhere to go.

QUESTIONS

J essup? I . . ."

"Yeah?"

She straightens up now, rocks back, kneeling over him, looking down into his eyes. He smiles at her and she smiles back, but then whatever she was going to say disappears.

"What?" he says.

"Nothing." She reaches down and holds the condom steady while she gets off him. It's awkward again, the two of them squashed into one seat. He peels the condom off, knots it, tosses it on the floor. He'll stop somewhere and chuck it in the trash on the way home. The wrapper, too. Has the image of Jewel finding the wrapper—or worse, the condom—and asking him what it is. Doesn't want to have *that* conversation.

She's curled up in his lap now, her arm around his neck. He can't believe how comfortable he is. He could sleep like this, but she seems wide awake.

"What were you going to say?" Jessup asks.

"Was that your dad? Sitting with your mom and your sister?"

Jessup can't stop himself from stiffening. She feels it.

"Was that what you were going to say?"

"Sorry," she says.

"No. It's okay. It's just . . ."

It's not something they've talked about. If anything, they've gone out of their way not to talk about it. They'd known each other before working at the movie theater together—film study at Coach Diggins's house, and even though the Diggins family moved to Cortaca only last year, Cortaca High School is less than 1,500 students, the size where nobody is really unfamiliar—but they'd never exchanged more than a few words until, suddenly, magically, they were dating.

"You don't have to," she says. "I shouldn't have asked."

"No," Jessup says. "It's complicated."

The crack of Corson's boot against Jessup's taillight, the thump of his body against the truck, the way his neck was turned, the dent in his head, Jessup on his knees in the snow puking up beer, the weight of Corson's body as he laid it in the car, metal and glass as the car hit the trees, and more, the grainy footage from the camera in the alley, David John sitting down next to Ricky and waiting for the cops, letters from Ricky—*I don't regret it none. You got to stand up for yourself. Like we always say: "We must secure the existence of our people and a future for white children."* Those fourteen words a rallying cry for white pride, Ricky writing home that what he did he did in self-defense, but he'd do it again so *"you and Jewel can be safe in this world, stopping them from taking away what little we have left."* Jessup's mom's eyes red-rimmed from crying, touching her wedding ring like a talisman, David John taking Jessup's hand at Kirby's, bowing heads, asking dear Jesus for a blessing, and then standing outside the restaurant, taking Jessup's hand again, shaking it like a man, "Proud of you," David John said. "Go have some fun."

"Jessup?"

"Sorry," he says. "Stepdad. He's not my dad. But he's a good guy."

"Isn't he . . . ?"

Even though she's right there, naked, the two of them in a small space, the heater blowing over both of them, he can feel that she's pulled away. He wants her to come back.

"Like I said, it's complicated."

"Tell me about it?"

So he does.

DAVID JOHN MICHAELS

I don't really remember what it was like before Mom and him got to-gether. I was five when they met, and they married quick. Ricky—my brother—remembers my mom drinking a lot before then, but I don't honestly know if she was a drunk or what. I mean, she goes to meetings like once a month or something, but it's never seemed like a problem to me. Maybe it was different back then—you talk to Ricky and he'll tell you that everything got better when David John came along—but it's hard for me to tell. The thing is, more than anything, you've got to understand, he's a good man. He works hard, taught us to work hard. He's always treated me and Ricky right, like we're his own kids. He dotes on Jewel, like she's a princess. And he loves my mom. I know that."

"You love him?" Deanne says.

Jessup stops. He's not sure he's really considered it before, but he doesn't have to pause long. "Yeah. I don't know why, but I always correct people when they call him my dad. Just did it a minute ago with you. Someone says 'dad' and I say 'stepdad.' And I shouldn't. I mean, he's not my blood, but he's never acted like my stepdad, never acted like anything other than my dad, so, yeah, I'd be lying if I didn't say I love him."

"Do you call him 'Dad' at home?"

He reaches up and cups the back of her neck. "It's going to be easier for me if you just let me tell it, okay?" She takes his wrist and pulls his hand around so she can kiss his palm, and he smiles.

"No. David John. Always. Ricky called him Dad. Don't know why I'm so stubborn about it. Anyway, I don't remember anything different than David John and my mom being married. It is what it is. You don't think anything of it. It just is the way it is, you know? You grow up and whatever it is in your house is what's normal, and it's only when you get older you start seeing that other people live other ways. I mean, you've always lived in a house, always had two parents around, and that's what's normal to you, but you'd probably look at my house and think it's a dump because it's a trailer."

"I—"

"I know, I know." He cuts her off as gently as he can. "Just . . . just let me, okay? If you want to know, just let me." She nods. "It's a nice trailer, double-wide, more than enough space, and we keep it up and we own the land and the trailer, which is more than a lot of people can say, but still, it's a mobile home. Which is a funny thing to say, because it's not going any-where. But a mobile home, no matter how nice it is, isn't the same thing as what people with money have."

He thinks of Victoria Wallace's house perched on the hilltop, the views over Cortaca and the lake, how it lets her and her parents look down upon the town like gods. The only way for him to get that high is to learn how to fly. Thinks, Icarus. Thinks, the sun.

"The point is, it never occurred to me to wonder why we live where we do. And same thing with David John. He came into our lives and that's the way it was.

"Maybe it was harder for Ricky." He shrugs. "Maybe. I don't know. No, I don't think so, because he took to David John right away, but then again, Ricky was nine . . . no, ten when Mom and David John got married. He was older than I was, and maybe it was more of a change with him? Because it *was* a change when they got married. At least that's what Ricky always says. We bounced around from apartment to apartment before that, chaotic, and David John's a discipline kind of guy."

Deanne pulls back a bit, something flittering across her face, and Jessup laughs. "Not like that," he says. "I don't mean Old Testament shit. Never laid a hand on any of us. Seriously. I'm sure he must have yelled at us some-times, but I can't think of an example. My mom can scream, but not David John. He's . . . gentle. 'Gentle' would be the right word. But firm, you know? When I say discipline, I just mean he's a 'do it right' kind of guy. Make your bed, clear the dishes, chores get done before you have free time. He believes hard work is the only salvation. Well, hard work and Jesus Christ. Discipline and hard work can be a drag sometimes, but mostly it's pretty good. I think kids crave discipline, you know? Order's not a bad thing. And Mom liked it, too. Turned things around for us. Ricky wasn't a troublemaker, not really, but he started doing better in school, and I guess I'd been acting out a bit before David John came along. And then they had Jewel and it was the five of us. David John worked hard, did okay with money—it's his trailer and land—and my mom mostly just stayed home and took care of Jewel, took care of me and Ricky.

"He's just . . . You know you got lucky with your dad, right?" He thinks of Coach Diggins handing him the game ball. "He's a good dude, and in some ways, I think, maybe he reminds me of David John."

GRACE

"Best thing I can think of to tell you about David John is that when I was eight, I broke my arm." He takes Deanne's hand, runs it up his left forearm. There's no scar, but he takes her fingers to his elbow and then backs them down two inches so that she can feel the small divot in the bone. "Football, actually. Stupid. Just bad luck. Only serious injury I've ever had playing. Got tangled up with two other boys. Just fell funny and was on the bottom of it. Felt my arm snap. Could hear it, and right away, I'm crying. And when I say I'm crying, I mean I'm wailing, full-on snot-bubbling-out-of-my-nose crying, the whole thing, rolling around on the ground and holding my arm against my chest. This happens, and David John just comes right on the field, scoops me up in his arms."

Her eyes go wide. She's the daughter of a football player and coach. Been around the game her whole life. Knows the code. Knows what it means that David John rushed onto the field.

"That's the thing about David John. He didn't care that you aren't supposed to do that. It's always been family first for him. Picks me up, carries me off the field cradled in his arms, right to the car. Has my mom drive us and holds me in his lap all the way to the hospital and then carries me into the ER. Never told me to suck it up or stop crying or anything, just held me the whole time, told me it was going to be okay, that he loved me, and I was his brave boy."

Jessup hears the way his words catch in his throat, but he doesn't want to stop. It's right there, in the truck with him: the smell of fresh-cut grass, the dirt rubbed into his skin, the whistles, the sound of pads and helmets, cold water in the heat of summer, the sharp pain as he hit the ground, and more than anything, how carefully David John carried him. "But I did stop crying, pretty much as soon as he picked me up, because what I remember from that day most clearly is that as soon as he had me in his arms, I knew I'd be okay. I didn't need him to say it. I just knew." And he *is* crying now. Nothing dramatic, though it's enough that Deanne can tell, and she leans in and kisses him, light, gentle, like grace itself.

GRACE ITSELF

And now that he's crying, he can't seem to get himself to stop, so he just gives himself time. Knows that Deanne's thinking about David John, thinking that there's something hard in Jessup that he doesn't call the man his father, but he's thinking about the sound his truck made, he's thinking of Corson's body, dead and gone, thinking of Corson's parents, thinking of what it's going to mean to carry this around with him for the rest of his life, so he lets himself cry, lets Deanne hold him.

It's not so long, a minute at most, but that's long enough.

WHERE YOU COME FROM

If you don't want to—"

"No. It's good," he says. He can't tell her about Corson. But he can tell her about David John. Do his best. "It's just, well, this is why it's hard. You don't get a choice in things, you know? You're born when you're born, your parents are who your parents are, and things happen the way they happen. Some of it's good and some of it's not. I can tell you everything about my entire life, but unless you were there, unless you were raised like me, it won't make sense. I know how it looks from the outside. Doesn't matter what Ricky was like as a kid or how David John was as a dad, people are always going to think we're a bunch of ignorant rednecks. I know that the only thing that matters to other people is . . . I'm not dumb."

"I know," she says. Her voice is soft. The heater rattles louder than she does, louder than Jessup's voice, too, but the hot air feels good blowing against his skin. He knows that early November is too soon for the snow and the cold to stay, that there will be a break in the weather again sometime before Thanksgiving, at least a few more days when he can leave his coat at home before the snow stays for good, the winter settling on Cortaca, but right now, in his truck, Deanne on his lap, cuddled against him, their naked skin a beacon in the night, the truck alone and hidden in the woods, the falling snow and the cold feel like the best part of winter, like sledding, hot chocolate, and sitting in front of the woodstove and watching cartoons as a kid, like waking up to school canceled, the trees coated, eight, ten inches of snow on the ground, the sky dropping an inch an hour, the world made new.

"I know you're not dumb," Deanne says. "That's one of the things I lo—" She smiles. "That's one of the things I like about you."

"I know how it looks from the outside," Jessup says again, speaking before he realizes what almost came out of her mouth, but he's talking again, and it's too late to stop. "I know what people think. I read what they had in the papers, heard what people on television said when everything happened, and the thing is, even though some of it's true, that's *not* what it was like at home. Mostly, when I think of David John, when people ask me about him, about Ricky, I think of my brother making me popcorn or making sure I finished my homework, of David John teaching me how to shoot and taking me hunting for the first time, of the way my mom seemed to light up every time he kissed her, and yeah, of the way he carried me off the field when I broke my arm. I mean, before . . . before the thing happened with Ricky, before they went to jail, our family was as close to all-American as it could be. After school was sports and homework, dinner as a family every night and then sitting together on the couch watching sitcoms. All of it. We did things right."

PRIDE

He looks at her, waits. She wants to say something, and he wants to give her the space to say it.

She starts off tentative: "I hear you. I do. I mean, he sounds like a good guy in so many ways. . . ."

"But?"

"I didn't say 'but,' Jessup."

"You're thinking it."

She puts her hands on his cheeks, kisses him gently, her lips lingering on his, just the slightest flick of her tongue. Pulls back. "I'm sorry. This isn't easy for me. I mean, you're telling me about how good of a guy he is, and you're telling me what he's like at home, but your brother . . ."

"Ricky."

"People say it was a hate crime. He had Nazi tattoos on him."

"They weren't Nazi tattoos," Jessup says. He says it too quick, too strident, doesn't want to say anything about the tattoos David John carries, the double SS lightning bolts on his left pec, the letters *F* and *R* and *G* and *N*, "For God, Race, Nation," inked below, the iron eagle with the swastika high up on his right shoulder. "And it wasn't a hate crime. *They* attacked *him* first," Jessup says.

Deanne retreats into herself. He feels like an ass, wants to apologize, but isn't sure what he's apologizing for. He didn't do anything wrong. Ricky didn't do anything wrong. He was just trying to protect himself.

Deanne speaks before Jessup can figure out what to say. "I guess what I'm trying to ask you, Jessup, what I'm trying to say, is that I've had a lot of kids tell me your family is into white power. And, you know," she coughs out a laugh, "for obvious reasons, that's not exactly easy for me to accept."

Jessup looks out the side window. With the falling snow, there's barely enough light for him to make out the dark sway of the trees. "But that's not me," he finally says. "I don't know what to tell you about my brother. He's my brother. He's not perfect, and he's going to be in prison until he's forty. And my stepfather did time, too. And yeah, the church my family went to—goes to—thinks that it's good to take pride in our skin. It's . . . it's not a white power thing, but I guess I can see how it looks. It's more of, like, pride in your heritage. A lot of talk. Like, at church, they'll say, what's wrong with being proud to be white? If you can sit with the black kids at lunch, or if the Jews can call themselves 'the chosen people,' what's the problem with wanting to hang out with people who are like you, who think that being white is a good thing? That kind of stuff. But that's not me."

"But that's *your* church," she says. She's not angry. She's trying to have a conversation.

"But it's not *my* church," Jessup says. "I haven't gone there in more than four years, not since what happened with my brother and my stepfather. That's not me. You know me. That's not me."

He stops. Thinks. It's true. At least, he thinks it's true.

He wants it to be true.

"I don't know what else to say. Here we are. It's not my church, but yeah, it's my family's church, my stepfather's church, and he's home now. And if I'm being honest, I'm happy to see him. I'm sorry, but it's true. And I get it if that means . . . I don't want to break up, but I guess I'd understand if . . ." He can't look at her. "It doesn't change anything having him home, not between you and me, but in a lot of ways it changes everything. I want to stay together, I mean, I'm so into you, Deanne. But I can't turn my back on my family. I'm not part of that church, but my mom takes my sister there. It's still my stepdad's church. I'm not part of that church anymore, but no matter how much I like you, and I like you so much that it makes me hurt sometimes—I can't even tell you how much I think about you—I'm still always going to be part of my family, and like it or not, they're always going to be part of that church. I don't know what I can do about that," he says. And then he adds, "It's complicated." Because he doesn't know what else to say.

ANSWERS

She's quiet for a minute. He can't look at her. Afraid of what she's thinking, so when she speaks, it's a relief, not just because of the words, but because of the end of silence.

"Jessup."

"Yeah?"

"Thanks for telling me that. It's important."

"Okay."

"I like you, Jessup."

"I like you, too."

"No," Deanne says. She bites her lip again, but it's different than the way she bit it while they were making love. "I mean, I *really* like you."

He realizes she's the one crying now. A dampness around her eyes that reflects the light from the dashboard and the stereo. He reaches up and thumbs off a tear.

"Deanne . . ."

"Are you going to make me say it first?"

But neither of them says it, so he pulls her close and kisses her for a few minutes and then they make love again—Jessup is vaguely aware that this is only something he can do again so soon because he's seventeen—and afterward Deanne asks him to drive her home. They don't talk much, just a few words about seeing each other at work, plans to go out after with Deanne's friends, but there's nothing uncomfortable. She holds his hand with both of hers, and when he drops her off in front of the church on Pearl Street, they spend several more minutes kissing. When she opens the door, it's all he can do not to grab her and stop her and tell her he loves her.

THE SLEEP OF THE JUST

By the time he gets home, it's close to two in the morning. He eases the door of the truck closed but can't do anything about the trailer shifting under his weight. He brushes his teeth, goes to the bathroom, strips naked, and climbs under the covers of his bed. He's expecting to be tortured by the sound of it, the soda-can crush of Corson's body against the truck bed, everything that's happened today, but as soon as his head touches the pillow the alarm on his phone goes off: 6:30 a.m.

He doesn't know what it says about him that he slept cleanly. And yet the moment he opens his eyes there's a weight that he didn't carry with him the day before: he's alive and Corson isn't.

The trailer is still, though Jessup imagines he can feel the difference in the air that comes with David John home. He does his best to be quiet, and he's out the door by 6:45. Sunrise isn't for another hour, and it's too dark to look at the back of his truck, to see what mark Corson's body left. At least that's what he tells himself.

He knows exactly where he's going—scouted it out months ago, spent a good chunk of last weekend in the same place—and he's parked by seven o'clock, sitting in his folding chair with his back to a tree, his Ruger bolt-action rifle across his lap five minutes later. He's wearing Carhartt coveralls over long underwear, his Timberland boots, his camo jacket, and an orange wool hat. He eats a banana and a Snickers bar, washes it down with some water, settles in. If he had access to private land, somewhere he could build a tree stand, it would be better, but this is a good spot. He's tucked into the trees but has a great view across an open field, 175 yards, 200 yards to where the trees begin again. For Wyatt this would be nothing, but for Jessup this is about as far as he's confident shooting. He can stay hidden from view while watching the tree line, just wait for a deer to step into the open. A clear shot from the darkness. Saw a dozen does and three bucks the previous weekend, two of them not worth anything, but one with a good rack, only it was back in the woods before he had a clean shot.

The snow has hung around overnight, and the woods are made fresh, the early-morning sun glistening where it slices through breaks in the canopy, the field a brilliance of early light off of ice. The temperature is on its way up, though, and in the stillness Jessup can hear the drip of the snow melting off branches. His rifle shoots .30-06, and he's got one in the chamber, four in the magazine, but he's settled in. All he has to do now is wait.

REAP

Normally he feels at peace out here, but this morning he keeps hearing the same thing over and over again: the thump of Corson's body against the body of his truck bed. Can feel the impact.

It's sacrilegious, but he finally digs out his phone, shoves in his earbuds, puts on Springsteen's *Nebraska*. The music is quiet, but it's enough to drown out his memories. He texts Deanne:

> hey. had a good time last night. maybe after we meet megan and brooke at the diner after work we can go for a drive again

Knows she won't be up for a couple of hours. Even though she wanted to come with him today, she thinks he's crazy for getting up early on a Saturday morning to go sit in the woods. Sends another text.

> anyway, just thinking about you

He plays through all of *Nebraska* and has moved on to Cash's *American IV: The Man Comes Around* when he sees the buck. He moves the rifle as slowly as he can. The deer is only partly out of the trees, its hindquarters still in darkness. It stands proud and tall, like there's nothing to be afraid of in this world of ours, none of the skittishness Jessup is used to seeing. The rack isn't going to set any records, but it's respectable, and Jessup figures there's enough meat to fill the freezer.

He's got the rifle up now, closes one eye to look through the scope. No wind to speak of, one seventy-five straight shot. The buck takes a few steps forward, turns broadside to him so Jessup has a clear shot for the heart, but the buck has his head turned toward Jessup. Through the glass, it looks like the deer is staring back at him. Jessup keeps his finger light on the trigger, breathes in, breathes out, in, out, in, out. Through the earbuds, the first sad thrum of Cash's cover of "Hurt."

The Ruger pushes back against his shoulder and the buck doesn't move. Jessup is still peering through the scope, and the deer is still staring back, but then Jessup sees something change on the buck's face. Jessup knows he's imagining it, that the deer can't possibly understand what has happened, but he could swear it's a look of betrayal, as if the buck knew Jessup was watching from the woods, as if the buck thought he could trust Jessup.

He expects the buck to bolt, figures he'll have to track him down, but the buck stays still for twenty, thirty seconds before its front legs suddenly fold, and then it's like the deer has simply decided to lie down in the snow, and even as he walks across the field, Jessup can see the way dark blood soaks into the whiteness.

He crouches, takes a picture of the buck that makes the rack look good, texts it to Wyatt. By the time he's stood back up and pulled out his knife, Wyatt has texted back.

nice! one shot?

one shot

how far?

Jessup types "175" but then erases it. When he's gone hunting with Wyatt, Wyatt has always pressed him to try to shoot from a distance that is farther than Jessup can comfortably hit.

200

pussy

Jessup chuckles. Wyatt shoots a Remington 700 he got from his grandfather, and he keeps it zeroed out to three hundred yards. Claims it's not worth hunting a deer closer than that. Of course, at the shooting range, Wyatt puts his grouping of bullets in a circle the size of a quarter from a hundred yards away, all the while joking that Jessup needs to cash a twenty-dollar bill.

He field-dresses the deer quickly. It's messy work, and once he's done, it takes him more than an hour to get it back to where he's parked. Now, with the sun out, there's no way for him to avoid looking at the back of the truck.

The plastic lens over the taillight is smashed, the bulb broken. And next to it, a foot forward, almost equidistant from the wheel and the back corner, there's a dent. It's small—he can cover it with his palm and does—but it's there. He painted the truck and cleaned it up best he could with his grandfather, but at the end of the day, it's still a heap of crap. Jessup knows this dent is new, can feel it bone deep that this one came from Corson. For a panicked moment, he thinks he sees blood, but he realizes it's from the buck, transferred off his glove.

But it's just a dent, he thinks. Not a burning arrow calling him out, nothing out of the ordinary on a truck like this, no reason to think it's anything other than one of many small accidents and mistakes that the truck has seen over the years.

Oh, Jesus. Get ahold of yourself, Jessup. He's squatting, rocking on his heels. The buck's head is turned, eyes bugged out, the dead deer watching him, judging him. Stop thinking about Corson, Jessup.

He stands up, drops the lift gate, and turns to the buck, muscles the dressed deer up into the bed. He's dirty and tired, and in manhandling the deer more blood leaks out. It's a thin trickle out the back of the truck, a dark blossom in the snow. He sticks his gloved hand underneath it, lets the blood drip onto his palm until his glove is covered. He wipes it clean on the broken plastic of the taillight lens, on the metal of the truck bed, over the dent and the rust.

Don't think about Corson.

Don't think about Corson.

Don't think about Corson.

He tries to close the gate, but the deer isn't in far enough, so he has to climb up in the truck bed. He grabs the buck's rack and pulls it all the way in. When he jumps back to the ground, he's breathing heavily. People who don't hunt think the hard part is bagging the deer, he thinks, stripping off his gloves and throwing them into the bed of the truck with the deer's carcass, but the hardest part is just getting it home.

SOW

He brings the buck to the processor, out in Brooktown. Near the Blessed Church of the White America compound, but no connection. No quarrel, either, and relatively cheap: he only charges sixty bucks including making sausages. The sixty bucks is worth it; Jessup processed his own deer last year, and it was rough work. Working an extra shift or two at the movie theater is an easy call. Still, he does the math in his head. He had twenty-five bucks in his wallet before he hit the ATM last night, took out sixty dollars, so there's eighty-five cash, back down to twenty-five when he returns to pick up the meat. Seventy-six dollars in the bank, going to need forty to replace the bulb and the taillight lens if he buys them from an auto-parts store. Should be getting paid from the movie theater this week, but that's not much since he only works somewhere between eight and ten hours a week, most of that money going to his mom to help with bills. He'll have to put off buying new boots for a while.

By the time he leaves the processor it's after ten. Decides to take a flyer on the junkyard on his way home, see if he can fix things on the cheap. He hits the jackpot almost immediately: a direct match for his truck. Same year, same model, the front a mangled wreck—he wonders if he looks inside the cabin if he'll see blood from the accident—but the back end is pristine. He salvages the lens and even finds an intact bulb; all told he's out of pocket less than three dollars. Lucky day. He pays and is starting the truck back up when his phone buzzes. Expects it to be Deanne, but it's his mom.

where are you?

hunting. got a buck. good one.

come home

on my way

now

She's not usually on his case like this. He feels the dizzy gulp of shame coming up from his stomach, the weight of his secret errand, but just as quickly he dismisses it. She can't possibly know. He figures with David John home, she wants to do something as a family. And he can oblige. Why not? He doesn't have to be at the movie theater until two o'clock, and even though he can always stand to work ahead, he's good on homework. He'll shower and be cleaned up by eleven, hang out with Jewel and his mom and David John until it's time to head to work, a happy family, everything right in the world.

It's not until he pulls in the driveway and sees the police cruiser outside the trailer that it comes crashing back to him how wrong he is.

BLOOD ON HIS HANDS

There are two cops in uniform standing in front of the cruiser, one black, one white, and they're talking to David John. The black cop turns and looks at Jessup, waves him in, so Jessup pulls past and parks with the nose of the truck almost touching the side of the trailer. He gets out, suddenly aware of how grungy he is. His coveralls are splattered with mud and blood. His jacket smells of the deer's death.

Both cops are turned to look at him, but Jessup is looking at David John, sees the quick, small shake of his head.

"Didn't I stop you last night?" the white cop says.

It's the same guy. Hawkins. "Yes, sir."

"Last person I stopped before my shift ended last night, first person this morning. Twice in twelve hours is a little much."

"A little more than twelve hours," Jessup says.

Hawkins isn't smiling. "Don't be a smart-ass. You're in some trouble here. And I thought you were going to get that taillight fixed first thing this morning."

"Yes, sir." He motions over. "Got a new lens and bulb right in the truck. Going to fix it right now."

The black cop has his hand resting on the butt of his gun. "You were out hunting?" Jessup nods. "Rifle in the truck?" Jessup nods again.

"Yes, sir. In a case. Unloaded. Trigger lock on it. It's behind the seats."

"You carrying anything else?"

Jessup feels like he's underwater. Everything is moving slowly. Hawkins is separated from his partner by ten, fifteen feet. The black cop is older, clearly the one calling the shots. He's only got the heel of his hand on the butt of the gun, but it's making Jessup nervous.

"What's this about?" he says.

"Answer the question," the cop says. "You carrying anything else?"

"Got a hunting knife in my jacket pocket. Multitool in my coveralls has a blade on it, too."

"Why don't you take those out and put them in the front seat of the truck, and then we'll talk, okay?"

Jessup complies. He doesn't hurry. Doesn't want to act nervous, plus it gives him a few seconds to think, run it through his head.

There's nothing. They've got nothing. He had gloves on when he picked up Corson, no fingerprints. And it would have looked like an accident. Wouldn't it have? That was the whole point of what he did. Everybody knew Corson was drunk. And Jessup left a good forty-five minutes after Corson and the rest of the Kilton Valley kids did, nobody out on the driveway to see Corson come back. No reason to believe that Jessup had anything to do with it. Just an accident, dumb luck for a dumb kid dumb enough to drive when he'd been drinking. Corson still jacked up and angry, coming back to the party to finish what he started with Jessup, and then just making a mistake and heading down the slope into the trees. Wear your seat belt, boys and girls. No, Jessup thinks. All they've got is people talking about Corson coming at him at the party, but even that leaves him clean. They didn't fight, nobody taking a swing. The only time anybody saw Jessup hit Corson was on the football field. Clean hit. Bang-bang play. Cops are only here because kids talk, because Ricky killed those two black boys in the alley, because David John is home, because word gets around about the Blessed Church of the White America and there's another black kid dead and Jessup's name comes up.

Doesn't matter what did or didn't happen with the truck, Jessup thinks. They can't know about that. He forces himself not to look back at the new dent at the rear of the truck.

Jessup closes the door, sees the black cop relax, his hand drifting off the gun.

Hawkins seems relaxed now, too, and Jessup knows they have nothing. Just talk.

"Where'd you go after I stopped you?" Hawkins says.

Jessup starts to answer, but the black cop cuts him off, his voice loud, jacked up.

"That blood on the truck?" he says, and his hand is now firmly on the pistol. Jessup can't stop himself from stepping back, lifts his hands, palms out. Same gesture of supplication he offered to Corson at the party. He's pressed back against the truck.

"Like I said, I was hunting," Jessup says. "Got a big buck." Sees the black cop squint at the word "buck." The cop knows exactly who David John is, exactly what church the family is going to tomorrow morning. But nothing Jessup can do about that except keep talking. "Just dropped it off at a processor's, but even field-dressed, probably two hundred pounds. Heck of a lot of work to get into the truck. Had blood all over my gloves. Some of it got on the truck, I guess. Hard not to get blood everywhere." He gestures at his coveralls, his jacket, careful not to move suddenly. "I need a shower, man. Guess I could stand to hose down the truck, too."

QUESTION

The black cop takes his hand off the gun, but he isn't relaxed. "Okay then. How about you answer the question."

"What question?"

Hawkins now: "Where'd you go after I stopped you last night?"

"What's this about?"

David John comes off the porch, walks over to where Jessup is standing. "Does he need a lawyer?"

The black cop shakes his head. "Not if he didn't do anything wrong. Now, Jessup, answer the question."

David John's voice is quiet, but it's firm. "I wasn't asking you. I was asking . . . What's your name again?"

Hawkins lets something approaching a smile come to his mouth. A secret coming to his lips. Jessup's reminded of Jewel as a toddler, the Easter Bunny, Santa Claus, his sister at four, five, six, fairy tales and bedtime stories, Disney princesses, Jessup telling her no, prison ain't so bad, just read what Daddy's written, he's getting good food, has friends, and Ricky misses you, too, but he's doing okay, and then somewhere in there, Jewel growing up, nah, I don't need a new bike for Christmas, knowing that it means extra shifts at Target for their mom, that it's Jessup sneaking into her room at night and slipping a dollar under her pillow, the Tooth Fairy in the form of her brother, understands exactly why it is her father's gone, where he is.

There's that tightness in his chest, a hard swallow, when did she grow up like that? No, he thinks, clenches his fists, digs his short fingernails into the skin, not the time or the place, think about Jewel later. Don't think about Jewel, don't think about Corson. Right now there's a snake in the garden. Take care of that.

Hawkins takes a few steps over until he's standing behind his partner.

He's got something approaching a smirk on his face now. "Hawkins. Paul Hawkins. You can have our badge numbers, too, if you want, Mr. Michaels."

Jessup thinks about what Hawkins told him last night. Blend in. Keep your head down until you're needed, see you at church. Thinks about Brandon Rogers on television, hair neatly combed, the optics of a suit and tie instead of a shaved head and neck tattoos. "Blessed Church of the White America" circling a flaming cross on David John's back, Ricky's back.

"I don't need your badge numbers," David John says, "but what do you think, Officer Hawkins? You think Jessup needs a lawyer?"

"No, Mr. Michaels. I don't think your son needs a lawyer. At least not right now."

Jessup wonders if Hawkins remembers that he's David Michael's stepson, not his son. Not that it matters. Nobody cares. What the hell is wrong with him? Why does he keep thinking about the wrong things?

Hawkins looks at Jessup now, the insolent smile wiped clean. Professional now. He's got a pad and pen out. Taking notes. "Maybe your son will need a lawyer at some point, Mr. Michaels, but how about we just have Jessup tell us what happened last night, where he went after I pulled him over for that taillight, and we'll see where that goes."

"I went to a party," Jessup says. "Girl from school. Victoria Wallace. Her boyfriend's on the football team. Aaron Burns. Victoria's house is past the university. Out in the country a bit. There were probably a hundred kids there."

The black cop takes the lead again. "You get in a fight last night? At this party?"

"No, sir," Jessup says.

"Really? You sure about that?"

"Yes, sir. There was a kid who gave me a hard time about . . . about my family history, but we didn't go at it or anything. Nothing physical."

"Who was this kid?"

"Kevin Corson. Black kid," Jessup says. He has to stop himself from flinching. Why did he have to say the second thing?

"You two didn't mix it up?"

"No, sir. He was pretty drunk. Drinking all night. Mad, too," Jessup adds. "Played for the team we beat last night, and I laid him out good at the end of the first half."

"Laid him out?"

"Yes, sir. Caught him right in the chest as he was trying to catch a ball. Came down on top of him and his helmet popped off. He dropped the ball, I picked it up and ran it in for a touchdown. He was puking on the sideline after. Pretty sure he had a concussion. Knocked him out of the game."

"Kevin Corson?"

"Yes, sir."

SMOKE SIGNALS

Jessup sees the curtain move in the living room window. Jewel peeking out. He wants to wave to her, to smile, to signal to her it's all going to be okay. Is this going to be her life?

Jessup tells the cops he left the party, got in his truck, drove to see his girlfriend, came home.

"You know Corson outside of football?"

"No, sir. Overlapped at a couple of football camps, but different sides of the ball. Enough to say 'hey,' but nothing more than that."

"Any problems in the past? Anything before the party last night?"

Jessup thinks about the parking lot, about Corson jabbing his finger into Jessup's breastbone. "He came up to me after the game. Said it was a dirty play. Kicked out my taillight."

The black cop is watching him closely, but behind him, Jessup sees Hawkins squint.

Fuck. He'd told Hawkins last night that he didn't know how it happened. That he'd come out of the game and just found the taillight shattered.

Hawkins doesn't say anything. Doesn't write anything in his paper pad.

"And what did you do?"

"Just drove away, sir."

"He kicked out your taillight, and you just drove away?" The black cop is baiting him. Scornful. All but calling him a pussy.

"That's correct, sir. I didn't want any trouble. I was going to meet my family at Kirby's. I was hungry and in a hurry. A burger sounded better than a fight." Jessup risks a smile.

"And last night? At the party? What happened with you and Corson?"

"Nothing happened."

"Nothing?"

"Nothing," Jessup says.

"Because we hear that you two had a scrap."

"No, sir," Jessup says. "He yelled at me, accused me of some things, but he didn't touch me, I didn't touch him, just a lot of talk."

"He *accused* you of things? Like what?"

Jessup stares at the cop. Pegs him at forty-five. Nothing like the fat cop they saw outside of Kirby's last night. This one—he can read the name tag now, says "Cunningham"—is clearly trying. Got an agenda. He's gone a bit soft, age creeping up, a small pudge over his belt, but Jessup bets he runs four, five times a week, lifts weights, but none of it enough to fight off the wrong side of forty. He's got a wedding ring on, so probably kids, too.

Jessup makes a decision.

"Said I wanted to call him a nigger."

The yard is quiet. There's the sound of a car heading away from them on the main road, but nothing else other than wind. Hawkins takes a step, his boots squeaking in the snow.

Cunningham narrows his eyes. "You called him the *N*-word?"

"No, sir," Jessup says. "I did not. He said I *wanted* to call him a nigger."

"Did you?"

Hawkins takes another step, grabs Cunningham's elbow. "Hey. Come on now, Marcus."

Jessup doesn't say anything. Cunningham keeps staring at him, and Jessup stares back, neither one willing to look away.

DAVID JOHN

I s that what this is about?" David John says. "Some boy is angry because he thought Jessup wanted to call him the *N*-word? That's enough to get the cops all the way out here in the country?" He doesn't emphasize the word "boy," says it like it's just part of the conversation, but he doesn't have to emphasize it.

Jessup says, "This is bullshit. I didn't call him anything. Corson's the one who said 'nigger,' not me. I don't say that word."

Cunningham looks like he'd be happy to draw down on both him and David John if he thought he could get away with it, if there wasn't anybody to see him. "For a word you don't say, you're saying it an awful lot," he says, his voice almost a growl. "You've said it three times in the last minute."

Hawkins still has his hand on his partner's elbow, and now he gently pulls, turning the black man a quarter turn. He says, "Come on, Marcus, let's talk for a minute."

Cunningham is reluctant, but after a few more seconds of staring at Jessup and David John, a hard, tight, deep look in his eyes, he and Hawkins walk down the lane toward the road. They stop at the edge of the driveway, Hawkins talking quickly, emphasizing, Cunningham saying something occasionally, his arms crossed, even from fifty yards away the fury in his body as easy to see as the sun in the sky.

David John stands his ground. Jessup is expecting anger from his stepfather, but there's only sadness.

"How much trouble are you in?" he says. "Did you get in a fight with this Corson kid at the party?"

"No, sir," Jessup says. And it's the truth. "Motherfucker came at me, talking shit about you and Ricky—"

David John cuts him off. "Watch your language."

The muscles in Jessup's chest go tight. There's a bruise on his ribs he hadn't noticed earlier. He bites his teeth together, remembers that the best thing he can do is take a breath, don't respond right away. Gives himself a second. Realizes that he's exhausted. Drained. Played his ass off, gave up his body on the field, everything that happened with Corson, with the truck, the party, the accident, dropping Corson's body into the car, staying out late with Deanne, up early with the sun flashing off the snow, dragging the deer out of the woods, and now this, standing in his yard, covered in blood. All he wants is a shower. All he wants is for all of this to go away.

He's still trying to decide what to say when David John softens. "Sorry," he says. "You're not a little kid. It's just, you know, one of the hardest things about being in jail is how much swearing there is. It's just not very Christian. Sets me on edge to hear it at home."

Jessup stifles a laugh. "Really? The swearing was one of the hardest things about being in jail?"

Jessup can see the quick change from earnestness to humor, David John taking a glance to the end of the driveway and then broadcasting a smile. "Okay. Yeah, that's as dumb as it sounds. But do me a favor, okay? Don't swear like that. Don't use the *N*-word. Don't say 'ain't.' Any of it. Don't talk like that. It makes you sound dumb. Don't give them any ammunition."

THEM

hem. Jessup knows David John isn't just talking about the cops. He's talking about all of them. The liberal elite, the pointy-head academics and fake-news journalists who talk about the Blessed Church of the White America like it's some fascinating study of inbreeding gone wrong, the black preachers grandstanding and calling what happened in the alley a hate crime, not once acknowledging that Ricky was minding his own business, that he was doing the right thing, coming into work late at night to fix a plumbing problem, simply changing his shirt when those two boys attacked him. *Them.* The mayor telling every reporter who would listen how Ricky and David John don't represent Cortaca, how Cortaca is a good town full of good people, how this should be considered a hate crime, Blessed Church of the White America a circus, everybody who goes there to pray a clown.

And David John isn't just talking about that, either; he's talking about every politician calling for good Americans to pull themselves up by their bootstraps without ever stopping to ask if they have any boots, every teacher Jessup has ever had looking at David John and Jessup's mom and seeing two parents who didn't go to college, who didn't grow up in a house where academic excellence was prioritized over paying the bills and making sure the heat and the water and the electricity stayed on, and conflating that with stupidity. *Them.* Because poor white always means dumb to them. They look and listen and think that a lack of a certain kind of knowledge—David John can fix almost anything, taught himself enough high school math to make sure Ricky got through algebra, can write letters home from prison that make Jessup's mom, Jessup's sister, Jessup himself feel like it's going to be okay, but he can't hang a diploma from a fancy university on the walls, can't live in a house with a formal dining room, can't drive a new car made with German engineering, can't come home from work with hands that are as clean as when he left the house—means a lack of intelligence.

That's one of the things Jessup suddenly realizes he should have told Deanne: how smart David John is, how hard he works, how infuriating it is to see in all of the articles, to hear from all of the blowhards on television, the assumption that his stepfather is a dirt-chewing moron, living in a trailer out in the country like an inbred, a plumber wallowing in shit, a God-fearing member of the Blessed Church of the White America because he's too stupid and lazy to think for himself. Every time somebody like David John—or Jessup or Jewel—says "ain't," says anything that makes them sound like their neighbors and kin, anything that shows that they are part of a tribe of people who don't have things handed to them, who have to work for everything, it's just proof to the people who were born on a greased chute of ease, every door opened, every opportunity given, every hand extended, that poor folks get what they deserve.

David John did everything right by his family, putting in sixty hours a week mucking up piss and shit, taking on two boys who weren't his blood and treating them like sons, a good husband, good father, teaching the kids to study, to work hard, salute the flag, and praise Jesus, and all of it, everything, balancing on a razor wire. Everything taken away because two black boys born into money—the sons of a police chief and a teacher, of two lawyers, their entire lives just handed to them on a platter—didn't like Ricky's tattoos. *Them.*

Jessup knows exactly who David John means when he says "them."

ANSWER

The cops are walking back over to Jessup and David John, but the black one peels off and gets into the squad car. He starts it up and backs the cruiser down to the end of the lane. Hawkins watches, waits, and then turns to David John and Jessup.

Jessup shakes his head, "I didn't—"

"Shut the fuck up." Hawkins is furious, almost feral. "I'm going to ask you this once, and I want you to tell me the truth. Honest answer, Jessup. You understand?" He looks at David John. "This can all go away, but only if your son tells me the truth. You got that? Is there anything I need to know about last night?"

Jessup glances at David John. David John gives the smallest nod possible. "Go ahead, Jessup. Paul's good people. You might not remember him because, well, for obvious reasons, being a cop and all, he tries to keep a bit of a low profile at the church. But he's church people."

Hawkins softens a bit. "I'm glad you're out," he says.

"Me too. Now, Jessup," David John says, looking at him, "what happened?"

Hawkins holds up his hand. "Hold on. Let me tell you what we've got, and then you tell me what happened. Want to make sure there's no mistakes here."

Jessup wonders if the world is unspooling around him. His legs feel shaky. All he's had to eat this morning has been a banana and a Snickers bar, running on three, four hours of sleep. He could use a shower, a sandwich, even a nap before he has to work. Instead, he's standing on the driveway, talking to . . .

Hawkins talking. Bunch of kids sleeping over at Victoria's, sleeping it off, one of them heading out in the morning and seeing the sun glinting off the metal and broken glass of the Mercedes smashed up at the edge of the woods down the hill from the driveway. Corson in there, no seat belt, going to be an autopsy and they'll check for alcohol and drugs. Assumption is that this is just a standard tragedy, kid turns off his car and puts it in neutral instead of park, too drunk to stop it. There's always some dumb teenager on a Friday night, at least nobody else was in the car. That's what they think at first, but Cortaca on a quiet Saturday morning means there's plenty of cops showing up at Victoria's, and plenty of cops means plenty of talking to plenty of kids, and Jessup's name comes up.

"So," Hawkins says, "first assumption is that this is just some stupid nigger"—Jessup realizes he has to stop himself from flinching, the familiar word so unfamiliar out of this uniformed cop's mouth, Jessup not lying when he told Cunningham it is a word he doesn't use—"who doesn't know how to use a parking brake, but with David John coming home yester-day . . ." He sighs. "We started roll yesterday morning with the chief of police talking about David John getting out of prison and that we should all be looking out, any excuse to pull you over. He's got it in for you, and the orders are, if we've got anything, if anything is hinky at all with you, let's make sure we get it on paper, cover our asses. And then, all of a sudden, here we go, it's Saturday morning and another dead nigger—"

David John interrupts. "We don't talk like that in my house. This is a Christian household."

Hawkins squints. "Fine. Another dead Negro, which would be a good start in my book, but we've got all these high school kids blurting out a name, and that name belongs to David John's kid. It's not a good look, Jessup. Let me ask you again, is there anything I need to know about what happened last night?"

There's only one answer Jessup can give.

"No."

FOREST, TREES

Hawkins makes a show of it for his partner watching from the cruiser, writing things down in his notebook as he asks Jessup to walk him through everything that happened last night, football game through right this minute.

"You don't leave anything out," Hawkins says. "You want to make this all go away, it's a lot easier if I don't get any surprises. Good or bad, you tell me."

"You can trust Paul," David John says.

Jessup wants it to be true, but he can't help but think about what it means that Hawkins hides himself behind a badge and a uniform. Lying in wait. He knows he can trust his stepfather, but this cop is different. Doesn't matter what David John says.

He mostly tells it straight. Jessup tells him about Corson kicking out the taillight in the parking lot, dinner at Kirby's, getting pulled over—though Hawkins obviously knows that part, doesn't correct Jessup or remind him that last night he said he didn't know what happened to the taillight—about Corson confronting him at the party.

"About when did this happen?"

"Eleven o'clock." He pulls out his phone. Looks at his texts to and from Deanne. "I texted my girlfriend at ten fifty-five. This was, at most, five minutes after that. The whole thing with Corson only lasted a couple of minutes."

Hawkins stops writing. Looks at Jessup. "Some girl at the party videoed most of it. Keep that in mind. When you talk about what happened, you stick to the truth."

For a moment, Jessup thinks he's going to be sick. He can picture the video in his head: the grainy darkness, the headlights of Corson's car, the interior light with the door open, the sick thud of Corson against the truck, the shaky movements of a girl holding her cell phone watching him lift Corson's body into the Mercedes. But that's not what Hawkins is talking about. The video isn't from what happened in the driveway. Nobody saw that.

Jessup tries to tell himself it's as if it never happened.

Hawkins continues. "You come off looking pretty good. You can tell Corson is drunk, and even though he's clearly trying to provoke you, you don't say or do anything dumb. Stand your ground without aggression, and the girl keeps it rolling. Even if you'd gotten into a scrap, that would have been okay. Anyway, the video follows Corson walking out the door with his friends, keeps shooting it until Corson gets in his car. Harder to see once she goes outside, but you can tell it's Corson getting in the car by himself, driving away. Time stamp runs it from ten fifty-nine to about eleven ten." He's got his pen back on the pad again, writing. "Then what?"

"I don't know. I was embarrassed," Jessup says. "Wanted to leave but thought that would look weak." He tells Hawkins about the beers, sees David John scowl at the drinking, but that's a conversation for another time. "Left about eleven forty-five."

"If we ask around, people will confirm that time frame?"

"Yeah. They should. I mean, I don't know how much kids were watching the clock." The picture! He can hear how excited he sounds, almost pitiful, like a puppy looking for attention. "There's a picture! Most of the guys from the team. Right before I left." He scrolls through until he finds it on his phone. Hawkins and David John look at it. Jessup points at the time: 11:43 p.m.

"And then you came straight home? Because there's some question that maybe Corson came back, looking to finish what he started, and it would be good if we knew where you are the rest of the night."

David John starts to say something, but Jessup cuts him off with a quick "no."

He knew what David John was going to say. His stepfather was about to vouch for him, to say that Jessup came in about midnight, that he remembers it was midnight because it was earlier than he expected, and he looked at the clock just as Jessup came through the door, and he'd be happy to get on a stand and swear the whole truth and nothing but the truth that Jessup came straight home from the party, no chance for anything to happen. Unbidden, the image of Ricky in the alley, the security camera filming at 7.5 frames per second, herky-jerky: David John looking at the camera, reaching into the truck, Holmes's body turned over, and then, whatever it is that happens out of sight of the camera. Nothing David John would admit to, but the cops finding a knife in Holmes's hand, only one set of prints, like it was wiped clean.

David John looks like he's going to try to speak again, so Jessup is even more forceful. "No." He hesitates. He doesn't want to bring Deanne into this, but if he doesn't . . . He can't ask it of David John. He can't do that to his mother, to Jewel. Not again. "I went right to my girlfriend's."

Hawkins clicks the ballpoint closed, open, closed, open. Writes something on the pad.

"Name?"

"She snuck out," Jessup says, evading the question. "I don't want her to get in trouble. But I texted her that I was already driving . . . uh, at . . . eleven fifty."

Seven minutes, Jessup thinks. Seven minutes from when he took the photo in the living room of Victoria Wallace's house until he texted Deanne back. And in that seven minutes it's like a black hole opened and swallowed his whole world. He needs to get those seven minutes back. He needs to rescue himself.

"With the snow, I was going slow, but I drove straight from the party, picked her up at"—he looks at the texts again—*here*—"eleven fifty-nine p.m. A minute shy of midnight." Shows Hawkins the phone.

"And then what?"

"We parked in the woods in the parking lot by the reservoir."

STEEL TRAP

Hawkins smirks. Clicks his pen again. Closed, open, closed, open. "Bet you weren't up there to go swimming. I don't suppose I have to ask what you did up there." Jessup can feel his face gone hot. "What time did you bring her home?"

"About quarter to two," Jessup says.

Hawkins asks him a few more questions, glances over his shoulder to the end of the lane, where Cunningham still sits in the car.

"If there's anything you're not telling me, it's important that—"

Jessup starts to speak, but Hawkins shoots out his hand, pissed. "I'm talking right now, not you. If there's anything you're not telling me, anything that needs to be kept quiet, you keep quiet about it. Keep your fucking mouth shut." Hawkins takes a deep breath.

"It doesn't matter what really happened. You need to understand that this is going to play like hell. After what happened with your brother and your dad"—Jessup glances at David John, and even in this exact moment he's got enough self-awareness to realize that for once he doesn't want to correct the misstatement—"this has some bad optics. You've got a good story there. Helps that there's the photo and the texts, and if I need to follow up beyond this, assuming your girlfriend can tell the story the same way, it'll turn out fine for you. But the medical examiner is in right now, doing an autopsy. If there's anything—and I mean *anything* at all—that looks off, we'll be back tomorrow with a search warrant and things will get ugly for you and your family."

He stares hard at Jessup. It's hard for him not to look away. There's something flat about Hawkins's eyes. Makes him think of a shark. He wonders if Hawkins is ex-military. He's got the look. A tour in the Middle East and then back home and wearing blue.

"I'm on your side in this, Jessup, and if you say you didn't do anything—"

"I didn't do anything." It's reflexive. Just bursts out of his mouth. He's not sure who he's trying to convince: Hawkins, David John, or himself.

Hawkins shrugs. "I honestly don't care, Jessup. I'm not going to cry myself to sleep over this. But what I'm saying is that there are people in the department and around the county who think that Ricky and David John got off too light with what happened. Nobody cares about the truth. They just care how it looks and how it plays in the news. I'm telling you this as a friend: if there's anything that looks off in the autopsy, things are going to go in a bad way for you. There will be Black Lives terrorists protesting downtown and television trucks and the mayor and every politician in the country is going to be on this. Sorry," he says, looking at David John. "You can't outrun the family name."

Jessup wants to scream. It's not even his goddamned name. He didn't do anything wrong. He says it: "I didn't do anything wrong."

Hawkins clicks the pen closed, tucks it with his notebook into his pocket. "You're not listening to me. I don't care if you had a hand in that boy's accident or not, Jessup, but there are a lot of people around here who will, who are just looking for an excuse to go after your family, to go after the church, so if there's something floating around that contradicts your story, something that you might not want to get looked at in a lab, you take care of that right now. Make sure it doesn't show up later. You understand me?"

He stares at Jessup until Jessup nods.

"Now," Hawkins says, "I'm not going to shake your hand, David John, because that isn't going to look right—we don't know each other, right?— but you make sure Jessup does what I say. Keep your heads down and this storm will pass over."

"Thanks," David John says. "I expect you won't be coming to church tomorrow, then?"

Hawkins grins, and now Jessup is sure that he's reminded of a shark. Dark waters hiding things.

"Expect not," Hawkins says. "As it is, risky for an officer of the law to come to services. Think I'll lay low for a while."

TELL ME

The cops pull out of the driveway. Jessup starts to head inside, but David John grabs his wrist.

"Tell me," he says. "All of it. Whatever happened, I need to know. If you want me to help you, I need to know everything. Tell me exactly what happened."

So Jessup does. He leaves nothing out.

BIBLE STUDY

He turns the water as hot as he can stand it. He's got a deep bruise on his side, the crown of a helmet leaving its mark, another bruise already turned yellow on his right biceps, a scab on his forearm. He doesn't remember any of them.

The water comes off cloudy at first, deer blood, dirt, the morning in the woods disappearing down the drain. He scrubs at his skin as if there might be more blood hiding there, thinks about the angle of Corson's neck, the dent in his skull.

He's huffing now, can't get air in, as if instead of standing in a shower he is underwater, drowning. The weight of the ocean above him, pushing him down. He places his palms hard against the plastic of the shower stall, willing himself to stay quiet, shaking, sobbing without sound, the running water covering what the thin walls of the trailer can't. It comes on him like a tidal wave, dragging him under, but he fights against it, swims up to the falling water again, says, whispers, prays, "Our Father, who art in heaven . . ."

He says the Lord's Prayer once, twice, ten times, twenty, thirty, working the soap like it's sandpaper, forgive us our trespasses, scouring his flesh, digging his short fingernails into the bar, forgive us our trespasses, turning the water hotter, the steam rising up like an offering, forgive us our trespasses, punching himself over and over in the thigh, forgive us our trespasses.

BAGMAN

Jewel is making grilled cheese sandwiches. The smell of melted butter fills the trailer.

Jessup hesitates as he hands David John the keys to his truck. "Do we have to?"

"Yes," David John says. They've already argued about getting rid of the truck. Jessup knows that David John is right, that it's the one thing that can tie him concretely to Corson's death, but it's hard for him to let go of the keys.

He's holding a garbage bag in his other hand, and he passes that over as well. His stepfather opens up the bag, looks inside.

"This all of it?" Jessup nods, and David John ties the bag. "Keys for the van are on the hook. Give me ten minutes." Walks out of the trailer, already holding his phone, dialing his brother.

Jewel is oblivious, but Jessup's mom is sitting on the couch, holding a book. Something from the library. Inspirational. She's not reading. Just watching. Doesn't say anything. Jessup wants to tell her not to worry, but he doesn't say anything either.

He's wearing wool socks and his sneakers, jeans, a Cortaca High School Football long-sleeved T-shirt: school logo with the word "Football" underneath, on the left breast, "One Team, One Family" on the back. His jacket is in the trash bag, along with his boots. He doesn't have another jacket, so he's got a hoodie. Cortaca Football, too, heavy and zip-up, black, warm enough until he can get to the thrift store for a new coat. He slips the sweatshirt on, zips it up.

"You got your shirt for work?"

His mom's eyes are bright. She pays attention. She's no dummy. At the stove, Jewel is humming something to herself. Happy. Her dad is home. All is right in the world. She slides the spatula under one of the sandwiches and puts it on a paper towel, hands it to Jessup.

"One grilled cheese sandwich, to go. Careful," she says. "It's hot."

"It's supposed to be," he says. He takes a bite.

Jewel pokes him in the stomach with the handle end of the spatula. "I think you mean 'Thank you, oh favorite sister of mine.'"

"You're my only sister," he says. They're both smiling, and he lifts the grilled cheese up, an acknowledgment of thanks, a salute, a signal that he loves her.

She's grown in the last year. She still looks like a little kid to him, but she belongs in middle school, in sixth grade. He knows that's going to change, though, sees what the other kids look like when he drops her off or picks her up, girls turning into young women as they move from sixth to seventh to eighth, knows that before he can stand it she'll be in high school, college, married, kids of her own. And he'll be off somewhere, too, university, a job, a life away from here.

He can't bear the thought that it might not work out that way. He'll do anything to make sure she breaks free. The both of them.

"Jessup?" his mom asks again. "Do you have your shirt for work?"

"Shoot. No. Thanks," he says. "Sorry." He walks back to his bedroom, eating the sandwich, pulls his collared Regal Cinemas shirt off a hanger, and walks back.

"You're off in your own world today," she says. Her voice is quiet. Let Jewel stay in her own private world, her voice says, hasn't it been hard enough for her with Ricky, with her dad? Not you, too, Jessup, not you. "You sure everything's going to be okay? I don't like any of this."

"I'm sure," he says.

When he and David John came inside, they sent Jewel to her room to listen to music while they told Jessup's mom what was going on. Most of it. Didn't tell her what he and David John talked about after the cops left. The soda-can crumple of Corson's body against the truck. The dead weight of getting him into the Mercedes. David John looking at the dent on his truck. Didn't tell his mother why he filled a garbage bag with his boots and coat, gloves, T-shirt and jeans, why David John has taken Jessup's truck to the compound.

She's not stupid, though.

"I've got to go. We'll meet you at the Creamery, okay?"

His mother nods. Goes back to pretending to read her book.

Ricky's not coming home anytime soon, David John back for less than twenty-four hours. She looks at Jessup, but she doesn't ask any other questions. Afraid of the answers.

He finishes his grilled cheese, chucks the paper towel in the trash, stops by the kitchen table, where Jewel is sitting. She's got a dog-eared book propped up in front of her plate. She's near the end of the book. She drops her sandwich on her plate, wipes her hand on her pants, gulps at her milk, and turns the page.

"Here," Jessup says, tearing off a clean paper towel and handing it to her. "Don't wipe your hands on your pants."

She rolls her eyes, but she takes the paper towel.

He puts his hand on her shoulder. "You reading that for school?"

"Yeah. Extra credit."

"What is it?" She sticks her finger in to mark her page and closes it so he can see. *The Penderwicks.* He doesn't recognize it. "What's it about?"

"This family goes on vacation," she says.

"And?"

"And a bunch of stuff happens. It's really good. It's funny and . . . I don't know. I like the family. I'm going to get the next one out of the library on Monday. You should read it. You'd like it," she says.

He kisses her on the top of her head. "See you soon," he says, but she's already back in her book.

BETWEEN THE GATE AND THE ROAD

It's warmed up enough that with the snowplows and the salt, the roads are clear, asphalt unmarred by the winter white. Straight shot from their house, ten minutes to Brooktown and the entrance to the compound.

The church doesn't have a sign. The driveway bends into the trees, hiding the fixed-up barn where they have services, the social hall, the preschool building, the garage, Earl's house, the other outbuildings, behind that, paths cut through the woods, a swimming pond, a firing range, a campsite, but nothing you can see from the road. The only thing you can see from the road is the heavy steel gate. Enough room between that and the asphalt for Jessup to pull the van in. David John is already there, leaning on the gate, holding a football. The game ball, Jessup realizes. He'd left it in the truck. David John is not alone. He's talking to his brother.

Earl saunters over, knocks on the glass. Jessup rolls down the window.

"Keep your mouth shut," Earl says. "We'll take care of it."

"I didn't do anything wrong."

Earl's eyes are like a hawk circling, a mouse scurrying in an open meadow, sharp talons, a missile headed to earth. They've got red-tailed hawks, osprey, peregrine falcons, kestrels, goshawks and others in upstate New York, more than a dozen different kinds of raptors. Golden eagles, bald eagles if you're lucky, turkey vultures. Jessup read somewhere that a peregrine falcon can hit 150 miles an hour as it plummets to the ground, its prey never standing a chance. That's what Earl looks like. He's not missing anything.

Earl knocks on the door of the van with his knuckles. Knock, knock. Who's there? The Big Bad Wolf. Let me in.

Jessup says it again. "I didn't do anything wrong."

Earl knocks again, says, "Exactly. Like I said, we'll take care of it." With his other hand, he holds something up for Jessup to see. The keys to Jessup's pickup truck. Then they are gone, stuffed into Earl's pocket. Disappeared.

Earl looks at David John. "And what does Hawkins know?"

"Doesn't know about Jessup hitting Corson with the truck. None of that stuff. Knows about before and after, but not what actually happened."

Earl nods. "Okay. Let's keep it that way. But I'm going to need to tell Brandon."

"What?" Jessup is alarmed. "No."

Earl gives him a cold, even look. "He's got money and he can get New York City lawyers involved in this. If he'd been around when your brother and David John had their mix-up, things might have been different." His cold look turns into something warmer, a laugh. "He's smart, I'll give you that. He'll get us some good Jew lawyers. They'll do anything if they get paid, and they're the best money can buy. Now, you two go off and enjoy your day while I figure out how to take care of things." Teeth, lips curled. "Trust me, Jessup."

MOTION

David John holds the football on his lap. He's quiet for the first mile. Jessup is quiet, too. Processing. He's driving the van, but he feels like he isn't going anywhere.

Finally, David John speaks. "He's my brother. I had to tell him."

Jessup feels like he's supposed to answer, but David John didn't ask him a question. Wants to tell his stepfather what it was like having Earl in the house while David John was gone. The same flat, dead eyes on his mother. Never said anything, did anything that Jessup could put his finger on. But still. His mother didn't have a problem with her brother-in-law, and Jewel was always happy to see Uncle Earl, but there was something about the man that set Jessup on edge.

"You can use the van today and tomorrow."

"I still think this was a bad idea. Getting rid of it just calls attention to things," Jessup says.

"If anybody asks, tell them your truck broke down." Which isn't much of a stretch. It's not much of an answer, either. "We'll figure out the week later," David John says, "see what happens with the cops."

Jessup keeps the van steady. White lines cutting the blacktop, leading them into town.

"Hell, Jessup, why did you have to . . ." His voice is the voice of somebody who hasn't slept in years, and it trails off into nothing, the tires thrumming against the road.

"I didn't *do* anything," Jessup says. "It was an accident." He knows that he's whining, that he sounds like a little kid trying to pass the blame.

And now David John sounds like what he is: a father comforting a child. "I know," he says. "I know. But there are things we can't change, and we've got what we've got. There's a dead kid and he's black and you're white, and if this goes south, people will string you up. Ricky didn't do anything wrong, either. *They* attacked him. He was just protecting himself. And I'll be an old man by the time he gets out." He doesn't say anything about the four years of his own life gone by.

"I don't want Brandon Rogers involved in this," Jessup says. "I don't trust him. Don't like him."

David John lifts the football up, spins it. "Game ball." He puts it back in his lap. "I don't know, Jessup. I think Earl has the right idea. Maybe it would have been different if we were rich. If I could have hired some smart New York City lawyer for me and Ricky."

By which Jessup knows that David John means some smart Jew.

David John hesitates, says, "Or maybe if I raised you all some different way. A different church."

It's still not a question, so Jessup still doesn't answer.

David John shakes his head. "Lawyers could have made a difference with your brother. Good lawyers. Expensive lawyers." He says it again: "Maybe if we were rich . . ."

But they weren't. They aren't.

THE CREAMERY

Jewel and his mom are waiting for them at the Creamery. There's only a couple of people in line, which is a surprise. They expanded the entire building the year before, tripling in size, and they offer breakfast and lunch now to go with the ice cream. It's been in the same spot for eighty years, a local institution, the kind of place that's featured in tourist brochures and that the university likes to suggest to visiting parents. It's Jewel's favorite place in town. A treat for her.

His phone buzzes while they are waiting. Wyatt.

wat the fuck

Jessup thinks it says something about him that his first thought is annoyance that Wyatt texts him "wat" instead of "what." The sloppiness bothers him.

can't talk talk later

Notices he's got a couple of missed texts from Deanne.

call me

call me

are you okay?

I'm scared. call me, please

He texts her back.

sorry. getting ice cream with family. see you at work

He watches the screen. Almost as soon as the text goes through he sees the thought bubbles, quick response.

what's going on? you okay?

> yes. nothing. it's nothing. I'll see you soon.
> everything's okay

you sure?

> yeah. don't worry.

can you come in early? want to see you. 145?

> okay

okay

Okay. Okay. Everything's going to be okay. Everything's going to be okay. Don't think about Corson. Don't think about Corson. He notices his sister watching him. He slips the phone away and then shoos her forward.

She orders a scoop of Cortaca Crunch in a chocolate-dipped waffle cone. Jessup's mom gets an ice-cream sandwich. David John just orders a coffee. Jessup doesn't feel like eating.

NUCLEAR FAMILY

Jessup waits at the counter for their order while his mom and David John and Jewel go sit at one of the tables in back. Jewel is talking brightly about something, moves from her chair to sit on David John's lap. He wraps her up, beaming, and Jewel keeps turning to look at her dad, like she's afraid he's going to disappear again.

The three of them look happy sitting at the table. Jessup's mom smiling, reaching out to take her husband's hand, Jewel leaning against her dad, the three of them a Norman Rockwell painting: "Saturday Afternoon at the Ice-Cream Parlor."

Jewel is wearing a pair of stretchy jeans and one of Jessup's hand-me-down sweatshirts, which makes her look even smaller. She eats well—she's never been picky, and they try to cook fresh vegetables, eat lots of fruit—but she's a skinny thing. She's about the same height as most of her friends, but she has the ungainly awkwardness that comes in the space between being a child and being a teenager, and it hurts Jessup to think how fragile she is. But right now she looks happy. Having her father back is her birthday and Christmas morning and hope springing eternal all dipped in chocolate. As good as it gets. Jessup's mom looks that way, too.

The boy behind the counter delivers the ice cream and David John's coffee, and Jessup brings them to the table. "I don't know how you take your coffee," Jessup says.

"Just sugar," David John says. "I've got it." He shifts Jewel off his lap and takes his coffee back to the counter. Jewel is already working on her cone. She offers Jessup a bite, but he turns it down.

His mom reaches out and puts her hand on his forehead to see if he feels hot. "Are you okay?"

It is, Jessup thinks, the most maternal action that has ever occurred in the course of human history. He's good-natured about it, but he brushes her hand off. "I'm fine," he says. "Just tired."

His mom looks off to the side and he follows her gaze. David John is holding his coffee and talking on the phone. He shakes his head and then nods, an active listener.

Jessup wishes it were something as simple as a fever, because the truth is, he does feel sick. He's sure that the phone call is about him. Can't get rid of the feeling that everything is about to shake itself to pieces.

But when David John comes back to the table, he's smiling. "Got a job already," he says. "Somebody in Cortaca Heights used a little too much force trying to turn off the water to the outside hose bib. Don't even know how they got my number, but I'll take it. Jessup, I'm going to need the van this afternoon. Do you think you can get a ride home after your shift?"

"Yeah," he says. "I'm going out with friends. Somebody will drive me home."

Jewel rotates her cone to take another lick. "You have to work, Dad? I thought we were going to—"

"I know, honey, but I'm not really in the position to turn down a job right now."

"But you just got home." She makes a pouty face, puffing out her lips.

He sits, pulls her back onto his lap. There's a part of Jessup that wonders if she's too old to be acting like this, but there's a bigger part of him that's glad she isn't.

"Now, honey," David John says, "I know. But it's not going to be easy to build up the business again, and this is a good job." Jokes, "How do you think we're going to pay for this ice cream?" He turns to look at Jessup. "You're going out with friends tonight?" It's a question. It's an accusation. "I don't like that."

Jessup doesn't say anything. Doesn't look away, either. He could just tell the truth, which is that he is going to spend time with Deanne, but that's another universe that he doesn't want explored.

David John relents. "If you can't get a ride, you call me. I'll come get you. But not too late. Church in the morning." He looks at his watch. "We better get moving. Why don't you drive the van up to the mall and we'll follow you?"

HUMMINGBIRD

Jewel decides she wants to ride in the van with Jessup. She's bouncing up and down in her seat, holding the football in both her hands. "Why did Dad take your truck? Where did he take your truck? What's wrong with it?"

"Engine trouble," he says, and that satisfies her, because now she's talking about a video she saw that featured two dogs playing tug-of-war with a plastic bottle of soda.

"And then it exploded, and they both yelped and ran away. It was pretty funny. I'll show it to you later."

She gets quiet for a second. Crosses her arms, hugging the football, and looks out the window at the cut of the highway up the hill.

"You okay?" Jessup reaches out and pats her leg.

"Why does he have to work today? He just got home."

"You know," Jessup says. Because she does. She's a good kid. Knows they're broke, knows that having David John home and working again means things will change. A cell phone for Christmas. A better car for their mom. Mom not constantly worrying about the bills. Space to breathe.

"One of the girls at school a couple of weeks ago said we was on welfare."

"Were," Jessup says. "Use proper grammar." It's an instinctual correction, and it gives him a few seconds to think. He's not a parent. He doesn't know what he's supposed to do. "What did you say?"

"Duh. I said we weren't." She shrugs. "She's a bitch."

"Jewel!"

"Well, she is," Jewel mutters. "I told Emily last week at church. She said . . ."

Emily is one of Jewel's friends from the Blessed Church of the White

America. She's slept over a couple of times. Goes to school in Brooktown. In Jessup's opinion, she's a little shit. Talks back to their mom. He hasn't met Emily's parents, but the way his mom avoids the subject of Emily and has insisted that Jewel have Emily to their house instead of Jewel going there makes Jessup skeptical.

"What? Why did you trail off like that? What did Emily say?"

"She said that only niggers go on welfare."

He squints at her. She's watching. Testing. Waiting for his reaction.

"Don't say that word." Tries to keep his voice from sounding sharp. "We don't use that word, okay?"

"Why did the cops come?" She's calm. Possessed. Sometimes she's a little kid, sometimes she might be forty.

"Nothing," he says.

"If it was nothing, I wouldn't have had to go to my room."

"Don't be a smart-ass. It's nothing. I mean, it's something, but it's not me. A kid got drunk at a party last night and drove his car into a tree."

"You shouldn't drink and drive."

"Oh really, little missy?" He takes his hand off the wheel to poke her in the side. "Is that a fact?"

She squirms and laughs. "Well, you shouldn't. Did he die?"

He's surprised, but he shouldn't be. "Yeah."

"What did the cops want with you, then?"

He takes the exit, waits for the light to turn green, and then turns left and then left again, into the mall parking lot, driving around the back to where the movie theater is. There's a small snowbank at the edge of the lot where the plows made a pile, but the pavement is clean, the afternoon sunlight doing its job.

"I don't know. Nothing," he says. "We were at the same party and he wanted to fight me, but I didn't fight him, didn't do anything, but it was loud, so my name came up. That's all. Cops are just doing what they do. Busybodies. Nothing to worry about."

"Why can't I say that word? Mom says it."

Jessup is surprised again. "She does? No, she doesn't. You know how David John is with our language."

"I heard her say it to Uncle Earl."

"When?"

"I don't know. Over the summer. They were talking about Ricky."

He pulls the van into a space in front of the theater. The parking lot is sparsely attended, most of the cars there for the budget gym that's across from the movie theater. It's too early in November for Christmas shopping.

"Just don't use that word, okay?"

"Why?"

"You're better than that. That's why."

THE WATER

But is she better than that? He says good-bye, hands the keys off to David John, asks him to put the game ball on his dresser, promises to be home at a decent hour ("Stay out of trouble," David John says. His voice is quiet. Jewel's in the van, Jessup's mom is in the car, but David John is careful that they don't hear. "Remember, they're just looking for an excuse"— and heads into the mall.

He worries about his sister. Baptized in the Blessed Church of the White America. She only knows what's around her. Only knows how she's been raised.

He should be worried about himself, too. The snow comes down and it covers everything, makes it look clean and fresh, but just because it hides things doesn't mean there isn't anything rotting underneath. Sooner or later the snow melts and turns into a river, the water washing away everything its path, uncovering what lies beneath.

But this could stay hidden. Nobody can say he laid a hand on Corson at the party. Nobody saw the way the truck slid, Corson crumpled on the driveway. Corson was just dumb and drunk and made a bad decision, nobody to say anything different. Nothing to stop Jessup from getting out of Cortaca, from leaving his history behind. He'll gladly trade his body on the football field for four years of college, a degree. College is an island; he's been swimming his whole life, trying to keep his head above water, and solid ground for a few years is all he can hope for.

But what about Jewel? If family history is a weight around his neck, what is Jewel? You don't hand a drowning man an anchor.

FOR YOUR VIEWING ENJOYMENT

It's 1:40 by his phone when he walks into the back office. He changes into his Regal Cinemas shirt, tucks it into his jeans, pins on his name tag. Shoves his long-sleeved T-shirt and hoodie into his locker. His manager, Norma, walks in. She's in a good mood. She's always in a good mood. She's somewhere in her sixties—"You kids don't need to know exactly how old"—and is working because she likes it. Her husband is retired military, and he's been driving her crazy at home, so the job at the theater and her two grandkids keep her out of the house. Claims the movie theater gig has saved her marriage. She sees Jessup, starts telling him about her granddaughter's dance recital. Jessup smiles and nods, pretends like he's listening.

Deanne comes in, says "Hi," puts her car keys in her coat and then her coat in her locker. Norma, oblivious to how fragile Deanne looks, says, "Oh, I'll head out into the lobby, give you two lovebirds a few minutes before your shift starts." Norma imagines herself a matchmaker, thinks it's "adorable" that Jessup and Deanne are an item; since she found out, she's been scheduling them so their shifts line up, start together, end together. Jessup likes working for Norma. Everybody likes working for Norma.

As soon as the door closes, Deanne crumbles. She's not gulping in air, but she's crying hard. Jessup freezes. He doesn't know what he's supposed to do, and he's relieved when she moves to him, presses against him. That makes it easy for him: he knows enough to know that he's got to put his arms around her, hold her tight.

"I just—" she tries to say, but chokes up. She gathers herself. Still crying, but she can talk: "I just, I got all these texts, and Megan called me and she said that Kristen was at the party and she said that you and the running back from Kilton Valley got into a fight and this morning they found his body and—"

"Hey, hey, no," Jessup says. "Just hold up." She has her face cradled between his neck and his shoulder. He feels like he's pretending to be an adult.

WORDS AND ACTIONS

Tﾠhere wasn't a fight."

"But Megan said that she heard—"

"I didn't get in a fight, Deanne. Okay?" He feels her nod against his neck. "Corson came at me. He was drunk and yelling, but I didn't do anything."

Her voice is quiet. "Megan said that it's going around that you called him . . ." He's holding her, but her body is stiff now. Fight or flight. "Did you call him the *N*-word?"

"Jesus, Deanne. No." Corson standing in front of him, shaking his finger, just say it. The word on the tip of Jessup's tongue. "I don't use that word. You know that. You know me."

"Because if you—"

"Deanne." He's pleading. "Please. Come on. I didn't do anything. Corson was drunk. He came at me because of my brother and my stepdad, okay? It's not like it's some secret what happened, my family history. Everybody thinks they know the story." Good God, his voice is shaking, his jaw trembling, too. Why can't it just be the two of them alone in this room, the world around them something imagined, a construct of their imagination, no past shackled to his ankle, his life unfettered, the chance for him to hold Deanne like this, hold her tight like nothing could ever be wrong, just him holding her, this girl he has fallen for?

"He was drunk, and he was yelling about my brother and my stepdad, and he was the one saying it, the *N*-word, accusing me of wanting to call him that. I mean, after the game last night, in the parking lot, he came up to me and said it was a dirty hit before halftime."

She sniffs. "That was a clean hit. He was behind the line of scrimmage and you got there at the same time as the ball anyway."

He tries to laugh. It comes out choked. "Coach's daughter, huh? He said it was a bullshit play, and then he kicked out my taillight."

She pulls back, looking up at him. Angry, but angry *for* him, not *at* him. "What? Really?"

Jessup shrugs. "Yeah. I was even pulled over on the way to the party. Got lucky and only ended up with a written warning. Actually," he says, realizing he can't tell her the real reason why he needs a ride, "I'm not supposed to drive it until I can get the taillight fixed. My mom wouldn't let me take it to work. Any chance you can give me a ride home tonight?"

"Sure."

"Thanks. I appreciate it."

"It's nothing. But what happened?"

"At the party? Look, he was drunk. Had a bug up his ass. Said a bunch of crap, and I didn't do anything. I didn't want any trouble. And then he and his friends left, and he was drunk, and he had an accident. Whatever you're hearing, you've got to trust me. I didn't say anything. It's not my fault Corson killed himself. It's not fair. I just . . ."

He's lying to her. But he can't tell her the truth. Not if he wants her to stay with him.

They are standing there, in the middle of this bleak room, crappy tiles and a wall full of small employee lockers, old movie posters covering every available surface, a ratty couch. But it's just them, and she's looking at him, listening, facing him, both of her hands in both of his, close enough that all he has to do is lean forward a few inches to kiss her. Her eyes are welled up with tears, and he knows his are the same.

"I'm sorry, Deanne. I can't do anything about my family. It is what it is. I'm not my stepfather, I'm not my brother, but they're part of my life, and that's going to follow me around."

She lets go of one of his hands, wipes her eyes. Takes a deep, shuddering breath, reaches out and touches her thumb to his lips. "You know, Jessup, for a seventeen-year-old boy, you're not so dumb."

"Thanks?" He has a crooked smile on his face and he does lean forward a few inches now. Their noses touch, their lips gentle, the air between them disappearing. They are like that for a few seconds before they hear the door opening.

BUTTER WITH THAT?

Deanne is at the ticket window. He's behind the concession stand with Julia, a sophomore who has a crush on Jessup. She's okay, not a girl he'd be interested in even if he and Deanne weren't dating—nice, but he likes girls who challenge him—but Deanne teases him about it anyway, thinks it's funny to ask Jessup if he wants to butter Julia's popcorn.

There is a slow but constant stream of customers, always three or four people in line. Large Sprite and small popcorn, medium popcorn and a large water, small Coke and a Butterfinger, two kids' deals with Sprites a large popcorn large Coke M&Ms and nachos, two large Diet Cokes a medium Coke a medium Sprite three medium popcorns a grape slushy and you'll bring the pizza into the movie theater for us?

When there are gaps between customers at the ticket counter, he sees Deanne looking over at him, and he smiles back. A few times, when she doesn't notice, he catches teenage boys, college students, even a few grown men, looking at her in admiration.

She *is* beautiful, but the funny thing is, if he had to describe her, even though a lot of the guys on the team would say the coach's daughter is hot, Jessup would say she looks healthy. She's fit, the muscular leanness you get from running cross-country and distance meets in track and field, and she comes by her athleticism honestly: aside from Coach Diggins, Mrs. Diggins was a D-I cross-country runner, runs half marathons and triathlons now for fun. He knows it's desperately unhip to think of his girlfriend as "healthy" instead of "hot" or "sexy," but he doesn't care. She is hot and sexy, but she's . . . wholesome.

She sees him staring, gives him a wink that feels decidedly unwholesome, and he's got a hot flashback to the pickup truck, her skin on his skin, the way she held him as he slid inside of her.

"I said no butter."

Jessup looks blankly at the woman in front of him. He apologizes and gets back to work.

DIGGINS

It's quarter to six when Coach Diggins walks in. They are in a lull between shows. There are fourteen screens at the movie theater, and Jessup's expecting things to pick up soon. Saturday night and all. He's glad Norma has him and Deanne scheduled to go off at eight o'clock. Four more teenagers are working now, getting ready for the rush. Jessup has just put a new scoop into the popcorn machine when he sees Coach Diggins stop by the ticket booth, say something to Deanne. Diggins looks around the open lobby. He sees Jessup watching, acknowledges him, but he's searching for someone else first. Deanne points out Norma. Coach and Norma talk for a minute or two, Norma looking at Jessup and then waving him over. He tells Julia to keep an eye on the popcorn, not to let it burn.

"Your coach says he needs to talk to you," Norma says.

"I've got popcorn going." He feels silly as soon as he says it, so he adds, "But Julia's watching it." Feels sillier.

Diggins is solid. Serious. His jacket is zipped up and there's a fine gloss of water on it. Rain or snow?

Jessup is trying to keep his heart rate down.

Norma is clearly hoping to hover, but Diggins excuses her with a polite, but firm, "if you can give us a few minutes."

She heads behind the counter, clearly torn between the competing instincts of nosiness and compliance.

Diggins walks the two of them over to the corner, out of the way. He's the kind of man who looks you directly in the eye. No shiftiness. No looking away from that. Jessup meets the stare.

"You have anything you need to tell me?" Diggins says. "Because I got a heads-up call from Chief Harris."

Jessup's never met Chief Harris, but he knows the man. He seemed plenty comfortable in front of a microphone in the days after Ricky and David John were arrested. Was quick to say that they were investigating what happened in the alley as a hate crime, but not so quick to say that Ricky was defending himself, that Liveson was the one to start it, hitting Ricky in the face with a beer bottle. Chief Harris is black.

Jessup asks, "What did he say?" Diggins narrows his eyes at Jessup, and after a beat, Jessup adds, "Sir."

"You sassing me?" Diggins's Mississippi comes through. Angry.

All Jessup feels is tired.

X'S AND O'S

W hat do you want me to tell you?" Jessup says. What he really wants to say is, what's the point? Diggins has had his mind made up from the jump. Otherwise, why wouldn't Jessup be a captain?

As if he's said it out loud, Diggins nods. "I know what you're thinking, but if you tell the truth, I'll stand behind you. I want to know what happened: did you have anything to do with Kevin Corson's accident?"

"What did Chief Harris say?" Jessup is surprised at the words coming out of his mouth. David John has always been big on respecting teachers and coaches. When Jessup was younger, the one time Jessup mouthed off to a coach—he can't remember what it was over, just that it was the week before David John and Ricky were arrested—his stepfather marched over from the bleachers and demanded the coach pull him from the game and sit him. Even then, even though he was small at the time, he was one of the better players, and David John said that meant he had more responsibility, that he had to set an example for the other players. You could disagree—you could even argue respectfully—but no mouthing off. There's a difference, and you know it, his stepfather said.

He's not sure if he's mouthing off now, just that he doesn't understand what Coach Diggins wants of him.

But what Diggins wants is the truth.

Jessup tells him something close to it. Runs through most of the night, mostly sticking to the facts.

"And you didn't see him again after the Kilton Valley boys walked out of the house?"

"No, sir."

"And you went straight home after you left the party?"

Jessup barely hesitates, but he knows his eyes flicker, a quick glance at

Deanne. "Yes, sir." He can't tell if Diggins notices him looking at his daughter. "Look, sir, I'm sorry about what happened to Corson, but I didn't do anything wrong."

I didn't do anything wrong. I didn't do anything wrong. I didn't do anything wrong.

BALANCE

Diggins asks him a few more questions, treads lightly on the question of alcohol at the party, of who was drinking, who wasn't, and then sighs.

"Look, Jessup, I know you don't think I've been fair to you." He shrugs. "I don't know what to tell you. Maybe it's not fair. Maybe I shouldn't have taken what happened with your brother and your dad into account, but I was trying to do what's best for the team."

There's a part of Jessup that falls on his knees and grabs Diggins's hands, cries, but what about me, what about me? But there's a bigger part of him that knows that he has to stand there and face him like a man.

"I understand, sir," he lies.

Diggins gives him a curt nod. "Okay. If it comes to it, I'll say you're a good kid. Never gave me any trouble. But you've got to understand, there's a lot of moving pieces. And if you aren't telling me the truth—if you're lying to me, about anything—I will hang you out to dry." His voice is suddenly very cold. It's the voice of somebody who stayed in the NFL through sheer force of will, who played as a pro because he was willing to do whatever it took to win. The voice of a man who understands what it means to drown and who isn't going to let Jessup pull him under. "You understand that?"

"Yes, sir," Jessup says. He wonders what would happen if he said the word to Coach Diggins. If Diggins stood in front of him, wagging his finger, telling him to say the word.

Diggins leaves, stopping to chat briefly with his daughter. When he's gone, Deanne stares at Jessup. He can't read the map of her face.

PUNCHING OUT

He's off a minute or two before Deanne. Punches out, changes back into his long-sleeved shirt, goes to the bathroom. By the time he's done, she's ready to go.

They don't say much as they walk to the parking lot. It's a couple of degrees warmer than the night before, and there's a light mist hanging in the air. Just damp enough to make things feel miserable, to slick the pavement. Jessup is cold with just the hoodie, wishes he had his jacket. Did Earl burn it?

Deanne unlocks her car. It's a small SUV, a Honda CRV that is about four years old, a hand-me-down from her mother, and she keeps it surprisingly neat for a teenager. When Jessup rides in Wyatt's truck, he always jokes that you'd need a shovel to clean out the cab properly. Plus, Wyatt's truck always smells like dirty socks. Sometimes Jessup thinks Kaylee is a saint for putting up with him. Sometimes Jessup wonders why Wyatt is his best friend, if Wyatt really is as close as a brother.

"Do you want me to just drive you home?" she says, starting up the car.

The words hurt. He tries not to show it. "Oh. Okay. I guess."

But she doesn't put the car in drive. Just sits there, windshield wipers making a lazy, intermittent circuit. The radio is on. Pop music. Something he doesn't recognize. He shuts it off.

"Deanne?"

"I'm sorry," she says. "That was kind of bitchy."

"It's okay."

"No. I'm . . . I'm just scared."

"Yeah," he says.

Her phone dings with a text. She smiles wryly. "Brooke is at the State Street Diner with Stanley. Again. Said she's got a big booth."

The phone dings again. The smile disappears.

"What?"

"She wants to know if you're coming."

"Oh." He's glad she doesn't read him the text verbatim. Pretty sure it's not an innocent question, that Brooke hopes the answer is no.

A car pulls into the spot next to them. An older couple, midforties, gets out. They are talking seriously about something, neither one of them seeming to notice Jessup and Deanne sitting in the CRV. The windshield wipers sweep back and forth. The thin film of moisture slowly settles on the glass, waiting for the next heartbeat of the wipers.

Deanne thumbs her phone. "I'm saying we're not going to make it."

"Okay."

"I don't really want to go to a diner with Brooke and Megan and their boyfriends," she says with a laugh. "I mean, not really."

"Yeah. Me either."

"I don't really want to take you home, either. Want to go somewhere?"

He reaches for her hand. She slides her fingers between his.

GARDEN

He's glad it's November. In July they'd have to find somewhere to hide, but in November it's full dark by eight fifteen, been dark for a while. "Hey," he says, "daylight saving tonight. We get an extra hour tomorrow." He's still holding her hand. She's comfortable behind the wheel, but she's only had her license for two months, so she drives carefully. Nothing like riding with Wyatt or any other guy he knows. He thinks teenage boys are idiots. Even if the snow from the day before is gone, the roads are wet; she only grazes the speed limit.

They go to the bird sanctuary. It's about a mile from campus, but it's still part of Cortaca University. Before last weekend, when he and Deanne went there for a walk, he'd only ever been there on field trips in elementary school, but it's cool. The Lab of Ornithology is supposed to be world-class, and the sanctuary is 220 acres—it doesn't escape Jessup that it's almost the same size as the acreage the Blessed Church of the White America sits on—and littered with trails. More important, it's also littered with pullouts. It's not as private as the parking lot by the reservoir, but there aren't any streetlights, so it's private enough.

She turns off the car and climbs into the back without saying anything. Jessup isn't dumb enough to hesitate. He follows her into the backseat, and before he's even settled she's on him with an urgency that he hadn't expected.

She kisses him hard, her teeth hitting his, her tongue darting into his mouth. He's pressed back against the door, and she's straddling one of his legs, pressing against his thigh. They stay with kissing for a few minutes, long enough that the windows start to fog. He's got his hand up her shirt and then pulls it over her head, works at her bra for a few seconds before she sits up, pushes his hand out of the way, and takes it off herself. He wants to reach up and turn on the interior light, marvel at the way she looks, stare at her body, give praise for this miracle, but instead he pulls her toward him so that he can kiss her breast, her nipple in his mouth. After a minute, she pulls at the hem of his shirt, peels it off him, skin on skin, her mouth on his. He slips his hand past her waistband, can't believe she gives him this. As his fingers touch her, she makes a sound that is both a gulp and a squeak, her nails raking the back of his neck, and then grabs his hair and holds him against her.

EDEN

She works off her pants and then the two of them clumsily roll over. It's both funny and urgent, the two of them laughing and smiling and gasping and hurrying, their bodies too big for the cramped space of the backseat. He's got his hand between her legs, and she's squirming and trying to undo the button of his jeans, so he helps her, kicking off his sneakers, his jeans, his underwear, until both of them are naked. She gets a condom and gives it to him. He unwraps it, puts it on. He hesitates for a beat, staring into her eyes, but she puts her hands on his hips, pulls him into her.

He can't stop himself from letting out something close to a whimper. Doesn't understand how there can be anything better than this, even with the awkwardness of the backseat, with the air inside the car starting to chill in the November night. He keeps most of his weight on his arms, aware of how much bigger he is than her, but the sounds she makes are close enough to discomfort that he asks her if she's okay.

"Yeah, this is good," she says. "You?"

"Yeah."

She has one of her legs down off the seat, the other wrapped up over his hip and across his ass. She kisses his neck, rocks her body with his.

He doesn't know why it is that he stops, but he does. The warmth of her body under and around him is almost overwhelming.

She kisses him and then looks at him, her nose touching his. "Are you okay?"

"Deanne," he says. It's as if he is flying, the heat enough to make him feel like he's about to touch the sun. His voice is quiet. Everything is quiet.

He says what he's been thinking.

She says it back like all she's ever done is wait for this moment.

SERPENT

Jessup is half asleep. The car is cool, the windows wet on the outside from the gentle mist, fogged up on the inside from the heat of their bodies. He knows they'll have to get up, get dressed, turn on the motor in a few minutes so they can run the heater, but for now, all he wants to do is lie there. The smallness of the backseat just means they are closer together.

The sound of Deanne's phone is jarring. A trill interrupting the quiet. But she doesn't move.

After five or six rings, the phone goes silent. She nuzzles against him, whispers in his ear. "Say it again."

"I love you." He's earnest, wants to kiss her, but she laughs so he pretends to pout. "You do realize that laughter is not the correct response to somebody telling you that they love you," he says.

"Sorry," she says. "I don't know why I'm laughing. I love—"

Her phone rings again, and with a sigh, she sits up and reaches into the front seat, grabs it off the console. "Crap. Sorry. It's my dad. I can ignore one call, but not two."

She answers, holds the phone up to her ear with one hand, scratches gently at Jessup's chest with the other.

"No," she says. "I told you I was meeting Megan and Brooke at the State Street Diner. I just got here. I'm still in the car. I'm about—" Her hand stops moving on his chest. She sits up straight. "What do you—Dad!"

She tosses her phone into the front seat and starts scrambling for her clothes. Jessup realizes that Coach Diggins has been tracking Deanne's phone at almost the exact moment that Deanne hisses, "He's here. Get dressed!"

As the headlights sweep over them, Jessup sees the fear in Deanne's eyes, assumes that he has the same look in his.

WEATHER

Mercifully, Coach Diggins parks his car behind them and waits while Jessup and Deanne get dressed. They try to stay low in the backseat, to get their clothing on with some modicum of decency, but the headlights are a garish glare, shadows thrown everywhere, eyes squinting against the light.

Deanne is shaking, but she isn't crying, and Jessup is grateful for that. She opens the door, gets out, straightening her shirt, zipping up her jacket. Jessup gets out after her. He's shivering, pulling on his hoodie, the sweatshirt not enough to keep him warm against the chill. The mist is heavier now, more rain than snow, cold, wet, insidious, the kind of weather that brings misery, that works its way under your clothes, through your skin, that settles into your bones. His muscles tense. He can feel the bruises and soreness from the football game the night before.

He stands a half step behind Deanne, not touching her, but in her orbit. Coach Diggins rolls down the window of his car. It's a Lexus SUV, the kind with three rows of seats, a big box, tall and menacing. Diggins doesn't have to get out of his car to have a commanding position.

Deanne speaks first. She's still shaking, and it shows in her voice, but Jessup realizes she isn't frightened. She's furious. "This is none of your business."

He's expecting Diggins to yell, but the coach's voice is surprisingly soft, calm. It reminds Jessup of David John's voice. "You're my daughter, Deanne. Everything is my business. And, I have to say, I'm disappointed in you. You lied to me."

Jessup has his hands in the pockets of his hoodie. His teeth are chattering. The wipers on the Lexus flip back and forth in some undetermined rhythm as the moisture accumulates. He wishes he'd done up the zipper on his sweatshirt, wants to put the hood up for warmth, but he also doesn't want to move. Doesn't want to call more attention to himself.

Deanne's face tightens, but she gathers herself. It's actually scary how composed she is for a sixteen-year-old girl who just got caught naked in a parked car with her boyfriend by her football coach father. "You promised that was just in case my phone was lost or something happened. Not to track me."

"And you said you were at the State Street Diner with your friends," Diggins says evenly. "We can have a conversation about this at home."

"I'm not going home. I promised Jessup a ride," she says, but Jessup can hear it in her voice: she's already used up what bravery she has.

"Yes, you are going home," he says. "Jessup?"

"Yes, sir?"

"Get in. I'll drive you home. We can have a little talk."

MILEAGE

Deanne squeezes his hand, and then he walks around and climbs up into the passenger seat of Coach Diggins's car. Coach leans out the window a bit. "Straight home," he says. Deanne doesn't say anything, just storms over to her car.

Diggins pulls out onto the road, waits for Deanne to back out, and then follows her CRV toward Highland Road. He glances at Jessup. "Where do you live?"

Jessup tells him, and at the corner, when Deanne turns right, Diggins turns left. He looks over again at Jessup, sees him shivering.

"There's a seat warmer," he says. Pushes a button on the wood-trimmed dashboard. After a few seconds, Jessup can feel the heat radiating through the leather seat.

"Thank you."

Neither one of them speaks for the first mile, Jessup not wanting to break the stillness, Diggins seeming to consider what he wants to say. The windshield wipers move of their own accord; some sort of automatic moisture detection that comes on fancy cars, Jessup realizes.

When Diggins does speak, it's not what Jessup expects. "I'm not going to yell at you. Deanne is old enough to make her own decisions. I have to respect those decisions even if I don't like what she is choosing to do. That being said, you understand, though, don't you, that it's different for a girl than it is for a guy? It means more for a girl. What you two were doing—and I don't want to know the details, don't really want to talk about it, I'll leave that for between Deanne and her mom—it's not something to be taken lightly."

He doesn't seem to want an answer, so Jessup stays quiet. He wonders what Diggins would say if Jessup told him that David John's brother,

Earl, likes to ask why it is that we acknowledge that men and women are different—men are stronger, women better as caregivers—but you can't say whites and blacks are different. Wouldn't it stand to reason that the different races might not be the same? He wonders what Diggins would say if Jessup told him that Wyatt calls Deanne an ebony, that Wyatt's girlfriend thinks Jessup is debasing himself with a black girl.

Diggins adjusts the temperature a degree. The road hums under the tires, a wet passage, the distance between them and Jessup's home splitting into infinity.

"Jessup, I want to believe you didn't say anything to Kevin Corson."

"I didn't." He blurts it out. Angry. Scared.

Diggins shakes his head. They pass under a streetlight. The LED lights have a blue tinge to them, and it makes Diggins's skin seem to glow.

"That's the thing, Jessup," Diggins says, his voice slow, quiet, sad. "It doesn't matter what really happened."

FORWARD MOTION

I'm sorry," Diggins says, "but it's the truth."

Jessup wants to scream. It's the exact same thing that Hawkins said in the driveway this morning. It doesn't matter what really happened. None of it matters, Jessup thinks. Not the time in the weight room, sweat dripping off him, his muscles quivering with exhaustion, not the wind sprints, the hours watching film, the willingness to sacrifice his body to stop a ball's forward motion. It doesn't matter that he's always been a good student, not just smart but diligent, up late, up early, keeping his work organized, reading ahead, extra-credit assignments. It doesn't matter that he's done everything right, that he's had no margin for error, that his classmates have Spanish tutors and math tutors, $1,500 SAT prep classes and private instruction for thousands more, science camp and math camp, internships with state representatives because Mom's sister knows somebody, an entire existence of parenting devoted to ensuring excellence, the American dream not something to aspire to but a birthright. It doesn't matter what Jessup has done, he knows; it's never going to be enough. The starting gun went off well before he was born, and no matter how fast he runs, he'll never win this race.

"But I didn't," Jessup says. "I didn't call him the *N*-word."

"And it doesn't matter whether or not I believe you, either. What matters is that kids are talking, and what's going around is that you used a racial slur," Diggins says. "Can I ask you a question, Jessup?" He glances at Jessup but then speaks without waiting for an answer. "Do you hate me?"

"What?"

"Do you hate me? Simple question."

"No," Jessup says. He thinks of the game ball. Wonders if David John has put it in his bedroom. "Of course not."

"What about that church you go to? It's a white power thing, isn't it?"

"I haven't gone there in years." Hesitates. Says, "You know about what happened with my brother and my stepdad?"

Diggins nods.

"I haven't gone there since any of that happened." Doesn't say that he's supposed to be going tomorrow with his family.

"What about that kid up there, the one in the coat and tie, goes to your church?"

"It's not my church."

Diggins ignores him. "What's his name? The one who's on CNN and Fox and always spouting off? Goes to Cortaca University. What is it? Buddy Rogers?"

"Brandon."

"Brandon, then. Does he hate me?"

"Probably," Jessup says. The truth is certainly more complicated, Jessup thinks, because if you listen to the way Brandon talks, it's not hate. It's not fear, either. It's something else. Like Brandon looks at black people and doesn't even think of them as people. Which is worse.

"I've seen him on the news, and he doesn't use the N-word. Doesn't blame the Jews or Mexicans. He does it nice and subtle. A dog whistle. Says 'urban violence,' or 'thug culture,' but we all know what he means."

Jessup can see the lights of the gas station in Tracker's Corners coming up. From there, it's a quarter mile until the turn, another quarter mile until his driveway.

"Why don't you let me out here," he says. "I'll walk."

HISTORY ONE

Diggins pulls into the gas station. He's off to the side of the pumps, the car running. He puts it in park and the locks click open. Jessup reaches for the door, but Diggins puts his hand on Jessup's shoulder.

"Jessup," he says. "This isn't about you."

"You can say that, sir, but it sure feels like it's about me."

"Look. I wasn't here when your brother and your dad killed—"

"He's not my dad." Jessup knows he's too sharp, and even as the words leave his mouth, shame washes over him. Judas. But he's already said it. "He's my stepfather."

"Okay." Diggins nods. "Stepfather. I wasn't here when your brother and stepfather killed those two kids, but people talk. Everybody knows your family is tied into that white power church, and what happened at the party is going to resonate. Even if Corson hadn't been drinking and driving— stupid, stupid kid—this would still have been a thing. You can't believe that the other kids at the party wouldn't talk?"

"I was eleven," Jessup says. He's not angry anymore, not ashamed either. He's broken and trying not to cry. Trying to be a man. "I was eleven when it happened."

"Sure," Diggins says. "It's not your fault. But it's going to follow you around. When a black kid says you called him the N-word, that's going to stick. There's no reason not to believe him."

HISTORY TWO

Jessup shakes Diggins's hand off his shoulder. "Can I go now?"

"You're going to stop seeing my daughter."

He shouldn't be shocked, but he is. He turns to look at Diggins, hoping that it's a joke, knowing that it isn't. Diggins is steely. No room for compromise.

"I thought you said she was old enough to make her own choices."

"Do the right thing."

"But I—"

Diggins cuts him off. "What? You're going to tell me you love her? You're seventeen, Jessup. What's the end game? Have you had her over to your house yet? Introduced her to your mother? Are you going to introduce her to your stepfather?" His voice is acid. "Hi, guys, this is my girlfriend, Deanne. Hope you don't notice that she's a nigger?" He steps hard on the word.

"I didn't—"

"But you will." Diggins is fierce. In the close space of the car, he's a beast and Jessup is cowering. He's bigger than Diggins, but it doesn't matter. Jessup is backed up against the door.

Diggins continues, "You'll say it sooner or later. You're thinking it right now, aren't you?"

"I'm not," Jessup says. But he is. He wants to tell Coach Diggins to go fuck himself, fuck you, you fucking—

"Of course you are. And when you're out with my daughter, it's always going to be there, too. Doesn't matter if it's right on the tip of your tongue or hidden in the depths. You've always got that word hidden in you, 'nigger,' ready to sneak its way out. American history right there, *boy*. That swamp isn't drained. I'll tell you, growing up in Mississippi, playing ball at

Alabama? You know what I liked? People there let me know *exactly* how they felt. 'Nigger,' 'boy,' 'coon,' I heard it all, right to my face. I had my fists clenched; the only thing that kept me from swinging was knowing what I had to lose. But when I was in the NFL, when I played for the Jets, the Vikings, when I was on the 49ers? When I was dating Melissa, me and this white girl out on the town in San Francisco? I was just guessing, trying to figure out who was thinking it." He takes a breath, and it's like a dragon getting ready to breathe more fire, but then, suddenly, for no reason that Jessup can tell, Coach Diggins seems to deflate. He sinks back into his seat, hands on the steering wheel. He's looking through the windshield now. Watching a Chevy Silverado pickup pull up to the gas pumps.

Diggins shakes his head. "At least that church you and your family go to has the balls to admit, to come out and say they want a white nation. Not trying to dress it up." He sighs. "I'm sorry, Jessup, but do you understand what I'm saying here? Do you understand why I don't want you with my daughter?"

"I never said it. I didn't say it to Corson last night. I never . . . I don't think that when I'm with Deanne. I *don't* say that word."

"But you will," Diggins says quietly. His voice is a whisper. He sounds tired. Jessup feels tired with him. "You will," he says again, louder. "I know all about you and your family. You can deny it, you can say he's your step-father instead of your father, but you can't hide from your history, your heritage."

"It's not *my* history," Jessup says.

"It is." He looks at Jessup, gathers his thoughts. "Do the right thing, Jessup. Be a man. Walk away from my daughter. You're still my player, and I'll stand up for you. If you want that, I'll do it. I'll stand up for you. You've got to understand, I'm not angry at you. I feel sorry for you, Jessup."

PAVEMENT

Jessup can't say anything. Diggins feels *sorry* for him? There's a part of him that understands that Diggins is fundamentally a good man, in the same way that David John is fundamentally a good man. In some different universe, the two would be friends. But there's a part of him, too, that is breaking in half. Coach Diggins is telling him to be a man, to do the right thing, but he has no earthly idea how to do either of those things. All he knows is that he doesn't want to—he can't—walk away from Deanne. He loves her. He knows that much is true.

He can't walk away from Deanne, he thinks, but he can walk away from her father. Jessup gets out of the SUV. He looks back after he's walked far enough away to be outside the halo of the gas station. Coach Diggins's car is still there, in the parking lot of the gas station, the lights on.

Jessup zips up his sweatshirt, pulls the hood over his head. It's not a mist anymore but a gentle rain mixed with wet snow, the temperature dropping with the night, but it's not enough to soak him through. Not yet. He realizes he's crying. Can't figure out when he started. With the weather, the sky is mostly covered, but there's just enough moon breaking through that he can see the road. He starts to run.

He breaks out too fast, and in forty-five seconds he's breathing hard. He slows down to a steady jog. Not a sprint, but not slow, an eight-minute mile. Figures it will keep him warm. Figures he has to do something, anything. There's no traffic, and soon enough it's just his breath and his sneakers against the pavement. He hits the corner and turns. Steps in a puddle, feels the cold seep through his shoe and sock.

He slows down to a walk again and pulls out his phone. The glow of the screen burns his eyes in the darkness. He checks his texts. He's got a bunch from guys on the football team, friends from wrestling, all some version of

"What's going on?" the word spreading quickly. Four texts from Wyatt and two from Kaylee, asking if he's okay, wanting to talk to him.

Nothing from Deanne. He touches her name, types:

I lo

Erases it.

WYATT

Jessup is forty, fifty yards from his driveway when the truck pulls out. It turns toward him, brights catching him and pinning him in the darkness before rolling to a stop, the window coming down. Jessup recognizes the truck before he sees Wyatt. It's a blue Ram crew cab, eight years old, but low miles, in good shape. Having a dad who's a mechanic doesn't hurt. There's a small Confederate flag sticker in the back window, but nothing else.

Wyatt doesn't have his normal smarmy smile. "How come you didn't text me back?"

"I was at work," Jessup says.

Wyatt blows his cheeks out, looks straight ahead. "Yeah, well. And then out with *Deanne?*"

The way he says her name is aggressive. Jessup's first reaction is anger, but he tries to tamp it down. Wyatt is on his side. Wyatt is his brother. Always has been. Decides to tell him the truth. "Yeah. Actually, parked up by the bird sanctuary. And, uh, Coach Diggins was tracking her phone. Caught us in the backseat."

Wyatt's face transforms, the joy of a friend getting in trouble. "Oh, shit! He must have been pissed."

"He wasn't happy," Jessup says. Decides not to say anything else. Already knows Wyatt's reaction if he does. "Were you waiting for me?"

Wyatt hesitates. Makes Jessup think of the time they were seven and snuck into the church kitchen and literally got caught with their hands in the cookie jar. Wyatt's dad gave him a spanking, but even though Jessup's mom was embarrassed, David John wouldn't let her paddle him. Doesn't believe in corporal punishment.

"You okay?" Wyatt says.

"Sure." Jessup notices that Wyatt didn't exactly answer the question, but he's cold, he's wet, he's tired, and he doesn't care. "I'm wiped out, man. I'll see you at church."

"Listen, Jessup," Wyatt says, "you be careful, okay?"

Wyatt's voice is unusually earnest. He's got a fever glint in his eyes, looks like there's more he wants to say, but he stops, nods.

"I will," Jessup says. "I'm trying."

"I'm serious. Be careful."

Jessup considers him. Wyatt sounds scared, but he sticks his hand out, taps his knuckles against Jessup's. "I love you, brother. You stay strong, okay? Stay strong."

Jessup watches him drive off and walks to where the mailbox marks the corner of his driveway. It occurs to him that Wyatt wasn't surprised that Jessup is going to church in the morning despite Jessup's long absence, but he forgets about it as soon as he turns: he's got other things to worry about.

THE LANE

The porch light is on. The car and the van are both there, but there are also three other vehicles: a truck he recognizes—Uncle Earl's ruby-red Ford F-150 SuperCrew—a car he doesn't—a low-slung, black BMW sedan—and a Cortaca Police Department cruiser.

The lights are on in Jewel's bedroom, light leaking through the closed curtains, but the curtains are open in the living room, and he can see his stepfather and his mom sitting on the couch, their backs to him.

There's a part of him that thinks he should turn around, just keep walking down the road, but he knows he doesn't have anywhere to go. He pulls out his phone again, looks at the time. It's half past nine. How can it only be nine thirty, he thinks? Not even twenty-four hours since the truck slid out on him.

As he walks past the cars, he can't help but notice the BMW is a 7 series. Fully loaded, it tops a hundred grand. A V-12 puts it past one fifty. People who drive cars like that don't spend a lot of time in double-wide trailers.

But really, he thinks, shouldn't it be the cop car he's worried about?

PASSAGE

They all stop talking when he comes through the door. David John and his mother are on the couch against the wall, the window catching their reflection. Earl is standing by the kitchen counter.

Jessup doesn't know if he should be relieved or not to see that the cruiser belongs to Paul Hawkins. He's still wearing his Cortaca PD uniform, but he's sitting in the recliner, the chair tilted back, feet up.

And on the love seat, Brandon Rogers. Usually, when Jessup has seen him, Brandon has been wearing a suit and tie, but tonight, even though he still looks slick, he's dressed more casually: dark, crisp jeans that look like they've been pressed, a pair of black dress shoes with bright blue soles that have to be expensive, a black button-down shirt layered with a black V-neck sweater. Of course, Jessup thinks, the BMW. He's never known anything but money, so why wouldn't he drive a good German car that Daddy can buy him?

Brandon pops to his feet. Sticks out his hand.

Reflex. Jessup shakes his hand.

"Why don't you grab a seat," Brandon says, as if it's his house, as if this is some meeting he is running. But maybe it is, Jessup thinks.

"Give me a second. I'm kind of damp. Let me just go get changed," he says.

David John says, "You get a ride home from Wyatt? Thought I saw his truck in the driveway."

Brandon chirps up, "Oh, that was for me. I just wanted to have a quick word with Wyatt and he was kind enough to meet me here. He's a good kid. Does his duty. Understands sacrifice. A real soldier for Christ and the white nation. One of the reasons I was the last one through the door. Well, last one other than our guest of honor."

There's something smug in the way Brandon says all of this. Judgmental. As if he's deliberately calling Jessup out for being late, for not being committed to the cause. Jessup wonders if Hawkins would arrest him if he punched Brandon in the face. He wonders what any of them would say if he told them he'd gotten a ride home from Coach Diggins, replayed the conversation for them. "No. Got a ride from a friend," he says. "I'll be back in a minute."

He slides through the room, smiles at his mom and David John—he's not sure if they see how tight the smile feels—and is down the hallway before anybody can say anything else. He steps into his bedroom, and as the door closes, he can hear the low hum of conversation restarting.

He closes his eyes and stands there for a moment. Just stands there. Breathes. He can feel a swarm of bees behind his eyes, and he can't tell if it's anger at coming home to Earl and Brandon and Hawkins in the living room, or if it's an overwhelming feeling of helplessness for the exact same reason.

Breathe.

Breathe.

He hangs his damp hoodie and his long-sleeved T-shirt on a hook on the back of the door and thinks about trying to take a quick shower—he smells like popcorn and condoms and sex—but knows they are out there waiting for him. Knows that would be pushing things. Grabs a clean T-shirt from his drawer and puts that on. Still cold. Pulls out a dry sweatshirt.

He unlocks his phone, opens his text messages. Still nothing from Deanne. He stares, waiting, as if that act alone will get her to acknowledge him.

BEDTIME STORIES

He takes a quick piss, brushes his teeth, splashes water on his face. In the hallway, he stops outside of Jewel's room. The door is cracked open, and he's about to knock, but he hears his mother's voice. Her low hum is soothing, a reminder of every night she tucked him in, of the way she nursed him through fevers and strep throat, of how she used to wake him up by rubbing his back and singing to him.

"Maybe in the afternoon," she says. "We can stop at the grocery store on the way home from church and get some then. Do you have any homework?"

"Nope. All done," Jewel says.

"What about the work you missed on Friday?"

"I did it in the car."

"Right." She laughs. "Why couldn't Ricky have been like this? I always used to have to chase after him to get to his homework, but both you and Jessup are so serious about school. You make it easy for me, pumpkin."

Jessup smiles, lets his knuckles dance on the door. "Hey," he says, leaning in.

Jewel sits up in bed. "Jessup!"

"Shouldn't you be sleeping?"

"It's early," she says scornfully. What do big brothers know about bedtime? What do big brothers know about being eleven? "And it's the weekend."

"It's not like you ever sleep in anyway. Latest you ever sleep is eight o'clock."

Their mom taps her finger against Jewel's nose. "She's going to sleep now, but she's not a teenager. I'm more worried about you getting up on time, Jessup."

"Me?" Jessup feigns being wounded. "I was up before the sun today."

"Yeah, but that was to go hunting. You're a little less eager for church."

Unsaid: that he's refused to go the past four years. Unsaid: that it's not up for discussion with David John. Unsaid: that she's not worried about his sleep.

He comes all the way into Jewel's room, sits next to his mother. Picks up the book that Jewel has on her lap. It's the same one from earlier. "Thought you'd finish this by now."

Jewel grabs it back, hesitates, then proffers it to him. "Will you read it to me? Just a chapter?"

Their mom gently pushes the book down. "Not tonight, honey. You need to go to sleep. And we need to have a talk with Jessup."

"How about a bedtime story? Just one."

"I've already told you one," she says. "Now lie down so I can tuck you in."

Jewel complies, but before Jessup can turn off the lamp, she looks at him and asks, "Is everything okay?"

"Of course," he says. Realizes he may have just told her another bedtime story. A fantasy. A fiction. Asks himself, what's one more lie? "Everything's going to be fine."

THE CURVE

His mom turns and goes into her bedroom, gesturing to Jessup to head back toward the kitchen, but Earl is waiting for him in the hallway. He wraps his hand around Jessup's right biceps. There's a bruise there from the football game that Jessup hadn't been aware of.

"Keep things straight," Earl says. His voice is a rough whisper, boot heels scuffed on cement, rats scuttling through drainpipes. "Everything just the way it happened, and when that nigger left the party, you didn't see him again."

Jessup's angry. Earl using that word affirms everything Coach Diggins said. Particularly here, in this house. In Jessup's house. He tries to match Earl's volume, spits, "I don't like this. Why is that cop here? And why is Brandon here?"

Earl is angry right back, but he keeps his voice low. "Brandon knows what really happened."

Jessup goes from angry to livid. "What the hell? What's wrong with you? Why the—"

"Shut up." Earl narrows his eyes, squeezes tighter. "My brother and I are just trying to do right by you," he says. "Don't want the same thing happening to you as happened to Ricky. Nobody's going to believe it was an accident. Brandon understands that, and he's helping. Hawkins is one of us, but he doesn't need to know the details. We're keeping this between you, me, David John, and Brandon. You got that? Now shut up and play your part if you want any hope of stopping your life from going down the toilet."

Jessup gives a sour nod. "Yes, sir."

The other three men are deep in conversation when Jessup walks into the room. Earl sits down beside David John on the couch, Hawkins and

Brandon still in the same places, the recliner and the love seat respectively. Jessup doesn't want to sit next to Brandon, so he pulls over a kitchen chair.

Hawkins is in the middle of talking, and he has the floor: "—first thing in the morning. Can't imagine they're going to have too much trouble finding a friendly judge. I'm telling you, when the medical examiner called and said he thought it looked suspicious, Harris couldn't have been happier than if somebody had given him a watermelon and bucket of fried chicken."

It's all Jessup can do not to wince. He can't pretend he's never heard that kind of talk before, but it's not his world anymore. Hasn't been his world in a long time, and all he can think of is Coach Diggins's sad voice, how sure he was that the *N*-word was going to come tripping off Jessup's tongue. And if he's honest with himself—he doesn't want to be honest with himself—he's not sure that Diggins was wrong.

"What do you mean 'suspicious'?" Jessup asks.

"Looks more like he got hit by a car, not that he was in one," Hawkins says evenly. "Not much to go on, but they're head-hunting. They'll be coming for your truck in the morning. Better hope Corson never touched it. They find DNA from Corson on your truck and they'll make your life a misery. You said he kicked out your taillight, Jessup, but if I were you, I'd make sure that truck is scrubbed down. Or better yet, disappeared."

Earl leans forward, leaning on his knees. He's wearing a pair of clean, pressed khakis and a white button-down dress shirt. His glasses are too big for his face, but they make him look earnest. He's got his hair cut short, just a bit longer than a buzz cut, gray working its way up his sideburns. "We owe you one, Paul."

"No kidding. But thought you'd want to get ahead of the curve on this."

"Damn right," Brandon says. "If we handle this right, it's going to play great."

Jessup can't help himself. "What?"

"You're the perfect martyr, Jessup. Young. Good-looking. You're all-American. Good student, right?"

"Honor roll," David John says proudly. He looks at Jessup with the same smile you give your son. Jessup doesn't know where to look. "He wrestles and runs track, too. He's a good kid."

"Exactly." Brandon Rogers talks with his hands, excited. He talks fast, too. Jessup understands why they love him on television. "I've already talked to my dad, and we've got lawyers lined up."

"Good ones?" David John asks.

"The best. A couple of Jews from Harvard." The four men laugh at that, but Brandon notices Jessup isn't laughing. "Don't worry," he says to Jessup. "We've got this under control."

WAR COUNCIL

W hat?" Jessup asks. He tries to keep the edge off his voice. Thinks he wouldn't mind teeing up on Brandon on a football field, driving his shoulder through him, pinning him to the dirt. "What do you have under control? I don't understand any of this."

Hawkins lowers the footrest, stands up. "I've got to take off," he says. "And, obviously, keep my name out of things."

"You working tomorrow?" Earl asks.

"Not supposed to. But Chief Harris has a hard-on and the mayor's already involved, so we'll see. Might be a lot of overtime in the department this weekend." He shakes Earl's hand, David John's, Brandon's, takes Jessup's hand in his. Hawkins squeezes hard, a macho handshake meant to show he's in charge. Jessup's expecting it, though, gets a better grip first, squeezes harder, torques the underside of Hawkins's hand so the bones grind, but he lets go quickly. Doesn't think he can get away with more than that.

The men are quiet until the door is closed, and Jessup hears Hawkins's footsteps, the police car's door open and slam shut, the throaty growl of the cruiser's engine.

Brandon speaks first. "The big thing is your truck. I'm sure they'll find Corson's DNA on your truck. Even if you scrub it down, it will be there. The science on that is incredible now. It's basically impossible to get rid of. Crime scene techs have gotten really good at catching it. They find DNA on your truck and everything goes out the window. We've got to get rid of the truck."

Jessup runs cold. A roller coaster cresting, the feeling of being sent to the principal's office, his truck fishtailing and the sound of a soda can crushed by a boot stomping down. He realizes he's breathing fast and shallow. Not sure if he's going to be sick or not.

Earl says, "It's taken care of."

Jessup's sure he must look sick, the roller coaster dropping straight down, everything swirling.

Brandon doesn't seem to notice. "It's just the four of us who know, right? Nobody outside of this room?" He looks at David John, Earl, Jessup, all three of them nodding in turn. "Good. And we aren't going to talk about it again. Ever. Never, ever speak about what happened. The official story— Corson left the party, Jessup never saw him again, just an accident—is the only story now. You tell the truth and Jessup is going to spend a long time behind bars. They'll make it out like a deliberate act. But you listen to me, and we'll come out ahead. If they don't have the truck and nobody's stupid enough to say what really happened, they don't have anything. Worst case a fine, a slap on the wrist for not providing the truck if they come with a warrant. So stick to the official story, that Corson was aggressive, you walked away, no idea how Corson managed to kill himself. This is how we're going to play it: it's a witch hunt. Pure and simple. Got it?"

They all nod again.

"They want to make an example out of you, Jessup. You caught the part about the warrant?" Jessup nods. He's tired of nodding. Brandon continues: "They'll be here early in the morning. They'll toss the trailer, go through everything. Looking for the clothes you wore last night. They'll want to impound your truck. You're sure that's taken care of, right?" Earl nods. Brandon continues, "they'll work up everything they find for DNA, going over Corson's body and car for DNA evidence, too. But I talked to one of the Jew lawyers already, and you're good with whatever they find on Corson or in his car."

"What?" Jessup thinks he might be sweating, which seems hilarious, because he's freezing.

"Well, you guys played football against each other last night, and my understanding is you knocked the shit out of him a couple of times, so yeah, of course there's DNA."

"Right," Jessup says. Thinks of the Mercedes. He was wearing gloves, his coat. Is there DNA? How does that work? What can they find in the car?

"Look," Brandon says, as if he's reading Jessup's mind, "you don't have to worry about anything. Any DNA on Corson, any on you or your clothes, even in his car. The only issue is the truck. We've got good lawyers, and I've seen the video that girl made at the party. That boy was out of control, and nobody in his right mind would have blamed you for popping him one. And everybody saw him get in the car and drive away. They are going to come in hot and heavy on this; they want to string you up because *they* can't get at *me*."

He looks again at Jessup, Earl, and David John in turn, waits for them to nod at him, to acknowledge how important he is, that none of this would be happening if "they" weren't out to get him. Jessup wants to ask who "they" are, but it doesn't matter. Brandon means all of them: the mayor, the police chief, the blacks, the Jews, the stupid white liberals who are selling out their own kin. Even though he hasn't been to church in a couple of years, Jessup's still been around it, can play Brandon out note for note.

Brandon shakes his head. "If I'd been here when your brother got jumped by those two boys, things would be different." He looks truly remorseful. "He'd be sitting right here with us right now. But you don't have to worry, Jessup. I'm going to take care of all of this. That's why I'm here. That's why Earl's here. But the thing is, Jessup, we've got a golden opportunity here. It's all about the spin."

THE SPIN

Brandon Rogers holds court.

He's got a good grasp of things from the game through the party until Corson drove off, tells it clean, and Jessup is taken aback by how well Brandon has it down. He thinks he's let his personal dislike of Brandon cloud his judgment: Brandon is sharp. Brandon says, "You left the party and went immediately to go be with your girlfriend. She'll back you up on that, Jessup? Can I speak to her?"

"No," Jessup says. "I mean, yeah, she'll back me up, but you can't speak to her, okay?"

He's panicked, tries not to show it. Deanne. Thinks about what Coach Diggins said. Walk away.

"She doesn't know you," Jessup says. "Besides, she snuck out. Wasn't supposed to be out, not with me, not at all. She'll be embarrassed, okay? We went up near the reservoir and parked in my truck."

The three men in the room smirk, and even though it's a friendly sort of smirk, the masculine braggadocio of sex, of we-can-guess-you-weren't-talking-politics-in-that-truck-of-yours, it makes Jessup run hot. He wants Deanne left out of this. Never mind that she's black, never mind any of that; he loves her, and what they have between the two of them is about him and her, nobody else. He doesn't want to share that. Doesn't want to share her. Doesn't want her name on Brandon's reptilian lips.

Brandon keeps his smarmy smile on his face, continues. "Fine. But the party line is Jessup didn't see Corson again, and it's not Jessup's fault that Corson managed to kill himself."

The spin is simple: this is the mainstream media and the radical, politically correct left trying once again to blame white people for a black person's failings.

Brandon has already called three different cable networks, all three of them promising to have satellite trucks down first thing in the morning. He spends a few minutes name-dropping, bragging about how much the television networks love him, how he has other calls out.

"Usual talking points. Liberals as jackbooted thugs, cops caving to political pressure instead of worrying about the real criminals, that whole thing. White folks are the victims. I'm thinking about calling for a rally. Some kind of a 'stand up in pride' sort of thing. We'll see about that, though."

"You trust those reporters?" David John asks.

"Hell, no. But I've got them in my pocket, and if we get lucky, one of the Cortaca cops will push a camera away or something while they're serving the warrant. Good television. Makes cops look like bullies. And the television people will come up to the church after they're done here, and we'll put on a good show, right? Make it look like we're just defending ourselves against government overreach, okay? Earl, we good with that, at the church? The men on board?"

There's something in the way he asks the question that makes Jessup uncomfortable—Brandon looks like a fox in a henhouse, too pleased with himself—but he chalks it up to excitement about the idea of being in front of cameras.

"Yep. We're good," Earl says.

"And the truck?"

"You keep asking, I keep telling: the truck's taken care of. It's not a problem." He has the same look on his face that Brandon does, but Brandon immediately turns his attention to Jessup.

"Now you," he says, "you make yourself presentable in the morning. Suit and tie. Sunday best, okay? You got a suit?"

Jessup wants to push back, but he's not even sure what he's pushing back against. It feels like everything has been taken out of his hands. He just nods. It's a secondhand suit he bought for a formal dance last year—eleven dollars at the Salvation Army, complete with shirt and tie, another six bucks for a pair of dress shoes in his size—but it's presentable.

"Good. Be ready early. I'll be here by seven." He stops, smiles. "And don't forget to set your clocks back. Daylight saving time."

THE SLEEP OF THE DEAD

The sound of the truck hitting Corson's body.

The sound of the truck hitting Corson's body.

The sound of the truck hitting Corson's body.

The sound of the truck hitting Kevin Corson.

Jessup wakes up white-hot, sweating, sheets tangled. For a moment, he thinks Corson is standing over him, but it's just the dark, shadowed shape of his dresser. Barely enough light for him to see the game ball resting on the dresser's top.

Four in the morning.

He thinks about the hit, the clean beauty of it. Corson's helmet popping off when Jessup drove him into the turf. The sound it made when he drove his shoulder into him. The sound of the truck hitting Corson's body. Wonders, did he mean to do it?

Don't think about Kevin Corson.

Don't think about Corson.

Don't think about Corson.

Don't think about Corson.

He doesn't remember falling asleep again.

THE MORNING SHIFT

David John wakes him at six thirty. "Give me your shirt," he says. "I'll iron it for you."

Jessup shaves, though the truth is it's not something he really needs to do. He shaved Friday morning, and he could easily go a few more days before he looks scruffy. His hand is shaking while he does it. Tries to be careful. Doesn't want to cut himself. Don't think about Corson. By the time he's out of the shower, David John has the shirt ready.

"Get dressed, and let's go outside for a bit," he says.

At quarter to seven, the sunrise is pure, flat light cutting over the trees. It's gray and bleak, colder again, the sky fat with clouds. Moisture waiting, early-season snow ready to burst again. In the ground under the trees, where the sun only glances, there are still patches of snow from Friday and Saturday, despite yesterday's brief respite and the freezing drizzle, spots of white awaiting companionship. Jessup is sore, bruised, but feeling good, all things considered. The football game seems like a lifetime ago, but it's not even been forty-eight hours.

David John is standing in front of his van. He's wearing his work jacket over his own suit. The pants are shiny with wear. He reaches out and grasps the knot of Jessup's tie. "Your tie's a bit of a mess. I'll redo that for you, okay?"

"Okay."

"You warm enough with that hoodie?" Doesn't wait for Jessup to answer. "We'll try to get to the store later. I'll borrow some money from Earl. You need a jacket. Or you can borrow one from him. His might be big enough for you. Not great, but good enough for a couple of days if we can't get to the store."

David John lets go of Jessup's tie, sighs. "Vultures are circling," he says.

Jessup follows his gaze to the end of the lane. There's a Fox News television van parked on the edge of the road.

"There's another one behind that," David John says. "I thought Brandon was full of it. Can't believe he actually came through with getting the media out here. . . ." He trails off, puts his hands in his pockets. Shakes his head. "I don't know about this."

He looks lost. For the first time in Jessup's life his stepfather looks small to him. It's hard to think of him that way. He wonders what David John will look like as an old man, tries to picture him at seventy, eighty. The picture doesn't come.

"Me either," Jessup says.

"You okay?" David John says.

"Not really." He says it without thinking, but David John smiles and then laughs, which makes Jessup smile and laugh, too.

It's a nice moment, but it's only a moment.

CAST IRON

You cold?"

"A little," Jessup says. "What did you end up doing with my coat?" It's a dumb question, he realizes. The wrong question. The wrong time.

David John shakes his head. "Let me tell you something, Jessup. This is just some bad luck, okay? Same as it was for Ricky. Think about if I'd been in the alley with him in the first place, or if I just hadn't texted him to meet me on the job, done it myself? You need to think of it that way. Bad luck, bad timing. Wrong place, wrong time. You did everything right, everything you could have to avoid this. That boy was pushing you, calling you names, calling you out, doing everything but daring you to fight him." He looks Jessup directly in the eyes. "I'm proud of you, son."

Jessup doesn't say anything. Can't say anything. What does it mean that Coach Diggins said the same thing to him, and then barely twenty-four hours later told Jessup to walk out of Deanne's life? What does it mean that David John, this man who is not his father, thinks of Jessup as his son? Jessup thinks he might cry if he speaks. Breaks off eye contact and looks at the gravel.

"I am," David John says. "I'm proud as hell. You didn't do anything wrong. It was an accident, pure and simple. And the truth is, nobody would have believed it, in the same way that nobody believed that Ricky was just protecting himself and nobody cared that I was simply standing by my son. What they cared about—all anybody cares about—is that we don't say things the way they want us to say them. You see those fraternity brothers at Cortaca University lined up in court in their thousand-dollar suits, and they can stand up and say it was just an accident. They've got the right parents and the right New York City lawyers, and if some kid dies from hazing or from drinking too much at a frat party, well, that's just a tragic accident and here's a slap on the wrist. But that's a different kind of family than us, isn't it? They've got money. And if you were poor and black or Mexican or Indian, there'd be plenty of help for you, people standing up and saying you're a victim of your circumstances. But nobody cares about us because we're poor and we're white. Might not be politically correct to say it, but it's true. And as far as all of them are concerned, if we ain't politically correct, then it means that we're wrong. That's how they see it. And that's why you did the right thing, Jessup. If you'd called the police, if you'd just fessed up and said it was an accident, you'd already be in jail. Both my kids locked up."

Jessup steals a glance and sees that David John is looking away now, gazing out toward the end of the driveway again. "Four years. Four years and all I ever did was run my business, work hard, raise you kids the best I could, go to church. And two black kids attack *my son*—they *attack* him—and he defends himself and I try to help, and they take me away. They attack my son and all he does is defend himself, and I do the same thing any father would do."

His voice is as calm as normal, but there's a heat to his words, real anger. "Take me away from you, from your mom, from Jewel, for four years. I'll never get that back. *We'll* never get that back."

He turns back to Jessup. "Look at me, son," he says. Jessup does. "You didn't do anything wrong. It was an accident, pure and simple, but even if you'd killed him on purpose, I'd have a hard time blaming you. I'd stand behind you. I don't condone violence. You know that. But that boy got what was coming. And the thing is, even though it's true, you can't ever say *that*. You know what happened, I know what happened, and Earl and Brandon know what happened. Nobody else. You got that?" Jessup nods.

"You keep your mouth shut. Stick to the official story and you'll be okay. You've got your whole life ahead of you, and I'm not letting them do what they did to Ricky, what they did to me. I think it might kill your mom to have you locked up. You understand?" Jessup nods again. His stepfather stands straight and strong. David John might as well be made from cast iron. "I'm not letting them do the same thing to you."

COMMUNITY AND CHRIST

He rubs at his head. "I am sorry, though. None of this is fair. And this is something you're going to have to live with. I'm glad you're going to church with us, Jessup. I hope you can find some solace in Jesus. He'll lift your burden, forgive your sins. If you go to Jesus with an open heart, you *will* be forgiven. Love, Jessup. Love heals everything, and you are going to have to carry the burden of what happened for the rest of your life, because the death of another human being—no matter whose fault it is, no matter what—is something that is a weight, but Jesus can help carry that weight. Jesus loves all of his children, knows that we are all sinners, and is willing to forgive us as long as we repent. Okay, son?"

This is one of those times when Jessup wishes there were other people around to see David John. If Deanne could witness this, if all of the politicians who called what happened with Ricky a hate crime, who blamed David John, if they could see this, maybe they'd see the David John that Jessup knows, because his stepfather's face is open, kind. Jessup can see that David John's heart is breaking, that he truly hurts for Jessup.

And yet . . . "How come . . ." Jessup says, "how come we go to church? Why the Blessed Church of the White America?" Jessup means, how can you tell me about love and belong to a church that preaches hate, how can you tell me that Jesus will take me in because he loves all his children but have those tattoos on your back?

But David John takes the question straight, isn't thinking of anything deeper in the question: "We go to church to praise Jesus, and we go to the Blessed Church of the White America because that's our home, our community. It's family, and I don't just mean because my brother is the one in the pulpit preaching the gospel. Church is about community as much as it is about Christ. You find people who are like you, who share your beliefs, and you form a family, and together you're stronger than anything. Jesus holds you up, but being part of a church means there are other hands to help. You've got me, your mom, your sister, but you've got the church, too, to lift you up."

GIVE THE DEVIL HIS DUE

David John stops talking, no chance for Jessup to ask another question, even if he could figure out exactly what it is he needs to ask his stepfather, because Brandon Rogers's BMW turns into the driveway. Brandon drives slow, the engine throaty and powerful, a call to attention. The car is a deep black, cleaner than any car has a right to be on a wet November morning, and the windows are dark enough that if Jessup didn't know who was driving, he'd be able to imagine the devil behind the wheel. The car goes off the gravel and turns onto the slick grass, the all-wheel drive handling things fine, the rear lights white as Brandon puts it into reverse and backs into a spot next to David John's van. The action of Brandon backing the car in pisses Jessup off. He doesn't know why, exactly, but something about it seems to sum up everything he dislikes about Brandon, the privilege, the clothes, the smugness of always knowing he's right. There's a part of him that wonders if he can get away with keying Brandon's expensive car.

He can hear music drifting from inside. It takes him a second to understand that Brandon is blasting opera. Wagner or something else that makes Brandon feel like a good Aryan, but whoever it is, it's pretentious and ridiculous and it's *opera* and Jessup just wants to smash Brandon's nose. He tries to calm himself down. Brandon is helping Jessup, isn't he? He shoves his hands into his pockets so that his balled fists aren't obvious.

But Brandon is oblivious to what's in Jessup's head, because he gets out of his car looking pleased with himself.

"I call, and they come running. Got those media fuckers in my pocket. I can take a shit on them one day and make them dance the next. They know I'm ratings gold. All I've got to do is promise a show and they're puppets on a string. We've already got Fox News *and* MSNBC, and I just got a text from my guy at CNN. They'll have a truck here in the next ten minutes. Got a couple of print people, too. *Washington Post* is sending somebody, and I think we might have the *Times*. A reporter from TakeBack, too, of course." He shakes David John's hand and then Jessup's. "We're going to have a good turnout."

The passenger door opens, and another young man, midtwenties and wearing a suit, gets out. He's small, five six, and skinny, holding an expensive-looking video camera with an attached microphone. He puts the camera up to his eye, a solid red light making clear that he's recording. Brandon waves his hand, clearly annoyed. "For Christ's sake, Carter, not yet."

Carter lowers the camera, the red light winking off.

All four of them turn at the sound of another car coming onto the gravel driveway. It's Earl's truck. Brandon nods. "Good, good," he says. He looks at Jessup, stops, tilts his head, the smile slipping a bit. "Going to have to fix your tie, Jessup."

David John laughs. Jessup can't stop himself from flinching, but it's a friendly laugh. His stepfather claps his hand on Jessup's back. "That's what I said."

Brandon nods. "Yeah, we want him looking neat. Put together. I want to see the coat, but I think this is going to be perfect. Neat, but not *too* neat. You can't look like you've got money. You've got to look like a good American going to church."

Jessup thinks, isn't that what I am, a good American going to church? But it's clear that Brandon doesn't care what Jessup thinks. He's already moved on to where Earl is parking, greeting David John's brother, telling them to head on inside while he goes and talks to the two news crews who are here, makes sure they have everything they need, helps them get set up so they're rolling when the cops show up to serve the warrant.

PAPERS

At twenty after seven, Brandon gets a text from Hawkins. "Ten minutes," he calls out. "Finish your eggs."

Jessup feels like he's choking them down. Goes into the bathroom to brush his teeth. His stomach feels loose, like everything might give way.

But what he sees in the mirror looks like a young man who has everything going for him. David John has fixed his tie, and with the suit coat buttoned and his shirt tucked in, he looks presentable. His hair neatly combed, clean-shaven, handsome, wholesome. He could be going to a dance. He thinks about Corson's father wearing a suit. Going to a funeral.

He barely gets the toilet lid up in time before he pukes. At least he has the presence of mind to hold back his tie.

He washes his face. Brushes his teeth again, swigs some mouthwash.

Stares into the mirror again. Keep it together, Jessup.

In the kitchen, Jewel is grumpy. "This dress is itchy." Their mom is brushing at her hair with an aggression that makes Jewel's head keep moving. "Ow!"

Jessup touches his mom's hand. "I'll do that if you need to finish getting ready."

His mom gives him the brush, thankful, hustling back to put on her makeup. "Braids, please," she calls out as she leaves. She's wearing a simple, modest black dress that falls just past her knees. It's one of her favorite dresses; she got it on deep clearance at Target, and she husbands its usage, saving it for special occasions.

"She looks pretty already," Jewel says. "She doesn't need makeup."

"Yeah, well, it makes her feel better, kiddo," he says. "She wears it like armor." He's less rushed than his mother is, brushes carefully, starts braiding. Jewel still squirms, but she isn't whining. "I think you're going to look like her when you're older."

Jewel is right. Their mom does look pretty. Sometimes Jessup forgets how young their mother is. She's only thirty-six. Fourteen when she had Ricky, nineteen for Jessup, twenty-five with Jewel. Most of the kids in Jessup's grade at school have parents in their late forties, early fifties. He's seen the way the fathers look at his mom when she comes to school events, football games, wrestling matches.

He finishes braiding, doubles up a hair tie. "Hold on," he says. Takes the blue ribbon on the table, winds it around the end of the braid, ties it in a quiet bow. He's actually better at doing Jewel's hair than their mom is. Too many mornings she's out the door early to go to work. He's spent more time than he cares to think about watching videos on the internet to learn how to do Jewel's hair right. "Looks good," he says. Pulls out his phone, takes a picture of the back of her head to show her. Jewel approves.

Brandon claps his hands. "Okay, it's time. Let's go. Mrs. Michaels, after you."

Obediently, Jessup's mom heads out the door, towing Jewel and then followed by David John and Jessup. Brandon has the four of them stand on the steps, arranges them like a family portrait, inserts Earl in the back. He looks at his minion, points his finger. "Okay, Carter. *Now* you should start filming."

He directs Carter back partway down the driveway so that he's got a good shot of the front of the trailer, and then runs a couple of one-twos to check for sound. Carter's got a headset on now, gives a thumbs-up.

The news crews have unloaded, too. Three camera setups, all of them trying to make sure that the others aren't in the shot. There's a print reporter, too, with a photographer, but Jessup can't remember who they are supposed to be, just that Brandon is excited for the attention.

Brandon signs off on everything, stands at the bottom of the steps, and waits.

He's got it timed perfectly, because it can't be more than a minute before three Cortaca PD vehicles turn into the driveway. Two cruisers and an

SUV. The SUV is the lead car, and when it stops, Chief Harris gets out of the passenger seat. He's holding some paper: the search warrant, Jessup realizes. The driver is the black cop from the day before, Cunningham. He turns off the car and steps onto the gravel, his hand resting on his pistol. Two cops get out of the first cruiser: a middle-aged woman who looks Latino and whom Jessup has seen around town occasionally, and a young, light-skinned black man. The black cop steps out of the passenger seat holding a shotgun. The woman was driving, and as soon as her boots hit the gravel, she pulls her pistol, leaves it hanging by her side. The two cops in the second car are white. Both of them built like football players gone to seed. Again, the one in the passenger seat is carrying a shotgun, the driver drawing his pistol and keeping it pointed at the ground.

Jessup can see Chief Harris realize too late how this is going to look on camera, the panicked look coming over his face about the same time that Brandon steps forward, raises his hands in a mocking gesture, and says, "Really? Is this necessary? You're coming here with guns drawn? We're just trying to go to church."

ROUND ONE

Chief Harris tells his cops to put their guns away, which leaves five cops standing behind him awkwardly, unsure what to do while Harris goes to hand David John the papers. Brandon makes a big show of taking the papers instead, reading them all the way through before handing them over to David John.

"You can search all you want," Brandon finally says, "but you're going to have to move your cars."

"Excuse me?" Cunningham looks at Brandon like he wishes it were just the two of them in a windowless room, Brandon cuffed to a table, Cunningham holding a sock full of batteries.

Brandon is playing to the cameras. "Like I said, we're just going to church. Are we under arrest?"

"This has nothing to do with you, Mr. *Rogers*," Chief Harris says. The woman cop snickers.

Jessup can tell that it bothers Brandon a bit, imagines him in a cardigan, trying to run a children's television show instead of wearing an expensive suit and putting himself forward as the new face of the movement.

He gathers himself nicely. "Well, then, if we're not under arrest, then why don't you move your vehicles out of the way so we can head to church. I think out on the road would do nicely."

"Where is Mr. Collins's pickup truck? I understand he has a 1994 Ford Ranger that he was driving Friday night. Our warrant includes Mr. Collins's truck as well as the premises."

Brandon looks genuinely confused. "Collins?"

David John quietly tells him that Jessup never changed his name. Brandon nods. There's a flash of irritation, something that he hadn't counted on, but he's more interested in Chief Harris and playing to the cameras.

"Well, as you can see, Jessup's truck isn't here. He spent some time doing ministry work at the church yesterday, and wouldn't you know it? Engine trouble. No, if you're looking for his truck, you'll have to come on out to the Blessed Church of the White America." He feigns a look of concern. "Oh. But then, I'm guessing you don't have a search warrant for the Blessed Church of the White America, do you? So sorry about the inconvenience, but I'm sure you can find one of your liberal judges—one who doesn't go to church—who's free on a Sunday morning. Now. About moving your cars?"

The cops grumble, but Harris shuts them up. While they are moving their police department vehicles, Brandon steps in front of the cameras, holds an impromptu news conference, which Jessup finds funny. In the movies, there's always a scrum. Here it's just three cameras, a slouchy middle-aged guy holding out a tape recorder, and a younger guy holding a notebook, his hair longer on top and buzzed on the side—must be from TakeBack, Jessup thinks—while Brandon acts like he's in front of a hundred cameras.

"—jackbooted thugs. We've got kids in hoodies selling drugs and carjacking law-abiding citizens, but instead of dealing with the problem of urban crime, the Cortaca Police Department has decided to come after a young man simply because our beliefs don't fit their liberal, global ideology. Jessup is a good kid. Honor roll, three-sport athlete, a literal choirboy at the church."

Jessup has to stifle a laugh. Choirboy. Brandon's an asshole, and he'd love to make the guy eat a fist, but he's good with the camera. Jessup stays off to the side, watches the cops coming back down the driveway.

"Look," Brandon continues, answering a question from the reporter from CNN, "there's video of this so-called incident on Friday night. And it shows clearly that Kevin Corson was a troublemaker, a common thug menacing a boy who did nothing wrong. And despite Corson's foul language and the unchecked animal aggression he displayed, Jessup stayed polite and calm."

The cops walk by stoically, making it a point not to look at the cameras. One of the big white cops hesitates, giving Jessup's mom a nod that seems to acknowledge how intrusive this is, a tacit apology for the fact that he's going to be pawing through the kitchen and trampling all over the trailer.

"The only reason—the *only* reason—the government is here is because we're white. If those roles had been reversed, if it had been a white boy yelling like that at a black kid, *all of it caught on video,* do you think the cops would be arresting the kid who got yelled at? Of course not. This is nothing more than a witch hunt, the Cortaca Police Department and the judge cowering behind political correctness."

Round one to Brandon.

CARAVAN

Brandon is another ten minutes with the reporters. He says a lot of things, even calls for a rally in Cortaca tomorrow night, says that they are going to set up on the pedestrian mall, stand up for the rights of oppressed white people everywhere, but mostly, Jessup thinks, Brandon repeats himself. He's only got a certain list of talking points. When the reporters start packing up, he comes to get Jessup and his family. "Okay," he says, "they might shoot a little B-roll, but they're all going to meet us at the church."

Jessup's family gets in the car and everybody else starts to wander off, leaving Jessup and Brandon alone for a moment. Jessup grabs Brandon's arm. "What the hell?"

Brandon immediately shakes him off, his face twisting, feral. "Get your fucking hands off me." He keeps his voice quiet. "And watch the cameras."

Jessup lets go. Takes a quick look. Nobody seems to have noticed. "You're calling for a rally?"

"I told you I was thinking of it." Calm now. Composed. A stone thrown in a pond, the ripples subsided, no telling how deep, how dark it is under the water.

"I'm not down with this. I don't want to be part—"

"Shut your mouth." He doesn't raise his voice—Jessup doubts anybody could hear them unless they were standing right next to the two of them—but it's so firm and so cold that Jessup does shut his mouth. Brandon continues. "I don't care what you want or don't want, Jessup. This is the way it's going to be. Now get in your damn car."

Brandon pulls out first, the black car riding low on the gravel, his camera-toting sycophant beside him, Earl's truck second. Jessup is in the backseat of his mom's car, sitting next to Jewel, their mom up front with David John, their car the last in line.

It takes Jessup a few minutes to calm down, to notice how quiet Jewel is. All four of them are quiet, but he's worried about Jewel. Doesn't want her here. Doesn't want any of this.

His mom keeps glancing at David John. They are nearly at the church when she finally asks. "Why did he say that about the truck?" She turns to look at Jessup, too. "Why did he say that about your truck? It's like . . . it's like he was daring them to come out to the church." She folds her arms, stares out the windshield.

David John's voice is quiet and steady. He's a rock for Jessup's mom to count on. Jessup knows that whatever happens to him, David John will move heaven and earth for Jewel, for his mother. "Don't worry about the truck. Earl's taken care of it. It's gone. It's not at the church. Look, Brandon knows what he's doing," he says. "Earl and him have something cooked up. I don't know all the details, but he's smart. We've just got to trust him, okay? And he's got good lawyers lined up. That's more than Ricky and I had. Jessup didn't do anything wrong, but it's a witch hunt. Brandon and Earl are trying to change the conversation, okay?"

GATEKEEPERS

The caravan backs up at the turn into the church. There are two men standing in the bed of a pickup truck parked off to the side behind the gate. Both of the men are wearing bulletproof vests in desert tan, an odd color choice, Jessup thinks, for upstate New York, and both are holding unmodified AR-15s that they must have already owned before the passage of the New York SAFE Act. One of the guns is wrapped in a camouflage skin, but it doesn't make the silhouette look any less like a military weapon. Wyatt's dad has an AR-15 and Wyatt and Jessup have taken it out a few times. It looks badass—it's just a civilian version of an M16—and it's fun, but Wyatt's a snob and always goes back to his Remington 700 for shooting from any distance.

Jessup's mom looks startled. "What are they doing?"

David John pats her leg. "Don't worry about it. Brandon and Earl think we might have some protesters today. They're just there for security. And to put on a show for the camera crews."

"I don't like the way it looks," she says. They are talking softly, the way adults talk in a car, as if there is some magic that makes it so the kids in the back won't listen in. "And I don't like Brody. I've told you that."

"Well, you don't have to like him," David John says. "The two of them are just there to keep things civil."

Jessup doesn't know the man holding the camouflaged rifle, but the other one is Brody Ellis. He's old, in his fifties, a huge guy, six foot, with a belly that makes him waddle. He looks ridiculous with his body armor. He's the kind of guy who tells little girls they're going to grow up to be lookers. He asked Jessup's mom out on a date a few months after David John went to jail. Didn't seem put off by the fact that he was close to twenty years older than her or that she was still married or that they were all part of the same congregation. He's got his AR-15 on a sling, the rifle pointed down, but he's got his fingers hovering over the trigger guard in a way that makes Jessup nervous. He doesn't like any of this. Brody gives a sloppy salute as the other guy hops down from the bed of the truck and opens the gate so their small caravan can drive through.

HOMECOMING

Jessup hasn't been through the gate in more than four years. Not since the day Ricky and David John were arrested. It wasn't a conscious protest—not at first. He just woke up the first Sunday and told his mom he wasn't going to church. She didn't press the issue too hard, and it became a habit.

If he is honest about it, he has missed going. It's a community. Every Sunday as long as he could remember. First going to the Bible school—really more of a babysitting service with small helpings of Jesus than anything—and then, as he got older, joining Ricky and David John and his mom in the barn for services. Him and Wyatt sneaking off sometimes after services to go play in the woods or shoot .22s on the firing range in the back acres, once a month sitting down at the long tables in the social hall for potluck dinners, mac and cheese, iceberg lettuce salads, fried chicken, Oriental coleslaw, oatmeal chocolate chip cookies, lemonade and iced tea, let us all bow our heads and pray, dear Jesus, remembers Jewel as a baby, six weeks old, in a white gown, christened in front of the congregation, mewling, her tiny fingers wrapped around Jessup's thumb.

The swings are still in front of the preschool building, the wood more weathered than he remembers, the plastic slide-and-fort combo seemingly reduced in size so that Jessup can now look over the top of the contraption. There's an addition on the preschool building that's new—Jessup's mom says it's been bursting at the seams because of babies and a growing congregation the past couple of years—and behind that, a big pavilion with forty picnic tables on a concrete slab that wasn't there the last time Jessup came to church.

Most everything else looks the same to him but also different, smaller, faded or with new paint that looks too fresh to him, neither way quite right.

Still, it's familiar: a homecoming of sorts. The open meadow looks warm, friendly, even with the flat light of this cloudy morning and the threat of snow, a few dollops of leftover white among the green. He wishes it were just a normal Sunday morning, that he were coming to sit in the barn, listen to Uncle Earl preach the gospel, get to his feet and belt out, "Will the Circle Be Unbroken," his voice rising in joy with three hundred other people.

The parking area has been expanded, gravel carefully graded, plenty of space for the whole congregation, and even though Brandon and Earl pull behind the house, David John parks right in front of the barn. "Good to be back," he says. There are a few cars and trucks already in the parking lot. Two likely belonging to the guys with the guns at the front gate, Jessup thinks, but he also recognizes Wyatt's pickup. Looks around but doesn't see Wyatt anywhere obvious.

CREATURE COMFORTS

arl's house is country nice: wide-plank pine floors worn smooth, a wood-fired stove in the sitting room, the rooms small by modern standards, but comfy. He got married when he was twenty, divorced at thirty, but in the dozen or so years that followed, he's kept his house clean with a fastidiousness that would have caused rumors if he hadn't worked his way through the single women in the congregation. For the past year, he's been dating a divorced mother of two about ten years his junior. Jewel isn't a fan of Earl's new girlfriend, says she's "picky," whatever that means.

Earl tells Jewel she can watch television as long as she keeps the volume down. "Have to finish my sermon, sweetheart," he says. He pats Jewel on the head, hands her the remote. He might set Jessup on edge, but he's been a good uncle, at least to Jewel. Jessup's never asked his mom or David John, but it suddenly occurs to him that if anything happened to them, Earl would be Jewel's guardian. He's already her godfather, which makes sense since he does have his own church. Earl disappears upstairs to his office, and Brandon excuses himself, says he has to make some phone calls, heads back outside.

Jessup goes into the kitchen with David John and his mom, who puts up a pot of coffee. The tie feels uncomfortable, and he tugs at it. His mom notices and swats at his hand.

"You leave that be," she says, and then looks at David John with a pained look. "You sure this is a good idea, with these reporters? And baiting the cops like that?"

David John takes out two coffee cups, looks at Jessup until Jessup shakes his head, closes the cabinet. "That's the plan, honey. Earl and Brandon think the best thing to do is make this a big story. Turn it so that it's not about Jessup, but so that it's about the church and how the police and the liberal politicians are always looking for somebody to blame. Brandon's good at this. He understands how the media works."

"But it *is* about Jessup."

"No, it's not," Jessup snaps. His voice is sharp enough that his mother is taken aback, and David John raises his eyebrows.

His stepfather doesn't raise his voice, though. "Don't talk to your mother like that."

The coffee machine is gurgling now, water dripping through the grounds, the black liquid rising in the glass pot.

"Sorry." He mutters it more than he says it, feels like a petulant child forced to apologize. Wants to act like a child. Wants to throw a tantrum right then and there, but instead he says, "I'm going to go for a walk, okay?"

David John nods, and his mom comes over, hugs him, holds him for a moment longer than is comfortable, and then kisses him on the cheek. As he walks through the sitting room and opens the door, Jewel doesn't look away from the television. He stops, takes one of Earl's coats off a hook by the door. It's a little small on him, but it's warm, better than his suit coat.

A WALK IN THE WOODS

He's careful to keep his feet dry. There are a couple of trails through the woods, one going back to a glorified junkyard where Earl keeps the burn barrels. The church has a Dumpster that gets picked up weekly, but Earl is country through and through. Jessup's pretty sure that one of the burn barrels contains a smoldering pile of ash that used to be his jacket and boots and gloves and everything else he was wearing Friday night. He goes the other way, past the campsites that the church youth group uses sometimes, down to the firing range.

There's a bite to the air—he thinks it's more likely to snow than to rain—but Earl's jacket is warm enough. He can hear the *pop* of somebody firing, isn't surprised when he sees it's Wyatt. Waits until Wyatt is reloading and then calls out. Wyatt's prone on a drop cloth, a sandbag on the ground to keep the rifle steady. He's wearing a pair of camouflage coveralls and a camouflage hunting jacket, has a dark knit cap pulled over his hair, pulls off his earmuffs.

"Little target practice before church?" Jessup asks. "Hunting for Christ?"

Wyatt carefully sets his rifle in the open case beside him, sits up. His serious look turns happy to see Jessup. "Hunters for Jesus," he says. "What would Jesus shoot?"

"How about 'camo for Christ'?"

"That's good," Wyatt says, laughing. "Could start a business out of that one. Christian hunting gear. Christian militia equipment. Body armor with a big cross on it, though maybe that's a little too close to putting a target on yourself."

He stands up and holds out his fist, bumps, gives Jessup a half hug.

Calling it a shooting range is being generous. It's an open alley through the woods, but it's long, cut off by a hill that climbs more than a hundred feet up, bullets going high no threat to carry. There are four standing stalls and two platforms for prone firing, target stands at 25, 50, 75, 100, 150, and 200 yards, the hill starting not long after that. He and Wyatt have spent hours out here, shooting metal silhouettes with .22s at 25 yards, metal plates at 100, the satisfying *gong* of metal telling them they'd gotten a hit, graduating to long-range shots at 200 yards, Jessup a literal hit or miss, Wyatt working harder at it until he can hit every time. Right now he's shooting at a target set out past the 200-yard marker, at the base of the hill, call it 225.

"You still come out here to shoot?"

"Yeah." Wyatt carefully closes up the case. "Earl doesn't mind, and it's easy to find an open time when the militia isn't out here and—"

"Wait. What? A militia? Seriously? I thought that was all talk. They really started the militia?"

"Yeah. Thanks to Brandon." Wyatt rolls his eyes. "Racial holy war. He wants us to be ready. I mean, I don't know if it's technically a militia or what, but they're calling themselves the White America Militia."

"WAM?"

Wyatt chuckles. "Yep. Started up last year. Come down here a couple times a week for target practice, do maneuvers in the woods. All that crap. Anyway, I don't like shooting with anybody from the congregation. They're either rednecks spraying bullets like they're holding a hose, or they're gun nuts. I mean, I like guns and all, but I'd rather be able to hit my shot than tell you why you need such and such a scope or whatever, and half the guys who can tell you everything about guns can't shoot worth crap either."

They both laugh. There's a couple who moved here from Arkansas sometime after Jessup stopped going to church, and Wyatt's told Jessup about the husband: brags about owning more than forty guns, and he's an equally crappy shot with all forty.

Wyatt closes up the case, sets it on a ledge in one of the stalls. "You just out for a walk?"

"Yeah. Trying to clear my head."

"Want company?"

Jessup hesitates. There's a part of him that does. He's known Wyatt his whole life. If there's anybody he can complain to about Brandon, about

Earl, even about David John, it's Wyatt. But even though Wyatt was at the party, knows about Deanne, knows everything about Jessup's life, has been his best friend since kindergarten, he can't tell Wyatt about those five minutes in the driveway, the swing of the truck, Corson's body on the ground. He can't. Can he?

"No," he says. "But thanks. I'm good. Brandon and Earl are making a circus out of this. They think everybody's going to be looking for a scapegoat, and with the family history, I'm an easy target, so they want to, to quote Brandon, 'control the narrative.'"

"Yeah. He's a shit weasel." He looks at Jessup, serious. "But he's not wrong about controlling the narrative. He's smart about that sort of stuff. You can't trust him, but he's got some tricks up his sleeve. This is a new world, and we're taking back what's ours. There's a lot of things I don't like about Brandon, but he's going to get us to where we need to be. It's our time. We're taking our country back."

Jessup tries not to let his surprise show. Wyatt's always been game to make fun of Brandon, but he's all in with this. Then again, while there was a time he seemed to be drifting away, at least for the last year or two, he's gone to church every Sunday; if Jessup was pressed, he'd have to say that Wyatt is a true believer. Not just in Jesus and salvation, but in the Blessed Church of the White America. Still, Jessup wasn't expecting such earnestness. It leaves him cold.

"This is a big moment for the movement. But don't worry. You'll see," Wyatt continues. "You'll come out of this okay. I've got your back, brother."

Jessup nods, heads off into the woods again.

EMOJI

He goes back and then left, heading over a small rise and stopping in front of the pond. It's not much of a pond as ponds go, not even fifty feet across, though that's big enough that kids swim in it during the summer, and it's oddly deep; Earl built a small dock with a diving board. Jessup goes out on the dock. There's no breeze, the water still. It's peaceful. It wouldn't translate to a photograph, but with the trees around the pond and the high grass circling the water, bits of snow here and there, it's got its own beauty. He wouldn't mind being out here with Deanne on a warm day, the two of them in swimsuits.

He winces. To bring Deanne here?

He pulls out his phone.

you up?

Stares at the screen. Wills the thought bubble to come up, but there's nothing. Puts it back in his pocket. He sees a small rock on the corner of the dock, grabs it, spins it in the palm of his hand. Nice and flat. Good weight. Pinches it between his thumb and index finger, wings it over the water, watches it bounce once, twice, three times, four, before wobbling a bit and popping up into the air, knifing under the water when it comes down.

His phone buzzes.

yeah. can't sleep. so mad

sorry

not at you. at my dad

oh

did he really tell you you can't see me anymore?

yes.

. . .

. . .

I had a big fight with him and my mom last
night when he got home. he was such an
asshole!

what did you say?

I told him I love you

The words make Jessup thrill, an electric pulse running through him.
He wants to shout it out, testify, wants to call it out to the world, wants to
hold her and kiss her and whisper into her ear. He settles for tapping his
thumbs on the screen.

I love you too

She replies with the heart emoji, and then kisses, and before he can respond she texts again:

where are you?

Jessup doesn't want to answer. Not honestly. How does he answer that
question honestly? Asks it right back instead.

where are YOU?

still in bed

hmm. pic?

! ha! no.

please

no. use your imagination. where are you?

He can't ignore the question a second time.

church

. . . the . . . what's it called?

Jessup?

Jessup?

what's it called

blessed church of the white America

oh

ALL APOLOGIES

J ust "oh." He waits a few seconds, but there's nothing else, so he types:

sorry. I told you. it's complicated

                                not really

He takes a deep breath. She came back with that reply awfully quickly, he thinks. He's trying to decide what to type when she texts again.

I'm sorry. that was kind of bitchy

                                it's okay

I saw the video

                                what video?

from the party

                                how?

somebody uploaded it. it's hard to watch

                                yeah

how come you just stood there?

        didn't want any trouble

is it true?

        **what? what Corson said? no. I told you. he
was drunk**

but you're there now. at the church. church of WHITE America

He almost corrects her, almost types back, *Blessed* Church of *the* White America, but he's smart enough to stop himself.

with my family. my stepdad wanted us to go as a family. it isn't me

        **if it isn't you, why are you there? can't you
just say you aren't going? you told me you
don't go, haven't gone in years**

but THEY still do. wanted me to come. important to them. made me come. I'm sorry. didn't really know how to say no

He waits, but she doesn't text anything. He thinks about the way she feels against him, the cinnamon gum in her mouth, the way the windows fogged up in her car last night, how good it felt to tell her he loves her, to have her say it back. He waits a few more seconds, but she still doesn't text, so he types:

I love you

. . .

I love you too

but you won't

He types it and sends it all in one fell swoop, tries to take it back as soon as it's gone, but it's too late.

????

TURNING POINTS

???

?

?

?

Jessup? what does that mean?

                    just promise me you won't believe every-
                    thing you hear, okay

what are you talking about?

                    about corson. about all of this

you're scaring me

                    I didn't do anything wrong. you have to
                    believe me

okay. I believe you

                    it's just . . . it's all stupid. I didn't do any-
                    thing, but everybody wants to make some-
                    thing out of this

everybody who

> everybody. cops and the mayor, want to make an example of me because of my family. and the people here at the church have their own thing. it's all so stupid. there are news trucks at the church with cameras. like a bunch of them cnn and fox and stuff

holy cow. really?

> yeah

what's going on?

He hears someone calling his name. A girl's voice. Jewel. He looks up from his phone, sees her standing up on the rise. She's huddled inside her coat.

"What?"

"You're supposed to come back to the house. There are protesters at the gates, and Brandon wants you to talk to a reporter."

"What?"

"Brandon wants you to talk to a reporter."

"No. The other thing."

"Protesters? You know, people with signs."

"I know what protesters are."

"Well, I'm supposed to tell you to come back."

"Okay. I'll be there in a couple of minutes."

She scowls. "I'm not leaving until you leave. I don't want them to yell at me for coming back without you."

"Jesus Christ."

"You shouldn't swear."

"Thanks, Jewel. That's super helpful advice." He feels crappy as soon as he says it. "I'm sorry." All he seems to be doing recently is apologizing to people he loves. "Give me a second." And now, another apology:

sorry. I've got to go. there are protesters here

what? why?

why do you think? You know what the name of the church is

He's typing his apology almost as soon as he hits send.

sorry

sorry

sorry

I'm so sorry. I'm an asshole

I'm on your side

I know. I'm sorry. it just feels like I don't have any control. I'm sup-posed to go talk to some reporter. I don't want to

then don't

it's not that easy. my stepfather, my uncle, and this guy brandon, they're handling it. lawyers, too, I guess. he's the one who invited the tv people so he can control the narrative

He feels slimy as soon as he types "control the narrative," but he doesn't know what else he's supposed to tell her. All he knows is that things have felt like they're spinning out of control, both literally and figuratively, ever since his truck slid out on the driveway. Or earlier, when he left the locker room after the football game Friday night. Or before that, when Ricky grabbed the pipe wrench, killed those two boys. Or earlier still, the first time David John brought him through the gates to the Blessed Church of the White America. Or before that, the day he was born, everything laid out so that no matter what he chose it would all go sour.

Deanne responds:

you don't have to do things their way if you don't want to. you're not a little kid. you're seventeen. you make your own decisions

SEVENTEEN

He's seventeen, but Friday night he killed another kid. Accident or not, there was a dead body lying on the snow, and he chose to lift Corson's body up, put him in the car, send it careening down that slope, instead of facing up to what happened. That was his decision, and right or wrong, he is going to have to live with it. He wishes he had David John's certainty that Jesus will help carry the burden, that Jessup will be forgiven. He doesn't know about that. He's only seventeen.

Seventeen. He glances up to where Jewel is waiting impatiently for him. Her hair is still pulled back and braided, the ribbon a flash of color in her hair. She's eleven, old in some ways, but painfully young in other ways. Has he been selfish, he wonders, focusing on getting himself out of Cortaca? Worrying about applying to universities and where he can play football, sacrificing his body in the hopes it will be a ticket out, studying late into the night and going into the library early, thinking about what kind of a future he might have, when leaving means leaving Jewel behind? And leaving her to what? To this? These people, this church?

Seventeen. Deanne can tell him he's old enough to make his own decisions all she wants, but he can't help but wonder: What happens if he makes his own decisions, if he walks away? Does he know better than Earl, than Brandon and his money and his New York City lawyers? Does he know better than David John? Because David John is damn sure that the only thing people are going to care about is laying blame. That's what happened with him and Ricky, and he doesn't want history repeating itself.

And if he can trust anybody in this world, he has to be able to trust David John. His stepfather would never do anything to deliberately hurt him. He owes his stepfather unwavering trust. Loyalty. David John has always done what he thought was best for his family.

Has he?

If that were true, Jessup wonders, would he be standing here?

For a moment, Jessup thinks about just jumping off the end of the diving board, letting himself sink to the bottom. The pond is easily fifteen feet deep there, cutting deep from the slopes. He could stay underwater for the rest of his life, dark and cool, quiet, safe, where nobody can touch him.

What's he supposed to tell his girlfriend? She says he's seventeen, says he's old enough to make his own decisions, but that's such an easy thing for her to say. No decision she makes has any consequence.

They're all like that. Not just Deanne but all of her friends, too. Megan and Brooke and their boyfriends, Josh Feinstein and Stanley, are just as bad. Victoria Wallace, too, all of them, Alyssa Robinson, none of them able to imagine a future that doesn't work out. Parents with good educations and good jobs, doing everything they can to make sure their children are a step ahead. It isn't that their parents love them any more than David John and his mom love Jessup and Jewel, it's just that when those parents sacrifice for their kids, that sacrifice puts a lot more in the till. All those other parents and kids shooting for the stars, never realizing that they are already standing on the moon.

Not a single one of them knows what it is to have something held out of reach.

It is easy for Deanne to say he's seventeen and he can make his own decisions: she thinks that to jump is to fly, can't understand a world of falling.

If she were here right now, watching him, she still wouldn't understand that if he steps off the edge of this dock he'll sink and never come back up.

Seventeen, but all Jessup can think of is David John carrying him off the football field, holding him on his lap all the way to the hospital, knows that however old he is, there is a part of him that will always be that kid, and right or wrong, he's going to trust David John. Has to.

Texts Deanne back:

I love you.

Doesn't wait for a response. Just puts his phone back in his pocket, walks up to where Jewel is, takes her hand, heads back to Earl's house.

LIGHTS

Brandon pulls him to the side, gives him a quick pep talk. "Look her directly in the eye. Don't look away, nothing shifty. Keep your hands still. Talk slowly and firmly. Don't say too much. We want to be the voice of reason here. Let the protesters get all angry."

"I don't understand why there are protesters here. How did they know about this?"

"I called them." Brandon chortles. "Anonymously, of course. It's an 'antihate' group up in town. They put out one of those ridiculous calls to action. Not a bad turnout, though. There's already twenty or thirty of them with more coming. Thought it would make for a good visual. Have them stomping around with signs and crap. There's nothing the news likes more than a bunch of snowflakes protesting. Means we'll get more airtime. If we get really lucky, they'll start coming in from the city to protest when we hold the rally on the pedestrian mall tomorrow night."

Jessup wonders if his mouth is hanging open. Tries to remind himself that Brandon is only three years older than him. But Brandon seems to have it all figured out, so sure of himself. He wants to say something, to tell Brandon this isn't what he signed up for, that all he wants is to take back that singular moment, the car sliding, the sound of Corson's body, Corson's body, Corson's body, but this moment, like that moment, gets away from him, and he doesn't know how it happened, but he's in the church, sitting on a pew next to a reporter.

The reporter is a woman from MSNBC who looks vaguely familiar to Jessup. He wonders if she was here when Ricky and David John were arrested. He's turned toward her. They're supposed to be sitting in a conversational manner. Natural, Jessup thinks, just a casual chat with a reporter in a church, like this is something he does all the time. The camera guy sets a couple of lights and what looks like a white umbrella, and then they're off.

Jessup feels like he barely says anything, a couple of "yes ma'ams," "no ma'ams," says he didn't say anything to Corson at the party, agrees that the video makes it look like Corson was the one being aggressive, no, he doesn't know what happened with Corson's accident, but yes, Corson seemed like he'd been drinking, and no, he doesn't know why the cops served a search warrant, and yes, since you bring it up, ma'am, it does seem like the cops are conducting a witch hunt, no the church doesn't preach violence, Jesus Christ is about love, no, he's not involved in the church's militia and can't really speak to that, yes, ma'am, my brother and stepfather did serve time, but it was self-defense, not like you're making it out to be, and no, ma'am, I don't spread hate, yes, ma'am, I'm proud to be white but that doesn't mean—

The camera guy stops rolling, snaps off the light, and he and the reporter stalk out of the church without another word. Jessup is stunned. He understands what the deer in the field must have felt like, the bullet ripping clean through without warning. It's all moving so fast. He doesn't have time to process: Brandon swoops in, clasps Jessup's hand, looks pleased.

"You're a natural," Brandon says. "If I didn't know better—and if I didn't have such a pretty face—I'd be worried you're going to take my place."

It's nine thirty. Close enough to the start of services that people are coming into the parking lot, drifting into the church. Brandon sees the look on Jessup's face, takes pity. "Come on. Why don't you go wait in the house for now? You can come back over right before church starts so you don't have to talk to anybody. It's going to be a busy day."

As Jessup walks across gravel, he can hear the sound of people chanting. He stops.

Brandon stops, too. "The protesters," he says. "Bunch of libtard college students and hippies from Cortaca. You'll see, though. There will be more of them later. As soon as this gets on television, the protest will grow. We'll get the social justice warriors driving up from the city, and mark my words, sooner or later you're going to have at least one Negro preacher grabbing the microphone. The news folks love this stuff, and it's like catnip to the eggheads and radical liberals. There's nothing those social justice warriors like more than a chance to get in front of a camera."

Brandon pats him twice on the back, like he's some sort of chum, and then gives a gentle push, steering Jessup toward the house before heading off to talk to the reporter and cameraman standing by the CNN satellite truck.

PEWS

At two minutes to ten, Jessup heads over to the barn with his mom and David John and Jewel. The church is almost full, and it feels like every man and woman sitting there is staring at him as he works his way up the aisle. It's only when they are already halfway up the aisle that Jessup realizes there's an empty space in the very front pew reserved for him and his family, right next to Brandon Rogers. The choir sits off to the left.

He sees Wyatt's girlfriend, Kaylee, sitting with her parents and her older brother, Peyton. Kaylee smiles and Peyton just tips his head. He's finishing up an associate degree in sustainable farming and food systems. He's the one who got Mr. and Mrs. Owen to take the farm organic, back when he was just a freshman in high school: he argues that the premium prices are worth the hassle and organic farming is the future if you want to make a living.

Some of the other faces are people he knows—old Mrs. Holland, who was old even when she was Jessup's first-grade teacher—but there are others who look familiar but he can't place, four years' absence enough to wipe the slate clean.

He sees Mr. and Mrs. Dunn seated with Wyatt's two younger brothers and his sister—she's a year younger than Jewel, and while they aren't besties like him and Wyatt, the two girls get along okay—but no Wyatt. And across the aisle from them, Leanne Gray, who's only two years older than Jessup, nineteen, but already married and, by the looks of things, about ready to pop out a baby. He used to have a crush on her something fierce when he was in middle school. Still has dreams about her sometimes.

They sit down, Jessup next to Brandon, and Jewel hops up into Jessup's lap. He doesn't mind it. Likes it, in fact. She's getting big, but he knows he won't be able to hold her like this for much longer, knows she won't want it soon, won't be caught dead on her big brother's lap in a year or two.

Uncle Earl comes out from the back.

Jessup's mom takes his hand, gently squeezes.

The service starts.

GRACE

Even though this is the first time he's gone since Ricky and David John were arrested, this church has been part of his life, and Jessup does have faith: he believes in God and Jesus and salvation. When he clasps hands with his brothers in the locker room, bows his head and prays, when he asks for protection for Jewel, for some relief for his mother, he believes. He believes in God's love and grace. He has to.

The entire congregation rises to their feet as one, singing out the praises of God. Despite his long absence, he settles into the rhythm: standing, singing, sitting, praying.

That familiarity, however, means that even though it feels like a homecoming, he's bored at times, his thoughts turning to Deanne and the way it feels to be with her, or to how happy his mother looks here, in this moment, with her family in church together—Ricky a permanent absence, always a shadow, but lessened now—but mostly, despite himself, he's happy. He's sitting with his family, a smile on his mom's face, David John's hand on her thigh, and next to him, Jewel sitting on the pew now, holding his hand, leaning against him.

He tries to ignore the fact that Brandon Rogers is on his other side.

Jessup puts his arm around Jewel. He remembers how when he was eleven, the age she is now, he'd lift her sleeping body from the car and carry her into the house, lay her gently in her bed, close the curtains and the door so that she could nap.

He'd do anything for her. He isn't a parent, but he understands it, understands how David John gave himself to the moment in the alley, the knife wiped clean of prints and shoved into that black kid's hand, understands how his mother works two jobs, catches an hour of sleep in her car between cleaning houses and standing at the register at Target.

He steals a glance over at David John. The man is shining with hope. Every one of his letters to Jessup talked about faith as refuge. Jessup has faith, but that's not the same as what David John has. David John has surety. Jessup's eleventh-grade social studies teacher, a Mormon, said there were all kinds of studies showing that religious people, specifically people who go to religious services, are happier. Jessup believes it.

SERMON ON THE MOUNT

He should have been expecting it, but Jessup is still taken aback when Earl focuses his attention on the front row. He goes through it quickly, how Jessup—his nephew, he calls him, no mention that Jessup is actually David John's stepson—is a victim, Corson provoking him but Jessup turning the other cheek. And now, even though it's clear that Jessup did nothing wrong, there has to be a scapegoat, doesn't there?

"Isn't that how it is today? No black man can die without it being some white man's fault," Earl says, shaking his head. It's clear that he's both amused and deeply sorry about the situation.

Somebody from the back yells out, "Dindu nuffin!" and there's an appreciative chuckle.

"That's right," Earl says. He leans forward in the pulpit, hands grasping the side of the podium. "We hear that all the time from black folks, don't we?" He looks around the church, makes eye contact. "I didn't do nothing."

Jessup tries not to stir. Doesn't want to call more attention to himself than what is already being thrown at him. He feels sick. An acid swelling in his throat. Whatever grace he felt is gone. He doesn't want to be here. Shouldn't be here. Doesn't belong here. This was a mistake. All of this. Everything from the moment of the thump of Corson's body against the truck.

What if he had simply stayed in his truck, driven away after the accident? But what then? Somebody would have found Corson's body on the driveway, called the cops that night, and Jessup would still be in the same place, a dent in his truck, a dead body, his own life hanging in the balance. What if he'd done the right thing right away: called the police on himself, told the truth, it was an accident, nothing more, taken his medicine? He's only seventeen and it was slippery with snow. He'd lose his license, community service. The police would understand. A slap on the wrist, the guilt enough, right?

But he glances over at David John, holding his mother's hand, hears Earl's voice, thinks about the Confederate flag sticker on the back window of Wyatt's truck, the tattoos on Ricky's back, the flaming cross, "eighty-eight" on Ricky's right shoulder, standing for the letter *H*, eighty-eight meaning HH, meaning Heil Hitler, and on his left shoulder, "pure blood," no explanation needed, David John's tattoos marking him just as clearly as Ricky, lightning bolts and swastika, unambiguous, the entire family marked, no matter that Jessup is clean of ink. He's stained anyway.

All this thinking of a different set of choices is fantasy. He knows that. There's nothing he could have done differently. Nothing that would have allowed him to walk away unscathed.

"We aren't asking for anything radical," Earl says. "Africa for Africans, Asia for Asians, America for Americans. Every other group can play identity politics, but when we do it, when we fight for the rights of good, white Christians, we get labeled as racists."

Jessup has heard all of this before, but he's aware of how tight his body feels right now. Every muscle clenched. He can feel the pulse of the congregation, the way they are leaning forward slightly, every word that Earl says soaking through them.

Earl raises his hand, open: "We aren't trying to take anything away from anybody. We just want to keep our God-given rights. If we don't fight against reverse discrimination, then we'll be left with nothing." His cadence has picked up, and his voice goes into a roar as he comes to the fourteen words: "We must secure the existence of our people and a future for white children!"

The congregants answer back, amens and applause, but Earl gestures for quiet. "This is an opportunity for us. We've got television crews here. Protesters on the road outside." A few boos. "You don't have to worry. We've got some of our brave soldiers out there"—he means the church's militia—"right now, keeping the peace. When you leave today, I want you to leave as Christians. I want you to be polite to those people outside of the gates." There's a smattering of unrest, sounds of dissent, but Earl isn't bothered.

"Let them be angry. Let the world see what the radical Left looks like. Besides, doesn't Jesus tell us to turn the other cheek? If the social justice warriors want to spend their Sunday mornings standing around with signs instead of praising the glory of our lord and savior, if those snowflakes think they don't need Jesus's blessing, well," Earl says, a wink, enough charm to explain why there is a church here at all, "I know *I'm* going to heaven, for I have faith. And to that, I say, let us pray. Our father . . ."

It's a sea of voices joining him.

Jessup is alone and adrift.

HONOR GUARD

Brandon has been checking his phone regularly throughout the service. He does so tastefully, keeping it down low by his leg, but it's hard for Jessup not to notice since they are sitting right next to each other. As Earl seems like he's winding down, Brandon reads something, and it seems like he's been shot through with electricity. He grabs Jessup's elbow. "They're here," he whispers. He makes a motion with his hand—discreetly—that catches Earl's attention.

Earl speeds up, has things wrapped up in record time, and then he's down in front of Jessup and Brandon, hustling them out. "Come on," he says. "Let's go."

They stop in the back room behind the pulpit to grab their coats—Jessup wonders how their coats got there, who had this planned out, but the answer is right in front of him—and Brandon already has his phone to his ear. Jessup assumes he's talking to his minion, Carter, because he asks the person if he's ready to film, tells him to make sure the news crews have their cameras rolling, lens on Brandon and Jessup "without fail. Without fail, okay? Just keep shooting the whole time. Record everything."

They are out in the parking lot, and even with Earl's borrowed coat on, it feels to Jessup like it's dropped a degree or two. There's still no wind, but there's a dark huddle of clouds, the afternoon no brighter than the morning. It smells like snow again, like the weather is tuning itself up for the coming winter, Friday night's snow a prelude for today. He wants to admire the way the sky is ready to burst open, but it's not a peaceful moment: he can hear the chanting of protesters.

David John slides next to Earl. "Are you sure about this?"

"A show of force," Earl says. "Nothing more. The militia is just there to show them they can't roll over us. Don't worry. We've got it under control."

Brandon hears this, speaks without looking back. "All we're doing is standing our ground. They have no reason to come on church land, warrant or no warrant, and we've got the cameras here. We're just making a statement."

But what, Jessup thinks, if he doesn't want to make a statement? He's quiet, though, and he follows behind, hating himself at every moment, not able to figure out any other choice.

As they turn the corner, he sees that there are now two pickup trucks parked in the grass off the road, one on either side, backed in so the beds are toward the gate. The gate itself is closed, with eight men standing in front of it. Another two or three are standing in each truck bed. All of them are armed: a mix of military-looking AR-15s, shotguns, hunting rifles. A couple of them are wearing bandannas over their faces, or balaclavas. Plenty have pistols in holsters on their hips. They are all wearing matching tan bulletproof vests, a uniform of sorts, and when Jessup gets closer, he can see they all have patches sewn onto the back left shoulder of their vests: the Blessed Church of the White America's flaming cross circled by the church's name.

They're bracing against what's on the other side of the gate: a swelling group of protesters and a convoy of police cars. The group of protesters has doubled in size, large enough now to be almost imposing, sixty, seventy people. It's a mix of college students and middle-aged and older men and women, professors, the kind of hippie Cortaca residents who keep the farmers' market afloat. Some younger kids, too, high school students, sons and daughters, people carrying signs and placards, some black people, more white. He thinks he sees his AP European History teacher, Mrs. Howard, in there, and recognizes at least two of the high-school-aged kids, the familiarity of a town the size of Cortaca. But the protesters aren't what captures Jessup's attention. What he's taken by are the cops: at least four Cortaca PD vehicles, four more from the county sheriff's office, and on the side of the main road, a giant truck marked "Cortaca Police S.W.A.T. Mobile Command." Mixed among all of it are the camera crews, and Jessup overhears a reporter talking earnestly into a microphone. Hears the words, "assault rifles" and "militia."

How did he get here?

He stops in his tracks, but even though he's five paces out in front, Brandon seems to sense it, turns, walks back to Jessup. "Come on," he says.

"This isn't what we talked about."

"Of course it is," Brandon says. "Smoke and mirrors, Jessup. Smoke and mirrors." He smiles, a cat with feathers in his teeth.

STANDOFF

he protesters are booing, chanting, making noise. Jessup looks at his sister. She's scared. He reaches out, chucks her chin, gives her a smile. Be brave, little one. She tries to smile back.

Chief Harris is waiting by the gate. He hands the papers to Earl, who glances at them and then, theatrically, crumples them up and drops the papers to the ground.

"This is private land. You aren't welcome here."

The cameras crowd in close, reporters thrusting microphones in.

"We have legal authority—"

Earl cuts him off. It's clear from Chief Harris's face that he's not a man used to being interrupted. "Not here you don't. Get off my land."

Jessup sees that Jewel is holding her father's hand now, that she's half tucked behind his body, and it makes him nervous. By his count, there are twenty police officers of one kind or another milling around the gate, a couple of more standing across the road on the edge of the farmer's field, behind the protesters. All of the cops have handguns, but there are at least eight geared up like soldiers in Afghanistan, holding M16 rifles that trickled down from the military. Jessup figures those are the cops from the SWAT truck. You can smell the macho in the air. Nothing's happened and it's already a disaster. Too many people, too much anger.

He wants Jewel gone. There's no need for her to be here. Wishes she were back home, in her own bed, reading that book she likes, warm and safe under her covers. Wishes he were back home, too, or somewhere else, with Deanne. Anywhere else. He slides over to his mom.

"Get Jewel out of here," he says. "You too. Both of you get out of here." She starts to protest, but before he can say anything else to his mom, Brandon Rogers grabs his arm.

"Come on," he says, pulling him to the pickup truck on the right. Tells the three men inside to hop down, then tells Jessup to climb up, follows right behind. It's just him and Jessup up there. A stage.

As soon as Chief Harris spots Jessup, he points. "You, son. If you don't comply with this warrant. Bring out your truck, son, or we'll have to arrest you."

"He's not your son," somebody shouts. It takes Jessup a moment to realize that it was David John. He's not used to his stepfather raising his voice. But despite his outburst, David John looks shaky, Jessup's mom and Jewel standing behind him. Why doesn't his mom leave with Jewel? She's clearly terrified.

"Now, Chief Harris, you have to understand, this is private property." Brandon is all smiles as he calls out over the crowd. The protesters have quieted down, watching, but the cops are definitely on edge. Brandon doesn't care: he's playing to the cameras, and Jessup can see that the reporters are thrilled. This is going to look good on television. He thinks of the Bundy standoff, Waco, Ruby Ridge, Charlottesville, the way events can spiral out of control, and the way, too, that Brandon is right: this is going to be the moment that makes him a star, that turns him into *the* face of the movement. He's got everything choreographed, down to the pickup truck backed up near the gate serving as a stage so that he can make sure there's a clear sight line for the cameras. Everything here is going to make Brandon Rogers look good.

And it might be this that bothers him the most about Brandon: Jessup doesn't know what Brandon *truly* believes in. Jessup can swear that he loves football and Jesus and, yes, Deanne, and he can swear that he'll do anything to protect his family, but he wonders if Brandon believes in anything other than himself.

"This is church land, and you can't just roll up here and do what you want. We're tired of the government deciding they can push around law-abiding citizens," Brandon says. "That's why I'm calling for a rally on the Cortaca pedestrian mall, tomorrow night at seven o'clock. A rally for white rights. Chief Harris, you and your fascist tactics are not welcome here, and we respectfully ask that you put your guns away and go home before some-body gets hurt."

To Chief Harris's credit, he stays calm. "We have reason to believe a crime occurred, and we have a warrant that allows us to search the prop-erty for a specific truck. This isn't about the church, Mr. Rogers. This is about the rule of law. And as for the guns, I think you might want to tell your men to lay down their weapons."

"Oh," Earl says, "I don't think so. We're on private property. Second Amendment rights apply to all of us."

SACRIFICIAL LAMB

Jessup is uncomfortable in the bed of the pickup truck. He doesn't know where to stand and starts to move to climb down, but Brandon grabs him. "You stay here," he says through clenched teeth. "Don't move."

Jessup stands back up. He knows that Brandon and Earl want him to look square at Chief Harris, but he can't keep his eyes from lowering. All he can think about is Deanne watching this at home.

Uncle Earl is still prattling about the Second Amendment, but then he looks over to Brandon. Brandon's quiet for a second. Jessup sees him looking across the road. There are a few cops standing off the asphalt at the edge of the plowed field, one and a half, two football fields of open land, and then a small rise filled thick by trees.

But Brandon recovers quickly. Stands next to Jessup, reaches behind him and grabs his jacket, holding him still, pinning him in place. It makes Jessup acutely aware that Earl's jacket is too small on him.

Chief Harris doesn't flinch. "We're here to serve a legally enforceable warrant, and I'm asking you to have your men put down their weapons."

Brandon takes charge again. "You can dress it up all you want, Chief Harris," Brandon says, "but the truth is you're coming in here with a SWAT team, with assault rifles and the full force and weight of the government behind you. Any violence that occurs here is on you and these protesters assembling unlawfully, blocking a *public* road. In fact, given the aggressiveness of these protesters and that our congregation is here peacefully, praising Jesus on a Sunday morning, shouldn't you be doing your job and arresting them for blocking the road? Because if you aren't going to do your job, I think it's completely reasonable that the members of our church have firearms, so they can protect themselves from these—"

Brandon spins, slams into Jessup. Their feet tangle up, and Jessup goes down like he's been tackled, Brandon on top of him. When he falls, Jessup smacks his elbow hard against the wall of the truck bed. He closes his eyes and turns his head as a shower of glass falls over him, the rear window of the truck shattered.

He processes falling and hitting the bed of the truck before he processes the sounds that accompanied Brandon's flailing, the glass breaking: three gunshots.

DAMAGE CONTROL

He's down in the bed of the truck with Brandon, but he hears Jewel's high scream, men yelling, a shotgun blast and at least two rifles chattering, could be more—he can't tell where any of it is coming from, only that he's sure he hasn't been shot—and Chief Harris shouting, "Stand down! Stand down!"

Even before the firing has stopped, before Chief Harris yells the command, Jessup is pushing Brandon off his body, scrambling over the side of the truck and jumping to the ground, shouting, "Jewel!"

It's pure chaos. Protesters screaming and running, somebody down in the road with a woman next to them, wailing, cops pointing pistols, the White America Militia at the gate already lowering their rifles, dropping to their knees, one of them—Brody Ellis, Jessup thinks, going by size alone—lying on his back, his face a smeared crater of blood, police officers in body armor running forward with M16s at their shoulders, others holding pistols raised, panic the only common element between the protesters, the church militia, and the police, Chief Harris continuing to yell, other cops joining in, drop your weapons, drop your weapons, on the ground, on the ground, but Jessup doesn't care, barely hears any of it, doesn't do more than take it all in with a quick look. The only thing he cares about is his family, and as soon as his feet hit the ground he's sprinting, looking for them.

What he sees is Jewel lying still on the ground with David John's body covering her, his body a shelter for hers, his mother right next to the two of them, on her side, crying, hysterical, reaching toward their daughter. For a frantic moment, Jessup is panicked—why isn't Jewel moving?—but then he sees her eyes open, sees her looking at him: she's fine, just scared.

"Are you okay?" he screams it, tries to calm himself down, catch his breath. A deliberate turn inward, not trying to make it worse for Jewel than it is already. Quieter. "Are you okay?"

There's yelling all over the place. He risks a glance back, sees the White America Militia members being shoved to the ground, separated from their weapons, the Cortaca cops and cops from the sheriff's department moving forward, aggressive containment now.

"We're fine, we're fine," David John says. He is spooked in a way that Jessup has never seen. "Are you okay?" David John asks. "You went down and . . ."

David John stops, gulps air.

Jessup looks at his stepfather. Is he . . . ? He is. He's crying. David John gets off Jewel, sits on the ground and buries his head in his hands. Jessup's mom gets to her feet, and Jessup reaches down and picks Jewel up. All of this takes five, ten seconds at most, and it's like being in the calm of the eye of the hurricane. He hears somebody screaming for an ambulance, two cops climbing up into the truck where he was standing with Brandon. Sees the line of men at the gate, guns on the ground, being shoved to their stomachs, hands on their heads with pistols and shotguns and M16s pointed in their faces, Brody Ellis bloodied and on his back, not moving, no point in offering medical help.

As he takes this in, he sees three cops in military body armor and carrying assault rifles barging toward him, fingers on their triggers.

"Down! Down! Down!" one of them screams, and Jessup complies. As he sinks to his knees, he sees the cameras trained on him, one of the reporters standing there with her mouth hanging open.

ECNALUBMA

The shouting and screaming continues for another couple of minutes, but Jessup is ordered to lie still. He's on his stomach, his hands behind his head. Jewel is between him and his mother, David John on the other side of his mother, same position as Jessup. They are all supplicants. There is only one cop watching them, pistol drawn, steady aim at Jessup.

Jewel is crying.

"Hey," he says. "It's okay. It's okay."

He can hear the sound of sirens in the distance. More cop cars. The first of the ambulances on their way.

Brandon Rogers, it turns out, is a screamer. One of the cops from the sheriff's office comes over to talk to the Cortaca cop holding the pistol on Jessup and his family, says it's just Brandon's shoulder. Not bad for a gunshot wound. He'll be fine. Shame it wasn't a gut shot. Worse for others: the militia member flat on his back at the gate with the bloody face, and the protester prone on the road, different sides, both equally dead. A couple of protesters wounded, but there's a lot going on and the cops are talking to each other, not Jessup, so it's hard to tell.

Jessup risks raising his head a bit. He can't see much, but he does have a clear view across the road. Sees two of the cops in SWAT gear standing together and looking across the field toward the woods on the hill, gesturing. Jessup tries to piece it together, understand where the first shots came from.

David John says, "I'm sorry, I'm sorry. Cindy, I'm so sorry," his voice breaking, the voice of a man who is broken. "I would never do anything to put you or the kids in . . . I'm sorry. I'm just so, so sorry." Jessup's mom risks reaching out, touching his hand, before the cop yells at her to put her hands back on her head and for all four of them to stay quiet.

Over the next five minutes, Chief Harris directs things. The men at the gate are all handcuffed and shuffled off across the road into the open field, their weapons collected and put in the trunk of one of the cruisers. Four cops are sent down the drive to stop congregants from coming out, trying to control the scene. There are, it turns out, three people who are shot besides Brandon and the two dead people. All three of them are protesters. One of them looks bad, shot in the stomach, but the other two seem minor, one in the lower leg, one in the thigh. The first ambulance comes screaming in, and the cops have already started triage. Brandon is not the top of the list. The EMTs are directed to the wounded protesters. Brandon can wait.

Finally, Chief Harris comes over with Earl to where Jessup is on the ground, tells Jessup and his family to get up. He motions for the cop to holster his pistol. High alert over. Turns to talk to Earl, who is asking something, pleading. Chief Harris looks shaken.

Jewel is still crying, more softly now, but with a sniffle, and once she's on her feet she turns to her parents. David John lifts her into his arm. She wraps her legs around him like she's a little kid again, and their mom swoops in, sandwiching Jewel between them.

Jessup stands there, alone.

AFTER ACTION REPORT

Earl comes over. "Why don't you head back to my house? For right now, the stuff with that Corson kid is the last thing they care about."

Jessup looks over Earl's shoulder. The body in the middle of the road and the body by the gate are still there. He's glad there are enough people milling around so that Jewel can't see. The EMTs already have one of the injured protesters on a gurney, an oxygen mask on her face, and one, two, three, and up into the back of the ambulance at the same time as a second ambulance comes in, sirens just one more thing to pierce the early afternoon.

The reporter for Fox News comes over trailing a cameraman, but one of the body-armored cops stops the reporter, says in no uncertain language to get out of the way.

Jessup's mom reaches out, touches the side of his neck. He flinches. "Ow," he says.

"You're bleeding."

He reaches up, touches it himself. Broken glass from where the rear window in the truck shattered. Safety glass, but still enough to leave little cuts. Feels like a sunburn. "It's nothing," he says.

His mom is suddenly shaking. "You could have been killed," she says.

Earl starts shooing them. "But he wasn't. Go on now. Head into the house."

David John's face is ashen. He's still holding Jewel. "This is my fault," he says. He has his hands tight around his daughter, as if he's worried she'll be pulled from him.

Earl shakes his head. "You didn't have anything to do with this. Some crazy person out there with a gun—"

David John is come to Jesus cutting Earl off. "It's my fault. I shouldn't have asked you for help. But I wanted to keep Jessup safe. Keep my family safe. My fault. I should have pushed back when you said we needed Brandon. If Brandon wouldn't have turned this into something big . . ." His voice is losing steam now. "I was trying to do the right thing by my family, but this, this . . . I made a mistake. This isn't the right place for us," he says, his voice so quiet now that Jessup isn't sure he catches the words completely.

His stepfather sounds lost. He *is* lost, Jessup realizes; David John has always used family and church as his compass, and the one might not survive the other.

David John figuring this out is too little, too late, Jessup thinks sourly, and he's immediately overcome with a sense of shame at how angry he is at David John. At Earl and Brandon and all of this, all of the things that he has never had any control over, but at David John especially. And shame because he's never questioned David John directly, never asked him how he could hold this hatred inside of him, how he could believe it would come with no cost to the people he loved. How could he fail to understand the sacrifice?

Sacrifice. The word rattles in him.

Earl's gentle in response to David John. "Go on to the house, now. Go on."

Sacrifice.

David John turns and starts walking to the house, Jessup's mom going with him.

Jessup doesn't move. He's thinking about what Brandon said last night, in his casual aside about meeting with Wyatt: that Wyatt "does his duty. Understands sacrifice."

Jessup takes one more look before he turns toward the house. There are two cops in the pickup truck where he and Brandon were standing. They're kneeling, so he can only see the top of their torsos, ostensibly giving Brandon first aid until another ambulance gets here. He looks past the truck to the field, where he sees several of the geared-up SWAT cops walking toward the trees, pointing, still holding their M16s. But he's not interested in the cops; he's looking at the edge of the field, where the land humps up and the trees are thick. Even though it's November, it's the kind of place where you can see out but people can't see in.

He thinks about sitting in the woods yesterday morning, staring across the field at the buck, taking his time and pulling the trigger. The hill across the open field, choked with trees, would be a good spot to hunt from, Jessup thinks.

MILLING

There are crowds of congregants in the parking lot, in front of the barn, milling near the entrance to the social hall. Mostly men, some wives, but all of them look concerned. There's a small group of Cortaca police officers standing at the exit of the parking lot, blocking off the driveway. They look menacing, out of place with their body armor and M16s. The congregants are dressed for church, winter coats covering a mix of suits and jeans with button-downs, women in dresses, here and there a few younger kids running around, oblivious to the concerns of their parents.

A group of somber men come over when they see Jessup's family. David John stops, kisses his wife, puts Jewel down on the ground, and joins the men. Jessup's mom takes Jewel's hand and heads toward Earl's house, shaking off a few women, but there are three who remain unshaken, who go with her; Jessup recognizes Wyatt's mom and Kaylee's mom, but he's not sure who the third woman is. His mom has a life at church that he doesn't know about, he realizes.

The men talking with David John are familiar, but Jessup can't honestly say he knows them. Those four years without church mean that even if he knew them before, he doesn't know them now. The whole group is serious, angry, full of bluster to shore up David John's unsteadiness. Leaning in toward each other. He hears Brody's name, other mumbles. To Jessup, it looks a lot like a football huddle, everybody following David John, listening to him speak. But the thing is, Jessup thinks, David John is no quarterback.

Which is uncharitable.

He wants to pull his stepfather aside, to hug him, to tell him he loves him, to say that he's proud of David John. Is that odd, telling this man who, by all rights except biological, can claim to be Jessup's father, that he's proud of him? Fathers tell their sons that they are proud of them, not the other way around, and yet Jessup doesn't have another word for it. That feeling, pride, comes over him so strongly that he can feel tears threatening to overwhelm him. He wants to say to David John that, no matter what else he has done or failed to do in his life, in that one single moment barely ten minutes ago, his actions were redemptive; when Jessup jumped off that truck, screaming Jewel's name, what he saw was a man who'd thrown his body over his daughter, who'd heard gunshots and gotten his family to the ground, whose first thought was to protect his family at all costs, to put himself in harm's way to keep his family safe. For David John, it was an easy and instinctual trade: his life for his daughter's. And Jessup knows that it's not the first time that David John has had the impulse: back in that alley, more than four years ago, with Ricky, David John was trying to protect his son, willing to do anything, including planting a knife, anything, anything to try to make things better for Jessup's brother.

And it makes Jessup feel like everything he's ever done has been made worthless because he hasn't told David John about this pride, how proud he is of how David John acts as a father, how glad he has been to have this man in his life, how much better he has made their lives in so many ways, and he wants to beg forgiveness for every single time he's called him "David John" instead of "Dad," every single time he's referred to him as his stepfather, because every single time has been a betrayal.

WYATT

While he's watching David John talking with the men, he sees something that catches his attention: Wyatt coming up the trail and out of the woods behind the barn. Wyatt's walking—strolling, really—with his hands in the pockets of his hunting jacket. He's wearing the same camouflage coveralls, the same jacket, even the same dark knit cap he was wearing earlier when Jessup came across him at the firing range. He's not hurrying, all the time in the world, and even from a distance, even with fifty people still milling about outside, he makes eye contact with Jessup.

Jessup wonders how that works, what it is in their relationship that allows Wyatt to find him so easily, that means they can find each other in a crowd. He knows he can do this with Jewel, can spot her onstage at a chorus concert, can pick her out of the group of kids breaking from school, knows where she is as simply as he can feel his own heartbeat. But it's been this way with him and Wyatt, too, from the beginning. Like brothers.

Wyatt takes a hand out of his pocket, points with two fingers to Earl's house.

Jessup walks around the outside of the parking lot, slipping away. He keeps his head down, shoulders bent, does his best to become invisible, a difficult task for a kid his size, in direct contradiction to everything David John has ever taught him: stand tall, talk steady, look straight.

One of the cops gives him a look, but Jessup keeps moving, and the cop is quickly distracted by somebody who wants to take their car out of the parking lot. Jessup can hear sirens drifting in from the road, wonders if an ambulance has come for Brandon Rogers yet. Wonders what the police are going to do with the two dead bodies. How long are they going to have to lie on the ground, blood pooling around them?

By the time he gets to Earl's house, Wyatt's already waiting for him by the porch.

"You okay?" Wyatt says. He touches Jessup's neck just like Jessup's mom did. His touch is gentle, thoughtful, and even though Jessup flinches a bit—it stings—he doesn't move away. "Looks raw."

"Glass from the rear window fell on me."

"You should clean that up." Wyatt moves his finger carefully over the side of Jessup's neck. "Doesn't feel to me like there's any glass stuck in there, but you want to go to a doctor or something?" He lowers his hand. "I can take you to the urgent-care clinic if you want."

"No. I think it's good. Just scraped up, really." Jessup touches his neck himself now. It feels tender and he wants to get a look at it, but he's pretty sure Wyatt's right. Doesn't seem like there's any glass embedded under his skin.

Jessup looks up and sees Wyatt's mom standing in the window of Earl's living room, looking down at them. He raises his hand in greeting, but she turns away.

"Shit," Wyatt says. "My mom's pissed at you."

"I didn't . . ." He sighs. He's tired of defending himself.

Wyatt shrugs. "Yeah. I know."

They both stand there, quiet, even though it's not quiet around them: one of the cops is standing in front of an SUV, telling the driver to turn around, not quite pointing his M16 at the man, but getting ready. Two other cops stand together talking about something. David John is listening to the collection of men; there's a lot of angry gesturing now, a roll of frustration coming from the group, heated glances at the cops, though David John just looks sad to Jessup, scared. There are other small clusters of congregants dissecting the morning's events, somebody's mother standing outside the front door of the social hall calling for her kid to come in, more sirens coming up the road, police or ambulance, Jessup doesn't know. The man in the SUV lays on the horn now, gesturing at the cop to move, the cop now raising his M16 and pointing it at the driver, cease and desist.

"Holy crap," Wyatt says. "This is nuts."

Jessup looks at him, shakes his head. "Why'd you do it?"

THROUGH THE WOODS, DOWN THE HILL, AROUND THE BEND, PAST THE POND, AND BACK AGAIN

They duck around behind Earl's house, avoiding the parking lot and the people still outside, cutting across the grass to the trail that leads into the woods. Fifty feet down the trail and it's already quieter, the trees muting the sounds. It's a mix that's heavy on sugar maples—whatever leaves were left denuded by Friday night's snowfall—and white pine trees, and the trail is spongy underfoot, small patches of snow still here and there. Judging by the way the temperature seems like it's dropping and the look of the sky, more snow is unquestionable.

Wyatt evidently has the same thought. "Going to snow," he says. "Couple inches, maybe."

They don't say anything else for a few minutes, just walking. An easy pace. Comfortable. Jessup thinks about how many hundreds of hours, no, thousands of hours he's spent with Wyatt. Church, elementary school—in the same class every year except fourth grade—and middle school, mostly taking the same schedule through high school until Jessup started loading up on AP classes, Jessup helping Wyatt keep up in math and science—Wyatt can hold his own in English and social studies—same football team from Pop Warner Tiny-Mite on up to now, wrestling, sleepovers on weekends in middle school, shared family vacations camping up in the Adirondacks before things went to hell with David John and Ricky, Jessup tagging along once Kaylee and Wyatt started dating in the eighth grade, from there, double dates with Wyatt and Kaylee and Jessup and whomever he was dating—though not Deanne, he thinks, not Deanne—and Wyatt losing his virginity in ninth grade, trying to tell Jessup what it felt like, Wyatt telling Jessup he was in love with Kaylee and going to marry this girl and when it comes time Jessup's going to be the best man. Wyatt his oldest friend and sometimes, Jessup thinks, the only friend who can possibly understand him.

Two hundred acres is enough for the Blessed Church of the White America to feel secluded, enough acreage for the path that winds through the trees to branch off here and there, to the pond, to the shooting range, to feel like the two of them could walk for hours, and right now, the outdoors feels like a sanctuary. More church than church itself.

Wyatt says, "You're going to film study this afternoon at Coach's house, right?"

Jessup scoffs. "Really? That's what you're thinking about? Football?"

"Yeah," Wyatt says, and his voice sounds off. He kicks at the ground with his boot, knocks a small rock. "I'm going to miss it. Ain't you going to miss it?"

"We've still got college," Jessup says, though that's hard to imagine right now. College seems like another world. Another entire universe.

"It won't be the same," Wyatt says. "High school's different. You know that. And, man, if I'm honest, the idea of college scares the crap out of me."

Not me, Jessup thinks. He doesn't say it, but there's a part of him that wants to stand on the pulpit and preach: Praise Jesus! College! A fresh start, a place where nobody looks at him and thinks of Ricky beating two black boys to death, where teachers don't already know that he belongs to a church that preaches ethnostates, where he can fall in love with a girl like Deanne without worrying about what that means. College! A whole life ahead of him.

Or at least, he thinks, there *was* a whole life ahead of him. Things are crumbling.

"Wyatt," he says, hesitant. "Why'd you do it?"

"How'd you know?"

"Come on, man. How long have we known each other? I'm not stupid. Why," Jessup asks, "did you shoot Brandon?"

"I didn't shoot Brandon," Wyatt says.

"Bullshit."

Wyatt can't help himself. He grins. It's a smile that Jessup has seen a hundred million times, but for some reason this is the first time it feels sharp to him, the first time he sees how different he and Wyatt are.

Wyatt says, "I didn't shoot Brandon. I missed and hit him. There's a difference."

Jessup stops walking. "What are you talking about?"

"Well, technically, I missed by hitting Brandon. I wasn't supposed to shoot Brandon." He looks so pleased with himself that it's all Jessup can do not to smile back.

"You hit Brandon on accident?" Jessup asks. "If you weren't trying to shoot Brandon, what were you trying to hit, then?"

"Not *what*," Wyatt says, "*who*. Brandon wanted me to shoot somebody else."

Jessup knows the answer before he asks, but he has to ask, has to hear Wyatt say it. "Who?"

"You," Wyatt says. "I was supposed to shoot you, Jessup."

HITS AND MISSES

Wyatt starts walking again, hesitates when he notices Jessup hasn't started up, but after a second, Jessup starts walking, too. Movement feels like everything to him. As if to stay still is to stand on quicksand, the world sucking him down, swallowing him alive, because he already feels like the ground is opening up beneath his feet.

"I was supposed to shoot you. Brandon wanted me to shoot you. He asked me to shoot you, so I said okay."

"You said okay?"

"You know you're just echoing me," Wyatt says. He starts to laugh.

"This isn't funny," Jessup says. He feels wretched. Doesn't understand how Wyatt can laugh.

"It's a little funny," Wyatt says. "Your face. But yeah, Brandon said, 'I need you to shoot Jessup,' and I said, 'Okay, sure.' There was a little more to it than that—I mean, he thinks I'm a good little soldier, and he's spent a lot of time cultivating me, getting to the point where he feels like he can trust me to follow orders—but basically, yeah, that's what happened."

"And even though you were supposed to shoot me, you missed and hit Brandon instead?"

"Yep," Wyatt says. "I was supposed to shoot you. I just missed. Bad shot. Wind or something."

Jessup thinks for a second, tries to replay Brandon spinning, his body tumbling into Jessup's, legs tangling up, the two of them going down hard, hitting the truck bed before the second shot took out the rearview window, before things turned to chaos. Thinks about the open field, the thick trees on the hillock. Easy to set up and hide. Thinks about the weather.

Jessup says, "It's going to snow later on, huh?"

"Think so."

"But it's calm. No wind. And there wasn't any wind earlier, either."

Wyatt agrees. "No wind. But there could have been a gust, couldn't there have been?"

"How far was the shot?" Jessup asks.

"How far did you say it was yesterday, that buck you bagged?"

"Two hundred. Actually, it was more like one seventy-five," Jessup admits, "but I told you two hundred because I knew you'd call me a pussy."

"I called you a pussy anyway."

"Yeah."

Wyatt laughs again, nods. He seems like he's happy. They're taking their time, walking, but clearly just trying to avoid having to talk about this face to face, and Wyatt is acting like it's nothing, but Jessup's known him long enough to know that Wyatt acting like it's nothing can still mean this conversation is everything. Wyatt's trying to tell him something he doesn't understand.

"Two hundred and twenty yards," Wyatt says. "Five yards shorter than it was supposed to be."

"You didn't miss, did you?"

"Not really," Wyatt says. Casual.

PIT VIPER

W hy didn't you tell me?" Jessup says.

"Because I knew you'd try to stop me," Wyatt says.

"What the hell, man? What were you thinking?"

They're on the path above the pond now, and it's Wyatt who stops walking this time. "I know you don't like Brandon and you don't trust him, but you're clueless, Jessup. You really don't understand, do you?"

"Why don't you educate me?" Jessup says, and he can hear how sharp his voice is. His first instinct is to apologize, but he holds against it. If he sounds pissed, it's because he *is* pissed.

"It's simple," Wyatt says. "A couple of summers ago, I think it was between eighth and ninth grade. I was dating Kaylee, I remember that, because I remember that she wasn't there, so it was either that summer or between ninth and tenth. Hot as hell, had to be ninety, ninety-five degrees. We went out behind your house, walking through the woods to public land and heading to the creek for a swim. Probably walked twenty minutes already, at most five minutes from the creek. We were right in the middle of thick woods, the shade giving us a little respite from the heat, and all of a sudden you jumped and let out a scream."

Jessup knows the story now. "It wasn't a scream."

Wyatt's amused. "Fine. A shriek, then. Either way, you sounded like a little girl."

"I almost stepped on a rattlesnake."

"First of all, it was a copperhead—"

"Bull," Jessup interrupts. "There are no copperheads around here. It was a timber rattlesnake. Rare, but not impossible."

"Okay," Wyatt says. "Fine, whatever. Copperhead, timber rattlesnake, whatever you want it to be. Point is, you jumped and screamed, and you were shaking like a chicken shitting razor blades."

"I wasn't—"

"I'm trying to tell you something, Jessup. Just let me talk, okay?" Wyatt's pleading. He's not joking around anymore, and the change in tone startles Jessup.

"Okay. Sorry."

"I guess what I'm trying to say is, the thing about it is, they're both vipers. Lay in wait and bite you when you ain't expecting it. You got that yellow 'Don't tread on me' flag, and that's got a timber rattlesnake on it, but it ought to have a copperhead coiled up on it because you don't see those sons of bitches until you already stepped on one. That's Brandon Rogers. He's smart as shit, but he's also a goddamned viper. He doesn't care about you. He only cares about making himself look good. You step on him and he'll bite you." Wyatt's talking with his hands, animated. Jessup thinks it's an affectation he's taken from Brandon Rogers. "You ask why I didn't tell you, Jessup, and that's easy. I didn't tell you because if I did, you'd have tried to stop me."

"I—"

"Dammit, Jessup. Shut up," Wyatt snaps. "I'm saving you from yourself. If I'd told you, you would have freaked out, or you would have made me promise not to do it, and Brandon would have coiled back up and waited, but he's a snake and he can't help his nature. Sooner or later he's going to strike. If I didn't do it, you really think he couldn't have found somebody else? And you really think they would have missed their shot?"

DON'T TREAD ON ME

Y ou understand what I'm saying?" Wyatt asks. "If I wouldn't have taken the shot, somebody else would have, and we wouldn't be here right now having this conversation." He takes a step forward, grabs Jessup's elbow. "He wanted a head shot. Wanted something brutal and bloody that would play on television until the end of time."

Jessup is shivering, but he's sure he's not cold. "But . . . why? Why the hell would he want me dead?"

Wyatt closes his eyes. His laugh this time is sad. "Oh, damn, Jessup. You don't understand a thing. He doesn't want *you* dead."

"Then why—"

"Man, come on. This isn't about *you*. Brandon couldn't care any less about you. This has absolutely nothing to do with you, Jessup. This is about him. His master plan. He wanted me to wait until you were standing right next to him and *then* have me shoot you. He's the face of everything and you're nobody, so everybody assumes that the shot just missed Brandon. Everything on video and he immediately calls it an assassination attempt; the radical Left trying to stop Brandon Rogers from speaking. You're dead but he's the one they pay attention to, because he's making the most noise. It immediately makes him the most important voice in the movement, makes him famous. Takes him from the fringes, man. Puts him in the center of everything."

Jessup is sure that he's supposed to say something, have some reaction to this, but he feels like the blood has drained out of him. What he wants more than anything right now is a bench, a chair, somewhere to sit. He's surprised not by Brandon's calculations—he's never trusted Brandon—but at how lucky he is that Brandon believed Wyatt's commitment to the cause meant he would be willing to sacrifice his best friend.

"You okay?" Wyatt says.

"No."

"You going to pass out, man? You look like crap."

Jessup bends over, puts his hands on his knees. Sucks air deep into his lungs, breathing like he's just finished wind sprints, has that same feeling of wanting to puke. "Yeah. Give me a minute."

Wyatt does.

Jessup stands there, staring at the ground beneath his feet, catching his breath. Finally, he can stand up straight again.

"So you shot Brandon instead?"

"Well, like I said, gust of wind. With all the cops and the SWAT fellows, I had to take that shot from four hundred yards—"

"You said two hundred and twenty."

"Four hundred," Wyatt says forcefully. "As far as Brandon knows, it was four hundred yards and the wind kicked up at just the wrong time, and man, I am *so* sorry about your shoulder."

"What if you'd missed for real? What if you'd killed him?"

Wyatt shakes his head. "Better him than you, brother."

ONE, TWO

You know better than that, though," Wyatt says. "I don't miss. Hit him right where I wanted, high, in the meaty part. Right shoulder. Had to make it look like I simply missed you. He's the only other person who knew what was supposed to happen, and I have to convince him that I did my best and we just got unlucky. He's going to need some rehab, but he should be okay."

"What did you shoot?"

"Like you said, what if I'd missed? Best rifle I've got for distance is the Remington. It's what I'm comfortable with."

The Remington means Wyatt shot a .30-06. Jessup says, "Could have used a .22. Would have done less damage."

"Nah. Not enough bullet for the distance. Would have been worried about being sloppy. Plus, Brandon Rogers might be a rich kid, but he's not an idiot. They tell him he got shot with a .22 and he'll know it wasn't a miss, that I did it on purpose. Nobody tries to go for a kill shot from two hundred yards with a .22. I'll take a .22 from fifty yards, but not from two-twenty, and hell, I'm telling him I shot from four hundred yards. Jesus, Jessup, how the hell do you ever bag a deer? And what, you're second-guessing me here? First you're pissed I shot Brandon, now you want me to have used a different rifle?"

"But it wasn't just Brandon, was it? What about the other people? One of the protesters got killed, a couple of them got shot. Was that you?"

"No." Wyatt shakes his head. He looks unhappy, scared. In that moment he looks his age, seventeen, just like Jessup. But that's almost old enough to go to war, Jessup thinks. At seventeen, rounding the corner to eighteen, Jessup's birthday in January, Wyatt's in March, they are almost the age to enlist—to be drafted in a different time—and go overseas to shoot and kill in the service of their country. "None of the protesters were me. I fired three shots. First one took Brandon, and it worked out perfect, because he took you down with him. Second into the rear window." He reaches out but doesn't touch Jessup's neck. Lets his hand drop. "I'm sorry about that. I just wanted it to look good. Figured the broken window would make it look like the shooter was trying."

Jessup doesn't want to ask. Has to ask. Wyatt is staring at him, waiting for him to ask. "That's two shots," Jessup says.

"Good counting."

"But you said you fired three shots. I remember three."

Wyatt doesn't blink. "Yeah."

Jessup thinks of the man with his face torn open, lying by the gate, his AR-15 on the ground beside him, body armor doing nothing to stop a head shot. He can't bring himself to ask explicitly, can only summon up the energy to say a single word: "Why?"

"Orders, man. Orders. It needed to look real," Wyatt says. "Brandon wanted it to look like the radical Left was starting a war. A real war. He said there had to be casualties and I had to kill somebody else along with you. To start a fire, first you've got to set a spark. We sacrifice two men, and in return we get thousands. I could get away with missing you by a few inches, but I couldn't pull that same trick twice. Not without Brandon figuring it out. Trust me, I only did this to protect you."

PROMISES MADE, PROMISES KEPT

No," Jessup says. "Don't lay this on me. You can't *kill* somebody and say you did it for me. This is on you, not me."

"You've got to understand," Wyatt says, his voice quavering, his mouth twitching. "I made a promise."

"To Brandon?"

Wyatt looks shocked. Like Jessup's got tentacles sprouting out of his face. Or, Jessup thinks, as if Jessup told him that he was in love with a black girl. "To Brandon? You think I'd care about a promise to Brandon? No, man. Look, I believe in the cause, but just because Brandon is part of it doesn't mean I owe him anything. Who cares what Brandon thinks? I made a promise to David John."

"He knew?" Jessup is furious. He doesn't even realize he's grabbing Wyatt's jacket until the fabric is bunched up in his fingers, Wyatt pulled close. But Wyatt doesn't do anything. Doesn't push Jessup's hand away, doesn't resist. Just meets Jessup's gaze with peace and love. It deflates Jessup's anger immediately.

"Don't be ridiculous. Of course David John didn't know," Wyatt says. He's clearly asking for forgiveness. Jessup doesn't let go of the jacket, but he doesn't do what he knows he *should* do, which is to wrap his arm around Wyatt and tell him it's okay, that he trusts him and he loves him, too, that blood doesn't matter when it comes to brothers.

"He would *never* have let you out there if he knew about this, never have brought Jewel or your mom. And anyway, you think David John would go along with something like this? That man's a fucking saint. He might be the best man I've ever met. I went to visit him, you know, a couple of times."

Jessup is stunned. One second he's thinking of Wyatt as his brother, the next he has to wonder if he knows Wyatt at all. He keeps his fist clenched on Wyatt's jacket, but he drops his head back, looks at the sky. The promise of snow still waiting to be delivered.

Wyatt's voice is low, hushed. He says, "You didn't know that, did you? That I went to visit him?"

Jessup can't look at him. "In prison?"

"Yeah."

"No. I didn't know that." He swallows. It hurts. "I never did."

"I know. And I get it, man, but I don't think you understand. All your dad tried to do was to keep Ricky safe, and—"

Jessup snaps his head down, turns on Wyatt, his voice a hard, quiet fury, pulling the jacket so that Wyatt stumbles into him. "Bullshit. This is *his* fault." Says it before he realizes that it is the word "dad" that triggers him. But he's already going: "All of it. You think Ricky would have been in that alley without David John, that he would have had those tattoos on him, that those . . ." He can feel the word splinter on his lips. Thinks of Deanne. Thinks of Coach Diggins telling him that it's just a matter of time before the word spills out of him. He can't say it. "And this, this . . ." He lets go and waves his hand, encompassing Wyatt, the woods, the trail, searching for the right word, fumbling, coming up with nothing better than to say, ". . . all of it. Blessed Church of the White America. This isn't normal. We might be rednecks, but neither one of us is stupid. You know this place isn't normal. If it *was* normal, none of this would have happened."

"Jessup." Wyatt meets Jessup's anger with an equanimity that seems to come from nowhere. It's the voice and calm of a man who is entirely certain he has done the right thing. "Jessup," he says again.

Jessup voice is glass. "What?"

"You know I love you. You know that, right?"

Jessup still has Wyatt's jacket grasped in one hand, and yet Wyatt hasn't pulled back, not once. Hasn't tried to separate himself from Jessup. Instead, Wyatt opens his arms, wraps them around Jessup, holds him like the brother he is, and Jessup doesn't know if Wyatt starts to cry because Jessup is already crying or if Jessup starts to cry because Wyatt is already crying, but it's just the two of them, the woods, the pond, the sky starting to open, snow beginning to flutter to the ground, the afternoon light dull and gray, nothing but Jessup and Wyatt, brothers holding each other in solace.

(STEP)FATHER

Wyatt's holding him tight, and Jessup holds firm, too. They hug for half a minute, which is an eternity, and finally, when they both let go and both step back, they meet each other with the same chagrined smile.

"I'd call you a pansy," Wyatt says, "but I think I'm the one who hugged you first."

"You said you love me, too," Jessup says, and they both laugh.

Wyatt is still laughing when he says, "I do love you, brother, but can I just tell you one thing? One thing about David John?"

Jessup looks up to the sky again. The snow is starting out light. Enough to look picturesque, not enough to be impressive. Later tonight, back in the trailer—assuming that's where he ends up, instead of in jail, he thinks, allowing himself the fantasy for a moment—if it keeps snowing, it will be nice to light a fire in the woodstove, put on a movie, sit in the love seat with Jewel, let his mom and David John have the couch. With the lights turned off inside, the blue glow of the television painting the walls, the snow outside will dance through the porch light, and he'll spend as much time watching that as he does watching the movie.

"Sure," Jessup says. "Tell me one thing about David John." He knows that he's gone from hugging his best friend and crying with him to sounding like a petulant child, but he can't help himself. He meant what he said. None of this would have happened if his mom and David John hadn't gotten together. But then again, none of the other stuff might have either: his mom quitting drinking, Jessup's grades and football, his ticket out of Cortaca. And he knows for sure that none of *this* would have happened: David John carrying him off the field in his arms, the way his mom smiles at David John, how happy he makes her. And above all else, Jewel. Without David John, he wouldn't have his sister.

"I went to visit him four times, I think, five times." Jessup opens his mouth but Wyatt rushes on. "Look, I'm not trying to make you feel bad. I do actually understand why you didn't visit, and I do understand that you're angry. It's just the two of us here, okay, and we've known each other long enough that we can drop the bullshit. This isn't about whether or not you went to visit him. This is about a promise." Wyatt looks up at the sky now, too. "Told you it would snow."

"Okay," Jessup says. "So? You went to visit my stepfather?"

Wyatt shakes his head. "I went with my mom, the few times your mom couldn't make it with Jewel. When she had the chicken pox, I think strep once or twice, something else. Your mom didn't want him to have to go without a visitor, and my mom offered, and she asked me if I'd keep her company. It was mostly just small talk. Him and my mom chatting. He'd ask me about school and football and stuff, but nothing serious. But every time I went, he'd tell my mom he wanted to talk to me alone. You know, man to man. Just for a few minutes. And every single time, he made me promise to take care of you."

Jessup feels like he should have seen it coming, but he's blindsided. "Take care of *me*?"

Wyatt has the temerity to laugh. "Come on, man. Everybody sees it but you. You're a big old marshmallow. He saw it. I see it. Everybody sees it. You can knock the snot out of somebody on the football field, and you're a mediocre wrestler—"

"Hey!"

"—and fast enough for high school track, but that's it. Ricky was skinny, but he was tough in a way you'll never be. He'll do his time and he'll be okay, but man, you could never do it. You wouldn't last a week in prison. You can take care of yourself physically, but that's not the half of it, not in life. You're not built for any of it."

"Come on, Wyatt."

"It's true, Jessup. That's why he asked me to look after you. Didn't ask, really," Wyatt says. "He made me promise. Every time I went to visit him he said the same thing. He said, 'Promise to watch out for Jessup. You promise to keep my son safe.'"

BACK INTO THE MAELSTROM

Wyatt shrugs. "Swore to God, swore to Jesus, swore on my mom that I'd take care of you, and, well, I did."

Jessup realizes his phone is buzzing. It's buzzed a bunch in the last twenty minutes, texts coming through. He hasn't checked, but now it's ringing, a call. He pulls it out and looks at it. His mom. But he's got a bunch of texts from Deanne, from Derek and Mike, a couple of other guys from school—what happened at the gate is on the news already, and everybody wants to know if he's okay—some texts from his mom and at least one from David John. Jessup sends the call to voicemail.

"We better head back," Jessup says.

Wyatt has his phone out, too. "Yeah. My mom is having kittens."

Jessup texts his mom to say he'll be back in a few minutes, looks up at Wyatt. "What do we tell them?"

"Nothing," Wyatt says. "We went for a walk because we were freaked out. They'll believe that. They're freaked out. The only person other than you who knows what *really* happened is Brandon, and I can't imagine he's going to tell the cops that the reason he got shot was because the guy he asked to shoot you in the head missed."

"You okay?" Jessup says. "I mean, you . . . Jesus. You killed Brody Ellis."

"I'll be okay," Wyatt says. "Besides, I didn't pick Brody. Brandon picked Brody. Whatever. I'm sure that I'm supposed to say all of this has fucked me up, but the truth of the matter is that, at least right now, I feel pretty good. I saved your life. You *owe* me. I'm serious. I saved your life. Think it through. If I'd said no, Brandon would have found somebody else and you'd be dead. And if I hadn't shot Brody Ellis, Brandon would have figured out that I didn't miss you on accident and he'd have me killed, afraid I'd tell somebody. Kill you, too, to protect himself."

"Seriously? You think Brandon Rogers has the stones to kill somebody?"

Wyatt shrugs. "Doubt he'd do it himself. More likely he'd find somebody to do his dirty work. It's not that hard to convince people that the ends justify the means. And I wouldn't underestimate what Brandon will do to save his own skin."

They start walking, back to Earl's house, faster now, a destination ahead of them, a purpose.

"But are you going to be okay?" Jessup asks.

Wyatt says, "Don't see that I have a choice."

Jessup shivers. "But what about the other people? There was somebody down on the road. A woman. And a couple of other protesters got shot."

"Like I said, not me," Wyatt said. "Our guys were jumpy. Couldn't tell who it was, but definitely our guys. They can call themselves a militia all they want, but they're a bunch of amateurs. Fingers on the trigger. As soon as I fired there were at least two, maybe three of them that let loose. Got to hand it to the cops. They actually held their shit together pretty well."

"Man," Jessup says. "This is going to be a spectacle."

"Yeah, well," Wyatt says. "People are going to go to jail over this. There's a dead protester, people shot. The cops will match ballistics and some of our guys are going to do time. This is national news, man. Somebody has to take a fall. The good thing, though, is that with all the noise, it won't be you. Maybe you can just slip through the cracks."

Dead bodies, Jessup thinks. He thinks of Corson. The sound of Corson's body. He doesn't deserve to be able to just walk away.

HOMEGOING

Inside Earl's house, Jessup's mom hugs him and then immediately starts to lecture him, tell him how scared she was, tell him he shouldn't have left like that, but she runs out of steam quickly. The television is on to Fox News, and Jessup catches a glimpse of himself standing on the truck next to Brandon, Brandon suddenly falling and knocking him down. It's unsettling to watch, and Earl turns it off.

Wyatt goes with his mom to find the rest of his family, and after a minute, David John and Jessup's mom usher Jessup and Jewel out. They want to go home. The cops are trying to get people off the compound, and the congregants of the Blessed Church of the White America are happy to oblige. It's not clear if people are angrier about the shootings at the gate than they are shell-shocked.

The parking lot is emptying rapidly by the time Jessup gets in his mom's car. Jewel is quiet, but at least she doesn't seem to be upset anymore. Mostly she's complaining about being hungry. Not for the first time Jessup is thankful for the resiliency of kids.

Traffic is backed up heading out—there's a checkpoint they have to go through and the news crews are still set up—but the car is nearly silent. Jewel borrows their mom's phone to play a game, and Jessup takes his own phone out. He starts with the easy texts, responding to his friends with the same short message that it's been crazy and he's okay and he'll tell them about it later. But even as he sends the texts he's not sure the conversations will ever happen. It's one thing to know about Jessup's history, about Ricky and David John and the Blessed Church of the White America, but it's another to deal with . . . this. Whatever this is.

Deanne is harder, though. He's not sure what to text her. Thinks about it while the car slowly creeps forward. He can see cops checking the trunks of cars, asking for driver's licenses, taking photos of the occupants. For an instant he panics, thinks of Wyatt's car, but then relaxes. Wyatt isn't dumb enough to try to sneak out his rifle right now. He's got to have it hidden somewhere.

He types:

I'm okay. sorry. it's been crazy. sorry I didn't text you or call you

don't know how much you know or what you saw. it's bad, though. not me. I'm okay. but the whole thing is messed up. I want to see you. please. I need to see you

Sends it, thinks for a second, types:

I love you

THE QUIET

It's weird to be back home.

David John goes into the kitchen and starts making sandwiches. Jessup's mom says she's going to lie down for a bit. Jewel turns on the television. For a second Jessup's afraid she's going to turn on the news, but she's eleven, not thinking about it, and it's a Sunday afternoon. She puts on the NFL, as if by reflex. The Giants are up two touchdowns.

Jessup goes into the kitchen and pulls down plates. Puts them on the counter next to where David John is making lunch.

David John glances at him. "Thanks."

"No problem."

"Want to talk about it?"

"Not really," Jessup says.

David John nods. "Okay."

Jessup starts to turn, but David John says, "Hey."

Jessup isn't sure what to expect, but all David John adds is "I'm sorry," and then he hugs Jessup, holds on for a few seconds, and then releases him.

KILLING TIME

He can't believe it's only two o'clock. He keeps looking at his phone, unlocking it, waiting, but nothing comes back from Deanne.

He does a bit of homework. He's mostly ahead of the game, but it never hurts to be prepared—he's smart and he's disciplined, but he's also taking all AP courses—and he doesn't want to watch football with Jewel and David John. Doesn't want to do anything, really, but better something than nothing.

Around two thirty he hears a knock on the front door. Looks out his bedroom window and sees David John telling a news crew to get lost. David John doesn't raise his voice, but he's firm. The reporter and cameraman trudge back down the driveway to their satellite truck.

A few minutes before three, he gets a group text from Coach Diggins. No film study today. Canceled in light of "recent events."

He opens his texts. Deanne hasn't responded. Decides to move from his desk to his bed, starts reading *The Merchant of Venice* for AP English.

At four fifteen he wakes up, startled. He doesn't remember falling asleep. Tries to figure out what woke him up. Something familiar. His phone. Dozens of texts, but only one he cares about, from Deanne:

I don't want to see you

CARRIER PIGEON

He doesn't do anything for a few minutes. Just keeps rereading the text from Deanne. He's got other texts, too, but he can't stomach any of it. He starts to go to the Fox News website and then stops. That's not where Deanne would be looking. Goes to the *New York Times*.

It's the top story. There's a photo of him standing next to Brandon Rogers, embedded video. Brandon is identified by name—"prominent white nationalist Brandon Rogers"—but Jessup isn't. He reads the story, watches the video of Brandon going down and taking Jessup with him, a short clip, thirty seconds long, pandemonium. It makes him feel sick

He goes to CNN's website, MSNBC's. The news sites aren't interested in him—the story is Brandon Rogers and the violence—but he's afraid to look anywhere else. Already knows what will happen if he looks at people he's connected to from school, his friends, doesn't want to see himself tagged over and over again, indelibly linked to what happened today.

There's no running from it. No pretending that people who know him aren't going to think he's at the center of this story.

That doesn't stop him from texting her.

please. can I just talk to you?

don't bother

please

please

Deanne, please

please

just give me a chance

please

please, Deanne. I love you

don't, Jessup. please don't

SUNDAY DINNER

Jewel comes to his room around five o'clock. She's got earbuds in and she doesn't say anything. Just curls up at the foot of his bed for a while. She closes her eyes, but Jessup doesn't think she's sleeping. He tries reading *The Merchant of Venice* again but can't concentrate.

Around six, their mom knocks on the door and calls them to dinner.

They leave the television on so they don't have to talk. The Arizona Cardinals at the San Francisco 49ers. Jessup thinks of Coach Diggins in a 49ers uniform. The chicken tastes mealy to him, green beans stringy. He's choking down the food, not really eating it. They are finishing up when the front door opens and Earl comes in. Snowflakes are on his coat and his hair like dandruff, already melting, the woodstove keeping the trailer warm. Earl looks tired. Jessup wants to hit him.

"Got anything left for me?" he says. Jessup's mom, obedient, jumps to her feet and makes him a plate.

Jessup excuses himself—homework, he says—goes back to his room. Twenty minutes after that, he hears the murmur of voices outside the trailer. Looks out his window and in the shadows he can make out Earl and David John.

It's still snowing, a light, drifting snow, steady but slight through the afternoon, an inch or two on the ground, enough to give a sense of freshness but not enough to be an inconvenience. The roads will be clear, Cortaca sending out the snowplows in full force, salt spread in even layers, blacktop gleaming through, the temperature only a couple of degrees below freezing. His stepfather and Earl are standing next to Earl's truck, the porch light sputtering out around them, just enough for Jessup to tell the two men apart. Earl is energetic, almost bouncing, left hand in the pocket of his coat, gesturing with his right hand.

David John is still. A statue. Jessup can imagine his stepfather standing like that all night, standing like that for the rest of Jessup's life. The snow piling on his shoulders, sloughing off his back, his arms, sun and moon rotating through, ice and rain, the trees budding and branching, the summer baking the ground, leaves drifting through the air, the snow coming again, an endless cycle of seasons and years, David John unmoving, constant. In some ways, that's what it's been like Jessup's entire life, as far back as he can remember—those first five years before his mom met David John a blank spot, nothing there—David John has been steady. Even for the four years he's been gone, he's been a constant, Jessup's mother cleaning houses and then working shifts at Target, Jessup cooking dinner, making sure Jewel did her homework, doing the laundry, cleaning their own house, splitting wood, whatever his mother couldn't do, and Jewel, sitting at the table, writing him letters, asking when he'll be home, his presence—and his absence—woven through their lives, discipline, rules, and yes, hope, hope and love and family, hard work can lift us up, believe in God, do what is asked of you and we'll be okay, we stick together, family above all.

Except David John does not stay still.

Earl punctuates whatever he is saying by shaking his finger and, so quick that Jessup at first thinks he's imagining it, David John lashes out.

It's a quick hook, snakebite fast, David John's right fist into the side of Earl's face. Earl takes a step back and then drops to the ground, rolls onto his back, lies there, holding his face.

David John steps forward, over his brother, and from where Jessup watches in his bedroom through the window, with the way the porch light casts shadows and the snow swirls down like sorcery, David John looms despite his size, smaller than Jessup, smaller than Earl, but ground down into something elemental, fierce, and Jessup is sure that if he were on the ground, in Earl's position, he would not dare to stand up.

And yet, after David John finishes speaking, Earl nods, and then David John reaches down, extends a hand, helps his brother to his feet. When Earl is standing, the two embrace, hold each other for several seconds, and when Earl gets into his truck, David John shuts the door for him, a sort of tenderness in saying good-bye.

KINDLING

J essup thinks about trying to go back to his homework. Thinks about joining Jewel in the living room—it sounds like she has a sitcom on the television now—or even calling Wyatt and seeing if he wants to do . . . something. Jessup doesn't know what. Doesn't know if he can face Wyatt again. But he hears the sound of David John working the woodpile, the heavy thud of the maul.

He goes out and pulls Earl's borrowed coat off the hook, slips on his sneakers. He doesn't see his mom, and Jewel doesn't bother looking up from the television, just grunts when he says "hey" to her.

The cold air feels good. The ground is slippery with new snow, and he wishes he had his boots, but he can feel some of his anxiety lifting simply from exiting the trailer. He follows David John's footprints around the side of the trailer. His stepfather has the floodlight on, a glare across the cleared ground in the backyard. There're two cords of wood stacked up here, wood that Jessup bought from Kaylee Owen's parents—her dad and brother cut wood during the winter, when the farm is quiet, hard work but good money—at a discount and hauled himself last spring. Enough to get them through the winter, the next, too, if they are careful, so much cheaper than the electric baseboards, turned on only as a last resort, the thermostat kept at fifty degrees so the pipes don't burst if it gets too cold during the day when he and Jewel are at school, his mom at work, the fire in the stove burned down.

David John lifts another log onto the stump, hefts the maul, slams it down. It hits true, splitting the log. He takes the larger of the two pieces, lines it up, hesitates, turns.

"We're good for kindling," Jessup says. "I split a bunch in the spring, when I stacked it."

"I know," David John says. "But I needed to get outside. Feels good, you know?"

"The exercise?"

David John is breathing hard. Jessup's not surprised. Splitting wood isn't easy. He drops the head of the maul to the ground, holds onto the handle with one hand, coughs, and then spits in the snow. "No. Yeah, sure, the exercise is good. That's pretty much all I did in prison. Worked out in my cell, worked out in the yard when I could, wrote you guys letters, read. I'm in the best shape of my life. I haven't done anything since I've gotten home, and I'm itchy, but no, I don't mean the exercise. I mean being outside. No fences. Nothing. I can go anywhere. Hard to believe I'm free."

Jessup blurts out, "I saw you hit Earl."

David John nods. "Yep."

"He okay?"

"Probably. He'll have a heck of a bruise." He holds up his right hand, flexes it theatrically. "I should know better than to punch him in the face. My hand's pretty sore."

"Why'd you punch him?" Jessup asks.

"You could have been killed today," he says. "Your mom. Jewel. I don't know. I punched him because I was angry. He told me he knew what he was doing, convinced me he and Brandon could take care of things, keep you safe. I shouldn't have done it, though. It was unchristian of me."

"But you helped him up. You hugged him after," Jessup says. David John looks at him keenly and Jessup blushes. "I was watching through the window."

"Yeah, well, I also told him to tell Brandon that if he ever comes to my house again I'll gut him."

"But you *hugged* him."

"He's my brother," David John says. "Look, you could have been killed. And Jewel. And your mom. That church has been . . . It doesn't matter. I— no, we—need some distance. You'd think that being in prison would have given me time to figure that out. That I wouldn't need to learn a lesson. But that's beside the point. What matters is that Earl's family."

David John looks miserable. "You know I'd do anything for you, right?"

Jessup nods.

"And your mom and your sister?"

Jessup nods again.

"Earl's my brother," David John says. "That don't change. But I told him that we're done with the church. We're not going back there."

JESUS

Jesus," Jessup says.

It's sacrilegious and instantly funny—David John laughs and Jessup does as well, despite himself—but it's all he can think to say.

"You know how a coyote will gnaw its own leg off to get out of a trap?" David John says. He moves the handle of the maul into his left hand and, with his right hand, taps his heart. "'For God, Race, and Nation.' FGRN. What a stupid fucking tattoo."

If Jessup was shocked to hear David John say he was willing to walk away from the Blessed Church of the White America, that's nothing compared to hearing David John swear. What a stupid fucking tattoo. The humor from just a few seconds ago melted into the night.

David John keeps speaking. "I had him put it right over my heart. 'For God, Race, and Nation'? If I could do it again, do you know what I'd get?"

He doesn't wait for Jessup to respond. Isn't even looking at Jessup now. Is just looking at the ground, at the head of the maul. "I'd get your mom's name inked right there. And Jewel's name and your name. That's what I should have had tattooed on my heart. My family. Close to my heart."

Jessup asks it softly: "And Ricky?"

It sounds like a hiccup. David John crying.

Jessup doesn't know what to do.

Thinks of David John carrying him off the field in his arms.

WEPT

S ounds: snow laying itself down like tissue paper unfolded; the wind rolling lightly against the tops of the trees; regret.

OWNERSHIP

David John wipes his eyes with the back of his free hand. He lifts the handle a few inches, lets the head of the maul thunk against the ground. Does it again.

"I'll own it," he says. "I've made some mistakes. And they've hurt you and your mom and your brother and your sister. But I'll own it, and we'll move forward. I don't know that there's anything I can do about Ricky. . . ."

Jessup thinks David John might start crying again, but his stepfather goes on: "I'm going to have to live with that. And don't forget that I have to live with what Ricky did as well. Two lives gone." He doesn't name them: Jermane Holmes and Blake Liveson. "No," he says. "Three lives gone. The men he killed, and your brother's. And I think of their parents sitting around their kitchen tables the same way we sit around the kitchen table. There's always an empty chair. You don't think that weighs me down? I have to own all of it. I might not be able to fix it, but I can try not to make it worse. That's all you can do, right? Try to make amends? Isn't that what I taught you your whole life? When you make a mistake, a real man stands up and takes responsibility, fixes what he can, tries to learn and be a better person, moves forward with his head held high. This church, it's . . . I can't undo what's happened, but I can help us figure out what comes next. I—"

David John stops speaking, looks out over Jessup's shoulder. Jessup turns, too, sees the sparkle of flashing lights.

PROTECTION

David John's face flashes dark. He hands Jessup the maul. "Put this away. I'm going to go see what's going on." He hesitates. "Once that's stowed, you come around front. Walk slow. Keep your hands empty, out of your pockets, where they can see them. Stay in the light. Can't be too careful, okay?"

Jessup hangs the maul up in the shed. He takes his time. He feels shaky. They've come for him, he thinks. It's over. But when he walks in front of the trailer, the lights on the cruiser are off and the two cops talking to David John don't seem too concerned with him. David John sees Jessup, motions him over.

"They're here to protect us," David John says.

"What?" He turns to look at the two cops, realizes they are the same two cops he saw outside of Kirby's on Friday night: the fat guy and the woman with the short hair. Both of them are white. They don't look friendly, but they don't look menacing, either.

The woman says, "You Jessup?" Jessup nods. She says, "Bomb threat for the high school got called in to Principal Stewart. Mentioned you specifically by name. Probably nothing. I expect there will be school in the morning. But in the meantime, Chief Harris wanted us to make sure there are no problems. Particularly after what happened today. We'll be parked out here all night."

For a moment, Jessup thinks she must be joking. But she's not joking, and after a minute or two, he and David John go inside. He sits down on the couch and David John calls Jessup's mom in, explains everything to her and Jewel. His mom is upset, angry, but David John calms her down. Jewel is excited at first, on her knees on the couch and looking out the window, waving to the fat cop until he waves back.

After a while, Jessup's mom turns the television back on, walks outside, and asks the two police officers if they want some coffee. They don't, and Jessup's mom comes back, sits on the love seat with David John. The four of them watch football highlights and then the first half hour of *Sunday Night Football*.

Around nine, with the Eagles down a field goal, she sends Jewel off to brush her teeth, to get ready for bed. Jessup doesn't have a bedtime—he hasn't had an official bedtime in years—but after his stepfather and mother tuck in Jewel, he goes into her room, kisses her, and then gets himself ready for bed all the same.

REPRESENT

He thinks about checking the news, but he can't stand it. Can't read about it anymore. He knows what he'll find: an avalanche of hate and blame directed at Brandon, at the church, at David John and Earl, and even though he hasn't been named, not explicitly, not yet, he won't be able to read it knowing that some of it is directed at him.

He's about to try texting Deanne again when he gets a text from Wyatt:

my mom says you've got police parked outside

> bomb threat at school. mentioned me. they're on like a security detail or something. just to be safe

whoa

> yeah

everybody okay?

> I guess. mom's pretty upset

think there's school tomorrow?

> cop in driveway said she thinks so

you going?

Jessup pauses. He hasn't thought about it. Hasn't gone that far ahead. Friday night, when he'd thought about school on Monday, he'd thought about returning triumphant. A playoff win. That hit on Corson and the fumble recovery, six points and putting the game out of reach, Jessup with the game ball. But too much had changed. Going back would be something different. People looking away, conversations stopping, teachers hesitant. And Deanne. He'll see her in the cafeteria, in the hall-way. And practice. Coach Diggins. Would he even be allowed at practice?

don't know

> yeah. you hear about the rally?

for football?

> wait. really?

no. jk.

> haha.

you mean brandon's rally, right?

> libtards have counterrally planned against us

No, Jessup thinks. Not us. There will be a rally downtown, but he can't think of it as *us*. But he doesn't type that. Doesn't reply. After a minute or two, Wyatt sends another text:

Brandon gave an interview from the hospital

> he's okay?

got released earlier. didn't even need surgery. he's crowing about it. assassination attempt. says it's a war wound. war to save white identity. says the radical left trying to stop him. says they fired the first shot and if they think whites are scared of standing up for what's theirs they've got another thing coming. he's calling the rally tomorrow night a unite the movement kind of moment. watershed. he's all over the news. been on like everything. fox and nbc and cnn and everywhere. message boards going nuts. got people flying in from all over and driving up. people already driving in from Tennessee, South Carolina, Virginia. Probably two hundred people already said they are coming to represent, plus whoever comes from church.

seriously?

going to be huge. you going?

to school?

no, dumbass. the rally. represent. pride, man. pride.

THE DEAD

He texts Deanne again:

can we just talk.

please.

give me a chance. I love you

He waits an hour, hour and a half, but there's no response from Deanne. Finally, he gives up, turns off his phone, goes to sleep.

Or he tries to sleep. There's the soft gurgle of the television, blue light leaking under the door of his room. Then the shift and step of David John and his mother going to bed. Past that, silence. Or something above silence: the sweep of snow carpeting upstate New York in a gentle but steady flow, dirt and grass disappearing with something less than urgency, the asphalt outside of the Blessed Church of the White America snow-coated, the spilled blood covered with white, the world around him covered entirely with white, cold and fresh, snow gliding from the heavens in an unhurried cadence, enough to keep the plows working through the night, but not enough to remake everything in the image of God.

Brody Ellis on his back. His face a pit of despair, gone. The protester—who was it? was it somebody he knew? Mrs. Howard? who?—unmoving. The glass falling over him, calling for his sister. She's still because she's scared. She's still because she's dead. Snow falls over all of them, covering bodies, covering blood, crosses in graveyards catching the snow, houses in Cortaca with roofs made pale and strange, the university campus inverted, the snow licking the surface of the lake, snow turning into dark, cold waters.

Snow covering Corson's body, the sound of the truck hitting Corson's body, Corson's body, Corson's body, don't think about Corson's body, Corson's body, don't think about Corson's body, don't think about Corson, don't think about Corson.

Don't.

The blankets are twisted around him, hot, his underwear damp from sweat, his hair slicked, the air around him cooling as the fire in the wood-stove goes low, but he can feel himself burning. He can feel himself ready to ignite.

But somewhere, in all of that, he does sleep, because it's morning.

THE LIVING

The first thing Jessup does is look out the window. In the ghostly morning light, he can see a Cortaca Police Department cruiser still in the driveway, but the cops in there are different from the night before. Two men. He thinks he recognizes both of them from yesterday at the compound. The cruiser is running, wisps coming from the exhaust, the two cops cozy in their car.

It's still snowing, but only barely. There are three or four inches on the ground, and he thinks how excited he would have been as a child to have snow like this so early in November. The possibilities piling up, sledding and snowballs, walking through the forest with Wyatt and a pair of shotguns, duck hunting, the snow a blank slate, the ducks calling for mercy as they launch into the sky, snow not yet an obligation, even shoveling seeming like a joy to a child.

Now the snowfall is weak, fluttering, but the sky is dark, the promise of more to come.

He turns his phone back on, and while it chugs to life he goes into the bathroom, relieves himself, brushes his teeth. He's about to turn on the shower when his phone buzzes. He thinks, *Deanne,* but there's a blizzard of texts, more than two hundred. Emails, too. A dozen voicemails. He doesn't know where to start.

It's the rally.

Wyatt wasn't kidding when he said it was going to be big. Everything that happened at the compound, the rally Brandon has called for tonight, the counterrally, it's the focus of everything. Front page of the *New York Times* website, the *Washington Post* website. The cable news channels losing their minds. Television trucks, network and cable alike, parked along the side of the pedestrian mall in a long row, six of them, more coming, waiting for the show. Counterprotesters already showing up on the pedestrian mall, twelve hours early, a feverish energy, ready to stand united against hate. Wyatt's texted a link to the TakeBack website, the news organization bankrolled by Brandon Rogers's father, and the main page is simply a black screen with "Day of Rage" scrawled in red, "Stand Up, Fight Back, Take-Back! Rally tonight in Cortaca, NY!" beneath it. Jessup clicks through, sees a call to action, a call to arms. Wyatt says he figures three hundred, even four hundred people coming to stand tall, an incredible number for such a last-minute event, white pride, baby, white power, the call going wide, every single white man who believes in a future for white children and who lives within five hundred miles on his way.

His other friends, guys from the team, a few girls, they text, too, but they don't know what to say, what to ask. Lots of *what the hell?* and *are you okay?* and *what's going on?* But many more texting *fuck you*, and *go fuck yourself*, and *Nazi piece of shit*.

But nothing from Deanne.

He showers, the rash on his neck from the glass stinging in the hot water, the ache from Friday's game carefully stretched out, shampoo, conditioner, soap, but he's in and out and pulls on underwear, a pair of jeans. Walks to his bedroom shirtless and sockless, a drip of water cold down his back. He goes to knock on Jewel's door to wake her up, their routine since David John went away, but the door's open and she's already up and dressed.

"Dad's making pancakes," she says.

As if it's just another day.

TEN

He puts on a white collared shirt, reconsiders, replaces it with a dark blue T-shirt, the color of dusk, tops it with a red Cortaca High School sweatshirt. He shovels his books and binders into his backpack, heads to the kitchen.

Jewel is at the table eating pancakes. She looks happy. Her hair is a mess—she hasn't brushed it at all—but she's wearing a pair of black leggings and a black sweater over a black T-shirt. Jessup smiles. "Looking pretty goth this morning, kiddo."

She grins, a gross, deliberately openmouthed grin, bits of pancake showing.

"Ugh," he says.

David John slides a plate onto the table. "Here you go," he says. "Syrup's on the table, cut-up melon in the bowl. No bacon or sausages. Sorry. You want an egg or something, too?"

"No. Thanks. I'm good. Where's Mom?"

"Sleeping," David John says. "She doesn't feel well. Going to take the day off."

Jessup takes a bite of the pancakes. Chews. Lets it sit. He can't think of the last time his mom missed work. She gets sick sometimes, a cold, a cough, but nothing serious, nothing that would make her miss a paycheck.

As if David John can read his mind, his stepfather puts a glass of water down in front of Jessup and says, "Don't worry. She's fine. Just tired, I think. She deserves a day off. Been busting her ass since I went to prison. I told her she needs to quit her job at Target. It's too much."

"We need the money," Jessup says.

David John's eyes go tight. "No," he says. "We don't. That's not what I care about right now." But he softens immediately. "I'm sorry. We've got a cop car camped outside. I'm worried. On edge."

"Me too," Jessup says.

David John rubs his head. His hair is bristly. Shorter than Jessup remembers him keeping it, though maybe that's because it's shot through with silver, though he doesn't really look any older. A wonder, Jessup thinks, after four years in prison. He knows the same won't be true of Ricky. Four years without seeing his brother. Is he going to go another sixteen without a visit?

While he's thinking, David John drops a set of keys on the table. "Take your mom's car," he says. "Can you get Jewel to school okay? I've got two jobs lined up this morning."

Jewel jumps up, says to Jessup, "I'm going to brush my teeth, and then can you do my hair, please?"

She doesn't wait for an answer. Just zips out of the room. Jessup picks up the keys, mutters, "Wish I had my truck."

"Get over it, Jessup. It's gone." He tries for a joke, pops his fingers together and says, "Poof. Gone, like magic." It falls flat. "What did you expect? Earl found somebody to get rid of it, no questions asked, nothing to come back to you. With that gone, you're good. All you got to do is stay quiet. Nothing to tie you to nothing."

Nothing, Jessup thinks, but the guilt. He'll always have that sound, the thump, Corson's body. That will never disappear.

David John reaches down and pushes the keys closer to Jessup. "You okay?"

Jessup isn't, but he nods.

He's thinking of what David John said the night before, about how David John has to take responsibility for his own part in Ricky's actions, about how he has to own not just Ricky's wasted life but Jermane Holmes's and Blake Liveson's lives as well. David John might have taken care of the truck, but as much as he'd do anything to protect Jessup, David John can't take care of this, can't ease the burden of guilt.

That's something that both Jessup and David John know to be true.

NINE

He lets Jewel put on country top-forty radio, even lets her crank it up loud while they drive to school. He brushed her hair for her, put it in a simple ponytail, and he thinks how beautiful she is. Fragile in some ways, but in other ways not. She's done well with everything that happened while David John was gone. The question, Jessup thinks, is if she'll do well now that he's back.

When he pulls into the drop-off zone at the middle school, he's struck with a bolt of anxiety. There are two police cars parked out front. But even though the cops are out of their cars, they are standing together tightly, looking like they are chatting rather than on high alert. A rote response to yesterday's bomb threat at the high school. None of the middle school students seem to care. They walk in crowds and individually, carrying backpacks and musical instruments in black cases, scooping up snow and throwing it into the sky. Somebody's built an anemic snowman on the grass by the front door.

It's the same at the high school: a casual acceptance that there's nothing to really worry about. As he turns into the lot, he sees a Cortaca police SUV parked next to a cruiser, three cops near the entrance. Buses are starting to unload, so there's a sea of students rolling off in waves.

He parks, grabs his bag, and shuffles through the cars. He has to work at keeping his head up. Knows that if he bows his head it's an admission of sorts, that it will be read as an acceptance of guilt. He also knows, though, that he's screwed either way. That to keep his head up, to look people in the eye could also be interpreted as pride, as a gleeful ownership of the violence over the weekend, of the rally planned for tonight, of everything that has happened or might happen.

He doesn't see Wyatt's truck in the parking lot. Could be he's missed it, but he hopes not. He knows it's selfish, but he doesn't want Wyatt here. Doesn't want anything else reminding people of his affiliations. Wyatt won't keep his head down, and while Wyatt won't spout off, he won't back down, either. Jessup knows that now. Wyatt's a different animal than he used to be. Metamorphosis. Wyatt isn't joking about a racial holy war, and he's willing to stand proud. But not Jessup. What he wants is a time machine. What he wants is a different life. What he wants is to be invisible.

But he can't be invisible. Not here. Not now. Maybe if he were smaller, but he stands out, his size, part of what makes him invincible, is part of what keeps him from being invisible. He sees students staring, groups of boys and girls recognizing him, somebody pointing. Hears somebody call out the word "racist," hears worse, but he doesn't look.

He hears footsteps, someone running, turns just in time to catch a glimpse of a familiar face, a teammate, Steve Silver, but he's not coming with a greeting. He's coming with a fist. He catches Jessup on the side of the head, on the temple.

Jessup goes down.

EIGHT

There's a lot of yelling. Two of the cops take Steve down, pin him to the ground, his face pressed against a patch of snow. The third cop stands over Jessup. Jessup can't tell if the cop is checking to make sure he's okay or ready to stop him from retaliating.

But he's not thinking about retaliating. The truth is that he's stunned. Steve's a senior, too. They've played together at Cortaca High School for four years. Were on teams together a couple of times through Pop Warner. Had he ever, even once, said anything, done anything to Steve?

He takes a second to sit back up. It hurts like hell where Steve nailed him. But when he sits up, he realizes there's a huge circle of students around them. Mostly they are gawking, but a few of them have looks on their faces that Jessup recognizes: hatred. Directed toward him.

"I didn't do anything," Jessup says. "He just hit me."

He looks around for a friend. The first person he sees that he knows is Alyssa Robinson. She meets his eyes, says calmly, loudly, evenly, "Go fuck yourself, you fucking Nazi."

The cop standing by Jessup yells, "Hey! All of you! Get to class. Now!"

The students start to disperse, but they aren't quiet. Alyssa isn't the only one to say something. The two cops have Steve cuffed now. He's lying on his stomach, looking at Jessup. Jessup knows that if Steve weren't cuffed, he'd try to hit Jessup again. He wants to rub at the spot where he was punched, but he doesn't want to give Steve the satisfaction. Instead he just stays seated, looks away. After a couple of minutes most of the students are gone. There's a steady trickle of kids getting dropped off or parking their cars, but mostly they just give curious looks and walk by. One kid stops to take a picture with his phone.

The cop standing over Jessup gives him a sharp look. "You okay?"

Jessup nods.

"Then get your ass to class."

He stops by his locker, stuffs the borrowed jacket away, heads to his first-period class, AP Spanish. He sits down and pulls out his phone. He isn't really doing anything on his phone, but it helps him pretend to be busy so he doesn't have to make eye contact, doesn't have to see the way people are looking at him. Señora Jenkins seems like she's oblivious to all of it, which makes sense, because she usually seems like she's oblivious to everything. She teaches Spanish by the book, which is fine, because, like most subjects, it comes easily to Jessup. Once the bell rings he's able to lose himself in the work; they are in the middle of their aesthetics and beauty unit, studying architecture in Barcelona. She runs a slide show for half the class, her notes clearly cribbed from the internet. The second half of the class is spent silently working on a persuasive essay.

In chemistry he sits in the back anyway, his benchmate a quiet kid who is only a junior and who has barely said a word to him all year. His jaw aches and he's got a soft hum in his ear from where Steve hit him. When it's time for gym class, he asks for a hall pass and goes to the nurse's office. The nurse is old—she's got to be close to retirement—but she's nice, and she doesn't take a lot of interest in Jessup. Gives him a bag of ice and lets him lie down on one of the vinyl couches. After a while, she asks him if he wants her to call his parents, and when he says no, she gently sends him on his way.

It's lunch, and he thinks about just going to the library and trying to hide, but he feels himself hardening, some stiffness in his bones that won't let him do it, David John's "stand straight, look people in the eye" echoing in his head, and he goes to the cafeteria.

When he passes through the doors, there's not a record-scratch of quiet, but there's a tonal shift, enough conversations shuttering to make Jessup self-conscious. There's a table with a couple of guys from the team, their girlfriends, and he can feel the tension rippling off them, the relief when he passes them by. There's an empty table off to the side, and he sits there, pulls out his lunch, pulls out his AP European History textbook. Camouflage.

He doesn't want to look like he's rushing, but he also doesn't think he could eat quickly if he tried; the sandwich sticks in his throat, dry wheat bread and sliced chicken left over from dinner, carrot sticks, an apple. He pretends to read the book, flips a page every minute or so, and soon enough it feels like the cafeteria is back to its normal buzz. But at some point he feels the table shift, someone sitting across from him.

Deanne.

SEVEN

She doesn't say anything, so he says, "Hey."

He wants to say so much more than just "Hey." Wants to get on his knees and bury his head in her lap, beg her for forgiveness, tell her he'll do anything to redeem himself—would he do anything? Stand on the table and shout his love. He wants to kiss her, wants to hold her against him, wants to taste her skin, wants to slip his hands up her shirt and undo her bra, feel the warmth of her body, the two of them alone in his truck, her car, the two of them alone anywhere, the desperation of being inside of her, of having her on top of him or being on top of her, of the way she looks at him, talks to him, the way she sees him. He wants to read her a poem, write her a poem, a song, an aria, wants to build a city around her, a thousand mirrors to catch the sunlight, to shine on her always.

"What's so funny?" she asks.

"Sorry. I'm . . . There's so much I want to say, and, you know, I lead with 'hey.' I guess it's funny. That's the best I can do."

She doesn't laugh, but there's movement at the corner of her lips. She's there. She's present.

"I heard Steve beat you up," she says.

He can't stop himself from bristling. "He didn't beat me up. He sucker-punched me." Instinctually, he touches the top of his jaw. It feels warm under the skin, the fist marking him invisibly.

"You okay?"

"You mean from this, or in general?"

"Do you want to tell your side of things?"

"Do you want me to?" he asks gently. He's trying not to be combative. And yet he can see that she's torn.

"No. Not now. Sorry."

He starts to reach out to take her hand, stops, pulls his hand back. "I understand," he says.

"Do you?"

"I don't know. Maybe?" He tries to smile and she tries to smile back. "I just . . ." He trails off. Tries again. "They aren't my people," he says.

"But you were there. Standing on the truck, Jessup. It's all over the news. It's everywhere. And you were part of it."

"I told you, it's complicated."

"No," she snaps. "It's not." She takes a deep breath, looks around. Jessup does, too. There are people watching them. Not as many as he would have thought, but enough. They lean in toward each other. Only a few days ago, they might have held hands across the table, and even now, he still wants to, wants to tell her he loves her. He does still love her, he does, but he also knows that if he says it right now, at this very second, he'll be met with silence.

"It's not complicated, Jessup. You can dress it up however you like, but there are two groups here. That church, those people"—he thinks how funny it is that she says "those people," how bad that would sound if he said it about black people, about the protesters, about the Jews, how the things that get thrown in his face can never be shot back—"they all think that white people are better. It doesn't matter what they call themselves, that they pretend to be some church, that they say they are true Christians. They're racist. And if you stand with them—no, if you don't stand against them—then you're just as bad. It's not complicated. It's simple. You're either with them or you're against them. There's no nuance, no middle ground. And you stood with them, Jessup. You stood up there with that awful, awful man. You can tell me that's not your church all you want, but *you* were *there.*"

"My family—"

"You think I give a *fuck* about your family?" she snaps at him. "What about my family? What about me? You're up there on a truck with that asshole who says that America is only for white people."

"Deanne," he says, his voice nearly a whisper. He can't talk any louder, can barely talk at all. Thinks of David John hugging Earl. "I can't," he says. "I can't turn my back on my family."

She stands up, all rush and fury. However much she loved him, she hates him now. Jessup can see it written all over her. Knows that there's nothing he can do, nothing he can say, no chance for redemption.

"That's fine, Jessup. You might not be able to turn your back on your family," she says, "but that means you've turned your back on me."

She's gone.

SIX

He sits there as long as he can, until people start filing out of the cafeteria to head to class, and then he packs his bag back up, goes to his locker, grabs Earl's jacket, walks out of the school. He doesn't sign out, doesn't do anything other than go to his mom's car, get in, and turn the key.

He's already at the gate to the compound before he understands what he's doing. Driving on autopilot. There's police tape fluttering in the breeze, strange tentacles of history. The gate's closed. He sits for a few minutes, looking, but there's nothing to see. No blood, no bodies. No men standing guard with AR-15s, the White America Militia in hiding.

The protester who was killed was a woman. Francine Nicholson. A sociology professor at Cortaca University. Unmarried. Thirty-three. She'd driven two of her graduate students with her to the protest. He's heard that the counterrally tonight is supposed to be in her honor. A memorial rally. A peace rally.

It's going to be a disaster. The Women's March on the pedestrian mall the weekend of President Trump's inauguration drew close to ten thousand people. Cortaca is that kind of town. And he knows Wyatt, knows the crowd of white supremacists that is going to come in response to Brandon's call, in response to TakeBack. They are going to be ugly. Brandon's people aren't coming for a peace rally. At least it's New York, he thinks. No open carry laws, concealed carry tough to come by in the county, too, maybe that will keep things under control. Or just the sheer number of counterprotesters. No matter how many people Wyatt thinks are coming—three hundred, four hundred, a thousand—no matter how much Brandon Rogers is pushing this, it's happening too quickly. It's a Monday and there isn't time for the white power groups to get here from all over the country; they will be outnumbered ten to one by counterprotesters.

Jessup closes his eyes, prays. He doesn't ask for forgiveness. He doesn't ask for anything for himself, just asks for the safety of his family, for Jesus to keep Jewel safe, to let Christ's love be a beacon to guide her, for his mother and David John to find some sort of peace together away from all of this. But most of all, he prays that tonight, on the pedestrian mall, there is not another woman left lying on the ground like Francine Nicholson.

FIVE

The van isn't parked in front of the trailer, so he's surprised to see David John sitting at the kitchen table when he walks through the front door.

David John has a book in front of him. A Bible. He's also got on a pair of reading glasses, which Jessup has never seen before. They make him look old.

"Why aren't you in school?" his stepfather asks, not unkindly, just a question, a solicitation of information.

"Some kid hit me."

"You hit him back?"

"No," Jessup says.

David John takes off his glasses, rests them on his Bible. "Good. Turn the other cheek. You hungry?"

"No, sir. I ate lunch."

"Jessup," David John says. His voice is soft. "I'm sorry."

"For what?"

But David John doesn't answer that question. Instead he asks, "You still with that girlfriend of yours? The coach's daughter?"

He's too surprised to try to dissemble. Doesn't deny it. Can only shake his head. He's sure he looks as miserable as he feels.

"Because of all of this?" David John asks.

"Yeah." Jessup is staring at the table. He looks up. "You knew?"

"Word gets around," he says. "Maybe if she wasn't a black girl nobody would have thought to say anything to me." He picks up the glasses again. He's careful with them, like they are a talisman of some kind, and when he puts them back on, Jessup has a sudden flash of what David John would have been like as a teacher. Gym. Or history. No, he thinks, social studies.

David John would have been a good teacher. He's patient. He can give himself in the service of another.

"Were you in love with her?" he asks. He watches Jessup for a beat and then says, "I remember what it was like to be your age. I'm not that old, you know. Your mom's young, and I'm only a few years older than her. Being young isn't so far in my past. Because you look miserable. You look like she broke your heart."

Jessup tries to control it, but he feels his shoulders start to shake, feels his breathing go away from him. He closes his eyes tight, his face twisting.

David John pulls his chair over, leans in, holds Jessup like a son.

FOUR

David John tells him to go lie down for a bit. Don't worry about Jewel, he says. He'll call Jessup's mom. She's at Wyatt's house, visiting with Wyatt's mom, but she's got to go to the grocery store anyway; she can grab Jewel on the way home.

He does. He doesn't expect to fall asleep, but as soon as he closes his eyes he's waking up, the afternoon gone by. He can hear the television, the gentle electricity of his mother laughing at something, Jewel asking a question, David John responding. It's light out still, but it's fading. It's not snowing anymore, a temporary break in the action, the sky still pregnant with clouds. He checks his phone. The forecast calls for two to four more inches overnight, cold tomorrow, but then warming up Wednesday. The weekend is supposed to be sunny and in the fifties. He'll go duck hunting.

Football practice.

He's missing practice. They're on the field right now. Still warming up, only half an hour in. If he hurries out the door right now, he can get there. He hasn't missed a single practice in high school, not once, and he thinks, if he just tells Coach Diggins . . . Tells him what?

He sits up, puts his feet on the floor, but he knows he's not going to practice. Not tonight. Tomorrow. Tomorrow he'll go. He'll ask Coach Diggins if he can talk to him before practice. He'll apologize. He'll be a man. Look him in the eye and say he wants to address the team, wants to tell them they are his brothers. All of them.

From out of nowhere he's overcome with thirst. As if he slept in the desert, the sun baking him, sucking the moisture from his body, and he wobbles to his feet. He goes to the bathroom, sticks his mouth to the faucet. The water is cold. Take me to the river, he thinks. Baptism.

When he walks into the kitchen, he sees his family sitting at the table.

David John is scrunched in next to Jewel, helping her with her math. He's got his reading glasses on again and is holding a pencil, working through the problem set with her. His mom is reading another library book. He can't tell what it is, but he knows her, knows it will be something inspirational. Something about faith and family. There's a bowl of popcorn on the table, and David John has his free hand in there, rooting around. He glances up and sees Jessup.

"How was your nap?"

"Good," Jessup says. And it was good. He needed it, he realizes. "I could have slept forever."

His mom reaches for him, takes his hand. "We need to talk. It's important. Can you sit down for a minute, honey?"

He does. David John and his mom are staring at him expectantly. It scares him, except Jewel is still working on her math. Whatever this is, she's heard it already.

"What is it?" He knows he should be afraid that the cops have figured out what happened with Corson, but that feels like it happened so long ago that it never even happened. Instead he's seized with the sudden fear that they are about to tell him that Ricky is dead.

But that's not it.

"We're moving," David John says.

THREE

It's so unexpected that Jessup can't process it. All he can do is smile with relief. It's not Ricky.

"You're okay with that?" his mom says.

"Sorry," Jessup says. "I just . . . I need a second. What do you mean we're moving?"

"It's not a new idea. Your mom and I have been talking about it for a year or so," David John says. "Just talk. A fresh start. But I haven't been able to get myself to do it. I didn't like the idea of leaving the church behind. There's a part of me that feels like I owe them. They were here for you when I wasn't, and they've welcomed me back like the prodigal son or, oh, something like that, something that Earl could probably say better. And the church has been something I could share with you and your mother and Jewel." He pats his chest with his hand, a twisted smile coming to his lips. "And Ricky, too. The church has been my home for so long that it's like a family. And that's the problem. Because the church isn't family. You are. We are. We're a family. Simple as that, really. Like I said last night, maybe I put the wrong things close to my heart. I know the idea is . . ."

Jessup's mom jumps in. "After what happened this weekend, we think it would be good. There's just . . . Well, it's all of this. A police car outside our house all night, to keep you safe? And some boy attacked you at school today?" She's still holding Jessup's hand, and now David John reaches out and takes his other hand. He should feel weird about it, but it's a familiar gesture, thousands of meals started with joined hands, bowed heads.

"Jessup," David John says, "when I say a fresh start, I mean it. I know you don't care about going to church—"

"That's not true."

"It is." Tender. Insistent. "I think you believe in Jesus—"

"I do."

"But I understand that the Church of the White America isn't your church. Not anymore. Hasn't been for a while. Not since Ricky killed those two boys. And that's okay. And after what happened this weekend, it's not our church either. I'm not . . ." He chokes up. Stops. Tries again. "You kids. Your mom. You come first. Family before anything. If I have to choose between the church or between Earl and you and your mom and your sister, that's the easiest decision of my life."

"What about Ricky?"

David John starts to speak, but Jessup's mom holds up her hand, cuts him off. This surprises Jessup as much as what she says: "It's too late for Ricky."

Nobody speaks. There's nothing to say.

It feels like both the worst thing and the best thing that's ever been said. Jessup feels an immediate sense of relief, and then shame at feeling relief, and he doesn't know what to do, so he looks closely at his mom, sees the puffiness around her eyes, sees the weight of the last few years on her face.

David John squeezes Jessup's hand and says, "When I say a fresh start, I mean it. For you. For Jewel. Somewhere away from here. Out west. Boise, Idaho. Guy I met in prison has a brother-in-law who has a plumbing business. He knows who I am, but he's a good Christian, believes in redemption. Said he'll hire me on. Give me a chance."

There is so much unsaid. So many things that Jessup knows he and David John will have to talk through in the coming years, but right now, that's not on the table. He looks over at his sister. She's looking back at him. She shrugs. "I don't care," she says. "I'll be fine."

And he knows it. Knows that she *will* be fine, but *only* if they leave, only if the Blessed Church of the White America is buried in their past, knows that the best thing he can do for his sister is to bless this, to make it easy for David John and his mother to follow through, to go to Boise, Idaho, to start a new life, unknown, unencumbered, her family history unshackled from anything that has happened here in a way that his can never be.

TWO

The details are sketchy. Boise is a college town, his parents say, like Cortaca, but four times as big. David John's talked with his prison friend's brother-in-law—his name is Quentin, a name that strikes Jessup as vaguely preposterous—and everything is set. Quentin can even get a rental house lined up for them. He'll front the first month's rent and will take it out of David John's paycheck in small increments over the next six months. A good Christian, David John says, and no, not affiliated, not in that way. Unitarian Universalist. He's offering a fresh start. A clean break.

His parents watch him, and he just leans back in the chair, trying to take it in. Finally Jessup says, "When?"

David John has already talked to his parole officer, already gotten approval—David John away from the Blessed Church of the White America? yes, please—and things are moving. Like he said, it isn't a new idea for him and Jessup's mom. The time line is aggressive.

Tomorrow, Tuesday, is for packing. Wyatt's dad has found them a used Jeep that's got a hundred thousand miles on it but has new tires and is in good shape. It will make the trip fine. Anything that can't fit in the Jeep or David John's work van gets left behind. Hit the road Wednesday first thing, drive through the night to save on a hotel, Jessup, David John, Jessup's mom rotating between the two vehicles, in Boise by Thursday night. Register Jessup and Jewel for school on Friday, take the weekend to get settled, and Monday they start their new lives.

If there's anything left over from the sale of the trailer after the mortgage is paid off and they pay back the Dunns for the Jeep, they'll start saving again for a new place. Or, depending on how work goes, they'll save instead for David John to strike out on his own again in a few years.

While they're talking, Jessup can feel his phone buzzing with intermittent texts. After a while, he excuses himself to go to the bathroom. He does go to the bathroom, but after he washes his hands he sits on the closed toilet seat, looks at his phone. Most of the texts he can ignore. Nothing from Deanne. One from Mike Crean, another from Derek Lemper. But there're six from Wyatt, the first five variants on the same theme:

you coming to the rally?

It's the sixth text that shakes him:

brother. I need you there. otherwise why did I do it? you owe me.

ONE

It's six fifteen when he asks David John if they can talk outside. Jewel is in her room reading or playing on her school-issued laptop, and his mom is at the stove, making pasta with red sauce, trying to use up the vegetables in the fridge.

Jessup shrugs the borrowed jacket on again—he'll need a new one for Idaho, boots too, the winters there making Cortaca look tropical, according to David John—and walks a bit up the driveway. After a minute, David John comes out.

The snow is still holding off, but the air reeks of it, and Jessup wonders when it will start coming down hard. He wonders, too, if he'll have a feel for the weather in Boise. He's never lived anywhere else. Never been farther from Cortaca than the northern edge of the Adirondacks, a five-hour drive.

David John is wearing his heavy work jacket, a pair of boots. He doesn't seem bothered by the cold. He's lived in the Cortaca area his whole life, too, except for those four years in prison, and even that was upstate New York.

"Sorry," Jessup says. "You know how it is in there. Hard to talk without Mom . . ."

"You want to go down to the pedestrian mall," David John says.

Jessup stares at him. Nods. "How'd you know?"

"It's not a good idea."

"I know. I just . . . I don't know." Jessup rocks back on his heels. He shrugs. "I want to see. I need to see, I guess."

"Why? You ain't going to march with Brandon Rogers and his kind. I know that. I've been paying attention. That's not you. Never has been, has it? And that's why we're moving. I'm trying to get you away from that."

"I'll be careful," Jessup says. "I don't know why, but I know I've got to, okay? I know I can't go to Idaho if I don't. I need to see it through. I can't just walk away."

David John studies him. "Yes, Jessup, you can. We are. If *I* can walk away from this, *you* can walk away from this. Don't you understand? We can give up anything if it means saving everything. You going down there? What do you want to see through? What do you think you're going to get by going down there?"

"For the life of me," Jessup says, "I can't tell you what I expect to get out of going." And then he starts to laugh, and after a pause David John laughs with him.

They stop laughing and Jessup waits. It takes a few seconds, but David John nods. "I don't like it, but if you really think it's important, I respect that."

"Thank you."

David John pulls the keys to his van out of his jacket pocket, holds them out. But when Jessup goes to take them, David John clasps his hands around Jessup's hand. "Can we pray first," he says, "please?"

They bow their heads, foreheads touching.

"Dear Jesus," David John says, "please guide Jessup. Please find him to safety. Please light the way to peace. Please allow him to forgive himself for his transgressions. Please allow him to ask for forgiveness."

He doesn't say Corson's name, but Jessup feels it within him. Knows that he'll be asking forgiveness the rest of his life, an angry kid with too much to drink and Jessup hitting the gas just a little too hard, something he should have owned up to but knows in his bones he never will, and now there's a ghost that will haunt him, will taunt him, and that sound, the truck hitting Corson's body, will be with him until the end of time, forever and ever, amen.

"Please, dear Jesus," David John says, "protect my son tonight, allow him to make good decisions, hold him in your love. Hold me, my wife, my daughter, my son." He pauses and looks at Jessup. "Because you are my son, no matter what you say, Jessup, you are always my son and always have been. Dear Jesus, hold him in your love. Amen."

And then David John steps forward and wraps his arms around Jessup, holding him, and all Jessup can think of is that day on the football field when he broke his arm, David John cradling him, carrying him, the knowledge that this man would give anything to keep him safe.

Jessup means it when he says it, "Amen."

ZERO

He can't get anywhere near the pedestrian mall. Traffic is backed up, people walking from all directions, singing, chanting, holding signs, smiling and serious, a flood of people. He parks David John's van in front of a dry cleaner's, the windows dark, two other cars pulling in after him.

In the spring there's the Cortaca Festival, and in the fall there's the Apple Harvest Festival. Food and art, carnival rides, bands playing in the pavilion at the center of the pedestrian mall, but he's never seen anything like this. As he gets closer, the already-swollen river of people thickens. People spill into the streets. The cars that are trying to get through are reduced to a crawl. He didn't go to the Women's March the weekend of President Trump's inauguration, but he saw photos—the photographer for the *Cortaca Journal* got a shot from the roof of the parking garage, the pedestrian mall unfolded below, people piled up like sand on a beach—and he has to imagine it was like this. He doesn't know how many people are here tonight. Thousands. Five thousand, ten thousand, enough to choke the roads, enough to mean that he has to turn sideways, slipping, juking, apologizing as he pushes his way through the crowd, trying to get closer to the center, to the pavilion.

It seems like everywhere he looks people are holding unlit candles, and it dawns on him that this isn't just a counterprotest, it's not just a memorial: it's a vigil. A college student, a girl, is standing on one of the concrete planters holding a cardboard box full of them, and she reaches down to hand one to Jessup. He takes the candle.

Even from a distance, he can hear the chanting, the drums. The protesters are making a joyous noise. He climbs up onto a bench, uses a tree to steady himself as he steps on the bench's backrest so that he can see over the crowd. He can see a group of men on the grand pavilion at the center of the pedestrian mall. Jessup doesn't know how to label them. Are Brandon and his ilk protesters? What, exactly, are they protesting?

He decides it doesn't matter. What matters is that even though he's still fifty yards back, from his vantage point he can see that there are hundreds of them. If he had to guess, he'd say three hundred men—all men as far as he can tell—with some of them wearing body armor over their jackets, a few Confederate flags, at least one Nazi flag that he can see, somebody else waving a giant white flag with the flaming cross and the words "Blessed Church of the White America," all crowded onto the grand pavilion stage at the center of the pedestrian mall, elevated above the packed crowd of people here to drown them out. Even from where he is standing he can see their anger. The snarls as they yell.

And for the first time in his life, Jessup sees how comical they are. How pathetic they look. That fury directed out into the ether. There are hundreds of them, a force, more of these men than he has seen in one place in his entire life, and yet they are little more than a dollop of land surrounded by the sea, whatever rage they have contained by the teeming masses, Cortaca police and state police and what feels like all of the police in the world forming a circle around them, a moat of sorts, the only thing keeping this ocean of people away from these pitiful men, and from where he perches precariously on the top of this bench, it does seem like the people are an ocean, moving in waves, in and out, chanting now in unison, their voices a glorious chorus.

He gets down from the bench, and even though the crowd tightens, bodies pressed together, men and women and even some children holding hands, he works his way through, closer and closer, until he's pressed up against a building, as close as he can get to the pavilion without breaking through the lines of police officers, as close as he can get without actually joining the men on the other side, and he sees Brandon Rogers at the center of it, elevated somehow on a box or a pedestal, his face bathed in floodlights, television cameras pointed in his direction, his right arm immobilized by a sling, a prop that seems both glorious and feeble, and around him, his acolytes pump their fists, screaming, spittle dripping, the men chanting something of their own now, faces turgid with blood, a grotesque lust, and then Jessup catches sight of Wyatt, his friend, the boy he's known since time immemorial, the boy who he's spent his entire life with, the boy who has been like a brother to him, who hasn't just been *like* a brother but has *been* a brother, years and years of history, the weight of history split by a rushing river coming at him, that boy, Wyatt, his brother always, his brother no more, at Brandon's feet, and whatever hesitation Wyatt has allowed in his life, whatever equivocation he seems to have felt about his place in the church, it is gone, because he looks at Brandon like he's looking at a god, his face shining with a joy so pure that it makes Jessup shiver, so that just for a moment Jessup wishes he were up there, too, that he could worship at the feet of this man, this movement, that he could make himself feel so big by making others feel small.

And then it happens.

It's just a spark, a few dozen lighters set to candles, barely enough for Jessup to notice, but as each candle is lit, the person holding it turns and lights the candle of whoever is next to them, hands cupping the flame, wick to wick, a tender gesture, the literal passing of the torch, and soon it is a hundred candles lit, and as these candles are lit, the fire flickering, jumping from hand to hand, people begin to kneel, falling to the ground, falling silent, and Jessup thinks that he was right to compare this to an ocean, because a wave washes over him, these lights, this quiet, the men on the podium still screaming, but instead of being overshadowed by chanting, they are drowned out by stillness, hundreds of candles lit, hundreds lighting hundreds more, thousands of protesters now, on their knees, holding candles in front of them, the guttering flames a bulwark against the darkness, like nothing Jessup has ever seen. But suddenly he realizes that he was wrong to think of the sea after all, to think of a wave, to think of these people like an ocean drowning out Brandon and Wyatt and all of these wretched men, because these lights, this peaceful reverie from the crowd of thousands is not at all like water, it is nothing like water, it is like nothing other than a constellation of stars, the snow slowly coming down now, a benediction, a blessing, snow drifting from the sky, falling among them, each candle a single star, and together thousands, tens of thousands, hundreds of thousands, millions of candles before him, and he can see this, he can see all of this, can see the way the light comes together, one flickering light barely a glow, but together it's stunning, overpowering, together these candles make a universe, and for what reason Jessup does not know, cannot tell, the men in the pavilion begin to fall silent now, too, as if they know their voices will not rise above joy and love and community, as if they know that what they have created for themselves is built only on tearing down, so they are silent now, even Brandon Rogers stopping, all of them, staring out at the vast expanse before them, looking over the ring of police and taking in the blinking heavens, and Jessup feels a sort of peace, because right there, right at the very front, he sees Deanne, sees her kneeling between her father and her mother, this first girl that he has loved, this girl who he will always love, and he moves carefully, stepping past a man and a small child, gently touching his hand to a woman's shoulder so he can get by her, feels people watching him, all of them, those kneeling and those up on the stage, Jessup caught between the two worlds, Wyatt watching him, offering his hand to help Jessup up to the pavilion stage, offering a hand to his brother, his friend, and in this moment, Jessup thinks about what it has meant to be caught up in the history of his life, to have been raised in this church, and Wyatt has made his choice, and here, now, Jessup is making his own choice, either to join or to depart, and no other choice will ever matter or hurt as much as this one. As he nears Deanne, he thinks, no, David John is right, you cannot turn your back on family. Since Wyatt is as a brother to him, that means that Jessup cannot turn his back on Wyatt. Since he cannot join him and he cannot turn his back on him, Jessup's only choice is to face Wyatt. So he makes his choice, stops in front of Deanne, looks at her and holds out his candle, holds it and waits, waits for her to light it, waits for the flame to catch, not asking for a declaration of love, not asking for redemption or forgiveness, asking for nothing other than the chance to face these men, to add a star to the night sky, the snow falling, the snow twisting, the snow glinting and ferocious in the dancing light of these thousand lights, and after what might be forever, Deanne touches her wick to his.

He kneels in silence, his candle another light against the darkness.

EPILOGUE

———•———

TELLING IT

Jessup is thirty-one.

It owns him as much as he owns it.

He speaks about it publicly. Not every day, not every week, but at least once a month. He stands in front of groups of teenagers, suburban mothers, black congregations in southern cities, high school teachers in midwestern towns, youth groups in Boston and D.C. and Denver and Seattle. He stands up and talks about the Blessed Church of the White America, tells people about the sound of Corson's body.

He tells them about sitting across the table from his mother. Tells them about David John bowing his head when Jessup gave him back his own words, saying, when you make a mistake, a real man stands up and takes responsibility, fixes what he can, tries to be a better person.

He tells the groups about Jewel. About trying to explain to her what happened. About what it felt like to have her turn away from him. About how hard he has worked to get her to turn back.

He tells them about Coach Diggins. Despite how he said he'd cut Jessup loose, Diggins was there for him: helping Jessup find a lawyer, meeting Jessup and David John and Jessup's mother at the police station, being the first one to reach his hand out, shaking David John's as they all stood in the vestibule. Diggins the one who called the coach at Yale, who explained . . .

Jessup can't help it. When he talks about Diggins, every single time, without fail, his voice breaks and he needs a moment to recover. Coach Diggins forgiving Jessup when Jessup can't forgive himself.

He tells the groups about how he took a deal, pleading to leaving the scene of a personal-injury accident, obstructing governmental administration, a laundry list of misdemeanors. Youthful-offender status because of his age, because there were no priors, because it was an accident, because Coach Diggins fights for him and because, with everything that happened at the church, it all became part of something bigger. Tells them how the court let him serve his jail time on weekends, so he could keep going to high school, working through the youthful-offender treatment program, community service, no criminal record. Tells them about moving to Boise and doing the youthful-offender program there—everybody agreeing a change of scenery, putting miles between Jessup and the Blessed Church of the White America, would be a good idea—and always gets a chuckle when he talks about the amount of paperwork *that* entailed.

Waits for the crowd to settle down and then waits for them to get uncomfortable with his stillness, and then waits another second or two before he tells them how *none* of that is fair, that he got off light for what happened, and that's one of the reasons he is here, now, in front of them, trying to own his actions, trying to make right.

He tells them all of it. He does this hundreds of times, standing in front of crowds of strangers and telling them the before and the after. He tells them who Kevin Corson was as a person, tells them what Kevin Corson's parents said to Jessup, their unwillingness to forgive, and how that's one of the things he has to hold inside himself, and that is part of why it is so important for him to be out here, claiming his mistake. He tells them about lighting a candle against the darkness. He owns it.

He doesn't tell them about Wyatt.

BROTHERS

He talks to Coach Diggins almost weekly, comes to Cortaca every year to talk to Diggins's team at the start of the season, and that means that he sees Deanne occasionally. This year's Christmas card has a picture of her with her husband and her two toddler daughters at the Apple Harvest Festival. She's a pediatrician. Still lives in Cortaca.

Wyatt still lives in Cortaca, too.

They haven't talked since Jessup got into the Jeep and started driving west to Boise. Jessup has reached out, but Wyatt won't speak to him. Jessup might as well be dead. But he has held Wyatt's silence. He has done at least that for Wyatt. He doesn't know what the cost has been to Wyatt—what it has meant for Wyatt to live with his own actions—but he knows what the cost of his own actions has been for himself. One thing it has meant is that he's lost two brothers. Wyatt and Ricky.

Twice a year, on top of his talks to Diggins's teams, Jessup flies to Syracuse, rents a car, drives two hours to the prison where Ricky is still incarcerated, takes a hotel room. The next morning, he signs in, goes through security, waits and waits, but Ricky won't see him. That's how it goes every time. He thinks of it as just another attempt to set things right.

Because Ricky won't see him, Jessup writes letters, but Ricky almost never writes back, and even then, when he does, the letters are vile, full of hatred, calls Jessup a traitor to the cause. Ricky has not been a model inmate. His sentence, originally twenty years, looks like it's going to stretch to twenty-five, thirty, an entire life gone by.

David John writes to Ricky every single day, but neither he nor Jessup's mom go to visit anymore. It makes both of them too sad. David John's shown Jessup copies of some of the letters he writes to Ricky; they are short but heartfelt, filled with small observations from his day, Bible verses, prayers that Ricky will find peace, family pictures. They are, David John says, meant to be a lifeline. All Ricky has to do is grab hold. But he doesn't. Ricky writes back to David John every few weeks, but it's clear to David John—clear to all of them—that Ricky is lost.

It's a permanent shadow over all of them.

LIFTOFF

Other than that, Jessup's parents are happy.

Of all things, his parents own a house that backs onto a golf course. It's become something they can do together, and they play as often as they can in the summer, bring their clubs when they go to visit Jessup in Montgomery.

Montgomery, Alabama. Coach Diggins went to bat for him there, too. Jessup sat out a year, working for David John, but Diggins called the football coach at Yale, told him everything that had happened, convinced him to give Jessup a chance. Yale and then law school at UCLA, and all of that led him to Montgomery. He still misses football, but he loves his job. He's a staff attorney for the Southern Poverty Law Center. He knows it's a penance, and he knows he'll never work it off. He's okay with that.

He's thirty-one and it's Christmas morning and it's snowing in Boise at his parents' house. Montgomery suits him better than he would have expected, but he misses the snow. That's one of the joys of visiting his parents over the holidays. Idaho at Christmas means snow. The other joy, of course, is seeing Jewel. She lives in Portland and is a consultant, finishing an MBA, too. She's tried to explain to him what she does, but it involves regression modeling or some other gobbledygook, and he can never do better than to tell people she helps figure out what people's salaries should be. All Jessup knows is that he's thirty-one and a lawyer and his kid sister makes more money than he does. They visit each other often, talk on the phone most days.

She's downstairs already. Jessup can hear her talking with their mom. Jewel has been dating a girl named Ophelia for about a year. Jessup likes her. Everybody likes Ophelia. She's funny. Sweet. She's working as a barista, mostly floating around, but her dad is some internet bajillionaire, so nobody seems too worked up about it. Jessup's parents go to Portland twice a year, same as they visit Jessup, and David John has been trying to teach Ophelia to golf. He doesn't hesitate to introduce her as his daughter's girlfriend.

And yet.

Jessup will never quite know what to say. He believes that you can unlearn the bad things you've been taught. His entire life since they left Cortaca has been based on that. But he still wonders if he'll ever escape the sound of the truck hitting Corson's body. There's something fundamentally unfair about the fact that he's been given a second chance, that David John has been given a second chance, while the dead men that they left in their wake have not.

All Jessup can do is atone.

ORBIT

It's an hour later in Montgomery than it is in Boise, so Jessup should already be up—he's an early riser, five every morning to work out with a group of buddies, except Sunday, when he'll sleep until eight or nine, depending on what he's done the night before—but he's on vacation, so he doesn't feel too guilty about lying in bed. Besides, it's barely seven o'clock. Christmas day or not, it's early enough for a house with no children in it.

The curtains are open, and he watches the snow tumble from the sky. It's hypnotizing. It makes a soft patter on the glass: big, light flakes, cotton-candy snow, something he never gets tired of seeing, particularly since he only sees it a few times a year now.

He feels the bed shift, Amy's body rolling against him, her arm over his shoulder, her hot breath on the back of his neck.

"Merry Christmas," she says.

He replies, "Happy Hanukkah."

"Hanukkah was over like a week ago, dumb-ass." She kisses the back of his neck, scratches indulgently at his back. She likes to joke that the only white supremacist at the Southern Poverty Law Center fell in love with the only Jew in Alabama.

They've been together close to two years. The wedding is in June.

Amy knows all of it. Every single part. No exceptions. Even about Wyatt.

She's a year younger than him, and she works on the Teaching Tolerance project. She told him that he'll carry it around with him forever. And she's right.

She's a good woman. Better than he deserves.

That's how it works sometimes.

And sometimes, late at night, in Montgomery, when it's raining, Jessup looks out the window and imagines that the rain is a cleansing rain, the world scoured clean, the world made new, but he knows it doesn't work like that. And even if it snowed in Montgomery, even if he could wake up to blankets of snow coating Alabama, covering everything, the world would not be made new. That's not how it works.

It works like this: the light swallows the darkness.

No one is born hating another person because of the colour of his skin, or his background, or his religion. People must learn to hate, and if they can learn to hate, they can be taught to love, for love comes more naturally to the human heart than its opposite.

—**Nelson Mandela,** *Long Walk to Freedom*

ACKNOWLEDGMENTS

Thank you to my literary agent, Bill Clegg. I am, and will always be, grateful for your voice. Thanks, as well, to all of the fine folks at The Clegg Agency: Marion Duvert for being an international force; and David Kambhu, Simon Toop, and Lilly Sandberg for all of the stuff that happens behind the scenes.

Thank you to my screen agent, Anna DeRoy, at WME. Fierce and fantastic.

Thank you to my editor, Laura Tisdel. Editing this book was a bit like playing Jenga, but instead of fifty-four blocks, it was 95,000 words. I still owe you a coffee mug that says "Okay. You're right. Damn it." Thank you to Amy Sun for all of the work that happens unseen but deserves credit. Thank you to Lynn Buckley for a cover that captures everything. Thank you to the countless people at Viking who help the ship sail.

Thank you to my friends and family. Thanks to the early crowd for keeping me sane, and to Shawn for always being willing to talk it through.

Thank you to my wife and kids for putting up with me when I'm in the middle of a project. This book, like all things, is for you.